BEST NEW
HORROR

BEST NEW
HORROR

Edited by
STEPHEN JONES
and
RAMSEY CAMPBELL

Carroll & Graf Publishers Inc.
New York

First published in Great Britain 1990
First Carroll & Graf Edition 1991

Carroll & Graf Publishers, Inc.
260 Fifth Avenue
New York
NY 10001

ISBN: 0–88184–630–9

Typset by Selectmove Ltd, London.
Printed by The Guernsey Press Co. Ltd., Guernsey, Channel Islands

CONTENTS

ACKNOWLEDGEMENTS

THE EDITORS WOULD like to thank Kim Newman, Jo Fletcher, Jessie Horsting, Dennis Etchison, Tammy Campbell and Kathy Gale for their help and support. Thanks are also due to the magazines *Locus* (Editor & Publisher Charles N. Brown, Locus Publications, P.O. Box 13305, Oakland, CA 94661, USA) and *Science Fiction Chronicle* (Editor & Publisher Andrew I. Porter, P.O. Box 2730, Brooklyn, NY 11202–0056, USA) which were used as reference sources in the Introduction and Necrology.

For
KARL EDWARD WAGNER
friend and fellow editor

INTRODUCTION: HORROR IN 1989

FOLLOWING THE EXPLOSION OF horror fiction in 1988, growth in the genre appeared to level off in 1989. However, horror still accounted for almost 15% of all the books published in America and 9% of the British total. According to the trade newspaper *Locus*, this is still a long way behind science fiction and fantasy (which each account for nearly 25% of the totals). However, the field is much more fruitful than during the first half of the decade.

1989 saw new novels from most of the big names: Stephen King followed up the commercial and critical success of *Misery* with an equally well-received tale of the horrors of authorship, *The Dark Half*; Clive Barker's *The Great and Secret Show* was the first part of a sprawling *magnum opus* that threw in almost everything but the kitchen sink; James Herbert turned his talents to the traditional ghost story in *Haunted*; *Ancient Images* by Ramsey Campbell combined the quest for a lost Boris Karloff and Bela Lugosi movie with something older and more dangerous; while Dean R. Koontz (not a horror writer, he insists) continued to please his crowds of fans with another bestseller, *Midnight*.

One of the most ambitious horror novels of the year was Dan Simmons's tale of psychic vampires, *Carrion Comfort*. Robert R. McCammon gave us a fast-moving combination of lycanthropy, espionage and Nazis in *The Wolf's Hour*. Two masters of the macabre moved closer to the suspense novel, Stephen Gallagher with *Down River* and Peter Straub with *Mystery*, while a master of suspense, James Elroy, moved towards horror with *The Big Nowhere*. Subtle terrors were also to be had from T.M. Wright (*The Place*), Robert Robinson (*Bad Dreams*) and Peter Ackroyd (*First Light*), the latter confirming the mastery of the supernatural novel which Ackroyd displayed in *Hawksmoor*. The Ackroyd and Robinson books were published as if they lay outside their field, and this was also true of Patrick McGrath's first novel *The Grotesque* and Katherine Dunn's extraordinary *Geek Love*, though Stephen Gregory's *The Woodwitch* was mysteriously transmuted into a horror novel as it crossed the ocean to America.

Several established horror writers produced enduring work: K.W. Jeter (*In the Land of the Dead* and *The Night Man*), Brian Lumley (*Necroscope III: The Source*), Chet Williamson (*Dreamthorp*) and Charles L. Grant (*In a Dark Dream* and *Dialing the Wind*). Nor should we forget Robert Bloch (*Lori*), Graham Masterton (*Walkers*), Joe R. Landsdale (*The Drive-In 2 [Not Just One of Them Sequels]*), Tim Powers (*The Stress of Her Regard*) and Jonathan Carroll (the remarkable *A Child Across the Sky*). Among the newer writers whose work attracted favourable comment were Mark Morris (*Toady*), Peter James (*Dreamer*), Michael Paine (*Owl Light*), Randall Boyll (*After Sundown*), Bruce McAllister (*Dream Baby*), David C. Smith (*The Fair Rules of Evil*), Scott Bradfield (*History of Luminescence*), Kim Newman (*The Night Mayor* and, as "Jack Yoevil", *Drachenfels*) and Nancy A. Collins (*Sunglasses After Dark*).

It was a good year for collections. Arkham House published a substantially corrected edition of H.P. Lovercraft's *The Horror in the Museum*, while the British publisher Equation brought out books of previously uncollected tales by E.F. Benson and Algernon Blackwood, among others. Living writers who published important collections included John Shirley (*Heatseeker*); Michael Blumlein (*The Brains of Rats*); Keith Roberts (*Winterwood and Other Hauntings*); Joe R. Lansdale (*By Bizarre Hands*); Robert R. McCammon (*Blue World*); F.

Paul Wilson (*Soft*); Christopher Fowler (*The Bureau of Lost Souls*); Laurence Staig (*Dark Toys and Consumer Goods*, published as children's fiction); and Robert Westall (*Antique Dust*, an adult book by a writer whose children's fiction has considerable adult appeal). And the much underrated Thomas Ligotti saw an expanded and revised edition of his acclaimed 1986 collection *Songs of a Dead Dreamer* from Robinson.

The anthology market fared less well. John Skipp and Craig Spector's *Book of the Dead* boasted contributions by King, McCammon, Schow, Winter and Lansdale, but despite the packaging, by no means all the contents were set in the world of George Romero's zombie trilogy. Ellen Datlow's *Blood is Not Enough* was a little too bloodless, and Graham Masterton's laudable charity collection, *Scare Care*, was a decidedly mixed bag of delights, as was *Hot Blood: Tales of Provocative Horror*, in which some of the tales chosen by Jeff Gelb and Lonn M. Friend seemed to be straining to rise to the book's subtitle. *Masques III* edited by J.N. Williamson, *Stalkers* edited by Ed Gorman and the ubiquitous Martin Greenberg, *Night Visions 7* (nominally edited by Stanley Wiater and containing tales by Richard Laymon, Chet Williamson and Gary Brander), *Post Mortem: New Tales of Ghostly Horror* edited by Paul F. Olson and David B. Silva, and the burgeoning *Pulphouse: the Hardback Magazine* anthologies included substantial material. Editor Joe R. Lansdale blended the western with horror (and virtually every other genre) in *Razored Saddles* (with Pat LoBrutto) and *New Frontiers*.

In Britain, the unstoppable *Pan Book of Horror Stories* limped into its 30th anniversary as the world's longest-running horror anthology series under the editorship of Clarence Paget, while Chris Morgan's *Dark Fantasies* tried to make a case for "quiet" horror. In *The Year's Best Fantasy Second Annual Collection* Ellen Datlow and Terri Windling provided a hefty grab-bag of fantasy and horror, and Karl Edward Wagner displayed more obscure gems in the seventeenth volume of his always-reliable *The Year's Best Horror*.

Not before time, contemporary women writers of horror and dark fantasy were showcased in Kathryn Ptacek's *Women of Darkness*, while Jessica Amanda Salmonson explored the tradition of feminist supernatural fiction in *What Did Miss Darrington See?*, both an excellent selection of reprints and an essential guide to further reading. Salmonson did much the same for fanzines and the small presses in her anthology *Tales By Moonlight II*.

On the magazine front we bid farewell to *Twilight Zone Magazine* (which followed its stable-mate *Night Cry* into oblivion) and *The Horror Show*, one of the best of the semi-professional journals. The occasional horror story turned up in the science fiction magazines, *Omni* and *Interzone* among them, as well as in more traditional outlets such as *Fantasy Tales*, *Fear* and the revived *Weird Tales*. However, the small press magazines dominated the field, with good material appearing in *2AM*, *Grue*, *Dagon*, *Midnight Graffiti*, *Haunts*, *Deathrealm*, *Ghosts & Scholars*, *Back Brain Recluse*, *Dark Regions*, *Eldritch Tales* and The British Fantasy Society's *Winter Chills*.

At times Clive Barker seemed to dominate the comics industry, with adaptions of his work appearing in *Tapping the Vein* Books One and Two and spin-off stories from his movie mythos turning up in the first volume of *Hellraiser*. Another British author, Neil Gaiman, used *Sandman*, and the willingness of DC Comics to deal with disturbing themes, to turn an old idea into some of the most daring and poetic fiction to appear in comic books in recent years. Bryan Talbot's ambitious and astonishing epic *The Adventures of Luther Arkwright*, which has much of awe and horror to offer, finally appeared in a collected edition. *Taboo* and *Fly In My Eye*, anthologies of new adult comics, were commendably determined to break new ground; the second issue of *Fly* even presented a graphic version of Ramsey Campbell's autobiography!

As usual, reference books ranged from the useful to the useless. Stephen King suffered further second-hand exposure in no less than three new volumes: *Feast of Fear*, a signed, boxed, numbered book of interviews edited by publishers Underwood-Miller; *The Stephen King Companion* edited by George Beahm; and Tyson Blue's *The Unseen King*. Emily Sunstein's biography *Mary Shelley*, subtitled *Romance and Reality*, explored the complex life of the teenage creator of Frankenstein. Brian J. Frost examined vampirism in literature in *The Monster With a Thousand Faces*, while Norine Dresser published *American Vampires*. Leonard Wolf's *Horror: A Connoisseur's Guide* was too sloppily researched to deserve its subtitle. By contrast, the revised and updated *Arkham House Companion* by Sheldon Jaffrey was indispensable. Kim Newman's revised *Nightmare Movies* was meticulously researched and thought-provoking, and *Horror: 100 Best Books*, edited by Newman and Stephen Jones, received a new lease of life in an American edition, its first edition having been all but aborted by the British publisher. Peter Cannon's *H.P. Lovecraft* was a terse and insightful introduction to the work of that controversial writer.

The most successful horror movie of 1989 was *Pet Sematary*, scripted by Stephen King from his own novel; it earned around $60 million at the box office. However, this was well behind top grossers *Batman*, *Indiana Jones and the Last Crusade* and *Honey, I Shrunk the Kids*. *The Fly II*, *Fright Night Part II*, *Ghostbusters II*, *Hellbound: Hellraiser II*, *Nightmare On Elm Street V*, *Hallowe'en V* and *Friday the 13th: Part VIII* all proved to be disappointments for their makers, and it looks as if the sequel as a species may go back into its hole for a while. Among the critical successes were *Paperhouse*, *Parents*, *Dead Ringers* and *The Dead Can't Lie* but, like other releases, such as *Phantom of the Opera*, *Lair of the White Worm*, *976-Evil*, *The Horror Show* and Wes Craven's hit-or-miss *Shocker*, all held the middle ground. It looks as if most horror films are still destined (many deservedly) to be cast straight into the outer darkness of video during the 1990s.

One of the most impressive movies of the year was Nigel Kneale's adaptation of Susan Hill's *The Woman in Black*, which was made for television, but with such fare as *Freddy's Nightmares*, *Monsters*, *Tales from the Darkside*, and the intermittently rewarding *Tales from the Crypt* and *Friday the 13th: The Series* clogging up the airwaves, television looks increasingly in need of real imagination. However, *Twin Peaks* is both disturbing and David Lynch's funniest work to date, and makes up for a good deal of dross elsewhere.

Ronald Chetwynd-Hayes and Ray Bradbury collected Life Achievement Awards at the second annual Bram Stoker Awards Weekend, staged by The Horror Writers of America in New York in June of last year. Superior Achievement in Novel was awarded to Thomas Harris's *The Silence of Lambs*; Kelley Wilde's *The Suiting* received the First Novel award, and Joe R. Lansdale's "Night They Missed the Horror Show" (from *Silver Scream*) the Short Story; David Morrell's "Orange is for Anguish, Blue for Insanity" (from *Prime Evil*) was the Novelette. Roger Anker's selection of tales by the late Charles Beaumont, some of them previously unpublished, was voted Fiction Collection of the year.

Ramsey Campbell's *The Influence* won the August Derleth Award for Best Novel at Fantasycon XIV, held in Birmingham, England in October 1989. Other British Fantasy Award winners were Brian Lumley's "Fruiting Bodies" (Best Short Story), *Beetlejuice* (Best Film), Carl T. Ford's *Dagon* magazine (Best Small Press), and Dave Carson (Best Artist). The Icarus Award for Best Newcomer went to John Gilbert, editor of *Fear*, and R. Chetwynd-Hayes collected the Special Award for services to the field.

At the World Fantasy Convention in Seattle later the same month Peter Straub received the World Fantasy Award for Best Novel of 1988 (*Koko*); George R.R. Martin's "The Skin Trade" was judged to be the Best Novella and John M. Ford's poem "Winter Solstice, Camelot Station" the Best Short Story; *The Year's Best Fantasy First Annual Collection* edited by Ellen Datlow and Terri Windling was found to be the Best Anthology. Harlan Ellison (*Angry Candy*) and Gene Wolfe (*Storeys from the Old Hotel*) tied in the Best Collection category, and Robert Weinberg and Terri Windling for the Special Professional Award. Edward Gorey was chosen as Best Artist, while *Pulphouse* publishers Kristine Katherine Rusch and Dean Wesley Smith won in the Special Non-Professional category. Evangeline Walton received the Life Achievement Award.

Perhaps not surprisingly, the 1989 Collectors Award issued by science fiction and fantasy bookseller Barry R. Levin went to Salman Rushdie as The Most Collectable Author of the Year—and that was surely the year's most frightening horror story.

1989 saw mixed fortunes for the horror genre. In America it looks as if the boom of recent years is on the wane, while in Britain—where trends in publishing tend to follow a year or two later—horror is still big business, and translations into european and oriental languages are multiplying. It remains to be seen if there is enough of a market to sustain the sheer volume of written and filmed material being produced—much of it patently sub-standard and aimed at a short shelf life between the covers of exploitative publishers or beneath the garish label of a quick-buck video.

To survive, the horror genre must move out of the mid-list category and, following the example set by a few of its best-known practioners, into the ranks of the bestseller or of recognised literature. As we head into the 1990s, with more new talent emerging within the ranks of the genre than ever before, we look set to see a true renaissance in this much-maligned field. We hope *Best New Horror* will reflect this.

THE EDITORS
APRIL, 1990

ROBERT R. McCAMMON

Pin

ROBERT R. McCAMMON was born in Birmingham, Alabama, where he lives with his wife Sally. He was just 26 years old when his first novel, *Baal*, was published. Since then he has produced a consistent string of best-selling horror novels, including *Bethany's Sin*, *The Nightboat*, *They Thirst*, *Mystery Walk*, *Usher's Passing*, *Swan Song*, *Stinger*, *Wolf's Hour* and *Mine*, as well as the collection *Blue World*.

"Pin" is a harrowing tale of psychological terror that pushes its point home with a vengeance.

I'M GOING TO DO IT.
   Yes. I am.

I hold the pin in my hand, and tonight I'm going to peer into the inner sun.

Then, when I'm filled up with all that glare and heat and my brain is on fire like a four-alarm blaze I'm going to take my Winchester rifle down to the McDonald's on the corner and we'll see who says what to who when.

There you go, talking to yourself. Well, there's nobody else around is there so who am I supposed to talk to? No, no; my friend's here. Right here, in my hand. You know. Pin.

I have a small sharp friend. Oh, look at that little point gleam. It hypnotizes you, Pin does. It says look at me look long and hard and in me you will see your future. It is a very sharp future, and there is pain in it. Pin is better than God, because I can hold Pin. God frets and moans in silence, somewhere . . . up there, somewhere. Way above the ceiling. Damn, I didn't know that crack was there. No wonder this bitching place leaks.

Now Johnny's an okay guy. I mean, I wouldn't shoot him. He's okay. The others at the shop—bam bam bam, dead in two seconds flat. I don't like the way they clam up when I walk past, like they've got secrets I'm not supposed to know anything about. Like you have secrets when you work on cars all day and fix tyres and brake shoes and get that gunk under your fingernails that won't ever wash out? Some secrets. Now Pin . . . Pin does have secrets. Tonight I'm going to learn them, and I'm going to share my knowledge with those people down on the corner eating their hamburgers in the safe safe world. I'll bet that damn roof doesn't leak I'll make it leak I'll put a bullet right through it so there.

I'm sweating. Hot in here. Summer night, so what else is new?

Pin, you're so pretty you make me want to cry.

The trick, I think, is not to blink. I've heard about people who did this before. They saw the inner sun, and they went out radiant. It's always dark in here. It's always dark in this town. I think they need a little sunlight, don't you?

Who're you talking to, anyway? Me myself and I. Pin makes four. Hell, I could play bridge if I wanted to. Lucas liked to play bridge, liked to cheat and call you names and what else did you have to do in that place anyway? Oh, those white white walls. I think white is Satan's colour, because it has no face. I saw that Baptist preacher on tv and he had on a white shirt with his sleeves rolled up. He said come down the aisle come on come on while you can and I'll show you the door to Heaven.

It's a big white door, he said. And he smiled when he said it and the way he smiled oh I knew I just knew he was really saying you're watching me aren't you, Joey? He was really saying, Joey you know all about big white doors don't you, and how when they swing shut you hear the latch fall and the key rattle and that big white door won't open again until somebody comes and opens it. There was always a long time between the closing and the opening.

I've always wanted to be a star. Like on tv or movies, somebody important with a lot of people nodding around you and saying you make a lot of sense. People like that always look like they know where they're going and they're always in a hurry to get there. Well, I know where I'm going now. Right down to the corner, where the golden arches are. Look out my window, I can see it. There goes a car turning in. Going to be full up on a Saturday night. Full up. My Winchester has a seven-shot magazine. Checkered American walnut. Satin finish. Rubber buttplate. It weighs seven pounds, a good weight. I have more bullets, too. Full up on a Saturday night. Date night, oh yes I hope she's there that girl you know the one she drives a blue Camaro and she has long blond hair and eyes like diamonds. Diamonds are hard, but you hit one with a bullet and it's not so hard anymore.

Pin, we won't think about her will we? Nope! If she's there it's Fate. Maybe I won't shoot her, and she'll see I'm a nice guy.

Hold Pin close. Closer. Closer still. Up against the right eye. I've thought a long time about this. It was a tough decision. Left or right? I'm right-handed, so it makes sense to use my right eye. I can already see the sun sparkle on the end of Pin, like a promise.

Oh, what I could do with a machine-gun. Eliot Ness, Untouchables, tommygun type thing. I sure could send a lot of people behind that big white door, couldn't I? See, the funny thing, I mean really funny thing is that everybody wants to go to Heaven but everybody's scared to die. That's what I'm going to say when the lights come on and that news guy sticks a microphone in my face. I need to shave first. I need to wear a tie. No, they won't know me with a tie on. I need to wear my grey uniform grey now there's a man's colour. Pick you up good on tv in grey.

Speak to me, Pin. Say it won't hurt.

Oh, you lying little bitch.

It has to be in the centre. In that black part. It has to go in deep. Real deep, and you have to keep pushing it in until you see the inner sun. You know, I'll bet that part's dead anyway. I'll bet you can't even feel any pain in the black part. Just push it in and keep pushing, and you'll see that sunburst and then you can go down and have a hamburger when it's all said and done.

Sweating. Hot night. That fan's not worth a damn it just makes a racket.

Are you ready?

Closer, Pin. Closer. I never knew the point could look so big. Closer. Almost touching. Don't blink! Cowards blink nobody can ever say Joey Shatterly's a coward no sir!

Wait. Wait. I think I need a mirror for this.

I smell under my arms. Ban Roll-On. You don't want to smell when they turn the lights on you what if it's not the guy but the girl who does the late news the one with big boobs and a smile like frostbite?

No, I don't need to shave I look fine. Oh hell I'm out of Ban. Old Spice that'll do. My dad used to use Old Spice everybody's dads did. Now that was a good day, when we saw the Reds play the Pirates and he bought me a bag of peanuts and said he was proud of me. That was a good day. Well, he was a fruitcake though a real Marine oh sure. I remember that Iwo Jima crap when he got crazy and drank all the time Iwo Jima Iwo Jima all the time I mean he lived it in his mind a million times. You got sick of hearing who all died at Iwo Jima and how come you ought to be proud to be an American and how things weren't how they used to be. Nothing is, is it? Except Old Spice. They still sell it, and the bottle's still the same. Iwo Jima Iwo Jima. And then he went and did it put the rope up in the garage and stepped off the ladder and me coming in to get my bike and that grin on his face that said Iwo Jima.

Oh Ma, I didn't mean to find him. Why didn't you go in there so you could hate yourself?

Now that was a good day, when we saw the Reds play the Pirates and he bought me a bag of peanuts and said he was proud of me. He was a real Marine.

The black part looks small in the mirror small as a dot. But Pin's smaller. Sharp as truth. My Winchester holds seven bullets. Magnificent seven I always liked Steve McQueen with that little sawed-off shotgun he died of cancer I think.

Pin, you're so beautiful. I want to learn things. I want to know secrets. In the glare of the inner sun I will walk tall and proud like a Marine on the hot sands of Iwo Jima. Closer, Pin. Closer still. Almost there. Close against the black part, the unblinking black. Look in the mirror, don't look at Pin. Don't blink! Closer. Steady, steady. Don't . . .

Dropped. Don't go down the sink! Get Pin, get it! Don't let it go . . .

There you are. Sweet Pin, sweet friend. My fingers are sweating. Wipe them off nice and neat on a towel. Holiday Inn. When did I stay at a Holiday Inn? When I went and visited Ma oh yes that's right. Somebody else lived in the old house a man and woman I never knew their names and Ma she just sat in that place with the rocking chairs and talked about Dad. She said Leo came to see her and I said Leo is in California and she said you hate Leo don't you? I don't hate Leo. Leo takes good care of Ma sends her money and keeps her in that place but I miss the old house. Nothing's how it used to be the whole world is turning faster and faster and sometimes I hold onto my bed because I'm scared the world is going to throw me off like an old shoe. So I hang on and my knuckles get white and pretty soon I can stand up and walk again. Baby steps.

Who blew that horn? Camaro, wasn't it? Blond girl at the wheel? Seven bullets. I'll make a lot of horns blow.

How straight and strong Pin is, like a little silver arrow. How were you made, and who made you? There are millions and millions of pins, but there is only one Pin. My friend, my key to light and truth. You shine and wink, and you say look into the inner sun and take your Winchester to the golden arches where Marines fear to tread.

I'm going to do it.

Yes. I am.

Closer. Closer.

Right up against the black. Shining silver, full of truth. Pin, my friend.

Look at the mirror. Don't blink. Oh ... sweating ... sweating. Don't blink!

Closer. Almost there. Silver, filling up the black. Almost. Almost.

You will not blink. No. You will not. Pin will take care of you. Pin will lead you. You. Will. Not. Blink.

Think about something else. Think about ... Iwo Jima.

Closer. Almost.

One jab. Quick.

Quick.

There.

Ow.

Ow. Don't. Don't. DON'T BLINK. Don't okay? Yes. Got it now. Ow. Hurts. Little bit. Pin, my friend. All silver. Hurts like truth. Yes it does. Another jab. Quick.

OH, JESUS. Deeper. Little bit deeper. Oh don't blink please please don't blink. Look right there there yes in the mirror push it deeper I was wrong the black part isn't dead.

Deeper.

Oh. Oh. Okay. Oh. GET IT OUT! No. Deeper. Got to see the inner sun I'm sweating Joey Shatterly's no coward no sir no sir. Deeper. Easy. easy. Oh. Streak of light that time. Blue light. Not a sunburst, a cold moon. Push it in. Oh. Oh. Hurting. Oh, it hurts. Blue light. Please don't blink push it in oh oh Dad where's my bike?

OH GOD GET IT OUT GET IT OUT OH IT HURTS GET IT . . .

No. Deeper.

My face. Twitching. Pain. Cold pain. Twitching. Seven bullets. Down to the golden arches and deeper still where is the inner s . . .

Oh . . . it . . . hurts . . . so . . . good . . .

Pin, sliding in. Slow. Cold steel. I love you, Dad. Pin show me the truth show me show me show . . .

Deeper. Through the pulse. Centre of the unblinking black. White's turned red. Seven bullets, seven names. Deeper, to the centre of the inner sun.

Oh! There! I saw it! See! Right there! I saw a flash of it push it deeper into the brain where the inner sun is right there! A flash of light! Pin, take me there. Pin . . . take me there . . .

Please.

Deeper. Past pain. Cold. Inner sun burning. Makes you smile. Almost there.

Push it in. Using all of Pin up. A mighty pain.

White light. Flashbulb. Hi, Ma! Oh . . . there . . . right . . . there . . .

Pin, sing to me.

Deeper.

I love you Dad Ma I'm so sorry I had to find him I didn't mean to I didn't . . .

One more push. A little one. Pin is almost gone. My eye is heavy, freighted with sight . . .

Pin, sing to me.

Dee

CHERRY WILDER

The House on Cemetery Street

CHERRY WILDER, a New Zealander, has confused biographers by living for years in Australia before moving to West Germany. Her strange stories have appeared in *Issac Asimov's Science Fiction Magazine, Interzone, New Terrors, Dark Voices 2* and other international anthologies.

Her novels include *Second Nature* (1982), the fantasy trilogy which began with *A Princess of the Chameln* (1984) and *Cruel Designs* (1988), a horror novel set in West Germany.

Although originally published in a science fiction magazine, the following story is a powerful and chilling memory of the Holocaust.

THE TWO YOUNGEST CHILDREN of the German author, August Fuller, spent eight years in California. After the war, their mother Vicki, his second wife, flew back as soon as ever she could to her husband's side. But there was no point in bringing the children back to Germany just yet ... the country was flattened and there was nothing to eat. So they stayed on until the end of 1947 with the family of Vicki's school friend, Estelle Bart O'Brien, and went back when Lucy had done her freshman year in college and Jo had completed the eighth grade.

They had left as Luisa and Joachim; they flew back in as Lucy and Jo. They were a couple of good-looking kids, but a little hard to place, bound to be exotics wherever they went. Jo at thirteen was short and slight with a smooth pre-adolescent beauty, large dark eyes, a mop of curly hair. Lucy at nearly eighteen was tall and slender, not built for sweaters. Her face was delicate, rather bony, her brown hair naturally-waved; her eyes were grey. She had had just enough dates to get along, but she knew that in certain circles she was classed as a dog.

It had taken an enormous amount of wire-pulling for them to fly at all. They were used to this hint of privilege and special treatment, and knew that it had to do with their father who worked miracles. Why, he had kept up a marvelous flow of letters throughout the war, postmarked Portugal at first, then U.S. Field Post. The children had received jointly over fifty letters—written in German, of course, but in the more readable English script. Vicki had set the letters carefully aside for future publication. Now it was getting on towards Christmas and they were sitting on the plane with a bunch of Air Force wives. They tried to brief each other on their lost childhood in the old country.

"Do you remember Christmas?" asked Lucy. "Do you remember the house at Christmas?"

It was something she herself could never forget. The northern Christmas, the cold, the delicious warmth, the suspense, the candlelight, had all sunk into her soul.

"The whole house smelled of cookies," said Jo. "There were green branches on the stairs. We were allowed to cut out Christmas cookies down in the kitchen. Aunt Helga sat at the corner of a huge table covered with oilcloth and ground Papa's coffee by hand."

"Did she?" said Lucy, surprised. "I remember the hall was too narrow, especially in winter with the coats and boots. There was a hallstand that Papa called 'the Bulgarian atrocity.' I thought it was rather pretty because of the lady painted on the mirror. Name six rooms that you truly remember and put someone you truly remember in each one."

"Papa in the study," said Jo, "that's easy. He let me sharpen pencils and spin the globe. Was the study upstairs?"

"It was on the landing, the mezzanine; it had a wreath on the door at Christmas."

"Okay. I remember Mom ringing the little silver bell in the room downstairs with blue curtains where they always had the tree. I remember Aunt Helga in the dining room carving the goose. Now we go upstairs. It's getting kind of foggy. Hey . . . Harald in a bedroom on the dark side of the house. I stood at the window looking out at a bunch of people in black, carrying flowers. He said 'It's a funeral, someone is being buried.' I really didn't know."

"I slept alone," said Lucy, "because poor Roswitha had gone away to University. I had the bedroom all to myself. It was across the corridor from the bedroom you shared with Harald."

Roswitha, their half-sister, had married the "decadent" painter Hans Molbe and had died in Paris, in exile, in 1940. Harald Fuller, their half-brother, had been in prison for his left-wing leanings; now he was working to build a democratic newspaper in the American zone.

"I remember Roswitha's wedding day," said Jo with shame. "I had to wear a *velvet suit*. Holy hell, that's one memory I kept quiet about!"

"I remember the wedding," said Lucy. "Hans had a beard and a bow tie. Harald got drunk on champagne, even Papa might have been a little bit plastered. Mom wore a long dress, a formal, in the middle of the day. Aunt Helga ran about so much that she had a nervous collapse in a wicker chair, under the oak."

She was beginning to see how weird and stiff and *Teutonic* the wedding had been. The older men had worn black frock coats and top hats. There were at least no uniforms, except for the band. Harald had sprung unsteadily onto a wrought iron garden seat and accused his father of bourgeois tendencies. Papa had passed it off with a silly joke in English "I represent that remark . . ."

Lucy was surprised by another memory of the wedding day. Outside the upstairs bathroom as she looked down at the sun-drenched landing. Aunt Helga took her by the arm. She had recovered from her swoon, and she towered over Luisa, her hair damp, her face unpowdered. "Your Papa is an innocent," she whispered, "an *innocent*. These people crowding into the house . . ." Which people? At the time Lucy had had no idea, but now she saw that there had been several undesirable elements at the wedding. Artists, socialists . . . with a sinking feeling, as the plane lost altitude, Lucy included the Jews. Mom was half Jewish, which was why they had had to go into exile in the first place.

There had been more wire-pulling. Papa made the decision to stay, as he explained in Letter Four, posted at Lisbon, December 1939. He must remain in the Deutsche Sprachraum, the area where German was spoken. The Nazis had left him alone after a token arrest in '41; he had his little retreat in Schleswig Holstein where he wrote but published nothing, and waited until the liberal spirit was reborn.

"I remember a great place," said Jo, "the attic. We had our *Geheimbutze* there, our secret clubhouse. We used to have a Christmas party with the toy animals and the dolls. There was an old dressmaker's dummy, shaped like a dame, you know, with no head and no arms. And a little door all covered with wallpaper."

"Honest to Betsy," said Lucy, rolling her eyes, "the things you remember, *Bruderherz*."

Actually, Lucy remembered the stifling, dust-smelling play-house in the attic very well. She had always been a little afraid of the dressmaker's dummy.

Then they were down in the cold at Rhein-Main, entirely surrounded by a reunion of Air Force husbands and wives. Two American kids in their best clothes—Jo had cuffed trousers, nicely creased, Lucy a pleated skirt and nylons. Now they appreciated the overcoats and boots that had seemed so dumb in California. They looked about nervously at their first German civilians. A tall man, emaciated, wearing a duffel coat with wooden toggles over an awful threadbare blue suit, came swinging through the crowd. He was questioned by an MP at whom he arrogantly waved documents. Lucy thought she would die.

"*Harald*!"

He was so *old*. He was so thin. His German was so hard to understand.

"Great God, look at the pair of you! Two spoiled brats from America!"

He shook hands with them both, painfully hard.

"Where's Mom?" demanded Jo. "Where's Papa?"

"Your mother hasn't renewed her driving license," said Harald. "Did you think *Papa* would appear in public? No, no *mein Lieber*, I have to undertake this unpleasant duty."

It *was* rather unpleasant, Lucy conceded. They took an hour to get out of the building. Harald bundled them into a queer old jalopy, an Opel, and they were whirled over the autobahn, past ruined factories and plantations of young firs, to the small town of Breitbach. There was a long high wall of pinkish stone; through an iron gate in the wall, they saw gravestones and grey monuments. The day was very still, grey and cold, but there was no snow. And there was the house, set back from the road on a deep, narrow site.

'Freidhof Strasse," announced Harald to his silent passengers. "Cemetery Street."

A tall woman with ash-blonde hair was sweeping the stone path.

"Your Aunt Helga," said Harald, "Frau Fuller Krantz."

"What happened to Uncle Markus?" asked Lucy.

She knew that it was all very sad. Her aunt had married late; Uncle Markus came back from the war and then died.

Harald scratched his head.

"Well, I'll give it to you straight," he said. "You'll get a lot of evasive nonsense in this house, but none from me, I swear it. Poor old Markus came back from the war . . ."

"Was he a Nazi?" asked Jo.

"No, of course not," snapped Harald. "He was a decent chap, son of a bookseller in Frankfurt. He was drafted into the Wehrmacht. He was lucky enough to get back from the Russian front in July '45. He committed suicide a week later."

"In the house?" whispered Lucy.

"Hung himself over the stairs," said Harald. "He was sick, exhausted . . . I don't know . . ."

"Was Papa at home?" asked Jo.

"No," said Harald. "Still up in his little *dacha* in the northern meadows. Helga was getting the house ready."

They struggled up the path with their suitcases while Harald stayed back, tinkering with the car. Lucy could not go any further; she rubbed her gloved hands and drew her turban of blue wool jersey down over her ears. The grass was dry, the trees were bare. Where was Mom? Why didn't she come out to meet them? The separation from her mother seemed as long and hard to bear as the lifetime she had spent away from Papa.

The house was broad and high, its dark yellow plaster peeled back in places to the bricks underneath. The windows had chocolate-brown shutters folded back upon the wall, and, in the center, over the front door, there was a deep balcony of the same brown wood. Lucy remembered the balcony and its window boxes stuck with evergreen twigs. Papa's study lay behind the balcony; she felt a rush of loving apprehension . . . after so long. . . .

She looked through a gap in the untidy cypress hedge and saw a ragged figure in black. A young man ran off among the tall grass and the grey monuments, flap, flap, he was gone, like a great black bird. She picked up her suitcase and caught up to Aunt Helga and Jo. Aunt Helga pushed back Jo's curls from his forehead and tucked them under his knitted cap. She took him by the shoulders, changing her grip, and held him at arm's length.

"Oh, he *will* be pleased!" she said. "Joachim at last! Joachim, the youngest child!"

Lucy recognized her aunt, and was shocked. Only the luxuriant hair was still as beautiful as ever. Helga's face had lengthened and set; there were heavy wrinkles on her brow. She was pale; even her lips were pale. Lucy realized that she wore no make-up; she had a naked face, as if she had just got out of bed in the morning, but she was a little bit dressed up, in a blue woollen dress and silver drop earings. Lucy herself was wearing powder over a rachel foundation and her peppermint-pink lipstick. Aunt Helga turned, stared, pursed her lips, and looked her niece up and down with a sigh.

"So, Luisa . . ."

She embraced her quickly.

"Go along."

She stood back with a motion of her broom and they heaved their suitcases into the house. There was Mom in the dark too-small hallway beside the Bulgarian atrocity, and she was in tears. Jo flung himself at his mother with a joyous shout.

"Ssh!" said Vicki Fuller. "Oh, my darlings, my darlings . . ."

As Lucy joined the family embrace, she remembered at last how things had been. They were hushed all day long because of Papa. But what did it matter now that they had Mom, their very own, pretty as the painted Jugendstil girl upon the hallstand mirror, girlish and slim, with Jo's dark eyes.

"Where's Papa?" cried Jo, shrugging out of his overcoat. "Is he in the study? I must go up!"

"Ssh!" said Aunt Helga as she came in. "You may go up quietly."

She laughed.

"Poor August . . . to have such a big boy burst in!"

"Go on," said Mom softly, "Go on, Jo do you know the way?"

Jo went thundering up the stairs and Lucy went to follow him, but Aunt Helga caught her by the wrist.

"Let him go," she said. "Let him go first. You must wash your face, Luisa. Your Papa doesn't like make-up."

Lucy shook off her aunt's hand. She saw that her mother was not wearing any make-up. She knew too that Mom would be no help. She never had been in certain situations.

"Now come," said Helga. "You look like a whore who runs after the Americans."

Mom said in a shocked voice, "Helga!"

Lucy ran lightly up the stairs without looking back at the two women. There was the study door, ajar; she went inside.

Jo had drawn up short of the huge desk where his father sat. Lucy saw that Papa had not changed at all. He looked just like his photograph on the book jackets: thick white hair, white since his fortieth year, a broad mild face. He brought his sentence to an end and looked up, shy and charming.

"Well, are you here?" he said.

He held out an arm on either side of his chair. Jo ran around the desk and was gathered up, but Lucy came more slowly. Her father stared at her as she approached.

"A film star," he said.

Then he held them, one on either side, and a wave of sadness passed over his face.

"I thought I would never see my little ones again."

"Papa," whispered Jo, "is Hitler really dead?"

"I hope so," said August Fuller devoutly.

"Papa, is it true about the horror camps?" asked Lucy, not to be outdone.

Even as she asked she realized what a foolish question it was. Harald, her own brother, was surely a victim of some camp. Had he been in *Belsen*?

"I will say this," said Papa, "I will say this, my dear children. The misery will never end. They will be counting the dead and arguing about the guilt for another fifty years."

"Papa," said Jo, "I'm going to give you an early present."

Their luggage was stuffed with presents. Now Jo drew from his trouser pocket a dime-store puzzle; tiny ball bearings had to be rolled into the eyes of a tiger. Lucy left them rolling the puzzle this way and that, and walked to the balcony doors. Far away there was a sound of children's voices, from a backyard or

15

a playground. She looked out at the head garden, and wished it would snow.

There was a gap two trees wide in the cypress hedge. A young man in black, perhaps the same who had flapped away at their approach, stood in the long grass of the cemetery, gazing up at the house. She could see his black curly hair and his pale face. He wore a long, black coat, not exactly an overcoat. Lucy could see neat graves with flowers and raked paths laid out beyond the wilderness.

Aunt Helga came to collect Lucy and Jo.

"Visiting time is over," she said briskly, like a hospital matron.

Jo was as balky as a six year old. He wanted to stay with Papa. He wrenched his arm away from Aunt Helga's firm grip and protested loudly in English.

"For crying out loud! We just got here!"

Lucy looked at her father. With a faint gentle smile, he laid aside the puzzle and picked up his fountain pen. Aunt Helga chased Jo around the desk. Papa sat like a man under a bell jar and let his sister hunt his youngest child out of the room. As they passed Lucy, Aunt Helga said, "You too! You too, Luisa!"

Lucy glanced down and saw that the young man in black had gone away. They followed Aunt Helga up to their old bedrooms, which they had shared with Harald and Roswitha. Lucy liked her room well enough, and tried not to think of the sunny bedroom at the O'Briens', all ruffles and polka-dots. The suitcases had been brought up, so Mom and Lucy unpacked and laughed and looked at farewell snapshots of Oakland, CA. When he had changed into his sneakers, Jo was allowed to go exploring. At last Mom went back to her typewriter downstairs and Aunt Helga said, "Come, Luisa!"

They carried the empty suitcases up to the third floor, where Helga slept, then up the narrow attic stair. There was a tiny landing with a window that looked out onto the slates. Lucy glanced anxiously at the stair rails, wondering about Uncle Markus. The long attic was partitioned off into small rooms, well-swept, and reeking of mothballs. The skylights were covered with brown paper. Sure enough, there was a version of their playhouse, with an old sofa and a heavy wardrobe against a partition. In one corner lurked the dressmaker's dummy, draped in a net curtain like a headless bride. There was a soft thump on the stairs and Jo came in, flushed with excitement.

"We used to play here!" he said. "I remember!"

"Oh, Joachim . . ." said Aunt Helga gently.

They stood beside her and saw that there was a field grey uniform stretched at full length upon the couch: nearby stood a pair of worn boots.

" A sad place for us all," she said. "My poor Markus . . ."

Subdued, they trooped out, and Aunt Helga locked the door at the top of the stairs.

"It would be pretty cold for a clubhouse, I guess," sighed Jo.

At five o'clock, they went down to the dining room for a meal of rye bread, margarine, plum jam, mettwurst, and awful sour plumcake covered with half-raw plums. Mom lit the first candle on the advent wreath of tannen and pine, decorated with gilded cones. There was nothing Lucy and Jo could drink except water. They tried disgusting peppermint tea and unrefrigerated skim milk. Jo spoke wistfully of Thanksgiving, and Aunt Helga asked, thanksgiving for *what*? At half past five, Aunt Helga cried, "Go up, go up, little Vicki . . . he will be waiting!"

Vicki carried up a tray to her husband. When Jo tried to follow, Aunt Helga held him in his chair with her hands on his shoulders.

"Hush," she said, "you must understand. It is their time together."

"Do *we* get any time with our father?" asked Lucy.

The irony was lost on Helga. She smiled benignly.

"I have been thinking," she said "You might be permitted to go along on August's walk."

"Permitted?" cried Jo, "are you mad? You're not my parent . . . *he* is!"

Aunt Helga smacked Jo across the face. Lucy, filled with instant strength, like Superman, sprang up from her place, pushed her aunt aside, and shielded her brother.

"How dare you!" she shouted. "Mom! Papa! She hit Jo in the face!"

No one came or questioned; the dining room was a long way from the study. Aunt Helga collapsed into her chair and burst into tears. Jo jumped up angrily and padded out of the room.

"I should not have hit the boy," said Aunt Helga, turning to Lucy with a dreadful tear-stained face. "Luisa, dearest child, it has been so difficult to care for your father. To give him conditions in which he could work, to protect him from interruption."

"Jo will go to Papa and Mom," said Lucy.

"Oh, August will send him away," said Aunt Helga. "It is his time alone with little Vicki."

She sipped her peppermint tea and said, "I was sure I would die when the arrest took place. August was so brave. We had a tip, we were always well-informed. He walked down the path carrying his hat and coat. He did not want them in the house."

"Who came for him?" asked Lucy. "What did they look like?"

"Two men in soft hats and raincoats," said Aunt Helga. "August said to me 'Such a cliché . . .' We had fugitives in the house, he sacrificed himself for them. He was speaking to the men; I was stationed at the front door; Frau Rothmeier and the children had fled into the back garden, then through the hedge into the cemetery. No one would look there, under the old trees. We did it at every serious alarm, but it was more difficult in winter."

Frau Fuller Krantz wept again, her face crumpled.

"Oh Luisa, it was so terrible . . ."

"Please, please don't cry," said Lucy, as warmly and sympathetically as she could. "Papa is fine. We're all here."

"I waited at the Praesidium in Darmstadt for thirty-six hours," said Aunt Helga. "Went to the ladies' toilet in a large store and washed my hands and face. Ate a bread roll and drank coffee. I came back to this house on the bus and managed to get through by telephone to an American businessman in Berlin, Mr. Walker. I didn't bother about secrecy, I said straight out:

'August Fuller has been arrested'. I lay down for a few hours just as I was, but I had Frau Rothmeier wake me. I changed my clothes and set out on my bicycle all over Breitbach, to the police, to the town hall, to a very cultivated man from the Labor Front, a party intellectual who had a villa on the Steinberg. I like to think it all helped. In three days, August was free. It was at this time, the autumn of '41, that we decided to go to Schleswig Holstein, to the little hut on the Mariensee."

"You saved Papa," said Lucy. "You were very brave, Aunt Helga."

Her aunt smiled at last. They sat in silence before clearing the table. It was dark outside, and there was only candlelight in the room, from the advent wreath. There was no heating, and a heavy chill was seeping into the house. Far away there were monotonous bursts of tapping and hammering, as if some amateur carpenter were patching some other house to keep out the cold. Suddenly, Lucy heard a wailing cry, dampened by distance, and a soft, horrible thump.

"Did you hear that?"

It was hardly necessary to ask; Aunt Helga had heard nothing.

"Really," said Lucy, "it sounded as if someone .. *fell down.*"

Helga's face became set and disapproving.

"I'm surprised at Harald, filing you up with these sad tales."

"What sad tales?"

"Enough!" said Aunt Helga. "We will clear, and if you are a good girl, you may have a tiny glass of elderberry wine."

They went down a few steps into the kitchen, which didn't smell of cookies any more. There was a pervading reek of smoke from the stove. All cleaners were in short supply: soap, washing powder, polish, spirits. There was sand to scour the pots and pans. When the washing up was done, Lucy opened the back door and looked into the yard. The night was undark; it was just beginning to snow. There was the old swing, moving to and fro as if Luisa, nine years old, had just run indoors.

"*Oh I remember. . . .*"

19

"I call it the children's playground," said Aunt Helga. "Joachim should see this. I strung up all the colored lights we had left. When I think how we filled this yard with colored lanterns in summer and colored lights in the Christmas season. I think of all the children: Roswitha, Harald, Luisa, Joachim . . ."

"There were children in the house, hiding . . ."

"Yes, even the little Rothmeiers. They were so quiet and good, but in the dusk they ran about like mad things. This yard can't be seen from the street."

Aunt Helga threw the switch and half a dozen colored bulbs flowered in the half darkness, strung from the clothesline to the garden shed. Lucy walked down into the garden among the phantom children running about so wildly. Roswitha was dead, Harald was thin and old, Jo was a displaced person, Luisa had become Lucy. Aunt Helga called and came after her. She put her into an old cloth coat and a pair of ankle boots.

"Aunt Helga, what became of the Rothmeiers?" asked Lucy.

Helga stood at the top of the steps, holding out her arms to the playground and the lights.

"They were saved!" she said. "We saved the family, your Papa and I. They all came safely to Palestine."

Lucy went stomping carefully across the lawn, which was lightly sprinkled with snow that was not sticking very well. The swing was in an iron frame painted white; the enamel was lumpy and rust-spotted. She stood against the back wall of ancient pinkish stone and turned to look at the house.

She was pierced with cold. She had never been so cold in her life. Her whole body was shivering, her teeth chattered, her face was stiff with cold. She could not stir from her place against the wall. The house was oddly lit, red and green in luminous patches from the colored lights. The figure of a man was standing on the roof, not far from the catwalk and the sloped iron ladder for the chimney sweep. In deathly silence, the man side-stepped and fell, face downwards, his black coat billowing out. Lucy knew the sounds that he had made: the wailing horrid cry, the brief passage of a body through the air, and the moist thump upon the snowy ground below.

She was trapped, unable to call for help, unable to think clearly about what she had seen. Gradually, the ordinary sounds of the night began to return. Aunt Helga shut a cupboard door. A car horn sounded, blocks away. A dog howled. Lucy ran shuddering for the back door and paused to glance around the corner of the house. Nothing lay on the ground.

She dragged herself back inside, hung up her coat, switched off the lights at Aunt Helga's command. She was like a sleepwalker. The bell rang at the front door.

"It is Harald," said Aunt Helga. "Let him in."

She fell against him in the hallway, gasping for breath.

"Now, now," he said. "How did you get so cold? What has upset you, Lucy?"

He dumped his coat and books in the library, where he slept. Then he led her into the warmed sitting room and sat her on the couch.

"What *is* all this?"

"What is the sad tale about someone who fell off the roof?"

Harald still carried his briefcase. Now he drew out a bottle of Coca-Cola and an opener. Lucy gulped the soda as if it were the elixir of life.

"It *is* a sad tale," said Harald, "and also a mystery. We are not even sure that he *did* fall off the roof. And if he did, no one has the least idea of what he was doing there. This gets unpleasant . . ."

He took a sip of Coke.

"He was not found, you see. The house was empty. Papa was in his lake-dwelling with Helga. I was in Theresienstadt. It was not until 1944 that Old Schultz, who used to do a bit of gardening here, came hunting for firewood. He found him lying there. He had been dead for years. His neck was broken."

"But who on earth *was* it?"

"Didn't I say? It was poor young Stein. Solomon Stein, Frau Rothmeier's brother. She used to slip out and meet him sometimes."

"But surely *someone* noticed that he was missing!"

"I'm sure they did," said Harald bitterly. "He was on some

deportation list, headed for the last round-up. His family were long gone."

"He was trying to shelter in the house," said Lucy firmly.

"Possibly."

"He *did* fall off the roof," she said, watching Harald very closely. "I heard the sounds and I saw him fall."

Harald shook his head from side to side.

"You are as bad as Papa and his nightmares!" he said.

She saw that she had come to some frontier that he could not cross; he was not battling with his unbelief, but with her unreason.

A voice cried joyfully, "Children! Helga!"

Vicki was calling; she walked slowly, majestically, down the stairs, arm in arm with August himself. Papa was making a special occasion, he was breaking his routine for them all. There was an instant response: Helga came with a bottle of wine, Harald stoked up the stove. Everyone spoke at once and crowded into the sitting room. The advent candle was lit again, the radio was switched on and a Strauss waltz was playing. Was it "Morning Papers?" "Wine, Women, and Song"?

"Wrong!" cried August. "It is Artists' Life!"

But where was Jo? Lucy ran up three flights and looked into his bedroom. In the feeble light of the bedside lamp he was lying curled up on his bed, sound asleep. His face had an unhealthy pallor, his forehead was damp. His hands lay palm upward, filthy with dust, the same thick dust that clung to the cuffs of his trousers. She shook him roughly awake.

"Jo! Jo! Papa is downstairs!"

Jo looked at her with unseeing eyes, black, glistening pools. He was always hard to wake.

"Are you okay?"

"I threw up," he said.

"Papa is downstairs. Will you stay sick or come down?"

He swung off the bed, and she followed him to the echoing bathroom. He washed his hands and face in cold water and stared into the glass. Lucy was impatient and frightened. He was only her kid brother, but who would be left for her if he slipped away?

22

They went down to the bosom of the family. August was in top form, playing up shamelessly to each of his children in turn. How they laughed. How Lucy blushed. How Harald's harsh jokes crackled from one end of the room to the other. Mom perched on the arm of Papa's big leather chair. Over the mantelpiece was a large aquarelle of a sweet-faced girl in a green dress melting into flowery depths of an orchard. It was Nina, the first wife, mother of poor Roswitha and of Harald. She had been Helga's schoolfriend.

Helga was persuaded to go to the piano at last, although she protested that it needed tuning. She began with "Stille Nacht," "Silent Night"; everyone joined in slowly, tentatively. Jo's beautiful unbroken alto rose up alongside August's fine light baritone and Helga's trained soprano. When the first verse was over they stopped, amazed. Vicki began to cry.

"It is *over*," said August. "It is really all over at last. We are all together again. We can start to live!"

Lucy was overcome by compassion. Poor things, she thought, poor old things. Aunt Helga swung into "O Tannenbaum" and Harald cried, "Now there's a good tune!" Then, intoxicated by the warmth and the wine and the Christmas music, they caroled away at "Every year the Christchild comes again" and "Ring, ring little bell," with Jo doing the solo for the Christchild who asks to be let in from the cold. Lucy and Jo and Mom began *a capella* with "White Christmas" and "Away in a Manger," but Aunt Helga soon played along. After a few bars she could fake it.

In a pause for refreshment after a bracket of Santa Claus numbers, Jo said, "Aunt Helga, what happened to my toy tiger?"

"Oh, Jo," said Mom.

"No, I need him," said Jo. "And there was a teddy and a wooden horse. A whole box of things we couldn't take."

"Hush," said Mom, "I expect they're somewhere about."

"Joachim, you're a big boy," said Aunt Helga. "Why in the world do you want those old toys?"

"I want to give them to the refugee children," said Jo, reddening. "There was an appeal, you know, on the radio."

Everyone was amused yet approving. Everyone but Lucy, who knew that for some reason Jo was lying, most persuasively.

23

"It does you credit, Joachim," said Aunt Helga in a quiet careful voice. "The toys have gone. They *were* given to refugee children. To the little Rothmeiers who stayed here."

It put an instant damper on the party. Harald said fiercely, "They were born and brought up in Germany and they became *refugees* overnight. Rosa and Benny Rothmeier and the baby. *Not* one of our greatest successes."

August was up in arms, arguing with Harald until they were both shouting. Poor organization! A complete farce! It couldn't be helped. Would he blame Helga? Frau Rothmeier herself had a grave responsibility. The wonder was that they did not *all* end up in prison!

"Aunt Helga," cried Lucy, "you said they were saved, that they all came safety to Palestine!"

"Make that the Promised Land," said Harald, "poor little devils . . ."

"I lied to you, Luisa," said Aunt Helga. "It is too sad."

The Rothmeier family had been picked up . . . arrested . . . on the edge of town, as they waited for the car that was taking them to the Swiss border.

"God, God, what could I do?" said Aunt Helga, wringing her hands. "I helped Frau Rothmeier button their coats and put on their overshoes. In the evening, when I was giving thanks for their escape, there came the telephone call from Herr Stein, the brother. The car had arrived late . . . he had seen his sister and the children arrested. Poor fellow, I think this sent him mad. Next day I went to take care of August. My bags were packed . . . It had taken weeks to get the necessary permit."

"Are you sure all the Rothmeiers . . . are gone?" whispered Vicki. "The mother and the three little children?"

"I'm sure!" snapped Harald.

"We have an inquiry running with the Red Cross," said August heavily. "I mentioned something of this in my letters to America. But it is foolish to hope."

Nevertheless Lucy did hope, from that moment. She found herself turning to the front windows of the house, upstairs or down. She looked out, dreaming, and saw them coming down the path. They were thin as Harald but grown into hardy waifs, twelve, ten, seven years old, clutching a toy tiger, a teddy bear, a little wooden horse.

She enjoyed this day-dreaming much more than her actual dreams, which were cold and filled with anxiety. She saw Jo with a dead look on his face, his lips moving as if in prayer. There was a tapping, scraping, boring sound that went on and on, and was sometimes like a voice, the Christchild or the lost children, wanting to come in. She woke at night hearing her father utter a strange roaring cry, coming out of his nightmare, and her mother soothing him to sleep again.

On the eve of the sixth of December, St. Nicholas's Day, everyone put out a shoe on the mezzanine near the door of the study. The adults persuaded the children to do so and vice versa. Lucy and Jo provided carefully chosen little gifts from their store, perfume, soap, socks, and what did they receive in return?

"They *have* to be kidding," said Jo.

"Ssh," said Lucy, sounding like Mom or Aunt Helga. "We get our real presents on Christmas Eve . . ."

It was an old joke that no one remembered. In the olden days, kids had to be satisfied with *much less* at Christmas: in fact, with an orange and a bag of nuts.

It was a quarter to six, bitterly cold, and pitch dark. The electricity would be off for another two hours: they had filled shoes and found their own presents with the help of Jo's flashlight. Soon Aunt Helga would come down to stoke up the banked kitchen range by candlelight. They sat on the stairs, fully dressed in trousers and sweaters under their dressing gowns, and sniffed at the oranges.

"I will go home," said Jo.

"You can't," said Lucy, not pretending to misunderstand. "You're too young. You have to stay with Mom."

"She'll see it my way," said Jo, with steely determination.

"Papa has plans for you."

"Papa can come and see me in America. He should have gone with us in the first place."

"Jo, they're all doing their best . . . even Aunt Helga."

"She's mean," said Jo, kneading his orange. "This is a creepy place. Think of Uncle Markus and the poor guy who fell off the roof."

"That was the war," said Lucy. "Jo, you have to stay here."

"This whole house is no better than one of those concentration camps."

Lucy was shocked and angry.

"You're out of your mind!" she said coldly. "Do you have any idea how bad it was in those places?"

"Yes!" said Jo.

Aunt Helga came down the creaking stairs and discovered the present in her old blue velvet slipper.

"Lavender soap!" she cried. "After all these years!"

August was driven out by Harald to give readings from his works, and radio interviews; he received his publishers' representatives in the study. There were other changes in routine because the children were being prepared to enter a German high school. Even Lucy must do a year in the *Gymnasium* before trying for a university place. Mom coached them in math and Harald in German grammar. It was generally conceded that the writing of perfect grammatical German was so difficult that Lucy and Jo might never master it sufficiently to qualify for certain professions.

August discovered—with a shocked look, one snowy afternoon as they trudged after him through the streets of Breitbach —that Lucy had read every one of his novels in the original and in translation. He set aside two hours, twice a week, to coach her in literature. They began to argue and expound very freely. Then each would stop, amazed: Lucy because this was the man, the author, who spoke, August because this fierce American girl was his own daughter. Aunt Helga, coming to end the seminar, had a proverb: "Children turn into People."

The snow was deeper now, and everyone was pleased, because Breitbach did not always have a white Christmas. The coldest months were those two generals who had defeated Napoleon further north: January and February. Lucy, ranging about the study one afternoon, looked from the window and became cold. The young man was much nearer, right in the grounds, staring up

26

at the house with an expression of misery and terror that froze the blood.

"Papa," she whispered, "there is someone in the garden!"

"What's the matter?" said August. "Is it someone after firewood?"

Far away in the reaches of the house there was a burst of tapping, a crescendo of little rapping sounds that rose up and then were still. They both heard the sounds, Lucy was sure of it.

"I see a young man with black hair," she said quickly. "He wears this long black coat . . . with a patch of yellow."

August gave a startled exclamation and hurried to the window. They looked down together, but the young man had gone. They were gazing at an unmarked patch of snow. They had both turned pale.

"It was Stein, young Stein," said August, "wearing his Star of David."

"He came from the cemetery," said Lucy.

"He is buried there," said August, "in the wilderness. That is the Jewish cemetery, divided from the rest. I think he was the very last to be buried in that place, after he was found . . . behind the house."

August sank down on the window seat beside the balcony door and put his head in his hands.

"I dream of him," he said. "It is one of my nightmares. I see him on the path and run towards him crying 'Come in, come in . . .' but he turns away from me because my house is accursed. My whole life, my work, my country, all accursed . . ."

"Do you hear . . . knocking sounds?" asked Lucy, very low.

"Yes," said August, "and scratching, and nibbling . . . the rats and mice working away at the foundations of the house . . ."

"Oh Papa," cried Lucy, taking him in her arms. "It will be all right again. Everything will be all right. Tomorrow is Christmas Eve!"

She looked down into the snowy garden again and screamed aloud. It was not young Stein who stood there, looking up with a terrible expression, but Jo, her brother. He flung a large snowball and it landed on the balcony. The next moment Aunt Helga came into the picture and hustled him away, raining smart little blows

27

upon the shoulders of his coat. Lucy saw that her scream had been too much for Papa, who hated loud noises. He returned to his desk, shaking his handsome head; their study of literature was finished for the day.

There was a problem about where to raise the tree. The small room downstairs with blue curtains was Vicki's typing room now, full of precious manuscripts. The tree was brought in semi-secretly by Harald and placed in the dining room. Aunt Helga shooed everyone away and set to work.

Late in the afternoon, Lucy sat with her mother in the typing room and Jo came to join them. It was Christmas Eve, so they were dressed in their best clothes. There was something very much the matter with Jo. He had grown two inches, his face was thin, he had an odd way of clenching his teeth when he spoke. All the grown-ups had spoken the word "puberty" in Lucy's presence, but she was not quite convinced. Well sure, puberty maybe, but what *else*? What was he up to? Now he sat with them, looking old and sick, a little like Harald, thumbing through the carbon copies of his father's letters to Luisa and Joachim in America.

They waited for the Christchild. Once Harald stuck his head into the room. He collected their wrapped presents to put under the tree and made everyone look for Aunt Helga's keys . . . she was turning the house upside down looking for her keys. He asked if they had their party pieces ready. Both Lucy and Jo, as the youngest, were expected to recite or read aloud at the feast.

"You needn't be afraid," said Mom nervously when Harald had gone. "Jo? I'm sure Lucy is not afraid."

"*Afraid*!" said Jo scornfully. "Afraid of reading something to those guys . . ."

Then he was sorry and he embraced Mom. Aunt Helga peeped in and said, "Vicki . . . Vicki . . . You must do your share!"

She smiled roguishly at Lucy and Jo.

"You two must wait for the ringing of the little silver bell."

When they were alone, Jo jumped up and said, "I always thought you had a lot of nerve for a girl."

His manner was desperate and strange; she knew he was asking for her help.

"Here," he said. "Read this page from Papa's letter. Read it to *them*. If you can't figure it out, Harald sure as hell will."

He had another present, a smallish cardboard carton clumsily wrapped in American Christmas paper.

"This is for the whole family," he said.

"Jo," she said, "Jo, if this is *running away*, it is truly a very dumb thing for you to do."

"It's not running away," he said. "Just the opposite. You can come too . . . where I'm going. Oh, I almost forgot . . . For Aunt Helga."

He fished in the pocket of his sports coat and drew out the bunch of keys. Then he snatched up Mom's beautiful vicuna lap robe and ran out of the room. Lucy heard him go upstairs. She began to read the page from Letter Twelve, which was dated November 1941.

"I have hidden away a great many books," wrote Papa, "to save them from the fire that is devouring our country. I think of all the secret places, in garden colonies, in the deep woods, in attics and cellars throughout the land, where men and women of goodwill have hidden those who are persecuted.

"A mother and her three children are hiding in our house, which I hope you still remember. I hardly know the children's names. When there is the least threat of danger they are hidden in a little room high up under the slates. They have learned to sit very still.

"I think of the oversized and inhuman monuments which this Warlord and his henchmen have set up in Germany. These vainglorious monuments will fall into dust and ashes. Only the secret places will abide, and the memory; the spirits of the men and women and the children who sheltered in these places will remain in them forever."

Lucy was puzzled and terrified. She was standing at the brink of an abyss. A sound began to penetrate . . . it was the ringing of the little silver bell. She walked slowly across the hall carrying Jo's package but she could not slip into the dining room unnoticed. Everyone was waiting, even Papa. Lucy received the full impact of the beautiful tree, just as she remembered it, blazing with real candles. She saw the strips of silver lammetta, the lovely baubles

29

of colored glass, the legions of wooden angels and the silver star at the top.

"Where is Jo?" they cried. "But where is Jo?"

"He had to go to the toilet," said Lucy. "He was nervous."

Everyone laughed. Aunt Helga had a very suitable proverb: "Eine schöne Bescherung," which meant "a fine howdy-do" as well as a fine sharing out of gifts at Christmas time.

"Lucy," said Harald, "what's the matter?"

Lucy still stood there, unable to move, clutching the messily swaddled package. The scene began to unfold in slow motion, so smoothly that she could almost believe in the intervention of some higher power.

Papa and Mom stood beside their chairs at the dining table, which was covered with plates of sweets, oranges, and nuts, one for every member of the family. Aunt Helga was the only one seated, fanning herself with a paper fan, warding off another nervous collapse after her exertions. Harald snatched the carbon of the letter from Lucy.

"Jo said you would understand," she whispered.

She went forward slowly to keep from sinking down onto the carpet. She placed the bunch of keys before Aunt Helga, and then put the package in the very centre of the table. She began stripping off the paper, and found that her guess was correct. The package smelled awful; it stank of dust and corruption. She wanted to rub her hands and arms where they had touched the wrapper. Her voice was loud, out of control.

"This is from Jo . . . for all the family"

"A key is missing!" said Aunt Helga.

"What in the name of God. . . ?" said Papa.

Lucy folded back the top of the carton, but she could only take out one thing and set it on the damask cloth. It was old and horribly stained, and there were dark threads adhering to the plush; it was a toy tiger. Harald uttered some growling sound and swiftly emptied the carton. There were six vile reeking dusty objects upon the table top.

"The children's overshoes. *Their overshoes*!" said Harald, his voice rising to a shout.

He felt among the overshoes and discovered that some of them were not empty. He snatched up a napkin and wiped his fingers. Then he handed Papa his own letter.

"What if Frau Rothmeier was picked up alone?" Harald said. "She went out to meet her brother, and left the children in their hiding place . . ."

"It's not possible," said Mom. "What you are saying is not possible. The children . . ."

After a long silence Papa said very gently:

"Helga. . . ?"

There was a sudden loud splashing sound, it went on and on, then a stink of hot urine filled the room. Aunt Helga turned brick-red and went into hysterics, half laughing, half crying. No one dared to slap her face. Lucy stepped backwards from the damp carpet; a red ball fell off the Christmas tree.

"I was going to August," said Aunt Helga. "My bags were packed. It had taken so long to get the permit . . ."

Lucy kept on walking backwards until she was at the door. Papa and Harald began to speak, both at once. She slipped out of the room and began to run up the stairs, softly, lightly, as if she were flying. She climbed up and up and the attic door was open, the key in the lock. She went in, breathing the mothball reek; the attic was bitterly cold; the skylights were crusted with frost flowers. Jo had candles stuck to an old plate; the couch was covered with a rug and the lap robe. She sat there quietly, and the door of the wardrobe moved. Jo came out. He sat beside her, and, without embarrassment, they held hands.

"There was a door covered with wallpaper," said Lucy. "She moved the wardrobe in front of it."

"Maybe they always did that," said Jo.

"You stole the key today or yesterday," she said. "How did you get in before that?"

"From the roof," he said. "Out the landing window and in through the skylight. It was always a secret clubhouse."

He might have fallen, she thought. He came here all alone and found his way into the hidden room. He found the children. He grew thin and old and said nothing.

". . . got a board off the back of the wardrobe," Jo was saying.

"Then I broke into the room. It wasn't so hard. I was just looking for the box of toys."

"Solomon Stein figured out where they were," said Lucy. "He was trying to save them. He was trying to get in."

Lucy began to weep at last; she felt hot tears running down her cold cheeks.

"I'm sorry," she whispered. "I can't help thinking . . ."

The icy cold. The darkness. They were very good, very still, but at last they began calling, tapping, scraping, like mice gnawing at the fabric of the house . . . the empty house.

"Is it very bad in there?" she asked. "Could I. . . ?"

What did she mean? Could I get in through the narrow door? Could I bear it? She thought of her dream or vision of Jo sitting at a table with a dead look. In the end, she opened the wardrobe and peered through the small opening behind it. Jo had broken the door off its hinges. Inside, he had made a small heap of tannen branches covering the bodies of the two older children, Rosa and Benny, and a smaller heap for the baby on its moldering pillow. The air was still very foul. The room was no bigger than a cupboard; it shared a corner of one large skylight. Looking into the room, you could *almost* feel what it must have been like for them . . .

"She knew their mother would never come back," said Jo. "She left them there and went away to take care of Papa, and never told anyone."

"Oh yes," said Lucy, "I think she did."

She turned her head to look at the poor dressmaker's dummy; Jo had draped the field grey army tunic around its shoulders.

"I think she told Uncle Markus."

She remembered what Harald had said. Markus Krantz was a decent fellow, and had committed suicide soon after returning home from the Russian front.

Presently, Jo said, "What will happen? What will they do?"

Lucy shook her head. She had lost the power to predict the actions of any of the adults. She could only identify with Jo and with the dead children.

They sat in the candlelight, waiting for a step upon the attic stairs.

STEPHEN GALLAGHER

The Horn

A GROUP OF travellers trapped by a snowstorm and lured into the night by *something* both beautiful and deadly . . . It's a classic horror scenario, and here rising star Stephen Gallagher enhances the tension with a bleak atmosphere of dread.

Born in Salford, Lancashire, and currently living in Blackburn, he became a full-time writer in 1980, scripting two adventures for BBC-TV's popular *Doctor Who* series. His short fiction has been published in *The Magazine of Fantasy & Science Fiction*, *Asimov's*, *Fantasy Tales*, *Ripper!*, *Shadows 9*, *Night Visions 8* and *Winter Chills*.

His early books included novelisations of his *Doctor Who* scripts and the movie *Saturn 3*, and were followed by *Chimera* (recently filmed as a four-part mini-series for television), *Follower*, *Valley of Lights*, *Oktober*, *Down River* and *Rain*.

E XTRACT FROM THE COURT RECORD, Crown v Robson, 24th September 1987:

Counsel: You lured her to this quiet spot on the pretext that you were going to run away together.

Robson: I never promised anything.

Counsel: Then you beat her senseless and left her for dead.

Robson: Hold on, chief! I tapped her once to calm her down, that's all.

Counsel: Are you now saying that you weren't responsible for her murder?

Robson: She was fit enough when I left her.

Counsel: So how do you suppose that she died?

Robson: That wouldn't be until the next morning.

Counsel: When, exactly?

Robson: Around the time they poured the concrete in, I expect.

"We've got heat, we've got light, we've got shelter," Mick said. "The lads even left us some dirty books. We've got everything we'll need to ride out the bad weather, so why don't we just sit tight until it all blows over?"

It was just then that the lights flickered and failed and the coal effect on the two-bar electric fire went terminally dark. The bars themselves went more slowly, and the three of us could only watch their fading glow with a kind of bleak desperation. Sub-zero winds were still hammering at the walls of the little roadside hut, and I felt about as well-protected as a mouse under a shoebox in the middle of a stampede. I was cold already. It was quickly going to get worse.

The single flame of Mick's gas lighter put giants' shadows on to the walls and ceiling. "Winds must've brought the line down," he said.

The other man, whose name was David something or other, said, "Anything we could fix?"

"Not me, pal. I'd rather live."

"What do we do, then? Burn the furniture?"

"Then we'd have nowhere to sit." The big man who'd told us

to call him Mick held the flame higher, and our shadows dived for cover. "Look, there's still candles and a gas ring. Nothing's altered. We can even have a brew."

"The kettle's electric and the water pipes are frozen," David said promptly. Mick looked at him, hard.

"I could really go off you," he said. "D'you know that?"

The candles were the dim, slow-burning kind in small tin dishes, and they'd been used before. The gas ring ran from a bottle under the table, and a kinked hose gave us a momentary problem in getting it going. The candles burned yellow, the gas burned blue, and our faces were white and scared-looking in the light that resulted.

Mick, David, me. Three separate stories of blizzard and breakdown and abandoned vehicles, three lifelines that probably wouldn't otherwise have crossed but which had come together in this fragile cabin at the side of a snowbound motorway.

"Well, here goes nothing," Mick said, and he grabbed a pan and went outside to get us some snow. The one called David went over to try the dead phone yet again.

I'd been the last to find the place, and I'd known immediately on entering that these two hadn't been travelling together. They were an unmatched and probably unmatchable pair. Mick weighed in at around eighteen stone and had the look of—well, there's no kind way of putting it—a slob, however you might dress and groom him. If you had to guess his line of work you might well place him as one of those vendors who stand with their push-along wagons near football grounds, selling hamburgers and hotdogs that have the look of having been poached in bodily fluids. David (he'd told me his second name, but it hadn't stuck in my mind) was more like one of those people you'll often see driving a company car with a spare shirt on a hanger in the back; he'd said that he was "in sales", which I took to mean that he was a salesman. He was about my own age, and had reddish-blond hair so fine that he seemed to have no eye-lashes. The story, as I understood it, was that Mick had been aiming for the big service area about two miles further along the road, but had found his way blocked and had been forced to abandon his van-load of rubber hose in order to walk back to the only light that he'd seen in miles. When he'd made it to the hut he'd found David already there, crouched before the electric fire with a workman's donkey jacket that he'd found and thrown around his shoulders. I'd joined them about half an hour after that, and no one had arrived since; the weather was worsening by the minute and it seemed unlikely that anybody else was going to make it through. The motorway must have been closed for some time now.

"Jesus wept!" Mick gasped when he'd fallen back in through the door three or four minutes later. I'd thought that he'd simply intended to take two steps out to fill the pan and then return and so I said, "What kept you?"

Some of the colour started to seep back into him as he stood over the heat of the gas ring, hands spread like he was making a blessing. He'd have made a pretty rough-looking priest. "I went down for a look at the road," he said, "just in case there was any sign of a gritter going through."

"See anything?"

"I'm lucky I even found the way back. I didn't get more than twenty yards, and it blew up so hard that I might as well have been blind. Nothing else is moving out there. Looks like we're in for the duration."

"Oh, great," David said heavily.

"You want to stick your nose outside before you say that," Mick suggested. "It's worse than before—it's like walking into razor blades, and I'll tell you something else. When the wind gets up in those wires, it's just like voices. You listen long enough and honest to God, you start hearing your own name. You know what I reckon?"

"What?" I said.

"It's all the dead people they've scraped up. They're all cold and lonely out there." And he winked at me as he said this, I suspect because his back was turned to David and David couldn't see.

"For Christ's sake," David muttered darkly, and he went over to the other side of the hut and started rummaging around in the cupboards for mugs and teabags.

Mick was grinning happily now, but I wasn't exactly sure

why. Lowering my voice so that David wouldn't hear me—he'd half-disappeared headfirst into one of the cupboards by now—I said, "What's all that about?"

"Haven't you seen the noticeboard?" Mick said, and he pointed to the wall behind me. "Take a look. We've found a right little Happy House to get ourselves snowed into. Desmond was reading all about it when I got here."

"It's David," corrected a muffled voice from somewhere inside the furniture.

Mick said, unruffled, "Of course it is."

I picked up one of the candles and took it over to the wall where the space alongside some lockers had been papered with old newspaper clippings. There were a few yellowing page three girls, but the rest of them were news stories. Some had photographs, and the photographs were all of mangled wreckage. It took me a moment to realise that they were all motorway crashes, and that the stretch of motorway where they'd taken place was the one that ran by under three feet of snow right outside.

"This must be where the lads wait for a call-out when there's something nasty," Mick said from just behind me. He'd come around and was inspecting the collection over my shoulder. "Some of the things they must have seen, eh? Rather them than me."

Amen to that, I thought, although even in the dim and unsteady candlelight I found that I was browsing through the details in some of the pieces with the kind of detached fascination that I always seem to be able to manage when it's a question of someone else's misery. Entire families wiped out. A teenaged girl decapitated. Lorry drivers crushed when their cabs folded around them like stepped-upon Coke cans. An unwanted mistress—this one really got me looking twice—an unwanted mistress dumped, Jimmy Hoffa-style, into the wire skeleton of a bridge piling that had been boxed-up ready to take concrete the next morning. ENTOMBED ALIVE! the headline said, but even that looked kind of pale next to the disaster involving the old folks' outing and the petfood truck full of offal.

I gathered from the collection that this hut was the base for the clean-up team who worked the road for some distance in either direction, and that they took an honest pride in their gruesome occupation. I imagined them trooping out to their breakdown wagon, whistling as they pulled on their jackets and thinking about next year's holidays. And then, at the other end of the drive, getting out with their bags and shovels to give their professional attention to the loved ones of some cheap-skate who'd saved the cost of a cabin on the car ferry or skipped a night in a hotel to drive on through and get an extra half-day out of the holiday flat. Where the team would be right now, I could only guess. I imagined that they'd have moved their base along to the service area as soon as the weather had started to clamp down, because the hut was no place to be marooned out of choice. The services would probably be starting to resemble a refugee centre by now, cut off but reasonably self-sufficient, and I wished that I could be there instead of here. The gas ring behind us was running with the valve wide-open, and still I could see my breath in the air in front of me.

David, over by the table, said, "Did you fill this?"

I tore myself away from the interesting stuff on the wall and followed Mick over to the ring, where David was peering into the aluminium pan. Where before it had been so over-filled with snow that it had looked like a big tub of ice-cream, now it held about an inch of water.

Mick observed, "It melts down to nothing, doesn't it?" And then the silence that followed was like the slow race in a restaurant to reach for the bill.

But then, finally, I said, "I'll get us some more."

I don't know how to describe the way the cold hit me as I stepped out of the hut. It was almost like walking into a wall, much worse than it had been when I'd made my way up there. The wind was the most disorienting factor, filling my eyes with hail and battering me around so hard that I could barely draw breath; but then, thankfully, it dropped a little, and the air cleared enough for me to see without being blinded.

Visibility was somewhere between fifty and a hundred yards, beyond which everything just greyed-out as if reality couldn't hold together any further. I could see about half a dozen of the overhead sodium lights marching off in either direction, their illumination blanketed and diffused by the amount of snow clouding the air. Of the motorway itself I could make out the parallel lines of the crash barriers as hardly more than pencil marks sketched on to the snow, and that was it. A few of the lightweight plastic cones that had been used earlier to close off lanes had been blown around and had lodged themselves here and there like erratic missiles, but nothing else broke the even cover.

I didn't see what Mick had been talking about. I didn't hear any voices, just the wind in the wires somewhere off the road and out of sight. The sound meant nothing special to me.

I had a baked bean can, catering size, that was the only other clean-looking container that I'd been able to find, and I stooped and tried to fill it with snow. The newly-fallen stuff was too fine, it just streamed away as I tried to load it in, but then I tried wedging it into snowball nuggets and did rather better. I was already starting to shake with the cold. I paused for a moment to wipe at my nose with the back of my glove, and realised with a kind of awe that I couldn't even feel the contact.

I fell back into the hut like a drowning man plucked from an icy sea. I'd been outside for less than a minute.

David looked up from the phone. I wouldn't have believed how welcoming the place could look with its candlelight and comparative warmth and the road gang's mugs set out ready, each with the name of an absent person written on the side in what looked like nail varnish. I did my best to make it look as if I had a grip on myself, and went over to set the rest of the snow to melt as Mick secured the door behind me.

"Still dead?" I said to David, with a nod at the phone.

"It's not exactly dead," he said, jiggling the cradle for about the hundredth time. "It's more like an open line with nothing on the other end."

"It'll be like a field telephone," Mick said from over by the door. "If nobody's plugged in, then there's no one to hear. How's it looking outside?"

"I'd still rather be in here than out there," I said.

Mick made the tea with a catering bag and some of that non-dairy whitener that looks and smells like paint. It was the worst

I'd ever tasted, and the most welcome. The three of us pulled our chairs in close to get into the circle of warmth around the gas ring, and we grew heady on the monoxide fumes. Inevitably, the conversation returned to the clippings on the wall.

"You want to see it from their point of view," Mick said. "It'll be like working in a morgue. You get bad dreams for the first few weeks and then after that, it's just another job."

"How would *you* know?" David asked.

"I've got a brother-in-law who's a nurse, he's just about seen it all. I mean, the likes of me and you, we don't know the half of what it's about."

David didn't comment, but I suspect that by then he was starting to read something personal into everything that Mick was saying. I believed that I'd recognised his type by now. Some people's reaction to pressure is to look around for someone convenient to dump on; they get angry, they get sarcastic, and if you pull through it tends to be in spite of them rather than with much in the way of help. I knew what Mick was talking about. I could imagine the team sitting there, patiently reading or playing cards while waiting for carnage. They were one up on us . . . we'd go through life telling ourselves that it was never going to happen, but they knew that it would and the knowledge wasn't even anything special to them.

Mick seemed to be the one who was holding us together, here. I'm not sure that right then I'd have wanted to rely on David for anything. He was frowning at the floor, his borrowed donkey jacket sitting uneasily on his shoulders. Had he really struggled from his car to the cabin with just a suit jacket and no overcoat? He must have seen the way that the weather was going before he set out, but he didn't look as if he'd taken any account of the possibility that he might have to step much beyond the warmth of a heated building or a moving car. Some people have too much faith in everything. I'm the opposite—I reckon that God intended few things to be immutable and that such things as designer luggage, golf shoes and the new shape of Volvo aren't among them.

I'd been heading for my girlfriend's place over in the next county when I'd come to my own unscheduled journey's end.

She was with a big retail chain who were moving her around and paying her peanuts, and I was just about holding down one of those jobs that they kept telling me might or might not turn out to be something permanent. The only way that we could ever get together was at weekends, hiding out from the landlady in her one-roomed flat. Mine must have been one of the last cars to get on to the road before they'd closed it. I'd had to stop as a jack-knifed articulated lorry had been cleared from the sliproad, and then it took two policemen to get me rolling again because my tyres wouldn't grip on the icy surface. They advised me to stay in low gear and to keep my revs down, and I remember their last words to me as I managed to get moving again—*Rather you than me, pal.* It got worse as I went on. After half an hour in first gear, following the crash barrier like a blind man following a rail, the temperature needle crept up into the red zone and then finally both hoses blew. I stopped and taped them and topped up the water, but the engine seized soon after that.

Mick was the only one who seemed to be listening as I told them the story. He said, "I've been driving this route since they opened it. I've never known it this bad. It looks like the end of the world."

"You've got a knack of seeing the bright side, Mick," I told him.

"You won't have seen that road train about half a mile on," he said. "A big new wagon and two trailers. It was blocking the road all the way across, that's why I had to give up and walk back to the last light I'd seen. Those things are like dinosaurs, they'll go on through anything. But it couldn't get through this. What do you reckon, Desmond?"

"*It's David!*" His sudden shout was startling in the enclosed space of the cabin, and I think even Mick was surprised by the reaction he got.

"All right," he said. "I'm sorry."

"Well, bloody get it right, then!"

"I said I'm sorry. I was only asking what you thought."

"I just want to get home," David said miserably, looking down at the floor as if he was embarrassed by his sudden outburst.

And then Mick said, with unexpected gentleness, "Nothing to argue with there, Dave."

It was then that the gas ring began to make a popping sound. We all turned to look and I heard somebody say *Oh, shit*, and then I realised that it had been me.

The flame didn't exactly go out, not right away, but it was obviously into some kind of terminal struggle. Mick reached under the table and heaved out the squat metal cylinder; when he raised it two-handed and gave it a shake, there sounded to be about a cupful of liquid sloshing around in the bottom.

"There's some left," David said hopefully.

"You always get some in the bottom," Mick said. "Still means it's empty."

There was another cylinder under the table and right at the back, but this one sounded just about the same. By now the ring was giving out no heat at all and making such a racket that nobody objected when Mick turned the valve to shut it off.

The silence got to us before the cold did. But the cold started getting to us a couple of minutes later.

We broke open the lockers in the hope of finding more coats or blankets, but all that we found were tools and empty lunch buckets and mud-encrusted work boots. David's earlier remark about burning the furniture no longer seemed like a joke, but the truth of it was that there wasn't much about the furniture that was combustible. The chairs were mostly tubular steel and the table was some kind of laminate over chipboard, which left a stack of soft-core porno magazines and a few paperbacks and one deck of cards. By now, the hut had turned from a haven into an icebox.

David was the one who put it into words.

He said, "We're going to have to go out and find somewhere else, aren't we?" He made it sound as if the place itself had done a number and betrayed us. "This is great," he said bitterly. "This really puts the fucking tin lid on it."

Possibly we could have stayed put, jogged on the spot a little, done our best to keep going in the sub-zero air until the worst of the weather receded and rescue came pushing through. But Mick was already going through the lockers for a second time, as if looking again for something that he'd already seen.

"The way I see it," he said, "there's only one thing we can do."

"The services?" I hazarded.

42

"We'd never make it that far. It's more than two miles and it might as well be twenty. I reckon we can do maybe a quarter of that, at the most."

"Which gets us nowhere," David said.

"It gets us as far as that big road train that's blocking the carriageway." So saying, Mick reached into the third locker and came out with a short, hooked wrecking bar. Holding up the jemmy he went on, "If we can get into that and get its engine running, we can sit tight in the cab with the heater on."

"Until the fuel runs out," I said, probably a touch too pessimistically.

"Those things never run out. They've got tanks like swimming pools. We can either wait for the snowplough to find us or else strike out again as the weather improves. What do you think?"

"It'll have a radio," David said, with a sense of discovery that seemed to surprise even him.

We both looked at him.

"A CB radio," he said. "Don't most of these big trucks carry them? We can tell someone where we are"

"That we can, Dave," Mick said with a note of approval, and then he looked from him to me. "Are you game?"

"Let's go," I said, sounding about four-hundred per cent more eager than I felt. But Mick raised a hand as if to say, *slow down*.

"Just wait on a minute," he said. "There's no point in all of us scrambling out together. What I reckon is, one of us strikes out and does the necessary, and then he leans on the horn as a signal for the others to follow."

"I wouldn't know what to do," David said bleakly.

"Me neither," I said.

"Well," Mick said, "since we're talking about breaking and entering and a little creative rewiring, I'd say that I'm the only one with the education in the appropriate subjects around here. Am I right?"

He was right, and as far as I was concerned he could make all the jibes about education that he wanted as long as he got us out of this. He turned up his collar and buttoned up his coat, and he pulled on his sheepskin gloves as I moved with him to the door.

David decided to give the phone yet another try as I made ready to let Mick out into the unwelcoming night.

I said, "You're mad, you know that?"

"I had my brain surgically removed," Mick said. "I've been feeling much better without it." Then he turned serious. "I'm going to get down to the crash barrier and follow it along, otherwise there's no knowing where I may end up. Keep listening for the horn." He glanced at David. "And keep an eye on him."

"He'll be all right."

"If he starts messing about, dump him. I mean it."

There was a blast of cold air for the brief second or so between Mick going out and me getting the door closed after him, and this time it stayed in there with us like some unwelcome dog that had dashed in and was standing its ground. David had slammed the phone down with a curse, as if its non-cooperation was a matter of deliberate choice, before settling on one of the chairs with his hands thrust deep into the pockets of his borrowed coat and the collar up over his nose to recirculate the heat of his breath. He looked like some odd kind of animal retreating into its blue worsted shell.

"I heard what he said, you know." His voice was muffled by the thick material, and sounded distant.

"He didn't mean anything by it."

"Yeah, I bet. And who does he think *he* is? Scott of the Antarctic?"

"I don't care if he thinks he's Scotty of the Enterprise. If he gets us out of trouble he'll be okay by me."

He settled in deeper. "Well, don't go worrying about me. I'm no deadweight."

"Never said I thought you were."

There was silence for a while.

Then he said, "Pretty serious, though, isn't it?"

Yes, I was thinking, it *was* pretty serious . . . but it could have been worse. Worse was being sliced in two at a combined speed of a hundred and fifty miles an hour, just because someone else chose the day of your trip to cross the central reservation and come looking for suicide in the oncoming traffic. Worse was being buried alive in concrete, so deep that even X-rays couldn't find you. It was sitting with your hands on the wheel while your head lay on the back seat. It was any one of the fifty or so examples of a messy and uncontrolled exit to be found in the road gang's private black museum over there on the wall.

"We've still got options," I said. "That puts us one step ahead."

"As long as he makes it," David said.

The next twenty or thirty minutes seemed to last for ever. David wasn't great company, particularly after the way that Mick's parting words had stung him. I wondered what I ought to expect; more of the ball-and-chain act, or would he become dangerously gung-ho? If the latter, then I was going to be happy to let him go out first.

Finally, the wind dropped a little and we heard the distant sound of a horn.

I said, with some relief, "Our call, I think."

David said that he was ready. I asked him if he wanted to take one last shot at the phone, but he said no.

"The greaseball was right in one thing," he said. "You listen for long enough, and you *do* start to hear them calling your name."

I let him go out ahead of me.

My spirit of optimism took an instant hammering as the door was banging shut behind us; compared to this brutal storm, the wind that had set the wires keening on my last excursion had been a precise and delicate instrument. All sound and sense were destroyed on contact, and I was beginning to panic when I felt David's rough grip on my arm, shoving me forward into the blind haze. The snow had drifted high in places, masking the contours of the ground beneath and making progress even more difficult; we stumbled and floundered downhill towards the road surface, and as we descended from the more exposed slopes the wind mercifully lessened. We got across to the central crash barrier, a constant mist of snow steaming from its knife-edged top, but by then I'd become as disoriented as if I'd been popped into a box and shaken.

"*Which way?*" I shouted, and David had to put his face right up to my ear to make himself heard.

"*Northbound!*" he roared.

"*What?*"

"*This way!*" And he gave me a hard push to get me moving.

I wouldn't have believed how heavy the going could be. It went from thigh-deep to waist-deep and then back to thigh-deep again, and the barrier disappeared for entire stretches so that we had to navigate by the yellow sodium lights above us. I'd break the trail for a while, and then David would move up and replace me. Any tracks that Mick might have left had been obliterated, but then there was the sound of the distant horn to lead us on whenever the storm took out a beat to let it through.

He'd made it. So would I.

I reckoned that we'd been going for about three hours, although a more rational part of my mind knew that it had actually been closer to fifteen minutes, when we reached the first place where we could stop and rest. It was a flyover bridge, too high and too wide to feel like much of a shelter but offering a respite from the cutting edge of the wind. We staggered in so all-over numb that we might as well have been on Novocaine drips for the last quarter hour, and we collapsed against the wall like footsoldiers in some forgotten war.

"Are you okay?" I said to David, my voice oddly flattened by the carpet of snow that had blown in under the bridge.

"You must be fucking joking," he gasped, and that was all I could get out of him.

I tried to knock off some of the dry snow that had crusted on to my clothing. I didn't want to risk any of it melting and soaking through only to re-freeze as we pushed on. It came off in chunks. David was hunkered down and hugging himself, presenting as small an area for heat loss as he could. If we stayed here for too long, we might end up staying here for good.

I listened for the horn.

Even though the bridge was open at the sides there was an enclosed, somehow isolated feeling about that few yards of shelter. It was brighter here than outside because there was nothing clouding the air between the sodium lights and the reflecting snow and, as I'd already noticed when I'd spoken to David, sounds went dead as if they'd run into something soft. There was scaffolding around the bridge-support across the carriageway, but I could still make out the spraycanned graffiti in amongst the repair work behind it as if through a grid; it read: ROBSON YOUR DEAD WHEN YOU GET OUT, and it had been written in red. My favourite piece of graffiti was one that I'd seen on a beach-front building, the simple and elegant I FEEL A BIT NORMAL TODAY, but it was a beach-front that seemed about a million miles away from the here and now.

The wind outside must have dropped a little because a snatch of the horn came through, and it sounded closer than ever. It acted on David like a goad. He suddenly lurched to his feet and set out again, stumbling and flailing his arms as if he hadn't quite brought his limbs under control yet. Wearily, I wondered if I'd ever be able to raise the energy to follow; but even as I was wondering, I was starting to move. David was muttering as he went, but I couldn't hear anything of what he was saying.

I stumbled, because there seemed to be all kinds of jumbled crap under the snow here; my foot hooked up what looked like a length of compressor hose, and I had to kick it off. Over on what would normally be the hard shoulder I could see the half-buried shapes of machinery, big generators with tow-hitches and a small dumper that might have been the answer to our prayers if it hadn't been jacked-up with a wheel missing. It looked as if, until the bad weather had intervened, they'd been drilling out the concrete like a bad tooth. Canvas on the scaffolding had concealed the work, but the material had been ripped by a through-wind to leave only a few flapping shreds around the hole. The cage of reinforcing wire inside the piling had been exposed, and the wire had been burst outward as if by a silent explosion. It looked as if they'd gone so far, and then the freeze-up had enlarged the hole further.

I suppose I could have thought about it harder. But there are some things, you can think about them as hard as you like but you'll never anticipate what you're actually going to see.

And the sight that I was concentrating on, to the exclusion of just about everything else, was that of the road train firming-up in the blizzard about a hundred yards ahead.

The first details that I made out were its hazard lights, and there were plenty of them; almost enough to define its shape, rather like those diagrams that take a scattered handful of stars and connect them up into some improbable-looking constellation. They were flashing on and off in time with the horn, and they were about the most welcome warning that I'd ever seen. Ahead of me, David was striding out like a wind-up toy that nothing could stop.

It was a big Continental articulated rig in three jack-knifed sections, a true monster of the road that would look like a landslide on the move. The distant *parp-parp* that had led us so far had now become a deep, regular airhorn bellow as we'd drawn closer. David tried to break into a run for the cab, but he had to be close to exhaustion by now.

We helped each other up and in. An alarm beeper was sounding off inside the cab and in synchronisation with the horn and the lights. There was no sign of Mick anywhere.

I said, "Where is he?"

"God knows," David said, studying a dash that looked like a piece of the space shuttle. "He might at least have left the engine running."

"Maybe he didn't get that far."

But David pointed to a bunch of wires that had been pulled out to hang behind the steering column. "What's that, then?" he said. "Heinz spaghetti? You check the radio."

I checked the radio.

"I don't think it's working," I said.

Sixty seconds after our entry, the alarms cut and the horn stopped. The silence almost hurt.

David had found the starter by now, and he was trying it; the first couple of times it stayed dead, but he jiggled the hanging wires like a child patting a balloon into the air and this must have helped some weak connection, because on the third attempt the engine somewhere beneath the cab floor turned over without any hesitation at all. After a few seconds, it caught; but then, almost immediately, it faded away and died again.

"Bastard thing," David said, and tried again, but there was no persuading it to catch for a second time.

He flopped back heavily in the driver's seat. I said, "Maybe we can just stay here anyway."

"There's still no heat," he said. "It may seem warmer, but

that's just the comparison with being outside. If we can't get the blowers going, I don't see any advantage over being back in the hut."

He tried the starter again, but still nothing.

"There's your reason why," he said suddenly, and pointed to a part of the dashboard display. If what he was pointing to was the fuel level readout, it was reading something like empty.

"These things never run out," he said bitterly, in what I assume he intended to be mimicry of Mick's voice. "They've got tanks like swimming pools." And he punched the steering wheel hard, and flopped back in the driver's seat again with a face as dark as a bruised plum.

And somewhere out in the night, another horn began to sound.

We both listened, lost it for a while as the wind howled, and then heard it again. Our signal was being repeated from somewhere further along the road.

"Here we go," David said wearily, and he opened the door on the far side of the cab to climb down. This time he didn't even flinch when the hail hit him. *All right*, I wanted to say, *case proven, you're no deadweight, now why don't we just try sticking it out here a while longer*, but instead I levered myself up and clambered awkwardly across the cab. I could have dropped and slept, right there. And probably died, ready-chilled and prepared for the morgue, but at that moment I hardly felt as if it would matter.

Mick's sheepskin gloves were on the cab floor.

I reached down and picked them up. I wasn't hallucinating them, they were real enough. He must have taken them off for the delicate work of hot-wiring . . . but how come he'd allowed himself to be parted from them? I was wearing my clumsy ski gloves, and even inside these my hands were feeling dead from the knuckles out. If Mick had gone the distance to the next stranded lorry, as the sounding of this second horn seemed to suggest, then I reckoned that he'd better not be planning any piano practice for a while.

I slid out of the cab and hit the snow again. I was now on the northern side of the big vehicle. David had launched off without me, hooked by the call like some deep-sea fish being drawn up to the gaff. The horn wasn't so regular this time, but it was coming through more clearly.

And me, I wasn't happy.

The forgotten gloves were only one part of it. Another part of it was the fact that you didn't put a rig and its cargo, total value anything from a quarter of a million up, into the hands of a driver who's going to be walking the hard shoulder with a can to get some diesel because he let the tanks get empty. And the radio—the radio should have been working, even if only to give out white noise to match the scene on the other side of the glass.

I was looking around the side of the road train when I fell over Mick's body in the snow. He was lying face-down and already he was half covered by drift, which for a moment gave me the absurd hope that he might have been insulated from the chilling effect of the wind and might be basically okay. But when I tried to turn him over he was as stiff as a wet sheet hung out in winter, and when I finally got him on to his back I could see that there was a spike of reinforcing wire from the concrete flyover driven right up under his chin. I could see it passing up through his open mouth as if his head were something spitted for a barbecue. His eyes were half-open, but plugged with ice. The short jemmy was still in his ungloved hand, held tightly like a defensive weapon that he'd never managed to use.

This had happened right by the big diesel tanks behind the cab. The tanks themselves had been slashed open so that all the oil had run out and gone straight down into the snow. And when I say slashed, I mean raked open in four parallel lines as if by fingernails, not just spiked or holed by something sharp.

David had stopped, and was looking back; but he was too far away to see anything and only just on the verge of being seen, a smudgy ghost painted in smoke. He beckoned me on with a big, broad gesture that looked like he was trying to hook something out of the air, and even though I yelled, "No! Don't go! It isn't him!" he simply shouted back something inaudible and turned away. He walked on, and the blizzard sucked him in.

And from somewhere beyond him came the sound of the

horn, the mating call of some dark mistress of nightmares with her skin oiled and her back arched and her long silver knives at the ready.

I started to run after him.

I call it running, although it wasn't much in the way of progress. I reckon you could have lit up a small town with the energy that I burned just to close up the distance between David and me. Close it up I did, but not enough. He didn't even glance back. I saw him duck at a near-miss from something windborne and I felt my heart stop for a moment, but I think it was only one of the plastic cones or some other piece of road debris. David couldn't have been distracted by nuns dancing naked in the air by that stage, because he was now within sight of the next truck.

The truck.

It was much older than the first one, and not so much of a giant. It was over on the far side of the barrier and facing my way; it looked as if it had come to a long, sliding halt before being abandoned and half-buried where it stood. It had a crouched, malevolent look, its engine running and breathing steam, pale headlamps like sick-bed eyes. David reached the cab and pounded on the side to be let in. I stopped at the crash barrier and could only watch. The horn ceased. The door opened. The cab's interior light blinked on, but the insides of the windows were all steamed up and runny and there was only the vague shape of someone visible. David had already hoisted himself half-way up with his foot in the stirrup over the wheel, but now I saw him hesitate. The door had swung out and was screening whatever confronted him . . . and then suddenly he was gone, jerked in at an impossible speed, and the door was slammed and the light went out. I winced at the loud, long and intense muffled screaming that began to come from the cab, but I knew there was nothing that I could do. I thought about those long slashes in the diesel tank and, for David's sake, I could only hope that whatever was happening would be over quickly.

It wasn't.

And when it finally ended, and after the long silence that followed, I saw the door opening out a crack like a trap being reset. Light streamed out into the snow-mist, a narrow slice falling like a rain of something solid. I looked up at the truck's windows and saw that the now-lit windshield had been sprayed red on the inside like the jug of a blender, and it was just starting a slow wash-down as the cab sweat began to trickle through it. I watched a while longer, but I couldn't see anything moving.

I was calculating my chances of making it through to the service area. What had seemed like a complete impossibility before now had the look of the most attractive available option. I had to have covered a good part of the distance already, didn't I? And having just had a glimpse of the alternative, I was suddenly finding that the prospect of pressing on had a certain appeal.

The first move would be to cross the carriageway and put as much distance as possible between me and the truck. There was nothing that I could do for David now, and it made no sense to stay out where the overhead lights made a tunnel of day through the blizzard. It was as I was striking out at an angle across a field of white that had once been the fast lane, a stumbling and deep-frozen body with a white-hot core of fear, that the horn began again.

That was okay, that suited me fine. As long as somebody was leaning on the button then they weren't out here with me, and that was exactly the way that I wanted it. I was trying to remember the route from the times that I'd driven it before. My guess was that I was just about to come to an exposed and elevated curve that would swing out to overlook a reservoir before entering the hills where the service area would be sheltered. I wouldn't be able to see much, if any, of this, but I'd know it because the intensity of the wind was bound to increase; high-sided vehicles took a battering on this stretch at the best of times, and this certainly wasn't one of those. I'd have to watch my footing. On a clear night I'd have been able to see right out to the lights of some mill town several miles out and below, but for now all that I could see was a dense white swirling. In my mind I could see myself holding one of those Christmas-scene paperweights, the kind that you shake and then watch as the contents settle, but in mine there was a tiny figure of David hammering on the glass and calling soundlessly to be let out. I saw myself shaking the globe once, and I saw the storm turn pink.

Stupid, I know—I wasn't responsible for anybody, and I certainly hadn't got behind him and boosted him up into the arms of whatever had been waiting in the cab. But I suppose that when you've just seen somebody meet an end roughly comparable to the act of walking into an aircraft propellor, it's bound to overheat your imagination just a little. Maybe that could explain some of what came later.

But somehow, I don't think so.

The truck horn was starting to recede behind me. The notes were longer now, like the moan of some trapped beast tiring of its struggles. Great, fine, I was thinking, you just stay there and keep at it, when the storm brightened and a dark figure suddenly rose before me.

It was my own shadow, cast forward into the blizzard way out beyond the edge of the road so that it seemed to stand in the air over nothing. I looked back and saw that there was some kind of a spotlight being operated from the cab of the truck, the kind that turns on a mount fixed to the body and stays however you leave it. This one was pointing straight at me; it went on past, and I realised that I was too small and too far away to spot with any ease. And there was probably so much snow sticking to me on the windward side that I'd be tough to spot even at close range.

Any relief that I felt was short-lived, though, because just a few seconds later the spotlight picked up the line of my trail through the snowfield. The bright light and the low angle exaggerated it and left no room for any doubt. The light stopped roving, and the horn stopped sounding only a moment later.

There followed a silence that I didn't like, filled with unstated menace.

And then the cab door opened, and its occupant stepped down to the road.

I don't know what I'd been expecting. Anything but this. She was small, and slight. Her light summer dress was torn and soiled and her hair was lank and dusty and blowing across her face. Her arms were bare, but she seemed oblivious to the cold and the wind. She started out towards the point where my trail angled out across the road, and I knew that I ought to be turning and running but I couldn't come unglued. She was walking barefoot on the snow and leaving no mark; I saw her bend to touch the barrier as she stepped over, and it might have been a stile out in the countryside somewhere in the warmest part of the spring.

I finally turned to run. I got a brief impression of another of those plastic cones tumbling by in the wind, and then it bopped me as I walked right into it. I went down. I tried to struggle to get up but it was as if I'd had my wires pulled and crossed so that none of the messages were getting through in the right order.

I could hear her light tread over the wind as she approached.

She came up and stood right over me. Her skin was as white as marble, and veined with blue; I couldn't see her face for the halo of light from the cab spotlight behind her. All I could see was her ruined hair blowing around a pitiless darkness in which something was watching me.

Louie, she whispered.

Louie? I thought. Who the fuck's Louie? Because listen, lady, it sure isn't me. I opened my mouth to say something similar and I think I made one tiny, almost inaudible croak. The wind dropped and the night grew still, and then it was like her eyes turned on like blazing torches in the ravaged pit of her face as she bent down towards me, and I could feel their heat and the breath of corruption warming my frost-bitten skin. I could see now that her hair was matted with concrete, and that patches of it had been torn out. The exposed skin was like that of a plucked grouse that had been hanging in a cellar for far too long a time.

Louie, she said again, this time with a kind of nightmare tenderness, and she took hold of my dead-feeling face in her dead-looking hands and I realised with terror that she was raising me up for a kiss. I saw the darkness roaring in like an airshaft straight down to hell and I wanted to scream, but instead I think I just peed myself.

She stopped only inches away. She lowered me again. I think she'd just realised that I wasn't the one she was looking for.

Then she raised her hand and I saw the state of her fingers, and I knew how she'd caused the damage that she'd done to the diesel tank. I shut my eyes because I knew that this was going to be it. I stayed with my eyes shut and I waited and I waited, and after I'd waited for what seemed like the entire running time of *Conan the Barbarian* I managed to unstick one eye and look up.

She was still there, but she wasn't looking at me. She seemed to be listening for something. I listened too, but all I could hear was the wind in the wires overhead.

And then, only once and very faintly, the single blast of a horn.

Louie? she said. And she started to rise.

Most of what I know now is what I've learned since. Louis Robson was a construction services manager who drove a Mercedes, and she was a supermarket checkout trainee. How she ever believed that he'd desert his wife and run away with her will be one of those eternal mysteries like, why do old cars run better when they've been washed and waxed; but he must have made the promise one time and she must have replayed it over and over until finally, he told her to meet him one night with her bags packed and a goodbye letter ready to mail. The place where she was to wait was one of his company's site offices by the new motorway; he'd pull in outside and sound the all clear on the car's horn. Except that it was a signal that she would have to wait a long time to hear because when she got there, he was already waiting in the dark with a lug wrench. He dropped her unconscious body into a prepared mould for a bridge piling and threw her cardboard suitcase after, and then he put the sealed letter into the post without realising that it mentioned him by name. This was all five years before.

I don't know if it was just the signal, or whether there was room for anything beyond obsession in the dark, tangled worm-pit of what was left of her mind; but she lurched stiffly upright and then, like a dead ship drawn to some distant beacon, she set off in what she thought was the direction of the sound.

The blade of the snowplough hit her square-on as she stepped out into the road.

She wasn't thrown; it was more like she exploded under gas pressure from within, a release of the bottled-up forces of five years' worth of corruption. She went up like an eyeball in a vacuum chamber, and the entire blade and windshield of the plough were sprayed with something that stuck like tar and stank like ordure. Rags of foul hide were flung over a hundred-yard radius, showering down on to the snow with a soft pattering sound. The destruction was so complete that nothing would ever be pieced together to suggest anything remotely human. The plough had stopped and I could see men in orange day-glo overjackets climbing out, stunned and uncertain of what they'd seen, and I managed to get up to my knees and to wave my arms over my head.

"Anybody else with you?" they asked me when we were all inside and I was holding a thermos cup of coffee so hot that it could have blanched meat. "No sign of anybody?"

I'd told them that I'd seen some kind of a bird fly into the blade, and it had all happened so fast that nobody had a better story to offer. They'd told me their names, and I'd recognised them from the tea mugs back in the hut that they'd been forced to abandon as a base for a while. I said that I hadn't seen anybody else. Then one of them asked me how long I'd been out there and I said, it seemed like forever.

"You know the police have jacked it in and closed the road for the night," one of them said. "We wouldn't have come out at all if it hadn't been for somebody hearing your horn solo one time when the wind dropped. You've got no idea how lucky you are."

I raised my face out of the steam. We all swayed as the big chained wheels turned the snow into dirt beneath us as we swung around for the return journey, and somebody put a hand out to the seat in front to steady himself. They'd find Mick and David when the thaw set in, and I'd say that I didn't know a damn thing about either of them. And did I really have no idea of how lucky I was?

"No," I said pleasantly. "I don't expect I do."

ALEX QUIROBA

Breaking Up

"I AIN'T NO Clive Barker or Ramsey Campbell," reveals Alex Quiroba, "but I know horror." And that noble sentiment is certainly borne out by the harrowing story of mental disintegration that follows.

Quiroba, who not too surprisingly hails from Los Angeles, California, has been published twice in *West/Word*, the literary magazine of The Writer's Programme at UCLA Extension. He once (briefly) belonged to a religious cult whose leaders tried to convince him that he was Edgar Allan Poe in one of his previous reincarnations. He cites those horror writers who have affected him most as Camus, Dostoevski, Orwell, and Charles Bukowski.

He adds: "I live a boring life—reading the names in the telephone book excites me." At the moment he is working on a first novel.

THEYRE IN NANCYS BEDROOM and shes just crawled under the covers in her long flannel gown with her tiny feet buried in thick grey ski socks and she scratches herself like a cat settling into its nap. Max stands in the bedside lamps weak light after doing fifty pushups and he peels off his black bikini briefs leaving salmon-colored lines cut into his flesh. His limp penis and wrinkled scrotum stick together and the cool air pimples his skin and he smells his own staleness as he climbs into bed to face Nancy whos on her stomach with her arms tucked under her and her eyes are closed. In a while she opens her eyes and their grey irises flecked with green make him want her—funny how its the little things that make him want her—funny how its the little things that make you want someone—but tonight he reads something different in her steady gaze.

He reaches over and with his thumb finds and presses the hard knot of muscle next to her right shoulder blade which usually has the effect of making her writhe with pain/pleasure and beg him to press harder. It took them weeks of inch by inch selfsurrender before they allowed any kind of vulnerability between one another so that they could share the secret knotted places in their bodies and in their lives.

Tonight she doesnt move and its as if he werent touching her and finally she shrugs off his hand and says I guess Im turning off to you. He watches her eyes with aching and he thinks Im going to remember this for a long time.

Because its been two months and were not going anywhere together. And when Im with you I feel too comfortable to look around for a husband. She closes her eyes. Im going to be thirty-eight this month and I havent got time to mess around and feel good. I want to get married and have a baby and I cant do those things with you because youre just not the kind of man I want you to be.

He peers at the smile wrinkles in her unsmiling face and then closes his eyes and after a while he feels shes watching him. His turn to say something but nothing comes to mind. He draws an empty sigh and gets up to begin dressing and his skin pimples again but he cant feel the cold. I think youre awfully dumb doing this just before you get your apartment painted he says through his sweater as he pulls it over his head. Thats a joke: he was going to paint her apartment the next weekend.

After he ties his Nikes with Nancy watching his back he goes into the kitchen for a glass of water because his mouth is suddenly so dry. Under the harsh naked light bulb Max has to support himself against the sink with the glass halfway to his mouth because it feels like his chest is caving in on itself. His body is being pulled downward and with the obscene reflected glare from the sink in his eyes he blindly grasps with his free hand to pull himself up and it fumbles into the Rubbermaid dishdrainer filled with dishes he washed tonight before Nancy got home and his fingers close comfortably around the rough cracked wood handle of the butcher knife and its solidity is somehow reassuring. He brings the knife to his face as close as a lover and the cold light from the blade calms him and the glass slips from his other hand to crack in the sink. Nancy walks up behind him. Max are you all right? You can stay the night on the sofa if you dont . . . quick as a flash he turns and the cold sharp light in his hand slices the air. First he sees her graygreen eyes go round like two little mouths saying oh! and then beneath her chin a red mouth opens in a ridiculous smile and Nancys flannel breasts are soaked in glistening crimson. Her hands flutter up like pale birds trying to hide her new smile and she turns and staggers off making wet choking sounds and still holding the knife he follows her telling her its all right she shouldnt be embarrassed with him because he loves her.

Max blinks slowly and finishes tying his Nikes and hes aware Nancy is watching him. He walks into the livingroom where his jacket is tossed over an arm of the sofa and Nancy follows him out. Max you dont have to leave right away if you want to talk about it. Nope gotta go says a strange and distant voice and then hes out the door and walking in a dream down the street until hes standing beside his parked Datsun. He gets in and sits wondering what he should do now. He tries thinking about whats just happened but hes preoccupied with the night outside and the sounds of passing cars and talking pedestrians that are muffled by the glass and metal of his Datsun to the point he cant tell if they are imagined or real. Shadow and light and sound are pieces of a jigsaw puzzle lying next to each other but not interlocked. Time passes—out there—but in his little car it is waiting and still and he imagines he could stay in here for years without getting hungry or without having to pee.

Max knows its cold but he cant feel it. When I feel the cold—he tells the cars dark and silent interior—Ill start the engine and drive home. After a while though its obvious the cold is teasing him by staying barely out of reach crouching down in the darkness as touchable as a rainbow and all Max can feel is the sucking emptiness in his chest. He leans forward putting his forehead against the steering wheel but there is no comfort there.

Max starts up his car and drives to the freeway where he heads west and hes aware that the car is really driving itself. Hes not surprised by this but hes curious about how the car knows where to go and how it manages to stay between the broken white lines. But of course—as a BMW scoots past on his left—its the lights, the lights! Ahead of him are scores of little red dots teasing his car forward and in his mirrors are the bright headlights pushing him along. He closes his eyes a couple seconds experimentally and opens them and yes the lights have kept him on course. He relaxes and flicks on the radio and pale green numbers in the dash sing to him—make me feel like paradise—while he cruises through the night. The song ends and the SoCal deejay comes on and Max wonders just how completely the lights are in control. He tightens his grip on the wheel to feel its resistance and then he cleverly relaxes his hold as if hes been lulled into sleep by the singing revolutions of the wheels on the pavement—and he jerks suddenly with his left arm. His Datsun streaks across two lanes to hit the concrete divider and it flips over onto its roof with a sickening crunch in the oncoming lanes. The car still echoes from the impact when Max observes through his shattered windshield distorted headlights growing larger and he hears brakes squeal over human screams and then a tremendous slam sets his car on its side. Max is also on his side and hes broken in pieces and held together only by his clothing and his pain. Theres a flash of light and heat near him and with great effort he turns his head in time to see a hungry tongue of flame snake towards him and as the fire licks its way over his clothes and across his face and as he hears the pop and crackle and smells his own flesh cook he realizes theres a pain worse than the emptiness in his chest and he screams.

Max shakes his head and hes been staring at the Toyota parked in front of him. He starts his engine and drives to the freeway where he heads west following the red tail-lights of other cars until he comes to his exit and soon hes in his own apartment looking dumbly around at the clutter as if he were a stranger here. He trudges dreamily into his unlit bedroom where he sits heavily on the bed and he manages to pull off his Nikes before falling over onto his side. He thinks maybe hell cry but theres nothing there so he gives it up and for 'a few minutes he just watches the sidewise world of his room with a streak of light from the living room dividing the dark floor and then everything goes away.

He wakes early next morning long before grey light filters through his bedroom window. Not much point getting up and doing all that silly crap he does every weekday morning so he just lays there watching the light against the curtain go from grey to rose to pale yellow and then he gets up and calls into work sick.

That night Max parks his car under a streetlamp in Venice that gives off a weird unworldly light that makes shadows more impenetrable and treacherous looking. He walks down the side street and turns the corner and walks into the porno theater and every pore in his body exudes alcohol because hes been staining his teeth and tongue since late morning with Gallo burgundy. Drinking wine didnt make sense then and coming here doesnt make sense now; but then theres nothing much seems to make any sense. An idea has occurred to Max: that if he does enough things sooner or later one of them will make sense and everything will fit together and the hole in his chest will be filled.

Max pushes a five under the window and gets back two quarters (that makes cents he thinks smiling madly) and he pulls open the door when it buzzes and he walks into the theater. Its a small room with a hundred seats in ten rows and the ceiling is high and the air is fetid with cigarette smoke and male sex sweat. Theres a screen the same size as the ones they had in school high on the front wall and on it are a man and a woman fucking in lurid color. On each side of the screen are hung stereo speakers from which come sounds of a womans tremulous moans almost synchronized with the in and out thrusting on the screen and disco music plays behind the thrusting of cock into cunt. Max looks nervously as the faces in the audience washed pale by the light from the screen turn toward him and hes reminded of how cats jerk their heads when they hear a can being opened. Sexual tension that is electric and heavy at the same time hangs in the room along with the smoke and sweat smells and from the far corner comes the rhythmic squeaking of a seat needing oil. Max sits midway in an empty row of seats and hears the whispers and sighs of restless vipers loose in the Stygian shadows around him and when he looks up he sees Nancy being pronged by a big-cocked stud. In the corner of his eye a ghost in the row behind stands and walks around the end of the seat-row and comes to sit down beside him. A hand finds his crotch and fingers like white worms probe urgently and without gentleness and as Max looks down in bewilderment they unzip his fly to burrow inside and surface grasping another pale worm. Max looks up at the screen trying to focus on Nancy so he can tell her this is all her fault but when he does focus its not Nancy but some blonde up there straddling eight inches pushed up her twat. Max is confused and he looks at the face next to him thats made grotesque by the shadows and flickering fleshlight and wonders if his face also looks so monstrous. The worms leave his lap and the man nods meaningfully and rises and walks to the end of the row where he goes to the front and disappears through a curtained doorway beneath the screen. Max zips up and also rises. He sidles clumsily to the aisle where he considers walking out of the theater but then he thinks theres really no use fighting whats happening and he too steps through the curtains beneath the screen. Hes in a tiny room lit by the lights from the softdrink and candy machines and an electric water fountain stands opposite the vending machines and beside it waits the man with the wormfingers. At the far end of the room is the door to the restroom and Max figures thats where theyre going so he walks up to the door and opens it. Inside are two men bathed in red light with one on his knees sucking the other ones cock and Max slams the door on this scene of worship because hes embarrassed with the guy by the water fountain watching him. He crosses the room to the fountain and bends over to feel the chilled splash of water on his tongue. The stranger is quickly behind him to reach arms around and undo Maxs jeans and shuck them down along with his briefs while Max holds onto the fountain now and then pressing the button to feel the reassuring cool water as he hears the man unzip behind him and then fingers are roughly spreading his butt and the guys other hand is pushing his hard thing against him but it wont go in—then theres the sound of spitting and he feels it split him open and it goes in. While the guy is pumping into him Max looks to the side and theres a good-looking young man watching them with his fly open and one hand on his prick and the other holding a vial to his nose and he thinks: Im not really here.

Max pushes his money under the window and gets back his change and he walks into the theater where he finds an empty seat far from anyone else. He falls into a drunken sleep and wakes to find someones hand on his thigh. He picks the hand off like a dead fish and exits the theater.

Back in his apartment he eases himself onto the floor with the deliberate carefulness of a drunk and he gazes up at his cottage cheese ceiling. A longlegged brown spider makes its upsidedown way across the rough terrain and Max watches but he has no inclination to get up and kill it as he normally would. Either from his pain or from his apathy he has learned compassion—live and let live—and anyhow it would take too much effort. The phone rings and he doesnt feel like answering but then a thought comes to him. He tells the spider maybe somebodys hurting and needs talking to. He pushes himself up off the floor muttering Im not a selfish man. Max? Well this *is* a surprise Nancy; what the hell can I do you for? Max are you okay?—you sound strange. Thats because I *am* strange—anyway you gotta reason for calling or you just feelin kind? He looks up and winks at the spider and sits back on the sofa. Dont be that way Max. She draws a rattling breath and he says nothing. Im not changing my mind about any of this Max but when you left last night you seemed so strange and Im worried about you. Thats the second time in thirty seconds youve called me strange—thats significant. He takes off his shoes. Dont do this Max—I really care for you and we can still be friends. We can still be friends he echoes and he pulls off one of his socks and picks at the black fuzz caught under his big toenail. Is that really what you want Nancy? Long silence. No thats not what I want—I really miss you even after what you did to me. He looks up from his toes. And I love you but thats just not enough because there are other things than love. Like what? There are practical things like income and ambition. I have practical things: remember youd come home dead tired and Id make you feel better and you can tell me things you cant tell another living soul? Max . . . And I have ambition because I want *you* after all and I dont know how a man can be more ambitious than that. Another silence. I could change you know. I dont know Max. Theres a change in her voice and he leans forward. Just say youre willing to try because if we both try we can do something but Christ dont just throw us away. Shes breathing hard and maybe crying and she says something he cant understand. What—whatre you saying? Its the blood—its so hard to talk with all the blood. He says nothing. All right maybe we can try it—she sighs wetly—but no promises.

When he returns from the porn theater he eases himself onto the floor of his apartment and watches the cottage cheese ceiling wheel slowly and he glances at the phone and imagines its harsh ring shattering the silence. He closes his eyes and maybe he sleeps a little; then he opens his eyes and stands awkwardly and he wavers into his little kitchen where tiny roaches scurry for cover when the light goes on. A whitecrusted faucet drips into a sinkful of crudded dishes. In the recess beneath the sink stand boxes and bottles of miracle things that help end toil and trouble and he picks up the Liquid Drano—if only there were something to clear up a life as if it were a hairclogged drain—and he carefully focuses his eyes to read the label of instructions with its warning of red letters swimming on a white background and then he reluctantly sets the bottle down and returns to the living room where he falls onto the sofa and regards the phone.

Five minutes—he says aloud—Ill give you five minutes.

Hes not aware of the pounding on his door until he hears his name shouted. Maxwell Griffin! Los Angeles Police—open up please!

He starts to get up to go answer the door but he reconsiders that if he doesnt answer theyll go away—and hes expecting Nancy to call in the next five minutes—and he relaxes back into the sofa.

Maxwell Griffin!

Max watches the phone and waits but it still doesnt ring.

RAMSEY CAMPBELL

It Helps If You Sing

IN A WRITING career that has spanned nearly thirty years (he sold his first story to August Derleth at the age of 16), Campbell has been described as "perhaps the finest living exponent of the British weird fiction tradition."

A winner of both the British and World Fantasy Awards, he has written an astonishing body of work that includes numerous short stories and fourteen novels. Forthcoming is a special issue of *Weird Tales* magazine which will include some new fiction, while in the meantime we have *Needing Ghosts*, a recent novella which he describes as "in some ways the strangest piece I've written so far," and his latest novel *Midnight Sun*.

"It Helps If You Sing" originally appeared in the anthology *Book of the Dead*, but this blackly humorous fable could hardly be further from the premise of George Romero's zombie movies.

THEY COULD BE ON THEIR summer holidays. If they were better able to afford one than he was, Bright wished them luck. Now that it was daylight, he could see into all the lowest rooms of the high-rise opposite, but there was no sign of life on the first two floors. Perhaps all the tenants were singing the hymns he could hear somewhere in the suburb. He took his time about making himself presentable, and then he went downstairs.

The lifts were out of order. Presumably it was a repairman who peered at him through the smeary window of one scrawled metal door on the landing below his. The blurred face startled him so much that he was glad to see people on the third floor. Weren't they from the building opposite, from one of the apartments that had stayed unlit last night? The woman they had come to visit was losing a smiling contest with them. She stepped back grudgingly, and Bright heard the bolt and chain slide home as he reached the stairs.

The public library was on the ground floor. First he strolled to the job center among the locked and armored shops. There was nothing for a printer on the cards, and cards that offered training in a new career were meant for people thirty years younger. They needed the work more than he did, even if they had no families to provide for. He ambled back to the library, whistling a wartime song.

The young job-hunters had finished with the newspapers. Bright started with the tabloids, saving the serious papers for the afternoon, though even those suggested that the world over the horizon was seething with disease and crime and promiscuity and wars. Good news wasn't news, he told himself, but the last girl he'd ever courted before he'd grown too set in his ways was out there somewhere, and the world must be better for her. Still, it was no wonder that most readers came to the library for fiction rather than for the news. He supposed the smiling couple who were filling cartons with books would take them to the housebound, although some of the titles he glimpsed seemed unsuitable for the easily offended. He watched the couple stalk away with the cartons, until the smoke of a distant bonfire obscured them.

The library closed at nine. Usually Bright would have been

home for hours and listening to his radio cassette player, to Elgar or Vera Lynn or the dance bands his father used to play on the wind-up record player, but something about the day had made him reluctant to be alone. He read about evolution until the librarian began to harrumph loudly and smite books on the shelves.

Perhaps Bright should have gone up sooner. When he hurried round the outside of the building to the lobby, he had never seen the suburb so lifeless. Identical gray terraces multiplied to the horizon under a charred sky; a pair of trampled books lay amid the breathless litter on the anonymous concrete walks. He thought he heard a cry, but it might have been the start of the hymn that immediately was all he could hear, wherever it was.

The lifts still weren't working; both sets of doors that gave onto the scribbled lobby were open, displaying thick cables encrusted with darkness. By the time he reached the second floor he was slowing, grasping any banisters that hadn't been prised out of the concrete. The few lights that were working had been spray-painted until they resembled dying coals. Gangs of shadows flattened themselves against the walls, waiting to mug him. As he climbed, a muffled sound of hymns made him feel even more isolated. They must be on television, he could hear them in so many apartments.

One pair of lift doors on the fifth floor had jammed open. Unless Bright's eyes were the worse for his climb, the cable was shaking. He labored upstairs to his landing, where the corresponding doors were open too. Once his head stopped swimming, he ventured to the edge of the unlit shaft. There was no movement, and nothing on the cable except the underside of the lift on the top floor. He turned toward his apartment. Two men were waiting for him.

Apparently they'd rung his bell. They were staring at his door and rubbing their hands stiffly. They wore black T-shirts and voluminous black overalls, and sandals on their otherwise bare feet. "What can I do for you?" Bright called.

They turned together, holding out their hands as if to show him how gray their palms looked under the stained lamp. Their narrow bland faces were already smiling. "Ask rather what we can do for you," one said.

Bright couldn't tell which of them had spoken, for neither smile gave an inch. They might be two men or even two women, despite their close-cropped hair. "You could let me at my front door," Bright said.

They gazed at him as if nothing he might say would stop them smiling, their eyes wide as old pennies stuck under the lids. When he pulled out his key and marched forward, they stepped aside, but only just. As he slipped the key into the lock, he sensed them close behind him, though he couldn't hear them. He pushed the door open, no wider than he needed to let himself in. They followed him.

"Whoa, whoa." He swung round in the stubby vestibule and made a grab at the door too late. His visitors came plodding in, bumping the door against the wall. Their expressions seemed more generalized than ever. "What the devil do you think you're doing?" Bright cried.

That brought their smiles momentarily alive, as though it were a line they'd heard before. "We haven't anything to do with him," their high flat voices said, one louder than the other.

"And we hope you won't have," one added while his companion mouthed. They seemed no surer who should talk than who should close the door behind them. The one by the hinges elbowed it shut, almost trapping the other before he was in, until the other blundered through and squashed his companion behind the door. They might be fun, Bright supposed, and he could do with some of that. They seemed harmless enough, so long as they didn't stumble against anything breakable. "I can't give you much time," he warned them.

They tried to lumber into the main room together. One barged through the doorway and the other stumped after him, and they stared about the room. Presumably the blankness of their eyes meant they found it wanting, the sofa piled with Bright's clothes awaiting ironing, the snaps he'd taken on his walks in France and Germany and Greece, the portrait of herself his last girlfriend had given him, the framed copy of the article he'd printed for the newspaper shortly before he'd been made redundant, about how life should be a hundred years from now, advances in technology giving people more control over their own lives. He resented the disapproval, but he was more disconcerted by how his visitors looked in the light of his apartment: gray from heads to toes, as if they needed dusting. "Who are you?" he demanded. "Where are you from?"

"We don't matter."

"Atter," the other agreed, and they said almost in unison: "We're just vessels of the Word."

"Better give it to me, then," Bright said, staying on his feet so as to deter them from sitting: God only knew how long it would take them to stand up. "I've a lot to do before I can lie down."

They turned to him as if they had to move their whole bodies to look. Whichever responded, the voice through the fixed smile sounded more pinched than ever. "What do you call your life?"

They had no reason to feel superior to him. The gray ingrained in their flesh suggested disuse rather than hard work, and disused was how they smelled in the small room. "I've had a fair life, and it's only right I should make way for someone who can work the new machines. I've had enough of a life to help me cope with the dole."

His visitors stared as if they meant to dull him into accepting whatever they were offering. The sight of their faces stretched tight by their smiles was so disagreeably fascinating that he jumped, having lost his sense of time passing, when one spoke. "Your life is empty until you let him in."

"Isn't two of you enough? Who's that, now?"

The figure on his left reached in a pocket, and the overalls pulled flat at the crotch. The jerky hand produced a videocassette that bore a picture of a priest. "I can't play that," Bright said.

His visitors pivoted sluggishly to survey the room. Their smiles turned away from him, turned back unchanged. They must have seen that his radio could play cassettes, for now the righthand visitor was holding one. "Listen before it's too late," they urged in unison.

"As soon as I've time." Bright would have promised more just then to rid himself of their locked smiles and their stale sweetish odor. He held open the door to the vestibule and shrank back as one floundered in the doorway while the other fumbled at the outer door. He held his breath as the second set of footsteps plodded through the vestibule, and let out a gasp of relief as the outer door slammed.

Perhaps deodorants were contrary to their faith. He opened the window and leaned into the night to breathe. More of the building opposite was unlit, as if a flood of darkness were rising through the floors, and he would have expected to see more houses lit by now. He could hear more than one muffled hymn, or perhaps the same one at different stages of its development. He was wondering where he'd seen the face of the priest on the videocassette.

When the smoke of a bonfire began to scrape his throat, he closed the window. He set up the ironing board and switched on the electric iron. It took him half an hour to press his clothes, and he still couldn't remember what he'd read about the priest. Perhaps he could remind himself. He carried the radio to his chair by the window.

As he lifted the cassette out of its plastic box, he winced. A sharp corner of the cassette had pricked him. He sucked his thumb and gnawed it to dislodge the sliver of plastic that had penetrated his skin. He dropped the cassette into the player and snapped the aperture shut, then he switched on, trying to ignore the ache in his thumb. He heard a hiss, the click of a microphone, a voice. "I am Father Lazarus. I'm going to tell you the whole truth," it said.

It was light as a disc jockey's voice, and virtually sexless. Bright knew the name; perhaps he would be able to place it now that the ache was fading. "If you knew the truth," the voice said, "wouldn't you want to help your fellow man by telling him?"

"Depends," Bright growled, blaming the voice for the injury to his thumb.

"And if you've just said no, don't you see that proves you don't know the truth?"

"Ho ho, very clever," Bright scoffed. The absence of the pain was unexpectedly comforting: it felt like a calm in which he need do nothing except let the voice reach him. "Get on with it," he muttered.

"Christ was the truth. He was the word that couldn't deny itself although they made him suffer all the torments of the damned. Why would they have treated him like that if they hadn't been afraid of the truth? He was the truth made flesh, born without the preamble of lust and never indulging in it himself, and we have only to become vessels of the truth to welcome him back before it's too late."

Not too late to recall where he'd seen the priest's face, Bright thought, if he didn't nod off first, he felt so numbed. "Look around you," the voice was saying, "and see how late it is. Look and see the world ending in corruption and lust and man's indifference."

The suggestion seemed knowing. If you looked out at the suburb, you would see the littered walkways where nobody walked at night except addicts and muggers and drunks. There was better elsewhere, Bright told himself, and managed to turn his head on its stiff neck toward the portrait photograph. "Can you want the world to end this way?" the priest demanded. "Isn't it true that you wish you could change it but feel helpless? Believe me, you can. Christ says you can. He had to suffer agonies for the truth, but we offer you the end of pain and the beginning of eternal life. The resurrection of the body has begun."

Not this body, Bright thought feebly. His injured hand alone felt as heavy as himself. Even when he realized that he'd left the iron switched on, it seemed insufficient reason for him to move. "Neither men nor women shall we be in the world to come," the voice was intoning. "The flesh shall be freed of the lusts that have blinded us to the truth."

He blamed sex for everything, Bright mused, and instantly he remembered. EVANGELIST IS VOODOO WIDOWER, the headline inside a tabloid had said, months ago. The priest had gone to Haiti to save his wife's people, only for her to return to her old faith and refuse to go home with him. Hadn't he been quoted in the paper as vowing to use his enemies' methods to defeat them? Certainly he'd announced that he was renaming himself Lazarus. His voice seemed to be growing louder, so loud that the speaker ought to be vibrating. "The Word of God will fill your emptiness. You will go forth to save your fellow man and be rewarded on the day of judgment. Man was made to praise God, and so he did until woman tempted him in the garden. When the sound of our praise is so great that it reaches heaven, our savior shall return."

Bright did feel emptied, hardly there at all. If giving in to the voice gave him back his strength, wouldn't that prove it was telling the truth? But he felt as if it wanted to take the place of his entire life. He gazed at the photograph, remembering the good-byes at the bus station, the last kiss and the pressure of her hands on his, the glow of the bus turning the buds on a tree into green fairy lights as the vehicle vanished over the crest of a hill, and then he realized that the priest's voice had stopped.

He felt as if he'd outwitted the tape until a choir began the hymn he had been hearing all day. The emptiness within him was urging him to join in, but he wouldn't while he had any strength. He managed to suck his bottom lip between his teeth and gnaw it, though he wasn't sure if he could feel even a distant ache. Voodoo widower, he chanted to himself to break up the oppressive repetition of the hymn, voodoo widower. He was fending off the hymn, though it seemed impossibly loud in his head, when he heard another sound. The outer door was opening.

He couldn't move, he couldn't even call out. The numbness that had spread from his thumb through his body had sculpted him to the chair. He heard the outer door slam as bodies blundered voicelessly about the vestibule. The door to the room inched open, then jerked wide, and the two overalled figures struggled into the room.

He'd known who they were as soon as he'd heard the outer door. The hymn on the tape must have been a signal that he was finished—that he was like them. They'd tampered with the latch on their way out, he realized dully. He seemed incapable of feeling or reacting, even when the larger of the figures leaned down to gaze into his eyes, presumably to check that they were blank, and Bright saw how the gray, stretched lips were fraying at the corners. For a moment Bright thought the man's eyes were going to pop out of their seedy sockets at him, yet he felt no inclination to flinch. Perhaps he was recognizing himself as he would be—yet didn't that mean he wasn't finished after all?

The man stood back from scrutinizing him and turned up the volume of the hymn. Bright thought the words were meant to fill his head, but he could still choose what to think. He wasn't that empty, he'd done his bit of good for the world, he'd stood aside to give someone else a chance. Whatever the priest had brought back from Haiti might have deadened Bright's body, but it hadn't quite deadened his mind. He fixed his gaze on the photograph and thought of the day he'd walked on a mountain with her. He was beginning to fight back toward his feelings when the other man came out of the kitchen, bearing the sharpest knife in the place.

They weren't supposed to make Bright suffer, the tape had said so. He could see no injuries on them. Suppose there were mutilations that weren't visible? "Neither men nor women shall we be in the world to come." At last Bright understood why his visitors seemed sexless. He tried to shrink back as the man who had turned up the hymn took hold of the electric iron.

The man grasped it by the point before he found the handle. Bright saw the gray skin of his fingers curl up like charred paper, but the man didn't react at all. He closed his free hand around the handle and waited while his companion plodded toward Bright, the edge of the knife blade glinting like a razor. "It helps if you sing," said the man with the knife. Though Bright had never been particularly religious, nobody could have prayed harder than he started to pray then. He was praying that by the time the first of them reached him, he would feel as little as they did.

LAURENCE STAIG

Closed Circuit

LAURENCE STAIG tries to live and write in Suffolk. A former arts administrator, he can often be found in The Star, Lidgate. He has been described as ". . . the Stephen King of teenage books . . .", and since he began writing for older children a few years ago he has produced such novels as *The Network, Digital Vampires, The Glimpses, The Companion* and *The Night Run*, as well as the genuinely quirky short story collections *Twisted Circuits, Electric Heroes,* and *Dark Toys and Consumer Goods*.

He is currently working on his first adult novel and for the past three years has been Writer in Residence for the USA Spoleto Festival in South Carolina.

Although "Closed Circuit" originally appeared in a collection aimed at young adults, its unsettling blend of techno-horror should leave the most blasé horror fan with sweaty palms.

THEIR MOTHER HAD ALWAYS been afraid of multi-storey car parks.

There was no particular reason for this, no easily identifiable explanation. She just was.

Something about mazes? Perhaps.

Now she would have to learn to love them.

The Anderson family had been awarded one of the remaining places in the Township. Happy Sterling was to be their new home. It had taken her husband years to accrue enough Government Credits to qualify for a Development Corporation place. She had even surrendered her own right to Employment Credits in order to hurry things along. The Ministry of Placing offered an entire range of incentives.

At last they were there, everything to hand and with no need to worry about disruptive minority groups such as the Rioters and the Campaigners. Just spoiling it for others. Besides, it seemed such a nice place to live.

She would have to try to live with the car park. There was nowhere else to shop and a car was the safest way to get around. In any case, Consumer Comfort Shopping Mall boasted that they could provide everything you would ever want, all under one roof.

It was an oppressive kind of day. The sky lay like a dirty grey blanket, threatening to flop down upon them at any moment. There had been a thickening of Meltdown Jetsam lately and that always played havoc with the weather, or so she had been told by a guard on the freeway. It would almost certainly rain, which could be the only good reason for getting "under cover".

Mrs Anderson took a deep breath and approached the ramp which led from Housing Zone Zero 9 to the Mall. The entrance peeped out from below a dark monolithic block of concrete. Windowless, it squatted, waiting, at the far end of the access lane.

At first they thought they were driving into an enormous silver fishing net. Only when the bonnet of the car was almost touching the gleaming chrome of the mesh did they realise that it was a portcullis.

They had reached the ticket dispenser. The car window wound

slowly down. A small plastic card slid from the yellow meter as if it were offering its tongue for inspection.

Mrs Anderson took the card.

A synthesised voice crooned, "Welcome to Happy Sterling, have a happy shopping trip," and a green light flashed through the chrome mesh. Overhead, angry clouds shifted uneasily, globules of burn-out floated through the ozone as a spatter of raindrops hit the windscreen.

After a few moments the car advanced beneath the rising gate. Cautiously it crept into a dimly lit concrete cavern of invisible corridors and brief instructions:

UP, DOWN, LEFT, RIGHT, NO ENTRY, STAIRCASE,
LEVEL 8

John had been silent until now.

A brilliantly lit sign flashed a reassuring message as they manoeuvred into the UP, LEVEL 8 Lane: "No vandalism here thanks to CONSUMER COMFORT SHOPPING CIRCUIT Ltd." Below these, there was a friendlier message in red:

"YOUR PEACE OF MIND IS OUR PEACE OF MIND."

"How can they stop vandalism?" asked John.

His mother had also noticed the sign.

"Did you see what we had to get through to get in here!"

"Oh."

To the left a further sign announced: "You have entered at Level 8."

The car park appeared to be almost full. It was vast and impersonal. Even cars which seemed to have their own character and appeal became cold and purely functional once they sat in a multi-storey.

Perhaps it was this that made her afraid.

The building was deserted except for the rows of vehicles, neatly positioned in their bays. There was an equal assortment of new and old cars, all shapes and sizes. John was prompted into considering the possible re-introduction of his car cleaning service.

There seemed to be a lot of cars in Happy Sterling. When they lived in the north he had supplemented his weekly pocket money by this little weekend enterprise. Only when they introduced the Class Zoning system did the bookings start to fall. Manchester and Liverpool had been classified as Resting Only sectors. His father had accrued enough Merits to be awarded a job, which meant they had to move south, along with everybody else who had earned that privileged status.

It seemed a good system to John; the Riot Class could all be kept together, out of the way of socially useful groups such as the Producers and the Investment City areas. Still, he was glad that he hadn't been born into an Investors' family group. He would have had to live in an Investors' sector like his phone-friend, Jimmy. They all wore special uniforms and always spoke "Computer". At least as a re-classified Consumer Class family the Andersons could wear what they liked. The area was noted for its islands of industry. Living standards here were really high. The Andersons were lucky. The Great Meltdown had given everyone the chance to start again, right from scratch.

John decided that the return of the "Anderson Car Cleaning Service" was a must. Many of the cars seemed very dirty, almost abandoned. He decided that the township must be full of either very lazy or very busy people.

"This is crazy!" said his mother suddenly.

John had been so preoccupied with the various models that he had not noticed their arrival at Level 1, the very top. John thought this a strange place to start numbering, surely you started at the bottom?

"Stay calm," whispered Mrs Anderson, "it'll make sense soon."

She took a deep breath and drove on.

Julie, John's little sister, had been asleep in the back seat. With a yawn she sat up and looked through the rear window. The had left the north very early that morning and Julie always slept a lot.

"Are we there, Mummy?"

Mrs Anderson searched the level. She looked desperately for a space, or even the tell-tale indicators of a departing car. There was nothing.

The outside wind howled through the air vents and echoed across the gallery, the only indication of the storm. Rows upon rows of silent cars waited, patiently.

This was the largest multi-storey car park they had ever seen.

"Can we get out and see where we are?" asked Julie. "Can we see our new house?"

"Don't be stupid!" snapped John. "This is an enclosed car park, there's nothing to see. Anyway there wouldn't be anything to look at. Our estate's access-way goes straight into the Mall, it overlaps, stupid."

Julie tried to picture this in her head, but gave up.

"Quiet, you kids," said their mother.

Her nerves tingled.

"The centre must be packed but we've at least got to get something to eat. Dad will be here tonight. The Development Corporation won't be delivering the packing cases till tomorrow. I guess it's down we go again."

"Aren't there any other shops?" groaned John. "I only want a hamburger."

"Not according to their little blue handbook," she replied.

They kept going down.

"CONSUMER COMFORT is the only place to shop as far as I can tell. Give me a break, John, we've only just moved here. I don't know the neighbourhood yet."

John threw himself back in his seat. He was bored. He thought of all those cars again and mentally tried to calculate how much he could make if he got the job of cleaning all the cars on one level.

Slowly, their old estate car crept back down through the levels. Large yellow arrows directed them into narrow lanes. These, in turn, sub-divided into UP or DOWN or HALT. The options were clear.

LEVEL 7
LEVEL 8

The car crawled around a sharp hairpin bend and stopped.

"John?" Mrs Anderson squinted through the wind-screen. "Is

it my imagination or what? I don't think I've seen one car leave since we got in here . . ." Her words faded and slowed.

For the first time she looked about her, taking in the setting and layout of the car park. Cautiously she lowered the window and listened. They could hear nothing except the chug of the car "tickover" and the polite rush of the air exchange system.

A sign on a nearby pillar indicated a direction:

EXIT TO LEVEL 8: BANKS AND FINANCE COMPLEX, GOODS DEPOSIT STATION (GROUND FLOOR ONLY).

She followed the direction of the arrow. It pointed to a large pair of port-holed swing doors. With a sharp command to the children to stay in the car, Mrs Anderson jumped out.

She crossed the vehicle lane towards the doors. Suddenly, she stopped. Through the stare of the double O were queues of people waiting at lifts. A corridor to the left was filled with a blur of figures pushing shopping trolleys. She laughed at herself for being so silly.

Of course there were other people here.

She skipped back to the car and got in.

"What is it, Mummy?" asked Julie.

"Nothing sweetheart, Mummy had a peculiar thought, that's all. It's going to be crowded. All our new neighbours must be doing their shopping today."

She reached into the glove compartment. There were still some chewing tablets there. John shared them out.

A voice in her head told her to stay strong. If you're a Consumer Class citizen you take the rough with the smooth. She would have to get tougher.

They drove down another ramp.

Again Mrs Anderson brought the car to a halt.

She counted in her head.

LEVEL 8, that was where they had started, ground level. The Consumer Comfort Mall was a twelve-level shopping centre according to the corporation guide book. But four levels underground?

"Mum!" whined John.

With a low whistle at the thought of "underground cities" she shrugged her shoulders, engaged gear and moved off.

LEVEL 9
LEVEL 10.

This level was darker than the others, many of the lights did not seem to work. A wall had been re-treated, a shadow of letters showed that graffiti had been daubed on it at some time.
She chewed harder.

LEVEL 11
LEVEL 12.

The last floor. There was space.
With an enormous sigh of relief Mrs Anderson manoeuvred the car into one of the bays and switched off the ignition. She had not noticed how wet her hands were. She whispered a sentence of self-congratulation. To get round a multi-storey was one thing but to run through twelve floors and end up parked underground was another.
They had parked next to a gleaming 1999 Westland Coupé. John jumped out first and rushed over. His fingers rested lightly on the paintwork and then admiringly stroked the highly glossed bonnet. This car wouldn't need his services. It was immaculate for the year, and regularly polished.
He would have almost cleaned it for nothing.
Almost.
He looked around him. Most of the cars seemed glossier on this level. The really dirty ones, he had noticed, had been on the top floor. It was almost as though they had been grouped according to their layers of dirt.
Their mother took Julie by the hand and helped her out of the car, then slammed the door shut. The thud bounced back from the other side of the bay. They paused for a moment in order to get their bearings. Level 12 was only half full.
Their footsteps rang out as they crossed to the exit.
They were about to see the attractions of the Mall.

As the double doors opened, an alarming blast of activity hit them.

"Good God," was Mrs Anderson's first reaction, under her breath.

The three of them stood together for a moment. They linked hands as if this might provide some protection against the chaos and commotion before them.

They had stepped out on to a wide balcony which circled an enormous indoor space. It was like overlooking an arena. The central floor was only a single flight of steps down. Around the balcony walkway was a continuous chain of shops. Every one had open access, without shop windows or doors. Customers spilled out on to the walkway. Neon signs flashed above each one, announcing their name and, usually, the availability of credit: Laser Light Ltd; Holograms to Order (easy terms). Antrobus Electronics; Home Help in a Microchip (all credits taken).

It was only when Mrs Anderson looked up that she became aware of the impossibility of the building. Further encircling balconies and galleries stretched upwards towards the dark and distant ceiling (if indeed there was a ceiling). It was like being at the bottom of a cylinder supported by a series of broad ribs at regular intervals. Each rib consisted of row upon row of shops and stores.

The noise was tremendous. Mrs Anderson could just detect the strain of an up-tempo melody, contradicting different layers of turmoil and din.

There were people everywhere.

Frantic chatter was mixed with the squeak and crash of the trolley baskets, which were being pushed urgently round in different directions.

Occasionally, two trolleys would meet in a head-on collision, then they would reverse and continue on their way like the dodgem cars the Andersons had seen in the fun-fair centres.

Mrs Anderson tightened her grip on the children's hands. They stared around them, wide-eyed in wonder, saying nothing. A young woman pushing an overfilled trolley rushed past them. One of the wheels caught in a crack in the paving stone. She struggled to raise the frame out of the gap, wrestling for a moment with an awkward castor.

Mrs Anderson caught the look on her face. She turned cold. She had seen an expression of utter despair. The woman nervously brushed away the hair which fell in front of her face, and tears began to well in the corners of her eyes.

The trolley spilled over with unwrapped cartons. Julie caught sight of some items of interest: milk shake machines, android dolls, hologram cameras and personal video eye-sets.

"Let me help," said Mrs Anderson, as she gently lifted the trolley. The woman stared back in astonishment. Somebody was helping her?

A large red box with a picture of a turbo food mixer fell out of the basket. The frightened look returned as the woman snatched the box up and replaced it in the trolley. She looked up again at Mrs Anderson, her lips mouthing something before she rushed away like a hunted rabbit.

Suddenly a hand caught Mrs Anderson's arm. Another face stared up into hers, but this time the anxious expression alternated with a grin. There was a young man dressed in a bright blue sweatshirt. The words CONSUMER COMFORT CLUB were written on the chest.

"It's almost 'Hurry Up' time," he said, "and I know what it's going to be."

His clenched fists shook with excitement. He pushed his face towards hers as if to share a secret. Beads of sweat were breaking out across his forehead.

"It'll be the talking towel rail. Don't tell anyone."

He raised a finger to his lips and made a "Shushhh", then ran off pulling two half-filled trolleys behind him.

John had once heard a book in which everybody seemed to race around getting nowhere. His mother had even shown him a picture from a real book she had had as a child, of a large-eared White Rabbit looking at a pocket watch and mumbling, "Oh dear." This was just like that.

Julie gently pulled her mother's sleeve.

"Come on, sweetheart," said Mrs Anderson, "this won't take long." John had gone very quiet indeed. Once, when he was much younger and they lived in Manchester, his father had taken him to a meeting in Albert Square. That was before they had been advised to join the Toe-the-Line Association. The square had been packed, just like the inside of the Mall.

John had watched as all around him people's faces had grown twisted and angry. A scuffle had broken out and the Peace Police had been summoned. John and his father had been carried through the Square by the natural surge of the crowd. It had moved as a single heaving body, breaking and re-shaping, until in anger it began to turn inwards and eat itself alive.

They had been lucky to escape. Most of the crowd had later been designated Riot Zone Class, the mindless disruptive sector.

It was strange. Those in the shopping centre were Consumer Category but their faces still reminded John of Albert Square. All that anxiety.

His mother led them to the edge of the balcony. The ground-floor arena was just below them, a teeming mosaic of bobbing heads and crashing wire trolleys.

A tall figure in a peaked cap and blue shirt had been watching them from the car-park doors. Large drop sun-shades hid his eyes, and part of his face, but it was still possible to make out an icy, detached expression.

He had been standing against the doors with his arms folded. Now he walked towards the trolley bay, which was a confused tangle of wire mesh and thick red handles. He shook one of the trolleys free from its clinging partners and advanced on Mrs Anderson and the children. With a grunt he pushed the trolley towards them.

"Er, no. Thank you," she stuttered, "we only want—"

His fist crashed against the side of the basket and again he pushed the trolley at her. This time much harder. Her hands let go of the children's as she managed to catch the front edge. A loose wire caught her thumb.

"Take it! Keep on shopping, damn you!"

He hit the side of the basket again. The message was clear.

John and Julie stood quite still.

The screech of a Parade Day whistle rang round the building. Everybody froze where they stood. The air filled with whispers and urgent hushes. Even the peak cap forgot his bullying and looked upwards. A synthesised Trumpet Voluntary stabbed the air, followed by an excited female voice:

"Brought to you by the Tomorrow chain of stores, it's— HURRY UP TIME!"

The sound of a drum roll flowed into a bouncing disco beat. There were cheers.

Above this, the voice continued its frenzied announcement.

"Even now, at this very minute, our friendly store staff at the Tomorrow chain are marking the star reduction of the hour. What will it be, folks—"

The crowd began its soft murmur, a swell of excitement surged within the mall.

"The Akoni, fully digital, talking towel rail."

A cry of awe and wonder escaped from every mouth like the release of a pressure valve.

"And—the first dozen sold, I repeat, the first dozen only, will have the rail personalised to speak their name."

The buzz of approval broke into pockets of discussion.

"The offer is only available in Tomorrow stores on levels 5, 7 and 12. Remember "Every Hour on the Hour with Hurry Up". Now off you go and—quiiiickkkkly now!"

The electronic twang of a synthesised note bounced through with perfect timing, a low bass riff bringing the melody to a conclusion. An elderly woman further down the balcony cried out in an ecstatic wail:

"I MUST have one! I MUST have one!"

The shoppers broke into a mad directionless swarm.

The peaked cap man disappeared, swept away like a bad dream. Mrs Anderson put her arms protectively around John and Julie as people hurried by. A burst of bongos and a chorus of silver tongues sang to a bossa nova beat:

> Can you live without your creature comforts,
> Can you afford to let good buys pass by,
> If you've a sharp eye for a bargain,
> Keep on shopping and let time drift by.
>
> Come on let's Hurry on Up.

Quiiiickkkkkllly now!

The crowd around her responded with a cry of "Keep on shopping!" as an army of fists shot into the air in time with the jingle.

Mrs Anderson trembled. She couldn't move, frozen with the fear of having to mingle with these people. This was evil. Pure undiluted greed.

Down on the ground floor a small group of blue-shirted men, wearing shades and peaked caps, were talking. It was obvious that they had some sort of security role. One of them looked up at her. She shivered.

They had to get out.

Julie had begun to cry. John, it seemed, had been struck dumb. He didn't know whether to laugh or not. Deep down he was fascinated.

"Now listen kids," Mrs Anderson spoke slowly but firmly as she walked them towards the exits. "This place isn't for us. It's too busy. Just do as Mummy says, we're going to go back to the car."

The first throb of the crowd had moved on. It was now much easier to get through to the other side of the balcony. They moved amongst the anxious empty faces.

From a doorway next to the car-park doors stepped the security guard bully.

"Damn, damn," said Mrs Anderson.

She manoeuvred John on to Julie's arm and grabbed an abandoned trolley. They changed direction, wheeling the trolley slowly towards another pair of doors set back between the first cluster of shops. Occasionally the wheels would stick in small cracks and crevices between the paving slabs. Mrs Anderson would stop and casually ease the trolley up and out of the fissure, but with eyes locked firmly on the swing doors.

Just as they passed Antrobus Electronics a large cardboard box suddenly fell into her basket. Behind the box had been a small balding man with a round pink face. He wore an outsize scruffy raincoat and his tie had been pulled up round his collar. Sweat trickled down his face as he drew breath in heavy laboured pants.

"I . . . I . . . I'm so sorry." He struggled to regain his speech. "I just didn't see you. I've got . . . to get this to Level 8 to deposit .. got to. We've bought three."

He took out a crumpled grey handkerchief from his raincoat pocket and dabbed his face. His eyes bulged, nervously trying to take in everything about him.

"It was very . . . cheap. They've still got some left I think . . . Electro-land, just over there. We might even . . . be able to get a couple more with a credit disc."

Mrs Anderson's nails dug into the red grip of the trolley. The neon shop signs began to blur and dance. She clenched her teeth, and a voice inside her head told her to hold on and act like one of them. With a blink she opened her eyes wide, becoming a talking doll.

"That's all right. I wasn't looking where I was going. What is it you've bought? It is nice, I must get one too."

The man pushed his handkerchief deep inside his pocket and embraced the box.

"Thank you, thank you. Shopping is so good, so good. It's a CBC Television. Super "Voice Activated" in seductive ebony and pink."

The word "pink" was muffled by the box as it fell towards his face. He scuttled away mumbling, "It's mine," as he went.

Mrs Anderson wondered why he had bought three televisions and what he would do with five.

The shops on this side of the balcony all seemed to be concerned with electrical goods. Mountains of food processors, toasters, home computers and the like were neatly stacked in blocks which poured out on to the walkway. Inside the brightly lit shops eager salesmen took plastic cards, credit discs, and asked for signatures in a continual loop of:

"Certainly, sir. Top of the range. Special this week. Certainly, sir. Please sign here."

The Andersons soon found themselves before an alcove which led to yet another large pair of oval-eyed doors. Just as Mrs Anderson pushed the door inwards, a tall blonde woman with half-frame spectacles charged through from the other side. She stopped and looked directly down her nose and into the trolley.

She wore a bright blue badge bearing the message "Keep on Shopping". She made a clicking sound with her tongue.

Piercing blue eyes held Mrs Anderson, pinning her to the spot.

"That will never do. You must do better than that. How do you expect to keep the country on its feet, eh? Tell me that. If you've run out of money it's simple, go to Level 8, two hundred credit ranges to choose from. You're privileged to be here, you know! We all have to do our bit when we first arrive. Off you go now. Keep on shopping."

She did not have a trolley, but held a clipboard and a wedge of credit-card coupons. She vanished into the crowd.

That was it! Enough was enough.

Mrs Anderson grabbed the children by the hands and rushed through the swing doors.

They stopped dead in their tracks.

They had entered a short brightly lit corridor. There was only one way out and that was into the open mouth of a steel grey lift.

She thought quickly. They were on the bottom floor, the lift could only go up. To hell with it, they had to get out. The car could be collected later, Bob could do it. They would go straight to the exit on Level 8 and leave.

Mrs Anderson pushed the children into the lift, the doors closed politely behind them. She saw only one illuminated square: 8. She pressed it. They could not be certain at first that the lift was moving. It shuddered, then an increasing whine could be heard.

They were startled by a loud hiss which came from the ceiling. A tape had started which was obviously worn and ran at varying speeds.

"Hiiii therrr, since you'rrrre visiting Level 8 call in on the Credit Forever counselling centrrrrre. Unit 199. Remember, Unit 199. Keeeep orrrrn shopping."

A fuzz of hard guitar chords and erratically crashing cymbals provided a background to another jingle:

Credit Forever is fast and quick,

Credit Forever will do the trick,
Buying things is kinda' fun,
Brings life's essentials to everyone!

At this point the cymbals wowed for several seconds and the hiss stopped.

A light above the door flashed 8.

When the lift yawned open a short corridor which mirrored the one on Level 12 greeted them. Mrs Anderson pulled the children down the passage and through the now familiar double doors. They stepped out on to another balcony.

The layout was frighteningly familiar too, but here the balcony did not overlook a central arena. Instead there was a vast space. Mrs Anderson rushed to the balcony rail and looked over.

She immediately pulled her head away.

"Oh my God," she said, "it's not possible, do they go on for ever?"

She looked up.

Everything swam.

Above her she counted seven huge concrete bands, each bustling with noise and activity. These were Levels 7 to 1, capped by a huge dark blue dome which seemed to sit above the last balcony. Again she looked down. She could make out other balconies and shopping chains. Lights flashed from the shops and various jingles spilled over into the abyss. Shafts of light crossed from one level to another. Many projected down and down and down.

It had to be an optical effect.

A blue-sleeved arm pulled her from the rail. She cried out as she caught her reflection in a large pair of drop shades.

"Are you all right? We don't want any "leapers". Ruins the shopping for some," he said.

He grinned, revealing a pattern of brilliant white and gold teeth (a Government perk). They alternated perfectly.

"Do you want credit?"

He nodded towards the long row of counters. The Andersons had stopped where the electrical shops had been on Level 12.

Mrs Anderson swallowed and wiped her nose on her sleeve.

"No, no thank you. Where is the exit, please?"

The grin vanished. The face said nothing for a moment.

"The exit?"

"Yes! Yes."

He did not seem to understand the question. Then the teeth appeared again.

"Oh, you mean the exit to the levels. To and from."

"*Yes*," she agreed, nodding furiously, "the exits!"

She would nod at anything. She just wanted to get away.

"Well, that's easy. Through those doors. That'll get you through to the lanes."

He pointed to a pair of yellow doors set back from the front of a Consumer Comfort Bank. Through the oval eyes she could make out the dim glow of the carpark lighting.

She mouthed a word of thanks and pulled the children. John's arm resisted the tug. She looked round. He was looking up at the guard. A smile glowed from his face.

"Keep on shopping," he said.

The guard smiled back.

They were the first words that John had spoken.

Julie laughed and repeated the words.

"Yes! Keep on shopping!" Then she giggled coyly.

"Nice kids," said the guard.

Mrs Anderson's heart leapt into her mouth. She almost gagged. She pulled harder, dragging the children towards the oval eyes of the doors. A voice called out behind her.

"Hey! The lift is easier, you know!"

Once through the double swing doors she fell back against the wall and closed her eyes. She shook with sobs as the sound echoed mockingly back across the car park.

Through the tears came distorted shapes and colours. The sign she had noticed when they had first arrived was still there.

But there was something wrong with it.

YOUR PIECE OF MIND IS OUR PIECE OF MIND.

There were signs that indicated DOWN to Level 9, or UP to Level 7. Signs that indicated which EXIT lane to which level.

Signs that told you where the lift or EXIT to the balcony was. But there was nothing which read WAY OUT, or just plain EXIT.

She began to take the EXIT lane to Level 9.

The children walked behind her, perfectly in step.

Their eyes were glazed and they smiled, quietly humming "Credit Forever".

Twenty minutes later they were all sitting in the car. Mrs Anderson crouched over the steering wheel. The air was hot and sticky. Had the storm finished? She was trying to remain calm, but it was difficult. She had driven back up to Level 8, but everything looked different and she had been unable to find a way out. The car had somehow got intó the wrong lane.

They were now at Level 10 having already been to the top and back. There must be another route out. Level 12 had to lead to a special exit lane, she had heard of something similar in the south-western multi-storeys. You had to drive through all the floors to get out. That must be it, mustn't it?

She pushed the accelerator down to the floor. The engine screamed.

She bit down hard on her tongue, her eyes fixed on the LEVEL 11 arrow.

With a roar the car catapulted down the ramp to Level 11.

Tyres tore as the white estate sought Level 12.

Almost unconsciously the car discovered EXIT TO LEVEL 13.

"Level 13?" she gasped.

Then she laughed.

And the children laughed.

Radio Mall One was really quite good after a while. It was the only radio station which the car's receiver would pick up, but that was perfectly understandable, being in a huge concrete car park.

There would be lots of "give-away" prizes with the hologram photograph demonstration at 7 p.m. on Level 2. She thought that sounded like fun.

There would also be free Radio Mall One T-shirts. Her hands were dry, her eyes bright and shining.

After an hour they had all learnt the words to the Hurry Up Song:

"Can you live without your creature comforts?"

A pretty tune. All three had sung it together, Julie had even made up a new verse. They would send that in.

They also knew the salute to "Keep on shopping". Might as well carry on until the petrol ran out. Curiosity really. A shopping Mall could be so welcoming. So warm.

After they left the EXIT lane from Level 50, the car slipped on to Level 1 again.

And again . . .

STEVE RASNIC TEM

Carnal House

STEVE RASNIC TEM was born in Pennington Gap, Virginia, in the heart of the Appalachian Mountains. He currently lives with his wife, the writer Melanie Tem, and children in a supposedly haunted Victorian house in Denver, Colorado.

He has contributed literally hundreds of stories and poems to small press magazines and anthologies, and forthcoming fiction includes tales in Tim Sullivan's *Cold Shocks*, Robert Bloch's *Psycho Paths*, Charles L. Grant's *Greystone Bay 3 and 4*, Bill Pronzini's western anthology *New Frontiers 2* and *Fantasy Tales*. In 1991, Rosemary Pardoe's Haunted Library will be publishing a booklet of five new traditional ghost stories entitled *Absences: Charlie Goode's Ghosts*.

The title of the story which follows aptly sums up its theme.

GENE'S phone rang again, the third time that evening. "Yes?" he asked again, as if the very ring were his name.

"Are you coming over, Gene? Could you come over?"

He held back any immediate reaction. He didn't want her to hear him sigh, or groan. He didn't want her to hear the catch he knew was waiting in his throat.

"Ruth," he said.

"Who else would it be?" she said, as if in accusation.

For just a second he felt like defying her, telling her about Jennie. The impulse chilled him. She couldn't know about Jennie. Not ever. "No other woman," he finally said.

She was silent for a time, but he knew she was still there. He could hear the wind worrying at the yellowed windowshade in her bedroom. Her window would be closed, he knew, but it would leak badly. There would be a draft that went right through the skin. But none of that would bother her.

"Come over, Gene," she finally said.

"Okay. I'll be there."

"I'll wait," she said, as if there were a choice. He hung up the phone.

The house was at the end of a long back street on the west end of town. It was one of the oldest in the area, its lines ornate, archaic, and free of the various remodeling fads that had passed through this neighborhood over the years. Gene had always appreciated the dignity of the Victorian style.

But he also knew that Victorians could be extraordinarily ugly, and this house was a perfect representative of that type. The exterior color seemed to be a mix of dark blue, dark green, and gray, which resulted in a burnt stew of a shade, a rotting vegetable porridge. The paint had been thickly applied, splatters and drips of it so complicating the porch lines and filigreed braces under the roof that they looked like dark, coated spiderwebs. The windows and doors were shadowed rectangles; he couldn't make out their details from the street.

All but a few of the houses along this tree-shadowed lane were abandoned. Some were boarded up, some burned out, some so overgrown with wild bushes and vines and weeds they were virtually impenetrable. Here and there a few houses had been torn down, the lots given over to bramble gardens or refuse heaps. And in the occasional house a light burned behind a yellowed shade, its tenders hidden.

Gene stood on the porch of her house for a very long time. He could feel Ruth inside that dark place, perhaps lying quietly on stiff white sheets, perhaps sitting up, motionless, listening. He imagined her listening a great deal these days, her entire body focused on the heartbeats of the mice in the corners, the night birds outside in the crooked trees. He imagined that focus broadening to include the systemic pulse of the moths beating against the dim bulb of the lone streetlight on the corner, the roaches crawling over the linoleum next door, his own nervous tics as he stood on this porch, hesitant to go in.

He imagined Jennie in a dark house like this, at the end of some other god-forsaken street, waiting, her eyes forced open, waiting for him. And he hated himself for imagining it.

At first he had been so pleased that Jennie had kicked the habit. He'd seen it as a cleansing when she'd gone through the house in a rage, looking for needles, spoons, all that other paraphernalia she'd always carefully kept hidden. But now she'd been ill for months. She wouldn't tell him what it was; she didn't have to. She would no longer make love to him. Last night she had refused to kiss him. And cleanliness to the point of sterility had become an obsession. They didn't talk about it.

Now, standing on this darkened porch in a shunned neighborhood, he could imagine it was Jennie he was visiting, not Ruth at all.

He was staring at the brown, flaking screen door when it lightened briefly. Pale skin pressed into the mesh from the other side. The lips, endlessly bisected, were almost as pale as the rest of the flesh, but with a hint of silver in their curves. "Coming in?" the lips said, in an almost toneless question.

As Gene stepped forward the pale flesh backed away, leaving the mesh as dark and empty as before. The hinges were oddly silent when he moved them, as if perfectly greased, but that seemed so unlikely his hand shook slightly before he let go of the greenish brass knob. The door fell back against the frame without sound.

The staircase climbed out of the dark burgundy well of the entrance hall into the smoky shadows of the second story. The paneled doors to the parlor on his left and the rooms ahead of him were closed, as they had been every time he had been here.

The woman standing on the staircase was nude, her flesh pasty, her face so pale and features so blurred that in the darkness Gene didn't know if it was Ruth or one of her companions. Her breasts were high and full, catching the available light on their upper curves. The nipples were shadows, as if half-remembered and only vaguely applied. Her pubic hair was so thick, so dark, that in this dimness it looked as if someone had blown a hole through her groin, and it was a triangular window on the dark staircase behind her he was seeing instead.

Her black hair suddenly moved across the pale shoulders like a snake. "Hurry," she whispered huskily in Ruth's voice. She turned and moved up the stairs, so effortlessly that her buttocks remained smooth and firm throughout the movement. After a moment he followed, his hands ahead of him, suddenly too anxious to stay trapped in his pockets. They groped and pawed their way through the darkness. Not for the first time he wished he could tell someone about all this. Anyone. He wished he had someone here with him, to tell him whether what he was seeing was real. He thought how, after all this time, he had so few friends.

That dwindling of friendships had all started in college. There had been Ruth, but she hadn't really been a friend, just the woman he'd always been pursuing. He had known Jennie back then, but only distantly. She had dated the friend of a friend, and he remembered her as someone always desperate for fun, as if she didn't have a serious thought in her skull.

First he had pursued Ruth, then he had pursued Jennie. There had never been any time to make friends.

"Kiss me," Ruth whispered, and Gene moved his lips slowly over hers. "Now bite," she said, and his teeth gently prodded her unyielding flesh.

Making love to her was strange. Making love to her was like a cutting, a notching of her hard, white, translucent flesh. Each time required more effort on his part before she could feel anything.

"There . . . there," she said. "I felt . . . something."

He rubbed against her rhythmically, slowly at first and then faster, but it felt less like a making of love than like a sandpapering, an attempt to wear away the old, dull skin in order to expose fresh nerves, in order to feel something.

He had a sudden urge to strike her unresponsive flesh, slap and pinch it, anything to bring it awake. He knew Ruth wouldn't mind. But he would.

He could not look into Ruth's eyes when he made love to her. He could not bear that faraway stare. He continued to scrape himself against her, cut into her, and her body felt like a pair of scissors squeezing him, cutting through flesh and nerves and bone.

Her odor was sour and animal-like. Her flesh seemed to melt into the stark white sheets. He had a sudden skirmish with the thick tangle of her hair, the twisted sheets, and came up gasping for air, thinking of Jennie.

Ruth stared up at him from her resting place (Had he ever imagined her anywhere else?), looking as if she could read his mind.

When he left before dawn Ruth stayed in her bed. Not sleeping, really. And yet not fully awake. This was the usual way. In the other upstairs rooms he thought Ruth's companions must be similarly greeting the departures of their lovers.

A shadow moved suddenly into the hall, staggering. The man raised his white face, eyes dark and hooded with fatigue. The man, as if embarrassed, turned his head away again and made his way quickly down the stairs.

As Gene walked off the porch the rest of the neighborhood seemed suddenly to burn into a new life. He turned back around to look at the house. Its windows stayed dark and shaded, the sun doing little to lighten its colors.

Jennie was still in bed when he got back to the apartment, only her head outside the sheet, the flesh drawn so tightly at temples and chin that her face looked hard, carved from wood. The bedroom shade was drawn to keep the morning light out.

"Jennie . . ." he whispered, but nothing came in reply.

The apartment was a mess. He could see the nest she must have made in front of the TV the night before. A U-shaped wall of firm cushions in front of the couch, the firmer the better to hold up her back and neck, the open space filled with blankets and pillows. Like the living room castles he used to build as a kid. A phalanx of overflowing ashtrays and snack trays had been arranged around the castle, but the food had been barely nibbled. Jennie always seemed to be consumed by this aimless hunger, and yet nothing would satisfy her. At times she could hardly eat anything at all. And yet the hunger still gnawed at her, and she kept loading up on the junk food, trying to find something she would eat.

Gene could picture her sitting here wrapped up in her blankets, her small face peering out at the TV, her nervous hands grabbing for cigarettes and snacks she would not eat. She seemed smaller with each passing day, more vulnerable, more and more like a kid. Less like a woman. He hated himself for thinking that way. As if Ruth were more than that.

Jennie wasn't the kind to sit up and wait—at least she never had been before. Their relationship had never been exclusive; that had never been part of the rules. Yet he kept thinking of her sitting up all night, and maybe, just maybe waiting up for him. And he hated himself for that as well.

Suddenly he felt starved. He went to the refrigerator and jerked the door open, the bottles and jars inside rubbing against each other musically. He reached for the quart bottle of orange juice.

When he started to open it he noticed that the lid wasn't on securely. He held the bottle up to the light from the narrow, curtainless kitchen window. As he turned it slowly he detected the faint impression of a lip print near the rim. She was just like a kid. More and more. He felt a sudden flash of anger, and poured out all the juice, discarded the bottle in the can under the sink. At first she'd been so careful, sterilizing her silverware, her cups and plates, making sure he didn't handle anything she'd had in her mouth. Like she was dirty.

They hadn't made love in some time. He couldn't even remember the last time they'd kissed.

Now he was ashamed of himself, looking at the discarded juice bottle. You can't catch it that way. He'd told all their friends that, his family who thought he should have nothing more to do with her. But he was scared. He knew better, but he was scared of Jennie.

And yet if he could love her illness away, kiss and rub it away, he would do it.

"I heard something." The voice behind him was so weak he hardly recognized it. "I didn't know you were home."

He turned around. She had the comforter wrapped tightly around her. The narrow muscles in her cheeks and throat trembled. He tried to smile at her, but couldn't quite get the idea up to his lips. "You should be in bed," he said. "You'll get cold."

"I'm always cold," she snapped.

"I know, Jennie." He went to her and put his arms around her. "I know." He squeezed her. After a moment's hesitation she squeezed back, or at least what passed as a squeeze for her.

"Hold me in bed?" she whispered.

"I'll hold you in bed," he said softly, leading her into the other room. "I'll hold you as long as you want. Forever if you want."

After an hour or so she was asleep again. Gene lay with her, massaging her back gently with his hands, feeling the lines of every muscle, every bone. And then the phone rang.

"Are you coming over?" He could hear Ruth's voice, and static, and wind.

"I was just there," he said quietly, watching Jennie stir in her sleep.

"But are you coming over? I need you to come over." Ruth's voice was steady, focused, obsessive.

"Ruth . . ."

"I need you."

He'd chased Ruth all through college. Every once in a while he would stop, and think how ridiculous he looked, what a fool he was, but those pauses for self-examination had been few and far between. She'd had the voice he heard in his dreams, gestures he could mimic in his sleep, skin that had felt like no other. He'd never wanted to think about whether his feelings for her were real, or whether this was truly a balanced, healthy relationship. Those questions simply had not applied. There had been nothing real about her, and he hadn't cared if there was a balance—he'd felt deliriously unbalanced. He'd simply had to have her.

He'd met her the first day of classes. The friend of a friend of a friend, although he could no longer remember which ones. He'd been introduced as a "math wizard."

"Then you'll have to tutor me sometime," she had said, with this simply amazing smile. And he had. If she'd asked him to, he'd have done all her work for her. There had never been "magic" before; now there was a magic he could not let go.

"I need you," she'd said, but it had meant something different back then. She'd needed his help with school, and she'd needed him to tell her how beautiful she was—so that she could be convinced that someone else might find her attractive. Even when she'd made love to him, it was to convince her that someone else—and that someone else seemed to change depending on her mood—would want to make love with her.

"You make me feel good," she'd say. "You make me feel alive." But she had never asked how she made him feel.

She should have asked. Because sometimes she had made him feel less than alive. He'd shied away from any other relationship, just in hope that she would be the one. He hadn't kept up his friendships. He'd convinced himself that his life would not work without her in it. He'd convinced himself that his relationship with her was a crucial turning point in his life, and that this was a relationship he dared not fail. Every woman he had met resembled her in some way. She'd become the measure for every female gesture, glance, or expression.

"Kiss me, Gene. There and there and there. Am I still beautiful?" He could hear noises in other parts of the house: Ruth's companions and their lovers.

"Yes," he said, with his lips urging her skin toward some vague warmth. "You've always been beautiful." He ran his fingers through her hair, and felt them go deep, too deep, into the dark waves that surrounded her depthless eyes, her pale, night-surrounding mouth.

"Good. That's good, Gene," Ruth whispered, holding him tighter and tighter within the scissors her body made. He wondered what she could possibly be thinking. It scared him that he could not even guess what she was thinking.

But then he'd never been able to guess what she was thinking. Even as she'd died, the thing that had haunted him the most was trying to figure out what she was thinking.

He'd been walking on the quadrangle at the center of campus. It had been a bright, sunny day, bright enough to burn away the haze that had accumulated the previous week. Both a haze of weather and the haze that had built up in his mind after several weeks of an unusually frenetic and unproductive pursuit of Ruth. In fact, the contrast had bothered him. The sunlight had felt just too bright, the campus setting too stark, too livid.

Suddenly there was a crash, screams. A large crowd had gathered near the stone wall that bordered South Drive. When he got there he saw a red Ford that had come up onto the sidewalk and knocked a third of the wall down.

He'd pushed his way through the crowd. Several people had been huddled over a woman on the sidewalk. Gene could see the long cuts on her legs, the nylons scraped away, the real skin scraped away below that, the shards of glass in her sides.

Then someone had shifted and Gene could see that it was Ruth lying on the sidewalk, that it was Ruth who had contained so much blood. Somehow he got through the crowd. He had said things, terrible and inarticulate things, but he could no longer remember what they were. And then it was *he* huddled over Ruth, the mask of her face *in his hands* and staring up at him, and it was a mask because the back of her head was gone, sprayed in carnival colors across the granite and marble of the rough wall.

But Gene had kept talking to her, holding the ruin of her head in his hands and sweet-talking her, kissing her open eyes and kissing her lips, passionately kissing her lips with tongue and tooth and caress as if to arouse her, then desperately rubbing at her breasts, even as her broken ribs caught on his shaking hands. Sweet-talking her, kissing and rubbing her, as if he were loving her awake after a long night asleep in his arms.

When they finally pulled him away from her Gene screamed as if they were taking him apart. But Gene could not remember that scream. What he would remember instead, and so vividly, was that sudden fantasy he'd had that his kisses had been working, that Ruth's eyes had just begun to focus.

"Gene?" And it had remained a fantasy until the evening she'd first called. "Could you come over?" Until she needed him to tell her how beautiful she was once again. "I need you, Gene." Until she needed him to put his hands, once again, into the thick waves of her dark hair. And to feel his fingers go too deeply through the hair into the space where the back of her skull should have been. Until she needed him to tell her she was still alive.

"There, there. I think I felt something. I'm sure I felt something." In desperate need to make her feel, he had bitten her left breast as hard as he could. It was like putting his teeth into leather. And still no blood would well, no bruise would form. "Don't leave now, Gene. So close. I could almost feel."

Passing the bedroom doors of Ruth's companions, he could hear their lovers softly weeping.

He'd decided that night that he would leave the phone off the hook. He'd prepare dinner, the biggest meal Jennie had had in some time if he had to cook all night. But he ended up spending more than an hour in the meat department of their local grocer, and still he wasn't able to choose anything. The chicken looked too pale, bloodless, as if it had all been dead too long. And you couldn't eat anything dead so long, could you? He was sure it would have no taste, no color.

And all the cuts of beef and pork looked somehow unreal to him. Too much red. Too much blood. He could not believe anything dead could have that much color.

Only the fatty parts looked real. The smooth, too-soft curves and hills of fat.

He rubbed each cut of meat through its sheer plastic covering. He thought he was close to knowing what they wanted from him—he could see it in the way their color changed when he pressed his living fingers into the meat through the plastic. But he couldn't quite bring himself to trust anything in that cold landscape of cut meats.

The lights were out in the apartment when he finally got back. Again, Jennie had left a mess, but he could hardly blame her for that. But she'd always been so orderly, almost obsessive about it, so he supposed this increasing laxness probably did not bode well.

"Jennie?" he whispered from the bedroom door. She said nothing, but the dim light that slipped beneath the bottom of the shade illuminated her head, the soft blond curls, the face that looked even more beautiful to him the paler it became.

She slept so soundly. He knew she would be in no mood for a meal. He could feel tears on his cheeks, running into the corners of his mouth.

Quietly he slipped out of his clothes and joined her under the covers. She did not stir, even when he pressed his cool body against her nakedness.

He began to kiss her, to taste her, and when she still did not respond he began to nip, to bite. He began to cry, massaging her breasts, probing her pubic area with his fingers, trying to kiss her, love her awake. But she remained cold and dry. The only air stirring in the room seemed to be his own, ragged breath.

Gene knocked on the dark screen door, and waited this time. This time, he knew, required a more definite invitation.

Her pale face appeared in the screen, her dark eyes taking in the bundle by his feet: the dull green blanket, the soft blond hair that still trapped the light, the pale skin with its tinge of silver.

"Is there room?" Gene whispered. "Room for her?"

Again Ruth looked at the bundle. Then her eyes floated up to hold him. "You'll still come? You'll be there when I call?"

Gene pulled his jacket closer, unable to keep warm. "Yes . . ." he said finally. "I'll be there when you call."

The screen door opened without sound, and the women inside the dark house dragged the bundle across the threshold.

It was two weeks before the next phone call. But he was there to pick up the receiver on the first ring.

"Hello," he said.

"Gene?" Jennie's voice said. "Are you coming over? I need you, Gene. I need you to come over."

KIM NEWMAN

Twitch Technicolor

KIM NEWMAN has recently updated his critical history of horror movies from 1968, *Nightmare Movies*, and completed an equally thorough volume on the western film; he has also contributed to *The Virgin Film Yearbook*, *The Macmillan Encyclopedia of Film* and revised editions of the Aurum Encyclopedias of *Horror* and *Science Fiction*.

A committed film buff, with his own weekly spot on British breakfast television, his avowed aversion to the process of "colorization" is given full vent in the following tale.

Newman's short fiction regularly turns up in *Interzone*, *Fantasy Tales* and various "Year's Best" anthologies; he is the co-editor of *Horror: 100 Best Books* and *Ghastly Beyond Belief*; his first novel, *The Night Mayor*, was published last year to great critical acclaim, and as "Jack Yeovil" he has a string of gaming novelisations appearing from GW Books.

He lives in Crouch End, London, and in the early 1980s he acted and played the kazoo in a cabaret band, "Club Whoopee." "It was wretched," he recalls.

P LAYING THE BUTTONS WAS all well and good, but Monte thought sometimes you had to get your hands in the colour. He had Bela Lugosi frame-frozen in mid-snarl, stretched black and white over the video easel, wooden stake jutting. Patiently, he combined film overlays in his plastette. Red was the key here. People like red best of all, and there would have to be a lot of it in the *Dracula* remix. It was integral to the property; perhaps a major factor in its lingering appeal. Finally satisfied, he inserted the plastette into the assessor, and sat back while the machine digitally encoded the precise shade that had struck him as proper. When it was done, the assessor pinged like an antique oven, and Monte plucked the now-primed squirtstylo from its lightwell.

He squeezed a blob of red onto the tip of his forefinger, and examined it. It was fine. Then he dabbed the electronic image/analog with the stylo, dribbling red between the re-production lines. The monochrome filled in, and gore gushed from the dead actor's starched shirtfront. The film looked better already. It was the personal touch that distinguished the Monte Video product from the competition's all-machine "enhanced" remix jobs. He plugged the stylo, and noticed phantom rinds of red under his nails. His hand looked as though it belonged to a murderer. He shook his fingers, and the red vanished in a static crackle. He adjusted his handiwork. He keyed ADVANCE and the film slow-forwarded a few frames. Lugosi completed his snarl, his hand clawed at the stake, blood flowed freely. The red grew, a blob in the centre of the image. It was fine. Monte keyed SAVE, and the colour took. The vampire's glowing eyes and skull-head cufflinks lit up, the exact red of the blood on his chest and about his mouth.

Michaelis Monte could remember the beginnings of the remix business, the ineffectually "colorised" films of the '80s. He had been among the first to test the potential of image/analog encoding, the process that enabled a skilled remix man to have an original moving picture reduced by the assessor to a particle chain of information bits and then rebuilt again in accordance with his own vision. With his own technologies, he had stolen the march on the majors, resisted many an attempted corporate rape, won all the Dickie awards going, and marked out an Ayatollah's share of the marketplace. Monte Video's *Dracula* was already a q-seller on advance orders. Securing the rights from the schizoid corporate descendents of Bram Stoker, Universal Studios, Hammer Films, the BBC and about twenty others who had dipped their claws into the property had been a lengthy and costly battle. With such an important acquisition, Monte might in any case have taken the time to handle the remix himself. Thanks to the Troubles, he was being forced to do the hands-on work personally. He was still the *numero uno* in the business.

Trevor, Ruby Gee, Consodine, and now Tarnaverro. All remaindered. Someone had it in for his remix men, or was trying for a strangehold on Monte Video.

He keyed PROCEED, and the assessor took over, absorbing Monte's decisions, replacing the drab grey of the original with dayglo colours. He liked to think that Monte Video's *Dracula* was the movie Tod Browning would have turned out in 1930 if he had been free from the censorship requirements of the day and had access to unlimited technical resources. Browning had been forced to have Van Helsing stake Dracula offscreen, with only a tame groan to mark the villain's death, but now the anti-climax could be fixed. Lugosi floundered through the vaulted crypt, eyes aflame like an electric Antichrist, pushing aside curtains of butterfly-winged/stained glass cobweb, recoiling from a succession of violently violet neon crucifixes. Then the vampire was down, and Peter Cushing was on top of him, hammering furiously, driving in deeper the killing stake.

Actually, Edward Van Sloan had played Van Helsing to Lugosi's Count Dracula, but since nobody remembered him any more, Monte had decided to mix in Cushing's definitive performance from the 1958 version. In fact, aside from Lugosi and Dwight Frye as the fly-eating Renfield, he had recast the whole film: James Dean as Jonathan Harker, Marilyn Monroe as the victim-cum-vampirette Lucy, and Meryl Streep as the heroine, Mina; he'd even stirred in Humphrey Bogart as the comic cockney asylum attendant. There weren't enough David Manners or Helen Chandler fans to make a dent in the marketplace, and Monte was always in favour of anything that added to the commercial afterlife of a property. His instincts had made him a rich man; rich enough to afford an unparalleled art collection—3-D religious postcards, popster necrophiliabilia, Woolworth's clown prints. Michaelis Monte was well-known as a man of influential tastes.

Onscreen, Dracula putrefied spectacularly, maggots bursting from his eyesockets. An entirely apt Jimi Hendrix guitar burst accompanied his deathscreams. Monte upped the zynth. More noise, more music, more scream. He infilled with more red. The last of Dracula should be a bloody pool on the lining of his opera cape, red on red. "Fuck you, Count," said Peter Cushing, "and the bat you rode in on." It was well said, and Monte's vocals people had taken a lot of care to perfect the actor's clipped voice pattern. Hendrix segued into Tchaikowsky, winding up the film with the snatch of *Swan Lake* that had been heard in the Transylvanian prologue, and the end titles strobe-flashed as Cushing led Dean and Streep out of the crypt into the rainbow-bright sunrise that lettered out "THE END" in the sky, and subliminally flashed an expensive ad for Coca-Drugs.

The message pore in the top right of the easel spiralled open. Monte saw an inset of his own doorstep, from the p.o.v. of the monitor-eyed stone eagle perched atop the lintel. Sally Rhodes stood on his WELCOME mat, drenchcoat belted tight, hat-brim pulled low over her domino breather. She looked the eagle in the eye and gave a tight smile. Monte pulled over the nearest slab, and ran the routine checks. The image in the pore proved true; a first-generation, unscrambled (he supposed that he only had himself to blame for the fact that you couldn't routinely trust anything you saw on television any more). The Household recognised her heat pattern, cross-checked the clearance of the Sally Rhodes Agency with the latest listings, and gave him a manual control over the door. He palm-printed an okay, and the pore closed as Sally Rhodes was admitted into his hallway.

Monte had scheduled this meeting for late evening in an attempt to avoid embarassment. He had, of course, been keeping the state police updated on his Troubles, as he was obliged by Law to do, but it was no secret that Monte Video was financially able to afford access to private sector policing. The Sally Rhodes Agency was known for its discretion, and Monte found that quality worth a hefty annual premium. He was even willing to overlook Sally Rhodes' tactless jibes about his business and taste in *objects d'art*. In a market rife with piracy, Monte Video rarely suffered from bootlegging, and the last large-scale operation to try infringing its copyrights had been permanently retired, thanks to Sally Rhodes.

Monte met her in the gallery. The paintings were asleep, but the room was a-whisper with their steady breathing. Sally Rhodes was admiring his shagpile Rothko. "There is some interesting work being done with sub-sentient jellies and acrylics at the moment, don't you think?" he ventured. The poised young woman turned and held up a hand in mock horror, waving it as if to ward off Dracula with a crucifix. He missed the point.

"That shirt," she gasped. "It's . . . it's . . ."

"It's called a Paisley pattern," he told her. "The lemon yellow and eggshell blue combination is my own idea."

"You didn't have to tell me, Miki. My grandmother told me about the 1960s. They must have been hell to live through."

"I wouldn't know. I was very small at the time."

"And now you're very big?"

"Quite." He adjusted his chrome and lucite love beads. "Are you in a position to make a report?"

"Only a preliminary. I note that you've lodged provisional declarations of war against Agfa-Daiei and Disney-McDonald's. You know what kind of commitment that will entail."

"What choice have I got? Someone's been singeing my remix men. With Tarnaverro gone, there's a severe crimp in my output. It has to be an alliance among the competition. They want me scuppered before Frankfurt."

"Perhaps," said Sally Rhodes. She peeled off her domino, and sniffed with distaste the herbal-scented air. "Do you have a roomscreen handy? I've got a tape to run for you."

He accessed the downstairs suite, which came complete with a full editing slab, and a glasswall display of Monte Video's topselling remix jobs: *Citizen Kane, Battleship Potemkin,*

Psycho, Faster Pussycat! Kill! KILL!, King Kong, High Noon, Double Indemnity, The Best of Sergeant Bilko, The Elvis Autopsy Video, The Seventh Seal, The Breakdancin' Nun. Monte thumb-signed the slab, and a framed poster for the Bob Dylan/Sylvester Stallone/Glenda Jackson/ Madonna *Women in Love* remix rose into its ceiling slot, revealing a milkwhite wallscreen. It was the only colourless thing in the house.

Sally Rhodes unscrambled the sequence lock on her brief-case, and produced a video cassette. It was a Monte Video Own Brand product. "This is from Tarnaverro's office," she said. "I've established that it was what he was working on when he was killed."

"Then it should be *Captain Blood*?"

"1935, Michael Curtiz, with Errol Flynn and Olivia de Havilland. Warner Brothers. Right?"

"Your pardon?" he double-taked. "Oh, forgive me, I always forget you're a, what are they called?, film *buff*." He spat the word with distaste, recalling the petitions that used to flood into his slab.

"Let's pass over that, shall we?" she said, shuffling fiche notes. "You've kept up on your autopsies, I trust?"

"Yes."

"But let me remind you. Tarnaverro was attacked by someone with a long, sharp, heavy blade. A carving knife, a machete, or a sword. He was almost literally hacked to pieces."

"Yes. That's why I suspect those Agfa-Daiei bastards. The multi-nats like to throw in a scare when they open hostilities." In his struggle to swallow Thorn-Futura-McAlpine before the combine swallowed him, Monte had authorized as bad or far worse. "And you know what the axis are like."

Being market leader was a precarious position. Since the Troubles started, with Trevor, Monte Video had lost over 20% of its employees to the marketplace. Even disemployment was better than being an unmourned casualty in a corporate skirmish.

"It may not be that simple, Miki. Have you ever thought to match the methods of assassination used against your people with the properties they were working on?"

Monte was startled. "No. Why should I?"

Sally Rhodes held up her fiche. "Trevor was the first. Two months ago. He was blown to bits by some kind of frag charge. He was remixing *Battleground*. Ruby Gee was expertly kicked and trampled to death. Her current assignment, *The Gold Diggers of 1933*. Consodine had his throat ripped out by some kind of animal. Remember the werewolf jokes in the newsies? His last property was *Lassie Come Home*. Do you see it?"

He wanted it keyed out for him.

Sally Rhodes slid *Captain Blood* into the VCR maw, and began to play the buttons. As always when you slot a cassette at random, the sex scene faded on. "This is the sequence Tarnaverro was remixing when they got him. We had to clean the blood and guts off the tape. The assessor was clogged."

Onscreen, Errol Flynn was extensively sodomizing the cabin boy. It had seemed wasteful not to feature the star's most legendary endowment in the film, and all the historical research proved that buggery would have been a way of life on the all-male pirate ships of the 17th Century. Besides, they had wanted to work up a role for the teenage David Bowie. There was a little ghosting, and Tarnaverro's green notation blips came and went in the corner of the image, but otherwise it was fine. It was an effective addition. Sally Rhodes was distracted, not looking at the action, but waiting for something else to appear. "Look, here it is, here's where it happens—" she framefroze "—look at this line." There was a thick band of different quality colour, crossing the screen like a ripple. She ADVANCED frame by frame, demonstrating the glitch's progression. It was a diagonal wipe from left to right. Inside the band, the colours were different: a little like the pastel shades of three-strip Technicolor, not very realistic and far too thin for Monte's taste. When the band had passed, all colour had gone. Bowie's face faded into Olivia de Havilland's, and, a cut later, Errol Flynn had his clothes on. There was a ruckus outside the cabin, and Flynn was bounding, cutlass in hand, to the door.

"So this is where Tarnaverro broke off? This is the original version?"

"Not quite," said Sally Rhodes, tapping a finger to the

screen, initiating PAUSE. A horde of pirate extras cowered in tableau as Captain Blood laid into them. They were typical Warner Bros, sea-dogs with earrings, three or four knives apiece, striped headscarves, leather boots, stupid expressions. But in the middle was a balding pirate with Coke-doke bottle glasses, and a twopiece whaleskin suit. It was Tarnaverro. The woman took her finger from the screen, and action resumed. In a long shot, Flynn threw off two huge attackers. Tarnaverro was in the mêlée, turning to run. His glasses fell off, and were kicked over the side by a sneering Basil Rathbone. The remix man made a dash for safety, and tripped over De Havilland's skirts. Flynn smiled, impossibly beautiful in the smoke of battle, and ran the interloper cleanly through. He heaved the body off his cutlass, and Tarnaverro fell into the sword-waving throng. The pirates hacked at him mercilessly. He even got his own close-up, still twitching, eyeballs free-floating, a coil of rope grey under his head. Then, he was out of the film—another dead extra—and Flynn was dancing up to Rathbone, jeering at the villain's frenchified ringlets.

Monte was appalled.

"Elaborate, isn't it?"

He had to agree. "It would take expert remixing to . . . do *that*. But it's pointless . . ."

The film went on. Monte waved down the sound, but the black and white figures still danced on the wall. He had to think.

"Mr Monte, do you know a Caspasian Kleinzack?"

"Of course. He's a remix man. With Agfa-Daiei. I've been trying to get to him. With the Troubles, we'll need to net a few top defectors to keep up our output. He's not up to my standards, or Tarnaverro's, but he's a professional jobber. Is A-D involved in this?"

"Unlikely. I mention Kleinzack because he's dead too. The newsies haven't got it yet, but he's definitely a casualty. I think A-D have had others, and there's been a total security clampdown at McDisneyworld. Someone doesn't like remix men. Kleinzack was shot. He was working on *My Darling Clementine*. Do you know the property?"

"1946, John Ford, with Henry Fonda as Wyatt Earp and Victor Mature as Doc Holliday. 20th Century Fox. You're not the only one who can remember things. A-D screwed me out of the rights in a nasty negotiation last year."

She smiled. "That's the one. A-D buy their policing from the Salvation Army. That's fundamentalism for you. I've got a few friends in The Sal, and I was leaked some fiche. According to them, Kleinzack was deleted with something exotic, a Buntline special. Ever heard of it? No reason you should. It was a white elephant showpiece of the Wild West, with an eleven-inch barrel. Wyatt Earp had one. Do you see the pattern? The Sal aren't saying any more, but it's my guess that if you were to screen Kleinzack's *Clementine*, you'd see a technicolor twitch, and it would wind up with a lab-coated Kraut remix man blundering into the crossfire at the OK corral and getting his globes shot out."

Later, after Sally Rhodes had gone, Michaelis Monte had a few stiff drugs. He was rattled, no doubt about it. In previous corporation wars, the higher echelons had been off-limits. You can't negotiate a peace with a frazzled corpse. But this new thing, this campaign of terror, didn't appear to be a particular respecter of the ethics of monetarist diplomacy. He found Sally Rhodes' conclusion unutterably creepy: "someone, *something*, doesn't like what you do Miki, and is taking extreme measures to shut you, and everyone else in your line, down."

He was safe in his Household. The defences were on, the grounds were secure. There were no human agents in the system to turn traitor, and the governing AI had had its loyalties freshly upgraded. Killflies were loose in the corridors of his retreat—he knew his employees referred to it behind his back as The House on Haunted Hill—and were coded to administer lethal injections to any moving thing that didn't match Monte's displacement configurations. He was as protected as a man could be.

He sat on the psychedelic bubble couch, and looked at his tiger-striped echt-Mondrian. The painting stirred in its sleep. He let the pleasant warmth of a soother seep through his body, calming him. As he watched, the painting's breathing grew ragged. It died, colours fading to grey, jelly congealing behind glass. It had happened before. A fault in the heating. There was nothing to worry about, the soother in his bloodstream told him. Deep in his brain, an unsoothed fragment of his consciousness screamed.

He floated back to his easel room. As he passed the sensors, his body heat registered. Overhead banks of lights lit up, then shut off when he had moved on. There was darkness in front and darkness behind, but he was always in the light. Safe, in white light.

Behind him, black eyes shone in the darkness.

Monte heard the swish, and turned. He couldn't see, but he had a strong afterimage. A tall man, with a heavy cloak.

He had to be alone. A 3-D wallplan proved it. He showed up as an orange pinpoint, winking in a corridor. There were no other warm bodies in the house.

He arrived in the easel room just too late. The twitch was disappearing off the lower right corner of the screen. A black and white picture remained. Monte stood over the easel, and watched as the camera tracked around an empty crypt. Lids fell off coffins, and creepy-crawlies—giant spiders, rats, an armadillo—scuttled in corners. Dracula's sad-eyed wives waited, infinitely patient, in long white shifts for their Master's return.

In his system, the soother reached the zenith of its effect. The tranquilising bulk of the pill had dissolved, putting a potentially dangerous dosage into him, and the emetic core spread in his gut. If he wanted to drug any more, he would have to empty his stomach. He wasn't soothed right now. Fear played his buttons, icy fingertips keyed his vertebrae. He would have to empty his stomach.

His bathroom was mirrored and luxurious, richly carpeted and hung with turquoise and scarlet silks. The design was copied from a Cecil B. DeMille spectacular of the 1920s he had rejected as too outmoded to be worth even a thorough remix. Jewel-encrusted gold taps shone against lime-green, veined marble sunken tubs. This was the focus, far more than his austere bedroom, of his fantasies and fulfilments.

Monte bent double over a puce and ginger toilet bowl, fashioned like a triton's horn, and vomited tidily. He slammed down the oyster-shaped lid and sat on it. The emetic had a calming side-effect. He felt bad, but was instantly better. He got up and walked to the sink—a mustard replica of the font in Salisbury Cathedral—and washed his face.

Behind him, a door silently opened.

Monte peered minutely at his face in the mirror. It was possible to be flabby and haggard at the same time. He bared his teeth. They were filmed yellow. Then, the thing took him. He saw the hand that gripped his jaw and felt the one in his hair, but neither showed in the mirror. He was held fast by emptiness. Arms like metal bands gripped him. Angling his eyes down, he could see the dark sleeve of a dinner jacket and the black folds of a cloak; but in the mirror (on-screen?) he was struggling only with himself. His Paisley collar was yanked away from his neck. Cold lips clamped to his throat, ice-chip teeth sank in . . .

The turquoise and scarlet faded first, turned dead and grey. Then, his shirt calmed down and resolved itself into a dingy, indeterminate smear. His vision slowly bled, the technicolor twitch passing from left to right before his eyes . . .

He felt himself emptying out. Feebly, he raised a hand to push away the unseen face pressed to his throat. He had no more feeling. His hand flapped, chilly and wet, in his field of vision.

The last things he saw were his fingers, stained forever with the black of his own blood.

GREGORY FROST

Lizaveta

GREGORY FROST is the author of three odd-titled fantasy novels (*Lyrec, Tain* and *Remscela*) and dozens of short stories, most of which qualify as horror, fantasy, or science fiction. He has been published in such magazines as *Asimov's, The Magazine of Fantasy & Science Fiction, Twilight Zone* and *Night Cry*, and the anthologies *Ripper!, Tropical Chills, Liavek* and *Invitation to Camelot*.

He reveals that "Lizaveta", a story of historical haunting first published in a science fiction magazine, came about as a result of reading Harrison E. Salisbury's study of the Russian revolutions of 1905–17, *Black Night, White Snow*.

Frost presently lives in Philadelphia with close companion Barbara and a cat the size of Staten Island. His favourite city, however, is Edinburgh, Scotland, where he holed up for a week once in a cold-water flat and read Kingsley Amis' *The Green Man* and Olaf Stapledon's *Starmaker*. He says he'd like to go back.

As HE STROLLED WITH his comrades along the fogbound filthy walk, Sergei Zarubkin wondered if the war with the Japanese were to blame for the eruptions of violence spreading through Moscow. The war had become a travesty in the failure of so vast a nation as Russia to devastate the upstart Orientals. Added to that, the hot August temperatures this year had inflamed tempers, fueled fights, even murders . . . as for instance last night in the Yama.

The Yama: the Pit, Moscow's Red Light District. Three blocks of ornate houses, with windows trimmed in carved scrollwork and lace curtains; where a woman cost three rubles for one hour of her time, ten rubles for a night; where boys of high-standing became men. But that quiet tradition had been suspended—because this night the Yama lay in darkness, in absolute stillness, with the houses all looted, their bright scrollwork smashed, lace curtains charred and hanging in tatters. All the whores had been beaten, killed, or driven out. And that was why four soldiers had to come here to the cesspool called Khitrovka Market in search of women for the night.

Zarubkin took a swig from the bottle of Smirnov's he carried, then passed it to Gladykin on his right, who lifted it, hailed it as a national treasure, and drank his fill before passing it on to Getz. From Zarubkin's left, Vanya handed him another bottle—he must have had it hidden inside his greatcoat. Zarubkin smiled to him, but recalled for an instant Vanya's despairing face, lit by the fires all around, last night in the Yama. Dragoons not unlike him had initiated the destruction: Two fools who decided they had been cheated out of three rubles by some madam; two men who had, because of tension and heat, impotency and drink, managed to stir a civilian army into looting and killing. Tonight those same civilians ran amok somewhere in Moscow, violence begetting violence. The disease of the mob had turned away from the whores, reshaping into something with a more sinister purpose: Zhidov, the new target. Jews.

Zarubkin, a captain in the Czar's guards, looked past his friends and into the fog. Why, he wondered, hadn't the zealots burned this pestilential place instead of the Yama? Even the police tended to avoid Khitrovka Market. The thick blanket of fog tonight hid much of the district's rot, but it carried the intense stench of the place, so that Zarubkin felt smeared with rheum. He took a hard pull from Vanya's bottle, then snarled, "To hell with the righteous citizens." It was they, after all, who had forced him and his friends to come here. Anywhere but where the mob was on this night off. Let those on duty look into the face of Hell. Not him, not two nights in a row.

Gladykin laughed and slapped his shoulder. "To hell with the righteous," he agreed, then added, "May they all burn for every one of us who carries crabs out of here tonight." And "Crabs!" cried Vanya, "To the crabs!"

They all drank to the health of lice and strode on. Their boots clopped like horses' hooves on the cobblestones in the dark.

Whatever evil had really dwelled in "The Pit," it hardly compared with Khitrovka. Here, as Zarubkin had learned from the heartfelt writings of Gilyarovski, the young girls were called *tyetki* when they advanced, at the age of ten or eleven, from begging to prostitution. Many had become alcoholics by that point, although their pimps—their "cats" — generally watered down the vodka. Few survived past their fourteenth year. Gilyarovski had found none in his search through the rubble. Because of two uniformed idiots, those hapless children would now have to match their indecent skills against professional prostitutes—the desperate survivors of last night's conflagration. How many of each, Zarubkin wondered, lurked in the fog ahead?

As the four men neared the heart of Khitrovka, beggars began to emerge from the darkness. The beggars choked the houses round about—thousands of soiled bodies wedged into a few blocks of space. Some were mutilated or deformed, unable to work. Some carried the corpses of babies in their arms as an appeal for sympathy in the form of coins even though with the child dead they had one less problem in their lives. Often the dead babies weren't even their own.

The sight of four large, well-fed guards in uniform sent most of the beggars scurrying back into shadow, the fog swirling after them. The four men walked on toward the building called Peresylny where the prostitutes had most likely found a haven. As he passed a curbstone fire, Zarubkin sensed someone watching him. The watcher turned out to be a scrawny creature warming its hands over the fire where another wretch, oblivious of him, cooked up a "dog's mess" of sausage and onions in a rusty iron pot. The creature staring so boldly was by appearances an ancient dwarf. The fire between his fingers revealed skin like parchment and a nearly hairless head that looked to have been smashed in on one side. The dwarf sneered at him, revealing brown and broken stubs, and gaps in the gums, like a child in the process of losing his baby teeth. His nose looked like a rotting carrot. By a trick of sound, the sizzle of the "dog's mess" seemed to emanate from the dwarf. Zarubkin looked away. He made himself relax, and discovered that his hand had closed over the butt of his revolver.

At that moment Gladykin announced, "I think it's time we separated, gentlemen. Together, we're going to scare off our nightingales. After last night the *tyetki*, I'm sure, expect us to burn their little world to the ground." He gestured at the fog, laughing as if to say that no sane man would waste his energy on such a task.

"All right," Getz agreed, "see you all inside Peresylny." Abruptly, he broke away from them and went up another street. They heard him walking long after he was lost to sight. Gladykin gave Zarubkin a wink, the turned and followed Getz like a bird in formation. "Later, my friend," his voice carried back. Zarubkin was going to share a humorous reply with Vanya, but he found that Vanya had quietly taken his leave, too. Zarubkin slowed and glanced around. Of the four of them, he had least wanted to venture on his own in this place, though soldiers would be quite safe. Especially, as Gladykin had said, after last night.

Pinpoints of light here and there revealed clusters of people, but the fog drank their voices and turned them into primeval lumps. The dwarf at curbside had vanished. Maybe the fog had swallowed him, too.

Zarubkin turned toward Peresylny, and a tall figure rushed toward him from a doorway on his left. He leaned away, his bottle held at the ready to smash down. Hands in fingerless lace gloves reached out for him. Delicate fingers closed on his wrist, over the neck of the bottle, pulling with the weight of a single body. The darkness swished. To his surprise, a woman pushed herself up against him. She stared into his face for a moment, her terror quite naked; then she glanced past him, all around, nervously.

Zarubkin guessed her age to be twenty-five. Vodka had puffed the skin beneath her eyes, adding some premature years there, but had not yet swelled her body or burst the capillaries in her nose. She was lean, her cheeks prominent and proud, her body like a whip in the dark décolleté dress that had blended with the fog. Her hair—it looked perhaps auburn—hung in disarray at her throat but also bore the signs of a coiffure not many days old.

When her attention returned to him he saw again the unrestrained terror in her dark eyes. What was after her in the fog? He could not help glancing around himself. Whoever wanted her, they would doubtless be less inclined to trouble one of the Czar's guard. Had she recognized that as he passed by? Was that why she had scurried to him? He smiled reassuringly, said, "Would you care for some vodka? It's not watered down—it's good Smirnov."

A smile trembled desperately on her lips, made little creases in her cheeks and revealed good white teeth. Of course, he realized then, this girl was from the Yama. No wonder she was terrified: in this place she played the part of the lamb in a field packed with wolves.

She drew nearer, like an intimate companion. "You're very kind, thank you." She took his bottle and drank deeply. He saw her looking over it into the fog once more, eyes searching, always moving.

Vodka glistened on her lips as she returned the bottle to him. Then she asked, "Would you stay the night with me, soldier?"

This nonplussed him: It was supposed to be his question to her, after all. As a Yama whore, she ought to have recognized the proprieties of their encounter. He politely took back his vodka.

She seemed to sense his withdrawal from the proposal. "Look," she said and dug fervidly into a small purse. "I have a ticket." She held up a yellow card. "Government approval."

He hesitated, but there was something about her, about her predicament, that he wanted to know. "Yes, all right," he said, found her staring out into the night again. She had made enemies here—probably, he thought, by trying to push her polished manners on the denizens. In Khitrovka she could disappear and no one might ever look for her. What was one whore more or less afloat in the stinking Yauza? She had to be scared to be so forward as to express *her* wants. The problem, as he saw it, lay in the fact that he had only enough money for an hour of her time if he was going to rejoin his friends for more drinking. In some embarrassment, he explained this. The woman started to laugh, very near hysteria. "Three rubles?" she said and pressed tightly against him. "My darling captain, with three rubles you can have me for life."

Zarubkin merely gaped. He had paid for a woman twice before, and he knew enough to know that this was not the way it was supposed to go. Then she buried her face against his collar and whispered, "Please stay with me this night, fair captain. Don't leave me to this . . . this horror."

She smelled of soap, and perfumed French soap at that. He wondered how so delicate a scent had survived a day amidst the ordure of the Market. The whore's breast rubbed against the back of his hand where he held the bottle to his chest. Her scent, her looks, her mystery aroused him. "Of course," he lied. "Of course I'll stay. Where do you live?"

The small room contained three beds wedged in around a scarred and warped washstand displaying a cracked ceramic pitcher and a brass oil lamp. Two of the beds had been stripped, and the whore assured him the other occupants would not be returning. "They fled the city this morning, Neva and Olenka. The landlords don't know that yet. I would have gone with them . . . they didn't wait." She hid her face where she could regain her composure. "I'm sorry. You delight that we're alone of course." She drew back the covers. Blotches and smears the color of rust stained the sheets but she swore that no vermin hid in the bedding. The business side of her came out as she undressed, her manner mechanical, any hints of nervous tension coming only at the end, as she removed the last of her shiny underclothes. Next she helped him remove his own clothing, her fingers quick but twitchy.

They lay down together. Her thin body shivered, but she smiled bravely, prepared to endure anything to have him. He found her peculiar forlornness arousing, and he pulled her to him. She stopped him briefly.

"My name is Lizaveta Ostrov," she said.

"I'm Zarubkin."

She looked questioningly into his eyes.

"Sergei," he added in compliance.

"Sergei," she replied flatly, and opened to him at last.

The warmth of the vodka seemed to shoot through him. Her love-making had urgency, as if she must race to the end before the whole world burst apart. It defied Zarubkin's knowledge of whores: usually, they feigned vague interest in their partner, and some not even that. He had always seen through the shallow façade and not cared. This woman treated him like a drink of water in the desert, or a last meal before execution. They made love three times in as many hours and polished off Vanya's bottle of vodka as well. She retrieved a bottle of her own from a small cupboard beneath the crooked window, crawling across the two other beds to get it. As she climbed back into bed and handed it to him, she apologized, "It's not as strong as yours. In the house in the Yama, the madam didn't wish for us to get so drunk as to forget to collect our fees."

"You'd prefer I paid you now, I understand."

The fright reappeared in her eyes. "Don't—don't pay until you leave. Not before day."

"What is it, is your 'cat' looking for you?"

She shook her head. "I represent myself here. Now that so many others have come, it's become more difficult. . . ."

He had to ponder that before the astonishing meaning became clear. "You came here *before* the Yama burned? Dear God, why? A beautiful woman like you, with your manners, your grace—"

"Oh, I did well. I learned very quickly, even though I'd arrived upon it so late, as a trade. You enjoy me?"

"Very much—I mean, three times is . . ." He looked around to cover his embarrassment. Her boldness in asking— that was like the whores he had known. "You became a prostitute recently then. Why did you choose—I mean, of all things to do with your life?"

"You're beside your whore this very minute—don't make it sound so foul, captain."

"I didn't mean—all right, yes, I suppose I did." He studied the creases in the sheet between his elbows.

Softly, Lizaveta said, "I was a teacher," and he glanced up. Her gaze had become distant. She drank long from the bottle of weak Smirnov's. "I loved children. I did." Slowly, she lay back beside him with her head against his shoulder. Her toes rested on the tops of his feet. She was nearly his height.

Zarubkin had intended to leave shortly, certain that his friends would tire of waiting and go off without him. Now he realized he would not be with them. He had asked his other whores to tell him about their lives, mildly curious. But the woman Lizaveta Ostrov did not act like any whore he had known. Her pose—if it was a pose—had him desiring the explication of her life as much as he had desired the union with her body. He really did want to know what had driven her here. What lay in the fog.

At first, when he asked, he thought she would not say anything. Then she sighed, leaned up and kissed him. "You'll stay with me, then?" There was, implicit in the question, the revelation that she had known his earlier lie for what it was.

"I'll stay. This time I swear I will, till light."

She covered her eyes with one hand, beneath which her lips trembled. The glistening of a tear crawled out into sight.

Unwilling to commit himself to her further, Zarubkin waited and drank, drank and waited. When she began to speak, it was so soft that she caught him completely off guard. She was telling him her story, and he had to ask her to begin again.

"When I graduated from the University," she said, "I was equipped to teach but could find no jobs in Moscow, so I returned to the University in the hope of inquiring after a job there. I should have done that at first, right away, because by then I think I must have been the last person in all the city to ask. What they gave me instead of a job was a list of places that needed teachers, and it wasn't a large list. A handful of jobs, all in distant places, too. Only one of them lay in the south, near the Kazakh border, in the foothills of the Urals. It sounded very lovely—warm and inviting—compared to the chill of Moscow, or of such places as Zhigansk and Obdorosk, which were among the remaining choices. I have always desired warmth, probably from having lived a cold childhood. We always want the other thing, the thing we don't have—don't you find people to be very polar in this way? I wrote a letter to the people petitioning, saying that I would take the job of teacher in their village, called Devashgorod. Next I waited—almost a month before the village replied. They sent back a letter of acceptance with directions on how to reach there.

"I left right away. A train took me to Orenburg, which was the closest civilized place to my new home, and that nearly a hundred kilometers away. I located a troika going into the Urals from there, a coach of odd travelers, and I secured a place on board, next to a man, a Persian I believe, just arrived from the Caspian Sea. He smelled of an alien sweetness and his Russian was terrible, but he smiled broadly, openly, with huge white teeth, whenever I looked his way. The others in the troika seemed to take offence at his presence and scorned me for befriending him even that little bit. No one spoke to me really the whole first day of the journey. I didn't care. I leaned back and watched the incredible scenery float by—the rolling steppes, whole hillsides covered in flowers, the mountains growing always larger and more distinct. By that second day the majority of the passengers had reached their various destinations or had gotten off at a crossroad to take a different path. Only three people remained: myself, the Persian, and a man who was going with the driver to some place on the Tobol River. 'This is old country,' he said to me. Left alone with us, I suppose he no longer felt the need to pretend indifference. He claimed this place we traveled through belonged to the oldest civilizations in the world. Time, he said, had hardly touched the land there. He could not understand why someone such as I traveled alone in such a place. So I told him about my teaching position, my first one. Where? In Devashgorod.

"The traveler to Tobol hadn't heard of it but the Persian beside me was plainly disturbed by the name. His faced pinched, and it furrowed like a plowed field, and he clutched my hand, saying, 'Must you go? Lady, must you go?' I answered that I had to, yes, or have no employment and a bad record. From that moment on, I became the outcast and he, the dark man, avoided me while the other man laughed contemptuously and called him a 'superstitious peasant,' but also quickly turned to reverie. Shortly after that he feigned sleep. Eventually, the wagon deposited me and my trunk at the intersection with the Devashgorod Road.

"A one-horse cart arrived. The driver greeted me with a great wave. He stood up in the cart, a huge man with long, shiny black hair and a heavy mustache. He had the cheeks of a Kazakh that looked set in place with a trowel. He wore a bright peasant shirt and rough trousers tucked into high boots, very worn. His name was Trifon, a curious name, I thought. As we drove to his village, he explained that he was the *ataman*, which is the chieftain of sorts, but with religious as well as judiciary duties. Every Kazaki village had an *ataman*, he informed me.

"The road took us up into the true foothills of the Urals. Peaks still had snow on them in May. The road became a trail, barely more than two ruts in the high grass. I experienced the moment that comes upon the threshold of a new life—of fear and doubt and a tingling excitement.

"The wagon bounced over the top of a ridge and there below me lay Devashgorod. Like a collection of dollhouses, quite lovely, colorful, it was a scene of utter serenity—or very nearly so. At the edge of the village nearest the road below us there was a great pit grown over by grass and flowers. From above I could look right down into that pit, and I found myself staring at the peaked roof of a house. It looked not very old, and I was amazed. 'What happened there?' I asked. Trifon replied quickly, 'Terrible. An earthquake, the ground opened up, the house was simply devoured by the earth. Most terrible day for our village. But here, look,' he said and pointed to a grove of fir trees nearby, where they had built their schoolhouse—no more than a shack really. 'That is where you will teach.' Trifon clapped his hands, just like a chieftain denying further discussion, and down into the valley we went."

Lizaveta paused to take a long pull from her watered vodka.

Puzzled somewhat, Zarubkin asked her, "But how did this drive you into whoring? Did Trifon rape—attack you?"

She laughed, dribbling a little vodka. "Oh, dear captain, no. As if such a thing would make you want more of it! I will tell you, it's coming, but let me do it naturally, please." She hugged against him to win his patience. Outside, someone shouted an angry string of invectives and someone else told him to shut up. Lizaveta ignored the noise and said, "Listen now. I began my teaching the next day. A local family called Shaldin took me in. They had a farm and a big house, and Trifon had prearranged everything with them. They had a son and a daughter who had each been schooled for some years. From them I learned of how my predecessor had approached teaching and some of the names of the students, the ones who were their friends. The daughter, Larissa, warned me to watch out for a boy named Akaky. He was apparently the ringleader for trouble. In all, only twenty-two students attended, a fact which hinted that there must be families who chose not to send their children, who taught them at home if at all, but who did not want them to know of the 'other world'.

"Early in the morning, before the children would arrive, I went to the schoolhouse. There I found stacks of papers and notebooks left by my predecessor. Dust coated the stacks and the desktop. I wondered how long the children had been without a teacher.

"While I finished cleaning off this area, the children began to file in. Most of them were shy, a bit afraid of me. Then, from outside, there came loud jeering, a teasing chorus of voices. I went to the doorway. At my appearance, they all fell silent and moved off—a dozen or so children. At first I thought they had been picking on an old man, but in a moment I saw that the old man was in fact a child, a victim of a terrible, withering disease that had made him age prematurely. I had heard of this, but never had I seen so pitiable a sight.

"He stood in a sort of hunch, as if the disease were pulling his body in upon itself. His head seemed too heavy for his neck. The purple veins showed under his skull, which was almost hairless. His skin had that quality of transparency that an onion has. Awful. His cold, bird-like eyes glared at me, and he hobbled past, still staring at me, wheezing as he climbed through the door, his right hand crippled up and pressed against his side. I could not believe the cruelty of these children, that they could openly taunt such an unfortunate. I resolved to change that if I accomplished nothing else. Children afflicted by this disease rarely live more than ten years, and I wanted above all to let this boy enjoy what time he had left.

"Once the children had taken their seats, I asked them each to tell me their names and how far they had advanced in their learning. When the time came for the wizened little boy, he refused to speak and just stared with his hard eyes straight ahead, as if he were deaf. I thought here was a poor victim, so harassed that he distrusted even me. I asked that someone tell me about him. Larissa Shaldin stood up. She made no sound, but the boy seemed to sense where she stood behind him. 'That is Akaky,' she told me in an incomprehensibly bitter tone. 'He rejects what you teach him and will continue to, no matter how hard you try. His family even despise him for—' she stopped and looked around herself '—for shunning everything.'

"'Why do you despise him, though?' And, though I addressed her, it was a question to the whole classroom. Larissa became dismayed by the question and sat down. Someone more daring called out from the back, 'You can see why—just look at him!' This engendered snickers from around the room. I saw that I couldn't carry the argument further without terribly embarrassing the child, so I left it at that and turned to instruction, working on their alphabets and handwriting skills. They knew barely half their letters. My predecessor had not been very qualified for her duties, it seemed.

"That evening I knocked on Larissa's door and went in to apologize for singling her out, which I hadn't meant to do. She sat on her bed in her undergarments and wouldn't look at me until I sat beside her. 'Child,' I said to her, 'you can't treat an unfortunate that way. It's morally wrong.'

"'An unfortunate?' she replied. Again virulence shot through her words. 'Akaky? He's everything he deserves to be, everything. Death would do us a service to take him.' She stopped speaking but her face expressed how much more she could have said. Her eyes moistened from this contained anger and she jerked her head away. 'You're just the same as the other one. You come here with your ideas about how things are. Everywhere is not like here. Please, I'm warning you now—let Akaky alone. Don't try to help him.'

"'But that's ridiculous, child. Why shouldn't—'

"'Do houses sink into the ground in your Moscow? Does the earth open up and devour people?' After that outburst she refused to say anything further. Her cheeks burned as if she were ashamed to have said any of this. I squeezed her hand quite uncomprehendingly and then left, thinking that her family must have put such ideas into her head. I could not imagine why. Had they branded him an outcast because of his disease? Did they think him contagious? Or were these people so backward in their thinking that they saw such physical calamity as a curse from God, a mark of evil? Questions such as that kept me awake a long time.

"The next morning, Larissa's father reinforced them for me. He confronted me in the hallway, blocking my way to the door. He said that, while he prided himself on doing his part for the village, there were rules in his house and one of these was that I was never to enter the children's bedrooms. I didn't know what to say. He went on, asking rhetorically, 'How would it have seemed if you had gone into my son's room last night to speak with him?'

"I answered that such a thing would have been unseemly without a doubt, but I added, 'Nevertheless, your son is but thirteen, sir.'

"'Well, and just so,' was his reply as though I had agreed with him. 'An impressionable age. And he is already infatuated with you. You didn't know? He's a romantic boy, my little Vald. He would mistake your attentions. Or he might think that he, too, had the right to pass into other people's bedrooms at night—his sister's for instance.'

"I could not believe this argument. Nevertheless, I deferred. I was, after all, a guest. But Shaldin could not leave the matter there. He went on, 'Just remember, madam, you may be the teacher in the school, but here I make the rules and it is only proper that you adjust to them. After all, what do we know of you, or you know of any of us?"

"'Very little,' I replied, 'but I know enough to see now that this is in some way connected to the incident with the child, Akaky.'

"I had known nothing of the sort, but the urge to say that seized me. Shaldin actually blanched as if I had uttered blasphemy. Then he pushed past me and went out of the house, slamming the door. The entire family must have heard the argument. The echo of the closing door banged all around the upstairs.

"I had no doubt now that Shaldin had forbidden any talk of the child in his house. Now I suspected there might be a blood feud between families involved. Everyone knows how strong are blood ties among the Kazaki. I've heard of disputes that lasted through generations, when the actual cause had been forgotten or even repaired. On the weight of that assessment alone, I determined to go see Akaky's family that afternoon.

"When the day's lessons had been completed, the children went off to help with family chores. There is always work in the fields and at home. I kept Akaky after all the others had gone, and I didn't tell him until then what I wanted of him. He did not even blink at my demand to see his family. That wrinkled mask of hatred became, if possible, more disdainful. I was struck with an extraordinary sense that all of this had happened before, that I was repeating the actions of my predecessor. The child climbed off his stool and shuffled out of the schoolhouse. I hurried after him, leaving my papers and things behind.

"I can remember my eyes stinging from the humid heat of the day as I hiked after him. I took to holding my hair off my neck and unbuttoned the collar of my blouse. The light breeze helped somewhat. Keeping up with Akaky proved no trouble despite my lace-up boots, which were hardly designed for rough hills. We passed sheep and goats—the stink of the goats clung with a particular tenacity to the steamy air. It pervaded my clothes."

The captain laughed. "There's surely no stink like it," he agreed, and passed the bottle back to her. She rose up to take a drink, and he saw her profile against the vague light of the window—saw the sparkle of moisture on her lips. She was, he reminded himself, really very lovely. In the street below Peresylny, he heard feet clatter on the cobblestones, and more shouting—spewed cries that sounded like alarms. He climbed past her, across the beds as she had done, and stared down through the grimy window. Fires spotted the night, but except for these small enclaves he could see nothing of Khitrovka no matter how he strained. The footsteps ran on, fading away.

Behind him, Lizaveta said, "It's like this here every night. Sometimes you hear it and you know someone's being murdered."

Zarubkin accepted that he would learn nothing from his watch and crawled back beside her. The bottle touched his hip, cold. He flinched and took it from her, took a drink, then settled back to listen to her. "You were going to his house," he prompted.

"Akaky's house," she said, "it was a hut actually. They had a large pen built on one side of it, but the animals inside were scrawny things. We had reached a rise slightly above the hut and as we descended, four people emerged from the doorway and stood in a row outside, waiting. They must have been watching for us. Akaky went up to his father and stopped. The child shrank into himself more than ever and glanced up at his father without raising his head. Then he pushed past his family and went inside. Only then did they all turn their attention to me—all staring with that same dark malignity the boy had. I tried to excuse their hostility by telling myself they must have felt cursed by his affliction. I told them who I was and that I was offering to help both the boy and them.

"The father snorted at me. 'Help us?' he said. "You wish to

help us, then kill that boy. You'll be helping the whole village *and* yourself, lady teacher."

"I couldn't believe what I heard. The man saw this, too, but all he did was shake his head sadly. Then he told me I was like the others, and that perhaps the next one would have a chance. "Maybe by then the boy will use himself up," he remarked. "Maybe he'll use himself up on you." Then he told me to go away. I turned to his wife, but she refused to look at me. His older sister—a girl who should have been married by then in that village—eyed me askance, as if daring me to try and address her. The grandmother beside her was the only one showing any sympathy in her face. Maybe she had traveled or at least understood that a world existed beyond Devashgorod. She said, "Best you should teach those who need your gifts." I thought then, my God, she could be Akaky's *wife*, he looks so ancient. The father inserted himself between us and repeated his order that I leave. What choice did I have?

"That evening no one in the Shaldin household said more than a few words to me, and even then they would not meet my eyes. Larissa's brother—the one who supposedly had a fondness for me—actually fled to his room when I encountered him on the stairs.

"I lay in bed that night, finding sleep impossible for hours. When I did finally drift off, I had vivid dreams. The sunken house had been resurrected, and I was walking through it, down wainscoted hallways. Ahead of me, doors on both sides of the halls swung open and closed.

"As I drifted along, I thought I heard a voice softly call my name. Drawn toward it, I waited for that door to open to me, then passed through it into a small room, the walls papered in burgundy, the curtains of white lace.

"A woman stood there. I thought at first that she must be a grandmother, but oddly, she wore clothes not unlike mine, clothes that a young woman would wear. The curtain fluttered around her. "Don't give in to him," she said. "He'll eat your life up to survive. Look at me." She turned more toward me, and I saw that her blouse below the collar shone with a wet darkness and seemed to be stuffed into a depression between her breasts, a hole. She might have said more, but the curtain came to life like a serpent. It wound around her throat and dragged her off her feet. I took a step toward her, but she held up her hand for me to stay away. Then the curtain snapped and she crashed back through the window. Beams of shadow, like an infernal opposite to sunlight, flooded the room. The floor splintered beneath me, and I dropped down into a pit.

"I awoke in my own room in the Shaldin house. The bedclothes stuck to me as I sat up, and I pushed them aside. My pulse raced like a horse. I threw off a great shiver. With the lamp turned up, I sat against the pillows and thought over the dream. The woman—I knew that she had been my predecessor at the school. What had he done to her, how had she been made to age like that? Akaky's grandmother came to mind. What if she were no older? The more I thought about this, the less it made sense to me. It was, I reminded myself, no more than a dream, which had conveniently assembled the things that were most unusual about the village into a narrative, but not a coherent reality. Feeling utterly foolish, I crawled back beneath the coves and went back to sleep; but I left the lamp burning brightly. I had no further dreams then that I remember.

"The child did not appear at the school that day, and another of the children informed me that Akaky had been too weak to come in today. The whole of the morning went uneventfully. In the afternoon, as I as returning home, I saw Trifon. He asked me how I found my new job, and I told him that it was going well, that the children needed a great deal of assistance because the last teacher had not done her work properly. "She was a weaker vessel than you," he replied, "but we shouldn't judge her too harshly, should we?" It was as though he could read my doubts, or had shared my nightmare. I agreed with him. He told me, "What she forgot was that not all children *need* special attention, that some are made to learn, and others not. There are children who will refuse to be helped. Though they are only children. You, I believe, understand not to invite problems." He bid me a good afternoon and went along the road. My hopes sank with that meeting, for I had expected that Trifon would give me answers where the others would not. Now I felt truly lost and a thousand miles away from the world I knew. I went to my room, closed the door, and began to cry. If anyone there heard me, they did not come to see what was the matter. Eventually, I cried myself to sleep.

"Immediately, a dream overtook me, vivid as the night before. At first I didn't know I was dreaming, because I was in my room still. But then I noticed how dark it was outside. The window across the room was open wide, the curtains drawn back. I could see stars for a moment, but then a shape blotted them out. The me in the dream got up and turned up the lamp, then carried it over to the window. The flame reflected me in the glass, but through myself I could see the child, Akaky, floating beyond, more hideous than ever, more withered and malicious. 'Let me in,' he said, 'you must help me.' I stepped back with the lamp, gesturing him through the window. He slid over the sill and settled on the floor. A mist curled over the ledge at his back. He stood hunched, grimacing in pain. I put the lamp down beside the bed and turned back to help him, remembering that he had been too weak to come to school, but he said, 'Lie down.' I found myself obeying him. A part of my mind watched me performing, but the rest of my will had been left outside the dream. He came to the foot of the bed and began picking up the discarded clothes lying there—the ones from the previous day—and my nightgown. Each item he held to his nose and sniffed, like a dog. Then he dropped each one and took another, until he had soiled everything. All the while, his liquid eyes glistened at me. Finally he came along the side of the bed and stood beside me. His crippled hand that he kept always curled at his side unfolded over my face. The fingers all ended in long, sharp nails like tiny blades. With his other hand he untied the bow at my throat, then grabbed the blouse and pulled it apart, exposing my breastbone. He turned the hand slowly and the nails hung above me. It no longer appeared deformed in any way. He let his hand descend slowly, savoring the moment. The promise of ecstasy gleamed in his cruel eyes—I've seen it in many lovers since. His hand dropped below my view, and I waited, not breathing, not thinking. Waiting. And then those nails sank into my skin. I went rigid. It was like terrible ice inside me. My back arched away from the bed until I thought it would snap, but I couldn't make myself move to stop him. He sighed, and

I could feel him wriggling his fingers down into my heart. That pain—how can I explain the sweet edge it had to it, pain that was almost unbearable pleasure. I began to scream and scream, trying to roll away from his clutch. He laughed—not a child at all, but a fiend. He rose up straighter. His eyes swelled, growing closer until they blotted out everything else.

"When I did wake up, the afternoon sun blinded me, coming in the window from just above the horizon. I got up, but rocked back from dizziness and had to catch my breath before I could stand. These nightmares, I thought, were draining my reserves. I went to the washstand to pour some water and cool myself, and I saw myself in the mirror. Between my breasts was a bruised ring of five tiny white scars. The bruises are gone now, but if I turned the lamp up I could show you the scars. I began to cry when I saw them. A moment later, Shaldin's wife called us all to dinner. I didn't know what to do. Should I tell them? There seemed no point; they would not be more sympathetic now than before. They might drive me from their home. I wiped away my tears and splashed my face, then buttoned and neatened my blouse.

"At dinner, I kept to myself, which seemed to satisfy them all. I must have eaten something, but I don't know what it was. The family made countless covert glances at me. Both children showed concern, but the parents had fear in their eyes. I had no energy left to cope with them, and I excused myself and retired.

"In the hallway outside my room, I heard Shaldin's caustic voice. 'I told Trifon I won't bring this on us,' he said. 'Some other house can have her, some other family can suffer on her account.' I had gone from guest to intrusive enemy. The man blamed me, even though he obviously had known of Akaky's powers beforehand. Why had he said nothing? I cursed him for his cowardice then and slammed my door so that he would know that I had heard.

"Once inside, I went to the window and latched the shutters before closing the window. The air would become stuffy. I hoped it would make me uncomfortable, and keep me awake, but it had just the opposite effect, and put me to sleep. But no one came into the room, and no dreams came to trouble me.

"In the morning, I sought out Trifon again. He sat in the corner of the store where they served pastries and tea. When I arrived, he was speaking with some others and his back was to me. I waited a short distance away. The men with Trifon grew uncomfortable and, one by one, they got up and left. He still had not turned to look at me, but he gestured over his shoulder for me to come and join him. I sat down. He took an empty cup and gave me tea. 'What is it?' he asked.

"'I will know all the things that you didn't tell me the other day.' He pursed his lips, then brushed the crumbs from his mustache. 'What would you know?' I said, 'Akaky.' I needed to say no more than that. Trifon was a huge man, but that name seemed to shrink him. He nodded as if he had long expected this, but he did not speak, so I prodded him further. 'Why do you all tolerate him?'

"'You know nothing of us, not even as much as you think you do,' he answered. 'We believe in God, yes, but also we believe that when a person is murdered, that soul enters the heart of the murderer to plague him.' I remarked that this was an interesting belief, but of no relevance I could see. 'Not relevant?' he said. 'It's the reason we've let the monster live. It's the reason he is the way he is. His father killed a neighbor—I'm sure it was an accident of emotion, but it happened. And the boy was born within weeks of that. Born evil, cruel, powerful, and desiring nothing more than to ruin himself and his family. The harm that he has done has been directed at them, at no one else. That is how we know whose soul he has, that's why his family lives in shame.'

"'How can you say he's harmed no one but them? What about the house out there that's sunk in the ground? What about that poor family?'

"Trifon stared at me as if to say I was a fool. 'That was *his* house. That was where *his* family lived. He brought it down.' As if to dismiss me, he shoved his cup away, but I had not finished.

"'What of my predecessor?' I demanded.

"'Her? She witnessed the event and fled from us. Nothing happened to her, just as nothing will happen to you. She lost her position. Akaky withdrew afterward, and no one here saw him. His family keeps away still in shame. They told us he had fallen into a trance and would die. We acted on that, believing—Merciful God, hoping for it. He should have died. We sent for you then. Now you're here and Akaky's weaker than before, so let him be, let him rot. Just don't run away in fright or we'll have to send for another teacher. Evil he is, but he won't do anything except frighten you. Especially at the house of Shaldin, because he fears Larissa—her gifts outshine his, and the rest of us. Oh, yes—you see, I told you that you knew less than you thought. We all have some powers like his. But we take precautions, and we don't use our gifts frivolously. If we did, we would all look like Akaky. Now you know why we put you there of all places in spite of Shaldin's objections.'

"'No,' I insisted, 'no, she didn't run away.'

"'What? Who didn't run away?'

"'Your last teacher. She's dead. Akaky sucked her life away.'

"'Rubbish—now you think him too powerful.'

"'Really?' I said. 'Well, let me tell you, wise *ataman*, the reason I know what Akaky did to the last outsider is that he is doing the same thing to me.' I wanted to show him the marks, the bruises and scars, but the high-necked blouse I had put on to hide them would not let me. He would have denied them, too, I was certain. He had his system of belief, as did the entire village—of witches or devils or whatever they were in Devashgorod. Angrily, I got up and marched out of the shop. I was no demon, nor had my predecessor been. We were something altogether different. We were prey.

"That afternoon I went into the church, as orthodox a church as you'd find in any village. I prayed for my soul, though I feared that I now dwelled somewhere that God did not visit. Afterward I returned to my room in Shaldin's house. My thoughts collided, but as I sat there I spied my trunk at the foot of the bed and I thought that I should obey my instincts and flee. I could steal a cart, but how could I drag the trunk out of here without the whole house knowing of it? The situation had trapped me, do you see, my captain? There was no way to leave and no hope of survival unless I could deal with Akaky. I thought then that perhaps I could make him leave me alone.

"At dinner I said nothing of my intention, but that night I dressed for bed and then opened the window into my room. A cool breeze from off the mountains blew in, and I settled back on the bed to wait. This time I hoped that the cold would keep me awake. For a while I tried to read some Gogol but could not concentrate, so I set it aside, lay back and waited.

"Even with the cold I eventually drifted to the edge of sleep. I might have dozed but it was at that moment that Akaky thumped against the window. Again a mist trailed in behind him. He was grinning. I sat up and said, 'I'll speak with you', as harshly as I could muster. My tone dismayed him for a moment, but then he sneered and came forward again. 'Lie back,' he said, 'I've no desire to speak with *you*. It's your life I want, not talk.' I fought his control over me, but my body obeyed against my will. Still, I could talk, and I said, 'You burn your own life up, doing this. Stop before you damn yourself.'

"He laughed, which turned into a cough. 'I burn either way,' he rasped. 'You can help me live a little longer.'

"'Why not stop, why not rest?' I asked him.

"'Because I love it too much. What would life be without the burning inside?' And his eyes rolled up in ecstasy as he lost himself in his own fire. In the room, as he did that, the furniture began to rattle and shift. The bed beneath me trembled, creaking. Then Akaky's rheumy eyes settled on me again. 'You can't imagine it,' he said. 'Or if you did, you'd give in to the pleasure with me—only your kind doesn't have the knowledge we do.'

"'Then why don't the rest burn themselves up, too?' I asked. 'Why aren't all the villagers out devastating their town for the sheer pleasure it brings?'

"'They're afraid. But I'm tired of talking to you. Be quiet now.' He uncurled that deformed hand of his and it was whole again, the nails glinting as if sharpened. The part of me that he controlled ached for him to insert them again. Terrified even of myself, I tried to roll free of him, but I might have been paralyzed. He undid the bow on my gown, exposing the bruise he had made. Then, behind him, a shape emerged from the shadows. Slender hands closed over his wrist above me and yanked him around. I found myself able to move, and I turned my head to see Larissa there. She whispered sharply in the Kazaki tongue, words I didn't know. What she said must have been a curse of some kind, because he reacted by spitting at her. With his free hand he swung at her face and knocked her against the door. Then he didn't touch her, only looked at her, but somehow this seemed to mash her against the wood of the door. She answered his assault, and he stumbled back a foot. She might have superior powers, but Akaky was willing to use his at a murderous level, which Larissa dared not. I thought of her withered and dried out from saving my life, and I couldn't let that happen.

"Akaky's head swiveled and his teeth creaked. He jerked with his neck and Larissa spun away, smashing against a chair and onto the floor. He seemed to expand, to rise almost to the ceiling. The house groaned and snapped. It must have spun somehow, because I was tossed across my bed.

"Larissa climbed up quickly. Blood was running out of her nose. 'Akaky,' she said, but he shook his head and replied, 'It's too late, you waited. I've new strength, from the teacher, and you shouldn't have picked now to try me, you shouldn't.' He closed the distance between them. I sat up, but reeled with dizziness, and I fell on my side, my face pressed against the cool binding of my book. The house lurched with a bounce. It would sink like the other one, and because of me. I grabbed the volume of Gogol in both hands, and I swung around and smashed it down across the back of his wretched skull. The blow drove him across to the door, and I heard something in him crack when he hit it. I thought I had killed him, but when Larissa and I turned him over we saw that only his nose had been broken. She could hardly stand and I made her sit in the chair she had fallen across, while I wiped the blood from her face. Beneath it, she had lines I'd never seen before—she had aged years from that short confrontation. 'He'll come again for you, night after night,' she assured me. 'In each generation here, there's one like him, who does damage until he perishes from his own obsession. Evil is always consumed by its own heat. But never before have there been outsiders. Now the evil will spread to the outside from us.'

"'The world has evil in it already, Larissa,' I told her.

"She nodded. 'True, but no evil before had your name on its lips.' I considered then finishing what I had started, killing the child. Larissa sensed this and told me that I would be foolish to do so. She believed the myth of her village. Perhaps I had come to as well.

"Larissa sighed, exhausted. I was surprised that no one else had stirred. She must have seen my distant look, because she said, 'They've been kept asleep. Akaky's magic. He wouldn't want to fight us all—it would drain him utterly.'

"'But why not destroy him like that?' I asked. Here they had what seemed to me the perfect solution to their problem; but Larissa shook her head. 'You don't understand us,' she said. 'He's evil, but he is of us nevertheless. We must tolerate him though we don't want him. In this way he destroys only himself, nothing else.'

"'Except me,' I pointed out.

"'Yes,' she agreed. 'He can destroy you. You should never have been allowed here before the village knew for certain that he had perished. And now you must go. I'll take you to the *ataman*, and he'll send you from here tonight.' She left my room to put on her clothes. I changed mine, stuffing my belongings into the trunk. When I came around the bed, Akaky's hand shot out and grabbed my ankle. 'Larissa!' he wheezed. 'I'll murder you. I'll wear you down till you're a rotting corpse.' He clutched my skirts, and dragged himself up me. Blood covered his lips and outlined the stubs of his teeth. I shoved him away, but he hung onto me with those fingers. I tried to reach the door, but he pulled me off balance. I fell, catching myself against the doorknob. Akaky was on his knees. I whirled around and slammed him against the wall. He growled, and his eyes rolled back, and a horrible pain opened in my breast. Akaky was grinning in pain and pleasure combined, his head back, the blood drawing lines up his face now. Frantically, I tore him from me, peeling his tiny hand away, crushing the fingers. He became weaker and more fragile by the moment. He laughed at me then, as if rejoicing in both our sufferings. I was not of their village; I could not block him out, and I could not endure this any longer. I slapped him as hard as I could. It was like hitting old, thin plaster. His cheekbone shattered under my hand. That whole side of his face caved in. He hissed, his breath foetid; but his hand went limp and he tumbled back across the chair.

"I stood there, shaking, waiting. If he had moved again, I would have taken something and beaten his head into the floor. Instead, he lay unmoving, as repellant a sight as if I had disinterred a corpse and brought it into my room. The stench of him seemed to fill the room.

"Larissa returned and saw him. In a mad rush I explained what had happened. Horrified, she bent over the chair. 'I think you've killed him,' she said. 'Come on, you have to get away now.' She grabbed my arm and pulled me from the room. I wanted to go back for my trunk but she insisted that someone else would get it. I was not to return to that room.

"Trifon listened to her story morosely. Was it me, I wondered, who shadowed the *ataman's* thoughts? But no, it was Akaky, for Trifon cursed him and spat. He agreed to hitch up his horses. My trunk was loaded on his wagon and I left Devashgorod in the dead of night, like a criminal, a spy. At the edge of town, Shaldin's house now stood canted to the right, as if the pit that had swallowed the neighboring house was growing, unseen.

"On the way along the road, Trifon handed me some money. 'This is payment for as much of the year as I can afford. You won't have a successor. Not till Akaky is taken care of.'

"I thought, *But he's dead. I've killed him, what of me?* I lost myself in gloom until I saw him. He stood beside the road as we went past. Trifon didn't see him, but I did. I saw the moonlight on his wild eyes, and I turned to watch him hobble into the dust after us. In terror I watched him recede into the night. When we reached the main road, Trifon wanted to leave me, but I wouldn't let him go. I pleaded with him to stay, not to leave me where Akaky could prey upon me. Trifon remained until morning, when he assured me in the sunlight that I was safe. Then he would not be kept there and drove off. His village needed him, he explained. Larissa Shaldin needed him. The troika was due around midday, or so he had claimed. I sat on the trunk, surveying the landscape for that hunched, repulsive shape. The trunk shifted under me, so gently at first that I didn't understand

139

what was happening. Then it shook violently. I jumped up at the instant that the latch burst. The lid flew open so hard that one hinge tore free. Clothing, all that I owned in the world, went spinning up like a fountain. At the center of it, a shape rose up—Akaky. His bleeding mouth drooled. The indented side of his face was purple and black. He scrabbled at me with those claws, but in his blind lunge he fell over the side of the box. I thought: Now is the time to finish him. I took a step. Should I kill him with a rock? Then he sprang from the ground, and his sharp fingers reached for my face. He missed but tangled them in my hair. I grabbed his wrist and tore myself free; his arm snapped and he wailed. I turned and ran.

"The troika picked me up later that day and I rode in the safety of the other passengers, saying nothing to them but protected by their presence, or so I hoped. But on the train to Moscow, I saw him outside the window twice, pressed to the glass like a fly on a wall. Where had he gotten the strength to do this? Had he killed someone else, drained their life to pursue me? I could not—did not want to—imagine it. And each time I saw him, he was more decrepit, more horrible. He looked like a mummified corpse, like nothing living. In Moscow I tried to go back to the University, but he sat on a bench by the door, knowing somehow that I would go there. In my despair I contemplated taking my own life, jumping into the river; but I haven't the courage.

"I don't know when I decided at last to go to the Yama. I think I just found myself there, wandering, and I saw the fine houses and realized that Akaky could never imagine I'd go there. It frightened me at first, but the women were kind, and understanding. Most of them had been through the same initial fears. The madam promised me that I had a cultured look that would appeal to her aristocratic clientele. I used most of my money to bribe an officer into getting me a yellow card, and the rest was, as the girls had assured me, just a matter of playing a role. I came to enjoy it. Hardly ever did I go out, but one man wanted a companion for the opera season, and I knew opera where the others did not, so the madam insisted. As I feared, Akaky found me. I saw him as I came from the opera one night, but he would not approach while the man was with me. Like a gnarled stick

140

creature, he hobbled along behind our carriage, following it all the way back to the Yama house.

"I escaped that night, dressed like a beggar, my clothes in a bag. No one paid me any mind and I saw nothing of Akaky. This became my refuge, a shabby room with two other whores; nights I've always had company, but now they've fled. Now I'm trapped in this pestilent hole. I must get out to work, to protect myself, but to go out is to invite Akaky to find me. I drink vodka and hope it will kill me, but it's too weak. All it can do is keep me from dreaming. He'll find me in my dreams. He'll get inside me again." She shivered. "Safety, I learned long ago, is an illusion. None of us is safe. All Moscow isn't big enough to hide me. He'll find me. The filth here feeds a million rats."

Zarubkin thought of the creatures outside in Khitrovka Market. He recalled the hideous dwarf where the sausage had been cooking. Dwarf! He sat up.

In the street something exploded. The lopsided square of the window lit up and the shutters rattled. Zarubkin jumped from the bed. Screams echoed from below, reports of gunfire. "What's going on?" he cried. He pressed against the glass. A few vague, scurrying silhouettes were all he could glimpse. Then came the rumbling that became hooves clopping on cobbles. Many horses. He could imagine them, the cavalry, like a wave. Shots sounded in a volley, a string of sound; and when that echo died down, it revealed a growing chant: "Bei zhidov! Bei zhidov!"

Zarubkin hurried to the bed and pulled on his trousers. He leaned back toward the window. Lizaveta sat up as if spellbound by the chanting. "The Jews," she said. Last night the whores, tonight the Jews. Here in Khitrovka lived all the usurers to whom so many of the soldiers owed money. The city, devolving into chaos, would take her captain from her. "No!" she cried. "You can't go, you promised to stay!" She stretched and grabbed his arm to make him look at her.

Footsteps pounded in the hall. Doors slammed open or closed. Zarubkin drew his pistol. A voice shouted his name—it was Vanya—and he answered, "Here!" by reflex, wishing even as he called out that he had kept silent. Lizaveta's hand slid away and he could not meet her gaze.

The door burst open to the whirlwind Vanya, his pistol also drawn. His wide eyes gleamed in the low light from the oil lamp; he looked to Zarubkin like a lost child. "It's a pogrom, Sergei! Come on, they're shooting Jews tonight. It's worse than ever." He glanced at Lizaveta with embarrassment. "Gladykin's already out there, 'for target practice', he said."

Zarubkin had known Gladykin for over a year—how had he tolerated the cruelty of the fellow for so long? Lizaveta rose, naked, from the bed suddenly and charged at Vanya. "You!" she shouted at him. "Here's a Jewess for you. Start with me."

Vanya's mouth hung open.

"Don't," Zarubkin protested in confusion.

"Here, you foul pig, here's all you could possibly want, both a whore and a Jew, one shot gets you double your prize. Where's your guts, oaf?"

Zarubkin said, "Lizaveta," harshly. She ignored him, closing on Vanya, who was trapped confusedly between two cogent thoughts and could not even move. She took his hand, caressing his wrist, the butt of his gun. "Help me with it," she implored him. A moment later the gun fired. It lit up the room for an instant like a sputtering candle. Lizaveta stumbled away from the horrified Vanya. Zarubkin caught her in his arms. Her head slid along his shoulder, into the crook of his elbow. "What did you do?" Her blood darkened his hand. "Why?"

She looked up at him and said, "Vodka's too slow." Her whole weight suddenly sagged against him.

"But—my God, Sergei, *she* did it," Vanya was stammering. This was worse than the deaths of anonymous peasants, this was a woman with a face and a name.

"Yes, Vanya, I know, I know." Zarubkin laid the body on the bed. He knelt beside her and held her hand. "God forgive her this terrible sin," he said finally. "Give her peace."

Outside more shots and cries resounded. The chant bounced from building to building, a cannonade. The air in the room seemed to stir around Zarubkin and he lifted his head. A cool draught brushed his cheek, then passed across the other. It breathed his name. He could barely believe what he understood then. She was with him still. Behind her presence, however, he could feel the smaller one pressing in. She clung to him for a moment, as she had in life. Then he lost the sense of her. He wanted to reach and bring her back. Sadly, he glanced at Vanya. The hairs on his neck crept up.

Vanya's mouth was turned down in a bitter scowl. The gleam in his eyes was no longer that of a scared child. It had become a feverish shine of the most intense hatred Zarubkin had ever seen. Vanya saw him watching and the scowl flattened smugly. Zarubkin had seen that face before. For a moment the pistol wavered in his direction before Vanya reholstered it. Jerkily, he turned away and walked out of the room, leaving the door open.

"Vanya!" Zarubkin cried. A shriek from down the hall answered him. Hastily, he grabbed up the rest of his uniform and charged out. Bullets filled the air like flies.

In Khitrovka Market, the horror had barely begun.

DONALD R. BURLESON

Snow Cancellations

DONALD R. BURLESON is a scholar of H.P. Lovecraft, although there is nothing of the Old Master's style in the tale of childhood terror that follows.

His fiction has appeared in *Twilight Zone*, *The Magazine of Fantasy & Science Fiction*, *The Horror Show*, *2AM*, *Eldritch Tales* and other magazines, as well as in the anthologies *The Year's Best Fantasy Stories* and *Post-Mortem*. He is the author of the books *H.P. Lovecraft: A Critical Study*, *Lovecraft: Disturbing the Universe*, many articles on HPL, and has even translated Lovecraft's "The Terrible Old Man" into Esperanto.

THE SNOW CAME SILENTLY to the window like the blind white groping hand of a mummy. Resting on his knees in bed and stretching toward the brittle panes, Jamie could just make out the vague outlines of the bird feeder on the edge of the deck, its once sharp wooden angles now muffled in white. Beyond, the pines and spruces that grew close to the back of the house were snow-shrouded ghosts waving in the wind, nodding to each other, whispering. It was going to turn out to be a big storm. Jamie liked that. Sort of. There was something nice about a lot of snow. But also something a little eerie, somehow.

Beyond the bedroom door, Mom had the radio on while she slammed around getting breakfast ready, and getting herself ready for work; Dad had the early shift at the mill and had left some time before. Jamie, still half asleep at the time, had heard him shovelling the driveway, crunching through the snow in his boots, scraping the shovel blade on the surface of the drive. It must have been snowing for a good part of the night, and the air visible through the frosted window was still a frenzy of flakes, falling thick and fast.

The bedroom door opened to admit his mother's face and a distant whiff of oatmeal cooking. "Jamie? Time to—oh, you're awake, good. You'd better hurry up and get dressed, and help me listen to the radio to see if they're calling school off. Come on, now."

Slipping his jeans and flannel shirt on and poking his feet into slippers that weren't really much warmer than the hardwood floor they had spent the night on, he made a trip to the bathroom and then to the kitchen, where his oatmeal was steaming on the table beside a glass of orange juice. From the shelf over the dishwasher, the radio was blaring, turned up loud so that Mom could hear it as she moved about the house.

"... a major snowstorm for southern New Hampshire and northeastern Massachusetts, with fifteen to eighteen inches accumulation possible by noon in some locations. If you have to go out, leave yourself a lot of extra time to get where you're going this morning, friends, because it's a real mess out there. And please drive with care, won't you—hey, we like you, and we want you to get there safe and sound. Better yet, if you don't *have to go out, why don't you just pour yourself another cup of that nice hot coffee and sit back and keep us company? Time is now 6:41, temperature outside our studios is twenty-four degrees. I'm Rick Phillips for Storm Center Radio, 1360 on your dial, coming to you from downtown Manchester. The cancellations are coming in, and we'll have a complete rundown for you following these messages, so stay tuned."*

Jamie ate his oatmeal and watched the snow through the kitchen window. Wow—maybe they were going to cancel school. He'd heard that it happened here in New England all the time. In Arizona, where they'd lived till this past year, they never, never cancelled school. Ever. The only time he'd even seen snow before was that one time in Colorado, when he was six.

"Mom?"

She paused in her trip past the door. "Yes, dear?"

"What if they do cancel school?"

She shrugged. "I'll just call Mrs. Carter to come over and sit with you. She only lives a couple of miles from here."

He knew Mrs. Carter well; she'd sat with him three or four times when Mom and Dad went out. She was okay, a little grumpy sometimes, but okay. Still—

"Mom? Maybe they'll close up at Sanborn's and you won't have to go to work."

She shook her head ruefully. "Are you kidding? Sanborn's wouldn't close if it was the end of the world. I have to go in. Listen, you'll be okay with Mrs. Carter. I'll be home an hour early, too, because I'll work through my lunch hour to make up the time." She withdrew.

Jamie worked on his oatmeal while the radio jangled its way through a series of commercials. He thought about the school building, ghostly and dark and empty of kids. Did the teachers come in anyway? He tried to imagine Miss Bouvier staying home, eating her breakfast in a house-coat and slippers with her hair up in curlers and no makeup on, but it was hard to think of a teacher that way.

". . . the list of cancellations that we have so far. We'll give them again at quarter past the hour. Now, we've had no chance

to put these in alphabetical order, so listen carefully. Here we go."
Jamie set his spoon down and listened. "*Manchester, no school, all schools. Manchester Senior Center craft classes scheduled for this morning have been cancelled. Litchfield, no school, all schools. Hudson, no schools, all schools. Concord, at least a ninety-minute delay, but keep listening, they may decide to cancel. Amherst, no school, all schools. Bedford, no school, all schools. Also, Bedford Senior Center is open but no transportation. Hooksett, no school, all schools.*" Come on, Jamie thought, finishing his cereal and trying not to chew too hard, so that he could hear clearly. Come on, who cares about all that stuff—what about Merrimack?

"*Derry, no school, all schools. Salem, no school, all schools. Ding Dong Bell Nursery School in Goffstown is closed today. Pelham, no school, all schools, but faculty will still meet at three o'clock unless further notice, stay tuned. This just in*"—Jamie had a feeling, and held his breath—"*Merrimack, no school, all schools.*"

"Mom?"

"I heard it, Jamie. I'm dialing Mrs. Carter now."

He put his bowl and spoon in the sink and went to the front window in the living room, glass of orange juice in hand, and stood watching the storm. The snow was beautiful in a way, but somehow also darkly suggestive, as if saying: see, you people think you're so smart, but I can shut you down any time I feel like it, and I feel like it right now.

Gazing across the front yard through the swirling gray-white air, he had to find the mailbox, now a shapeless muff of snow standing on a post at the end of the driveway, before he could tell where the yard ended out there and where the street began. Somewhere nearby, snowplows were thundering their way through the streets, but they hadn't gotten to this street yet. He remembered seeing a snowplow that one time before, in Colorado, a lumbering metal dinosaur with great shining eyes, nosing its way through the snowdrifts. His mom was talking on the phone now, but he couldn't hear her over the rumble of the plow that had just swung the corner onto this street and was barreling past, pushing a sliding mountain of snow with its enormous blade.

"Jamie."

He turned. "Mom! The snowplow piled snow up at the end of the drive. I'll get my coat and boots on and go out and shovel it for you."

She shook her head. "No, I don't want you out there, Jamie, not when you just got over a fever. Thanks anyway, dear, but I can do it. Or maybe I'll just drive over it. Anyhow, what I wanted to tell you was that Mrs. Carter can't come over to sit with you today." *Mrs. Carter has been cancelled*, Jamie thought; *stay tuned.* "There's nobody else I can get, so I guess you'll have to be here by yourself. That'll be okay, won't it—you're nine now, you can handle it, can't you?"

He shrugged. "Sure, Mom, it's okay." He wasn't really sure how he felt about it. In a way it was exciting, the prospect of being on his own for the day, but then again. . . .

He must have let his thoughts show on his face, because now she was making assurances to him. "You can watch television or play records or run your train set or do anything you like. And when you get hungry for lunch, you can make yourself a peanut butter and jelly sandwich, I know that's your favorite."

He warmed to that idea readily enough. "Can I make more than one?"

She laughed, but looked at him warily. "All right, but don't you go eating yourself sick, do you hear me, Jamie Hutchins?"

"Yes, ma'am. I mean, no, ma'am, I won't."

She was pulling her overcoat and boots on. "You can make a couple of sandwiches if you want, and there's a bag of potato chips in the pantry. And if you're still hungry, you can have an apple. There's a big bottle of soda too, in the fridge, for later, but you drink a glass of milk with your lunch, understand?"

"Yes, ma'am."

"And don't make a mess in the kitchen, and don't fool around with the oven or the microwave. And don't go outside in this cold."

"No, ma'am."

"Okay. I know you'll be all right. Here's my number at work"—she scribbled it on the back of an envelope and left it on the coffee table—"in case you need to call, and I'll call you at lunchtime. I have to run."

"Okay, Mom. 'Bye."

"Bye, dear." She was out the door, and he saw her trudging through the mounting snow to her car in the drive. He watched from the window while she brushed the snow off the car and shoveled the end of the drive. He watched as she backed the car out, watched until her taillights winked red through the windswept falling flakes and were gone around the corner.

Then he was alone. Alone in the house, alone with the snow.

Outside the window, the wind swirled into a dismal-sounding howl and rippled the snow like a curtain. Jamie stepped closer to the window, sipping his orange juice, and heard the floorboards creek faintly as he shifted his weight on them. Funny, how quiet, how empty a house could sound.

Well. He finished the juice, deposited the glass in the kitchen sink, and went down the hall to his room. Sliding the top dresser drawer open, he fumbled through the mess of socks and underwear and uncovered his emergency supply of candy bars, taking three of them and closing the drawer. Then he went to his parents' bedroom farther down the hall.

Kicking his slippers off, he folded back the bed-covers and crawled onto the bed and sat crosslegged in the middle facing the snow-crusted window and arranged the sheets snugly around his legs like a bird's nest. He had decided on this room rather than his own because this was where the other phone was. He was going to call Kevin Riley.

He unwrapped a candy bar and took a bite and leaned across to the phone beside the bed. Tapping out Kevin's number, he straightened back out in his nest with the phone in hand. A kid's voice answered on the other end.

"Lo?"

"Hey, Kevin, your mother licks armpits."

"Cheez. Hey, Jamie, you're gay."

"You're a fat slob, Kevin."

"You wet your bed, Jamie."

"You're spastic, Kevin."

"Hey, Jamie, your mother eats dog boogers."

At this they both collapsed into wild laughter. When they had got their breath back, Kevin said, "Great about school bein' closed, huh? What're you doin'?"

"Sitting here talking to you on the phone, what do you think I'm doing?"

"Your folks home?"

"No," Jamie said. "Yours?"

"Naw," Kevin said, "they both had to go to work. Wicked neat bein' home by yourself, huh?"

"Yeah," Jamie said, "yeah, I guess so."

Kevin guffawed so loud that Jamie had to back the phone off his ear an inch or two. "Whadda ya mean, you guess so? You scared bein' alone, Jamie? Hah?"

"No, no, I'm not scared. What's there to be scared of?"

"Yeah, I bet you're not scared. I bet you're gonna pee your pants."

"Up yours, Kevin."

"Bite my dong, Jamie."

"Hey." Jamie had just realized that the radio was still going, in the kitchen. "Hey, hold on, I'm gonna go get the radio and bring it in here so I can listen to it in the bed."

"You in bed, Jamie? What a pussy."

Jamie put the receiver down on a pillow and went for the radio. When he had it plugged in and playing on the bureau, with the volume down a little so that he could hear Kevin, he resettled himself in the middle of the bed and picked the phone up. "I'm back."

"What did you have to go get the radio for?" Kevin asked.

Jamie took another bite of the candy bar and talked with his mouth full. "Wanta listen to the cancellations."

"How come, you dumb ass? You already know they cancelled school. You're home, ain't you?"

Jamie watched the snow falling ever harder and faster beyond the windowpanes. "I thought maybe if it got bad enough they might close the mill early and—"

"And our dads would come home, right? I told you you were scared, you chickenshit."

"Stick it in your ear, Kevin."

"What station you listenin' to?" Kevin asked. Jamie could hear him tuning a radio across the dial, a jumble of stations fading in and out.

"It's at 1360," he said, "that Manchester station."

"Got it," Kevin said, and Jamie could hear the radio sound over the phone slide into agreement with his own radio.

"*. . . as storm-related information continues to come in, so stay with us and we'll keep you up to date on what's happening here in southern New Hampshire on this miserable day. Have another cup of coffee for me, won't you? Time now at Storm Center Radio is 7:28, and we have some basketball scores for you—ah, but first, this just in, schools in Londonderry are closed, that's Londonderry, no school, all schools. And I'm told now that schools in Concord and Laconia have been closed after all. That's Concord, no school, all schools, and Laconia, no school, all schools. Here's another one just in—Saint Anselm's College is closed today, both day and evening classes. We'll update you on the whole list of cancellations at 7:40, but first here's Tom Michaud with local sports news. Tell us, Tom, what happened with that basketball game at Rivier College last night?*"

"Hey, Jamie, this is neat. The whole town's covered up with snow."

Jamie had been to Kevin's apartment building across town several times after school or on Saturdays, and knew that you could see just about the whole town from Kevin's fourteenth-floor living room window.

"Kevin?"

"Huh?"

"Can you see Sanborn's from there?"

"Sanborn's? Yeah. Of course I can see Sanborn's. It's got snow all over the roof. What's the matter, puddin'-face' oo miss oo mommy?"

"Smell my farts, Kevin."

"Smell 'em yourself."

They were quiet for a while, their radios murmuring the same commercials, the same chatter. Jamie couldn't think of anything to say, and apparently Kevin couldn't either.

"*. . . cancelled, and also the meeting of the Franco-American*

*Friendship Club scheduled for this evening has been cancelled.
The Manchester Public Library is open this morning, but there
is no bus transportation for the Tiny Tots Storytime, and the
library will close at noon. Those are the newest ones in. Here's
a complete list of public school cancellations again now as we have
them, we'll be reading them again for the last time at 8:05. Here
we go. Manchester, no school, all schools. Nashua, no school, all
schools. . . ."*

"Hey, Kevin?"

"Mm?"

"Listen, you don't have to hang on the line if you got things
you want to do."

A moment of silence. Then: "Naw, I don't have nothin'
I wanta do. I'll stay on."

Jamie thought: I bet I know why, too. He said, "Sort of nice
havin' somebody to talk to, right?"

"You sayin' I'm spooked bein' here by myself?"

"I didn't say that," Jamie replied. "All I said was it's good to
have somebody to talk to."

More silence on Kevin's end, then: "Yeah, I guess it is, kind
of. Even if I have to talk to some numb-nuts like you."

They became thoughtful again, neither speaking for a good
while. Outside Jamie's parents' bedroom window, the snow
seemed heavier, more insistent, every minute. It brushed against
the frosty panes with jittery fingers of white, worrying at the
glass, whispering. He could scarcely see far enough out now to
make out the pines, except when the snow would lift a moment,
rearranged by the wind. He ventured a remark to Kevin, bracing
for the taunting reply it would bring.

"Something about the snow's kinda eerie, isn't it?"

Kevin was slow in replying, and, surprisingly, he said, "Yeah.
Kind of."

What do you know, Jamie thought—he feels it too. "Kevin,
can you see the mill?"

"Yeah, just barely. It's a long way off. I can just see it. Looks
like a ghost."

*". . . and Storm Center Radio will bring you all the details
throughout the day, so stay tuned. I'm Rick Phillips for Radio*

1360, Manchester, your information station for southern New Hampshire." Then music, some whimpy-sounding song like the old-fashioned stuff grownups listened to.

Odd.

Odd, the way that voice had sounded. Something— different about it.

"Kevin?"

"Mm."

"Did you think that guy on the radio sounded kind of strange?"

Kevin seemed to be thinking about this. "I guess I wasn't payin' much attention to him. I was watchin' the snow."

"Well, let's listen to him when he comes back on again."

"Okay," Kevin said. Somehow Kevin seemed different too, now, more serious. Jamie had almost never known Kevin to be serious about much of anything. The music droned its way to a conclusion, and the voice was back.

"*A little bit of Mel Tormé for a snowy morning, nice, don't you think? Time now is 8:25, that snow keeps coming on down. And do we have some new cancellations for you!*"

Jamie drew the sheets closer around his legs, feeling suddenly colder. The wind outside the window moaned and shifted the snow in crazy-looking patterns. That voice was different, and he didn't like the way it sounded. It was—what? A little like some kind of cartoon-character villain, sort of half-mocking like. Sort of . . . unreal.

"I see what you mean," he heard Kevin say. "He's . . ."

"Shh, listen."

"*Here's the big one, friends, listen carefully.*" He pronounced *carefully* the way Bela Lugosi might say it in a Dracula movie, drawing the first vowel out long with a final lilt. "*Here it is. Merrimack Valley Mill is cancelled.*" The radio went immediately to music again, some love song.

For a long while neither boy spoke. It was Kevin who finally broke the silence. "Jamie?"

"I'm here."

"Jamie, I'm lookin' out the window and somethin' looks funny."

"What do you mean, something looks funny?"

Kevin waited a long time before answering, and when he did, he sounded awestruck. "This ain't right. I can see Pennacook Park."

"So what's the big deal about seein' Pennacook Park?"

"I never could see it before. Not from here."

"Aw, c'mon, Kevin, it's as big as a football field. Bigger. You must of seen it."

"No, no, I'm tellin' you, Jamie, I never could see it before. I can barely see it now, just when the snow lets up a second, but it's there, all right. And"—Jamie could hear him draw in a shocked-sounding breath; Kevin, Kevin sounding shocked, Kevin who never sounded shocked— "and I just figured out why. It's because the mill ain't there."

Jamie laughed, but the laugh came out a little hollow. "Give me a break, Kevin. Of course the mill is there. What are you talking about?"

"Look, Jamie, I ought to know where that mill is, from my own window, and I'm tellin' you, it ain't there. That's why I can see the park, because the mill ain't hidin' it anymore."

Outside Jamie's parents' window, the wind whooped up into a deranged-sounding howl and threw snow against the panes. "Kevin, what are you saying? My dad works there."

Kevin was quiet for a long time, then said, "So does mine."

"Kevin, look—hey, ssh, the guy's on the radio again."

"*. . . hope you enjoyed that one by Dean Martin. At 8:39, this is Radio 1360, your voice of the storm.*" The voice had that lilting, mocking tone again, more so than before. "*And in case you thought we were through with cancellations, consider this one, my friends. This just in—Sanborn's in Merrimack. Sanborn's has been cancelled.*" Immediately, more music.

"Kevin?"

"I'm here."

"Kevin, my mom works at Sanborn's."

"I know."

"Kevin, can you see Sanborn's?"

After a moment, Kevin replied, "I can't tell, there's so much snow."

"Kevin, look, I'm going to hang up for a minute. I'll call you back."

"Promise?"

"Promise." Jamie clicked the receiver down and raced to the living room and retrieved the envelope from the coffee table and returned to the bedroom. He punched out the digits his mom had scribbled on the envelope, feeling oddly moved by the sight of her handwriting. As he listened for the phone to ring on the other end, strained to hear that soft burring sound, he heard only a blank hissing on the line, and the murmuring of the wind outside, where, he could see, the snow was falling harder than ever. Finally he gave up and dialed Kevin back. Kevin answered before the first ring was finished. "Jamie?"

"Yeah, it's me. Look, I tried to call my mom, but there's was no answer. It doesn't even ring."

Kevin coughed and seemed about to say something, when the voice returned to the radio.

"*We hope you're staying tuned, because we have another update on the snow cancellations. Exotron Technologies has been cancelled. Compton Industries has been cancelled. Pennacook Mall has been cancelled.*"

"Jamie!"

"I heard."

"Jamie, my mom works at Pennacook Mall."

"I know."

"Jamie—there's somethin' awful wrong. The downtown, out my window. There's, like, parts of it gone. I mean, really gone. Like holes in it."

"Kevin, I'm getting sc. . ."

"Shh. Jamie. Listen."

"*. . . and still more Storm Center Radio update for you. Ready for this one?*" The voice sounded thick, gloating, dreadful. "*Reeds Ferry Apartments, in Merrimack, cancelled.*" Music; some woman was singing, "Let it snow, let it snow, let it snow."

A brittle finger of ice wormed its way up Jamie's spine. Kevin lived in the Reeds Ferry Apartments complex. He swallowed hard to get his voice back.

"Kevin?"

Nothing.

"Kevin?"

Nothing at all.

"Kevin!"

Nothing on the line at all but a dead, dry hissing, like the sound that might come out of the grinning and remorseless mouth of a reptile.

"Kevin. Please be there. Please."

Silence. Silence on the phone, and the radio crooning along, unconcerned.

He hung up the phone and sat looking out at the snow, which had grown into a nightmare whiteness pressing at the window, blotting everything out, swirling in the madness of the wind.

He looked at the two remaining candy bars on the pillow, and at the envelope where his mom had written her phone number those eons ago. Pulling the sheets closer around him and pressing the envelope to his cheek, he sat in the bed and waited for the music to end.

NICHOLAS ROYLE

Archway

NICHOLAS ROYLE was born in Sale, Cheshire, and currently lives in North London. He has published more than 35 stories to date in a wide variety of books and magazines, including *Cutting Edge*, *Book of the Dead*, *The Year's Best Horror Stories*, *The Truth*, *Reader's Digest* and *Gorezone*.

He recently edited *Darklands*, an original anthology of horror stories by British writers, and currently has two novels looking for a publisher, *Counterparts* and *Saxophone Dreams*.

Royle was unemployed and living in a poorly maintained rented flat when writing "Archway": "While I could see a light at the end of the tunnel," he explains, "many can't. Because there isn't always one. And since I wrote the story, conditions have deteriorated thanks to benefit changes and mishandling of the economy."

I N RESPECT OF THE WEATHER, as she would later discover, it was a typical Archway day, the Friday that Bella moved into the flat. How terribly British of her to talk about the weather, Bella's sister wrote in reply to the letter Bella had sent a few days after moving in. Not at all like her, wrote Jan. What did she know? thought Bella. Jan had always sought arguments on trivial matters. Her provocations were best ignored.

She crumpled up the letter and looked out of the kitchen window. The sun was casting sharp rectangles of light on the huddled walls and buildings; large black-grey clouds moved in from the south-west like airships to obscure the light. The weather followed the same pattern every day: bright intervals followed by the intrusion of these heavy grey clouds, which were soon blown over by the ever-persistent wind. Bella had become something of a weather-watcher, it was true, but not because she responded to the Britishness of the occupation; rather, it served as a distraction.

She threw Jan's letter in the bin and crossed the kitchen. Her finger alighting on the percolator switch, she froze. There was that noise again. She'd heard it a few times that week and had been able neither to locate it, nor with any certainty identify it. Sometimes it was like an asthmatic's wheezing, sometimes an old man's derisive laugh. Asthmatics and old men there may well have been in the upper and lower flats and on either side, but the noise sounded as though it came from within her walls. Just an acoustic trick, she assured herself, the source of which would no doubt one day soon come to light.

"There you are then. You can have a day to think about it if you want," the landlord had said after giving his lightning tour of the flat. "But the sooner you decide the better. I don't know if you know what the present housing situation is like, but . . ."

"I know exactly what it's like," she interrupted him. "I've been looking for over a month and some of the places I've seen, well, I wouldn't live in them if you paid me."

"There's plenty would. Can't turn your nose up these days. Anyway, that's another matter. This is a good flat and I'll have no trouble finding someone for it. So, when can you tell me?"

Bella thought quickly. It was the first flat she'd seen which satisfied all her requirements—self-contained, own front door, bath fitted, telephone already in, adequately furnished, ten minutes from the tube, rent just within her means provided she got the housing benefit.

"I'll take it," she said, surprised at how easy it was, not believing the search was over.

"Right. You can move in on Friday. A month's rent in advance, a month deposit. When can you let me have a reference?"

"Pardon?"

"Reference. From your employer."

"Oh, by the end of this week, I should imagine." She should be able to get it by then. In fact, the matter of a reference had slipped her mind, but it was of course essential. She remembered the miles of cards in newsagents' windows which repeatedly stressed "No DHSS" and "Professional people only".

Bella straightened the framed photograph which had drawn her attention. Now at the white wall she fingered the crack. It was nothing to worry about, the landlord had said in his booming voice. But she found she was able to slide her finger into the gap—she was sure she hadn't been able to do that before. She heard the photograph move and reached to straighten it again. The crack widened a fraction and a solid lump of darkness fell into the room. Bella stooped to pick it up but it dissolved in her hand like it was nothing. Suddenly the light in the room dimmed as black light dribbled from the crack. The crack gaped and a great absence of light seemed to pour into the room, thick and viscous like tar, yet neither liquid nor solid.

It laughed at her.

Bella rose from contemplation of her breakfast, depressed after a bad night, and straightened the photograph on the wall. As she touched the frame she felt a tug of familiarity. She didn't remember anything else until some time later when she was on her way out of the door and she heard somebody laugh where nobody could have been.

Lunch was busier than usual at the restaurant. Again she felt glad she was not a waitress, rushing around with never enough time to do all that was demanded. Bella was happier sitting at the cash desk, steadily working through hundreds of pounds and as many indecipherable bills. Not that she was content, however. The cash system at the restaurant she'd worked at before coming here had been much more straightforward, and her work as a result had been more efficient. But that restaurant had closed for refurbishment work only a couple of weeks ago, its employees effusively thanked and put out on the street. So she'd asked around and found a job here. The wages were better, which was good, now that she had the flat to pay for. As for the reference, she was sitting on it. The manageress had typed up a short note which was now in the back pocket of Bella's jeans.

The telephone rang shrilly. It was for Marilyn. Bella called her, although she wasn't supposed to pass calls on to the staff. Not a word of thanks. But that was nothing new: these waitresses were not really disposed to friendliness. Bella regretted having not swapped numbers with the friends she'd made in the old place.

When Bella climbed out of the underground at Archway, the sky was almost completely blacked out by thick cloud, like a domed lid propped from the earth in the east by high-rise blocks silhouetted against brilliant white. As she stood at the exit the rain began to fall, heaving heavy drops onto the litter-strewn pavement.

"It's always the way, isn't it?" she said to a middle-aged woman who slipped away, bowing her head to protect the cigarette which clung mollusc-like to her bottom lip. A tramp moved slowly through the flow of people towards the station entrance. Seeing Bella standing there he held out a hopeful hand. She turned away and walked home through the rain and dirty streets. A crowd of boys collected at the end of Fairbridge Road. They wore training shoes, jeans slashed a little way up the side seams at the ankle, Paisley shirts whose tails hung out, gold chains and expensive haircuts. The rain had stopped; the clouds fled eastwards as if scared of the light which once more seeped into the streets. Bella counted sixteen boarded-up houses on Fairbridge Road. She began to wonder at the landlord's audacity in describing this area of Upper Holloway as "desirable".

Her resolution not forgotten, Bella searched the flat for a possible source of the noise which had frightened her. She was examining the bedroom door hinges when the laughter rang out clearly from the bathroom. She ran through immediately and pulled the blind up onto its runner. The ventilator groaned as it turned in the breeze; it slowed to a wheezing trickle; then laughed as a squall sent it spinning. She leaned over the toilet to pull the cord to shut it up. Below, a face turned from Bella's direction and a figure slipped across the waste ground into the shadow of a wall. "Nosy creep," muttered Bella as she let the blind unroll back into place.

It was just an ordinary salt cellar—metal top, glass body, almost full, a few grains of salt clinging to the downward slope of the silver top—but Bella could not tear her eyes from it. It was safe, reassuring, unambiguous.

She had been moving an easy chair from the living room to the bedroom and had dragged it across the bamboo curtain. The noise it produced—like a rattling of bones—had scared her, set her nerves on edge, even though she knew it was harmless. That being the first ambiguous sound, each new sound was exaggerated and misinterpreted. She'd positioned the chair in her bedroom and straightening up had given a little cry. But the face looking in at her had been her own. She'd pulled the curtains across and had sat down in the chair to try and relax. But the immersion heater had sighed like an old man. She'd stood up to straighten the photograph on the wall. Hadn't she done that before? she'd asked herself. So, she had come to the kitchen, sat down at the table and focused on the salt cellar.

At the edge of her field of vision hung the black oblong of the uncurtained kitchen window. Orange fog loomed outside, pressing at the glass, trying to force a way in. The conversations of her neighbours, muffled through the thin walls, became sinister. A radio played in the flat above but seemed to come from within her own rooms. What could she do to remain calm? She would call someone. Who could she call? There wasn't anybody. She'd lost touch. Her sister; she'd call Jan. As she touched the receiver the telephone rang. Bella jumped back and hit her head against the wall. This was ridiculous: she was being terrorized by *nothing* in her own home. She collected her wits together and picked up the receiver. A man's voice asked for Deirdre, insisted that Bella was she, would not be dissuaded. Bella hung up; she would have to get the number changed. She no longer wished to use the telephone. Jan would only say she was being hysterical. She retreated to the bedroom, away from the billowing fog wiping itself over the kitchen window, and to distract herself opened a book. There was a gaping black divide in the wall, out of focus beyond the pages of the book. Bella looked up but the crack was no more than three or four millimetres wide. Tiredness was causing her to hallucinate. She undressed and got into bed.

"What do you mean you can't manage to keep my shifts open?" she asked of the manageress.

Cheryl said: "Your figures aren't balancing, Bella."

"But that's not my fault. It's the antiquated till and that stupid system. I'm sorry, but it really is a stupid system. And that business of me having to keep the waitresses' money as well. I don't know what they write on their tip cards. I'd suggest you watch some of them before giving me the sack."

"I'm sorry, Bella. Don't you think this is very difficult for me? I'm only doing what I've been told to do."

They all said that, thought Bella. Their hypocrisy had always distressed her. Don't let the staff have phone calls, Cheryl had said. She'd accepted her own calls though. Standing there gossiping with her friends while Bella tried to do two jobs at once. There was much about the restaurant which was undesirable; however, Bella needed the job.

"I need the job," she told Cheryl. "You can't just get rid of me."

"I'm afraid that's the situation, Bella. We are no longer in a position where we have need of you."

It was becoming obvious that the management were not to be budged.

"Well, sod you, then!" Bella shouted and stormed out of the office.

Leicester Square tube station. Northern Line. Three trains had thundered into the station and rattled out again while Bella remained seated, trying to calm her anger and nerves. Feeling a little less violent by the time the fourth train arrived, she got on. A crowded tube train was not the best place to be when feeling angry and resentful. Bella had a tendency, when in that state of mind, to misinterpret dim-witted behaviour as antagonistic. And the tube was a great one for dulling the responses.

The clouds raced overhead at Archway. Bella felt insignificant beneath them. A vicious wind hurled itself along Junction Road and buffeted pedestrians emerging from the station. Bella didn't feel up to going back to the flat; she chose to walk about until she regained her calm. A tattered wretch of a man was stopping passers-by and asking for money. Bella turned and walked towards Highgate Hill. Brooding was pointless, she realized. She was in a mess though. No job, no money. Think positive! She would have to sign on the dole. There could be no immediate prospect of finding another job. She'd been lucky to get the one she'd just lost. Even if she found a vacancy, she'd be in a mess if they checked up on her reference. Why did you leave your last job? They sacked me on suspicion of dipping into the till. She wished now she had done so, if only to validate her dismissal and to give her something to show for it. She turned right into Hornsey Lane. Northbound lorries hurtled up the Archway Road under the overpass, under the Archway. The sky was re-forming: the remaining dark clouds drew together and formed a band joining the horizons. Bella felt small. She walked down the little path to the Archway

Road and stood in the shadow of the Archway and felt smaller still.

She had to wait fifteen minutes before it was her turn. Yes, she wanted to sign on. Yes, she'd signed on before, but years ago, and not here. She was claiming from today and would sign on whichever day suited them. Yes, she needed to have her rent paid. Yes, she would fill in the BI and take it to the DHSS in person rather than post it.

She took the BI home. "Claim Supplementary Benefit on this form," it said at the top. There were eight pages of questions. The walls of the room bowed in above her. A dull creeping light from the window hung over the mismatched furniture. A car turned a corner but the fly which buzzed around the lampshade was louder. She got up to make a cup of tea and passed by the kitchen window. Down below on the patch of waste ground a figure turned its face up to her window. Bella froze to the spot. The face just stared, its eyes quite clearly defined. Bella's flesh crawled, her scalp tightened. She shivered, and a change came over the face. It became elongated as the mouth opened and formed a black triangle. Symmetrical lines deepened about the eyes and mouth, accentuating the apex at the chin and reducing the eyes to black slits. The features formed a hideous triangular mask and became fixed in that image. It was the mime artist's version of an evil sneer; malice and twisted pleasure. The person had gone when Bella looked out again.

The BI presented its problems. "Why did you leave this job?" The walls around her began to press, the air to thicken. "What is the name and address of your landlord, landlady, or council?" Bella's temples ached. The light had deteriorated. "Is your home very difficult to heat because of things like damp or very large rooms?" Another early firework exploded outside. "Are you, or any of the people you are claiming for, pregnant? Who is pregnant?" A fly buzzed over the butterdish. "Who is blind?" "Who needs to have extra washing done? Please tell us why. If you wash at home how many loads of washing do you do each week? How much do you think this costs you each week for washing powder, hot water and electricity? Do you, or any of the people you are claiming for, have any other illness or disability which you would like us to know about? Who is ill or disabled? What is the illness or disability? Remember that if you deliberately give false information you may be prosecuted." "Excuse me." It was Bella speaking. "I've got a question about the BI form you gave me yesterday. It asks for the landlord's name and address. Does this mean you'll be writing to him to check the rent paid and so on?"

"I don't know," said the girl, her hand straying to a pile of cards. "It's not us who pays you."

"Well who pays me?"

"DHSS."

"Yes, but I just want. . . ."

"Look, if you take it to the DHSS they'll explain it for you."

"I don't need it explained. I just want to know if my landlord will be contacted. He doesn't know I'm unemployed, you see. He'd kick me out if he did."

"George." The girl leaned around the partition. "Lady wants to know if the DHSS will contact her landlord."

"Can't say. You'd have to ask them," said George, edging round to face Bella.

"Well, how do I do that? I don't want to put the form in till I'm sure. If the landlord knows he'll kick me out. No one lets to the unemployed, you know. Not if they can help it. Scum of the earth, as far as they're concerned."

"You'd better go to the DHSS, love. Archway Tower. Tenth floor. Ask there."

On her way out of the unemployment office, bewildered and annoyed, Bella scanned the long queues static before the unforgiving windows, and a familiar face revealed itself to her from shadows. She rushed out, clutching her BI, imagining the face grinning horribly at her back.

She hoped a bath would cheer her up and prove fortifying for her jaunt up the Archway Tower. There was nothing—or very little—to equal the pleasure of total immersion in hot foamy water. And somehow the prospect seemed extra attractive in the middle of the day.

The steam condensed on the windows so that she didn't have to drop the blind and resort to artificial light. She began to ease her body gradually into the water, but experience had taught her to opt instead for immediate total submersion: it was always a shock but you soon got used to it. She lay there for ten minutes without moving, without cares; simply enjoying the sensation of the hot water holding her body in its grasp. She brushed her palm over her thigh and thrilled at the tingling feeling produced. Her body was important; she enjoyed the indulgence of its desires. It was a long time since she'd had a man. Her hand floated between her legs. Water splashed out of the bath and onto her slippers. She trembled and lay back; the water regained its stillness; all was very quiet, so that the laughter was particularly shocking when it suddenly rattled through the ventilator. Bella jumped in fright and turned to the window. The ventilator spun and groaned. A dark shape loomed on the other side of the glass. Her first thought was simply that she'd been seen, and guilt filled her; then, as a patch of condensation cleared, she recognized the mad triangular face.

Bella took the lift to the tenth floor and made her way to enquiries. The room distressed her. Rows of benches on which slumped tired, unhappy claimants. Some tramps sat at the back with an upsetting air of permanence and propriety. All the faces in the room were devoid of hope; cheerless, lacking vitality, staring at the partitioned windows, only one of which was being used. There was no apparent queueing system, no ticket distributor, no future in hanging around, thought Bella. She did try to discover from one person whether or not there was any system, but the eyes which turned upon her were so empty and lifeless that Bella could not have stood waiting for an answer without loss of self-control and tears of pity and frustration.

She left the room and stood on the landing opposite the lift doors. These suddenly opened and a piteous group of people moved slowly over to the room Bella had just left—they seemed as if drawn there on an ever-shortening thread.

Over to the left Bella saw a door to another room. The door was unlocked, but the room empty. Rows of benches faced two windows above which was a sign bearing the words: "Appointment holders wait here. Your name will be called at the appointed time." You could wait here a lifetime and never have satisfaction. Here was a system supposed to care for and help those who needed it. Instead it gave you nothing. No, that wasn't true, it didn't dare give you nothing. That would be too definite, too cut-and-dried, too much like an answer to your plea. Instead it gave you the forms, the questions you didn't know how to answer, the delay before the inevitable mistake or refusal.

"It is dangerous to allow children on the windowsill," read another notice underneath the window. Bella looked down and saw the people moving below, crawling like carrion flies over the shit-heap carcass of their city. There would be a poetic justice about it all—the city getting the filth it deserved, and the flies by similar token winning their carrion—were it not for the fact that the flies were actually people; a fact which dwindled to a possibility, easily refutable, from this ivory tower.

There was a second door on the other side of the room. Bella went through into a long, narrow room, partitioned on the left of the aisle into cubicles. Chair, glass, desk, chair; six times repeated. No people, no papers, nothing. At the end a cubicle was sectioned off by walls and two doors. From within came a noise, scuffling and muffled sounds of movement. Bella beat a hasty retreat, not wishing to be apprehended where she probably was not supposed to be.

Back on the landing Bella waited for the lift to come. She looked out of the window down to the roof of the Archway Tavern where a person stood looking up at her. Even at that distance she recognized the laughing face. She swung round and nearly bumped into a man emerging from a door which could only lead to the room where she'd heard the noise. He pointed hideous grinning features at her. The lift arrived and she dived into it. The face was in the lift. She thrust her hands back through the gap and forced the doors open to let her out. She looked about wildly and saw a sign, "Fire Exit". The swing doors banged behind her and she clattered down the cold stone steps.

Her eye was drawn to the yellow stickers which decorated the grey walls of the staircase. "ASBESTOS," she read. "This material must not be worked in any way without written permission from the PSA District Works Officer. Accidental damage should be reported immediately to line manager." Here within the skeleton of the building one became aware of the rotten core, potentially mortally dangerous; the truth to which the lift passengers, ferried up and down through the bowels and guts of the tower, remained oblivious.

Bella came out into Junction Road and was accosted by a red-faced derelict who asked her for twenty pence. She stepped aside—he would only drink it—and left him to the charity of wealthier pedestrians.

Twice she walked back past the church—her mind all indecision—before actually going in for the Friday evening service. Her parents had brought her up to believe. She hadn't set foot inside a church, however, for as long as she could remember. The faces around her were solemn, the service also. She'd come for solace—there was little enough to be found elsewhere—and ended up condemning her naîvety in thinking that the old lie, if believed in, might help when other sources couldn't. When she came out of the church the sharp pointed face on the other side of the road laughed at her before retreating into the shadows of a dark alleyway. She was made to feel humiliated for trespassing where she didn't belong, like a wounded soldier seeking help in the enemy camp. Guilt followed close upon this shame and she was unable to shake it off, even when home with the doors locked and blinds down. Solitary in her prison she felt threatened from without; lonely yet not alone.

Loneliness had proved the stronger and Bella had wrapped herself up in a warm coat and gone out. She'd found one pub off Holloway Road which wasn't, as the others had appeared to be, colonized by drunken Irishmen. She'd made herself be congenial and had accepted the offer of a drink which a man called Brian Monkton had made her.

"These are my friends here. Colleagues really," said Monkton. "We're journalists."

"Right," said Bella. "I've never met any journalists before, I don't think."

"Well, I hope you like us. We're going to a party soon. Not far from here. You can come too if you like."

"Thanks, I think I will."

"What do you do, then? Sorry, what's your name again?"

"Bella."

"Bella. That's right. Lovely name. So, anyway, Bella, what do you do?"

She felt unable to admit she was unemployed. It might be a stigma among these journalists, whose company was better than none.

"I work in the restaurant business."

"Oh right, what, waitress?"

"Yes, well no, cashier. Nearly the same thing. But a bit different." Her words trailed off, confused, but it didn't matter: Monkton didn't appear to be paying much attention to what she was saying. He was looking where her T-shirt hinted at the divide between her breasts. Didn't men realize, she wondered, that women know exactly where their eyes are looking? Maybe they did and they thought women liked it. Could they really be that stupid? She supposed they could—but their intelligence needn't concern her tonight. There would be a party; she could meet people, have a few drinks, relax, forget her worries, forget that mocking face that seemed to be following her about. The man was talking to her:

"Come on, then, er, Bella. Everyone's here. We can go."

They walked in a large group north up Holloway Road. The night was crisp; Bella pulled her collar up. Cars sped by, burning trails of light onto her retinas; the occasional bus, its steamed-up windows yellow rectangles. A few Asian-owned grocery shops still spread their fruit and vegetables out onto the pavement.

A tramp curled himself into a ball in a shop doorway as they walked past on their way to a party. Bella felt a twinge of guilt, but reminded herself that she had troubles of her own and this would help her forget them for a while, might even make them go away, one never knew.

A man with long hair in a ponytail, who had introduced himself as Terry, passed a rolled and lighted cigarette to Bella. She took it between thumb and index finger and inhaled deeply. Too deeply, it seemed, for she shuddered a little as she held the smoke in her lungs. Her head swam as she exhaled. Terry was talking to her about his new play, about schematic problems he was having with act three; but she wasn't a very attentive listener. She'd drunk several glasses of wine, three cups of tea (of very dubious content), and had shared three, or was it four, cigarettes. Anyway, Terry didn't seem to be aware of her inattentiveness; he watched his fingernails as he spoke. He didn't seem to hear when she excused herself to go to the toilet. She looked back from the doorway and saw that he retained the same position and his lips appeared still to be moving—she giggled and left the room.

The hall was even more congested than the room she'd just left. She managed to pick her way through people sitting on the floor and reach the stairs. The toilet was on the first floor and amazingly there was no queue. She locked the door, pushed her jeans and briefs down, and took a seat. It was good to go, a relief. She wondered if Terry was still talking to his nails. She might not have seen it if it hadn't moved: in the corner to her right, almost hidden by curtains, a disfigured triangular face caught the light with a slight movement. Bella screamed and leapt to her feet, tugging at her jeans. The creature was laughing at her back, she knew, as she yanked the door open and fled downstairs, over the heads in the hall, and out the front door.

She didn't have her coat but wouldn't go back in; she'd come and retrieve it another time. Digging her hands deep in the pockets of her jeans, she trudged homewards. She didn't have far to walk, but the cold bit through her thin sweater, making her shiver. The party had been a mistake; she remembered the derelict they'd strode past on Holloway Road and flushed with guilt.

As she turned a corner she caught a glimpse of someone behind her on the other side of the road. The pursuer drew level on the opposite pavement and kept pace with her. She glanced across and her heart leapt onto her tongue. The grinning head bobbed on a black-clad body, scarcely visible in the dark, which pranced with a lunatic's gaiety. The face turned to her, glowing under the orange lamps, but glowing yellow, and not just the face, the whole head. Sobriety had returned, thanks to the cold, so what caused the apparition of this grinning dancing demon? There must have been something in the tea; those had looked like very big tea leaves, if leaves at all, at the bottom of her cup. She was hallucinating, that's why the dancing head glowed yellow under the orange lights which killed colour; it wasn't the source of its own light, but the product of whatever drugs Bella had consciously or unconsciously consumed.

Still the head kept pace with her, teetering above its stalk-like body, despite the advance of her rationale. If she turned a corner, it turned also, but kept the same distance between them. Thoughts fluttered around her skull: was the thing being cautious in not approaching? was it content to laugh from a safe distance? Deciding to risk it, Bella dived into a narrow passageway which she had used in daylight as a short cut. She denied herself the luxury of looking back and so didn't perceive that she was being pursued until she heard footsteps approaching at speed. They didn't stop at a respectful distance behind her. A hand clamped down on her shoulder and she wheeled round.

"Oh God!" It was Monkton from the pub. "What are you playing at? You terrified me."

"Sorry," said the newcomer, breathing alcohol through the mist into her face. "I didn't think. But then I'm hardly in a state to be thinking. You left so suddenly. Good party. Why d'you leave?"

"I, er . . . I had a headache, needed some air," Bella said, looking over Monkton's shoulder but seeing nothing in the orange mist.

"Right. Well. You going home, then? Got far to go? Can't let you go on your own."

Monkton was eager and Bella would be glad of company, in the general sense if not the particular. The threat she felt from the face seemed to have grown since its disappearance and replacement by Monkton.

"Thanks," she said. "It's not far."

One thing had led to another. Bella's gratitude to Monkton for walking her home, not fully expressed, for she couldn't tell him about the face; and Monkton's assumption that Bella would be grateful to him for looking after her. She'd invited him to come in and offered him the choice of cold beer or black coffee. He'd chosen beer, so she took two beers out of the fridge, thinking, what the hell, she was lonely.

"Don't worry about it, Brian," Bella had tried to comfort him. "You've had a lot to drink."

"It's not the damn drink," he'd said sharply.

The delay had been caused by Monkton's inability to come, despite his sustained erection. Since he didn't immediately put the blame on Bella, as she imagined most men would if they thought they could get away with it, she reasoned that it must have been a continuing problem, which Monkton was aware of and duly upset by. Bella was determined not to let the episode be a total failure. Her aggression hadn't worked, so she would invite a change in the balance of power. She cajoled Monkton to rise above the problem and by so doing end it. He had sat astride her and entered, no less firm in his intention than before. If he'd kept his eyes closed it might have been all right, but he'd opened them to sneak a look. The uncovered window was above the head of the bed. Watching through half-closed eyes Bella knew Monkton had seen someone watching him from the opposite pavement. Laughing at him.

"Bastard," shouted Monkton.

Bella knew. She only opened her eyes properly because she was supposed to. Dismay welled up inside her. A twitching insinuation of complicity plucked at her mind, born out of a responsibility felt. This must have read on her face; it was the only explanation for Monkton hitting her, as he did, three times across the face.

"You don't fuck with me!" he shouted. "Nobody fucks with me!" How one's real face showed itself. "Laughing at me. Bitch! Don't laugh at me!" he added with venom as he clambered from the bed and reached for his clothes. Bella felt consciousness disintegrating. She heard him mutter thickly about her not having seen the last of him, as he left the flat with a slamming of doors. Pulling herself over, she looked out of the window: the man who'd hit her marched away; otherwise the street was deserted.

The crack in the wall opened wider than before and seemed to drown the room with its absence. Bella turned to the window. Tarpaulins stretched over skips drooped tails which were derelicts whose coats flapped as they congregated to watch her. Through the lifeless mob a vital angry presence stalked. It was only a matter of time before he stepped through the divide in the wall on a mission of vengeance for his useless erection.

Bella walked the streets looking for a job. No one needed a cashier. One restaurant offered her part-time dishwashing which she refused. Back on Holloway Road a tramp asked her to help him with his bus fare so he could get to hospital. She brushed it aside, as she had all previous requests. But once imprisoned in the orange misty darkness of the side streets, she felt guilty. She shouldn't have turned down the job; she should have helped the tramp. Society and its governing powers wouldn't help him—on her shoulders she felt their absolved responsibility weighing heavily, like the pound coin in her pocket. She would turn back and look for the tramp to give him what little she had, but the sharp report of footsteps reverberated in her wake. It could be anyone. Or it could be Monkton, angry after his humiliation, seeking revenge, the only way masculine aggression knew how. She took a circuitous route and lost her pursuer, if indeed there had ever been one.

*

Bella no longer trusted the veneer of reality which had once sufficed to seduce her into belief, acceptance, submission. Within a week she saw its corners turning up, patches worn thin, like an old photograph on a book cover. She went back to the Archway Tower. The streets were crawling with derelicts, they were multiplying, the world was spinning its last; what about the other people around me, she questioned, is it ending for them as well?

She pushed past a tramp choosing his dinner from a dustbin and stepped onto the platform of a bus. She sat upstairs and watched the pavement creep by. A one-legged tramp hauled himself through the crowds on crutches. The bus stood for an age at traffic lights. The Tower loomed ahead, poking its head into the slate roof of clouds. Bella got off and walked. Footsteps resounded at her back; she stopped and turned and an anonymous swarm of people surged past her. She turned back again and watched the ground as she walked. Into her field of vision came a man beneath whose army greatcoat only one foot showed, and that didn't touch the ground. Now it did; now it didn't. His crutches echoed like nails in shoes. Abruptly he swung round on his metal sticks and extended a begging hand in Bella's direction. But she felt threatened and couldn't even bring herself to look at him. All she saw as she skirted his crutches and left him hanging there were the tattered military ribbons on his greatcoat.

She stood outside the Tower and gazed up at its vastness. The BI was in her pocket, but any meaning it may have once had no longer existed. The door swung open easily beneath her hand. She scorned the hypocrisy of the lifts and found the staircase. Footsteps followed her up the stairs, stopping when she did; they were her own. She needn't fear footsteps in any case; only herself, her own worst enemy.

Out of breath at the ninth floor, she rested her forehead against the whitewashed plastered wall. Her own footsteps still reverberated around the corners. Beneath her hand in the wall she felt a crack which opened at her touch. Black spilled onto the white and the footsteps grew louder. "Accidental damage should be reported immediately to line manager." The crack gaped ever wider. Bella fled upstairs and banged through the swing doors on the tenth floor. A door across the landing stood open; she ran to it and into a familiar room. Empty of people, filled with benches, vacant counter windows and one solitary chair. "Report to receptionist ten minutes after your appointment time if your name has not been called." The door on the other side of the room opened and into the room came a man wearing a sober suit and a grinning triangular mask for a face. Bella groped for the chair and propelled it at the window. The area of impact splintered, and she climbed onto the window ledge, kicking at the glass. "It is dangerous to allow children on the window sill."

She had to find him—not that he was of any particular importance—but she would be able to impose a token amount of order, to put one little thing right. She couldn't hope to solve anything, but could maybe purge a little of her guilt. It seemed to her that if she could remove a part of the guilt, there being still time, she might wipe some of the smile from the laughing face.

There were so many derelicts, however, so many homeless, she could look for ever. Dragging her shattered leg impeded her, all the more so for the lack of support in her spine, which she estimated to have snapped in three places. Instinct drew her on. Loss of blood onto the pavement was alarming pedestrians, but she could neither stop nor hide in a doorway.

Fifty yards away she caught sight of his back. His crutches glinted in the harsh sunlight, his foot scuffed the ground uselessly. She dug into her pocket for coins, but her hand sank into a raw gash. She knew as she tore her hand free of the muscle that it was too little too late. The tramp turned round and raised a crutch in defence. She knew what face she would see if she looked, even though it didn't belong there. So she wouldn't validate its existence by looking; she wouldn't give it the pleasure. Instead, she would have the last laugh and accept the responsibility. She tore at her own eyes with her nails and blood ran into the hollows of her cheeks, accentuating the geometry described by the two bloody sockets in relation to the smashed hanging jaw.

THOMAS LIGOTTI

The Strange Design of Master Rignolo

THOMAS LIGOTTI was born in Detroit and currently lives in nearby Michigan. He has worked as a grocery store clerk, in the circulation department of a local newspaper, as a telephone interviewer for a marketing research firm, as an assistant teacher for the Government Employment Programme, and in various editorial capacities for a reference book publisher.

All of which have probably had no effect whatsoever on his uniquely bizarre tales of fantasy and dread which have been appearing in the small press magazines over the past decade. More recently his fiction has been finding its way between book covers with the anthologies *Prime Evil*, Ramsey Campbell's *Stories That Scared Me*, *The Best Horror from Fantasy Tales*, and his own acclaimed collection, *Songs of a Dead Dreamer*.

It's pretty hard to describe the story that follows, so we'll leave you to soak up the atmosphere and rich prose that is unmistakably Ligotti's, and let the horror creep up on you.

IT WAS WELL INTO EVENING and for some time Nolon had been seated at a small table in a kind of park. This was a long, thin stretch of land—vaguely triangular in shape, like a piece of broken glass—bordered by three streets of varying breadth, varying evenness of surface, and of varying stages of disintegration as each thoroughfare succumbed in its own way and in its own time to the subtle but continuous movements of the slumbering earth beneath. From the far end of the park a tiny figure in a dark overcoat was approaching Nolon's table, and it appeared there was going to be a meeting of some sort.

There were other tables here and there, all of them unoccupied, but most of the park was unused ground covered with a plush, fuzzy kind of turf. In the moonlight this densely-woven pile of vegetation turned a softly glowing shade of aquamarine, almost radiant. Beyond the thinning trees, stars were bright but without luster, as if they were made of luminous paper. Around the park, a jagged line of high roofs, black and featureless, crossed the clouded sky like the uneven teeth of an old saw.

Nolon was resting his hands at the edge of the small, nearly circular table. In the middle of the table a piece of candle flickered inside a misshapen bubble of green glass, and Nolon's face was bathed in a restless green glare. He too was wearing a dark overcoat, unbuttoned at the top to reveal a scarf of lighter shade stuffed inside it. The scarf was wrapped about Nolon's neck right to the base of his chin. Every so often Nolon glanced up, not at the outline of Grissul moving across the park, but to try and catch sight of something in that lighted window across the street—a silhouette which at regular intervals slipped in and out of view. Above the window was a long, low roof surmounted by a board which appeared to be a sign or marquee. The words, or possibly it was only a single word, on this board were entirely unreadable, their paint washed out by some great deluge or deliberately effaced or . . . But the image of two tall, thin bottles could still be seen, their slender necks angled festively this way and that.

Grissul sat down.

"Have you been here long?" he asked, resting his hands upon the table.

Nolon calmly pulled out a watch from deep inside his coat. He stared at it for a few moments, tapped the glass once or twice, then gently pushed the watch back inside his coat.

"Someone must have known I was thinking about seeing you," Grissul continued, "because I've got a little story I could tell."

Nolon again glanced over at the lighted window across the street. Grissul noticed this and twisted his head around, saying, "Well, someone's there after all. Do you think tonight we could get, you know, a little service of some kind?"

"Maybe you could go across yourself and see what our chances are," Nolon replied.

"All the same to me," Grissul insisted, twisting his head to face Nolon. "I've still got my news."

"Is that specifically why this meeting is taking place?"

A blank expression fell across Grisul's face. "Not that I know of," he replied. "As far as I'm concerned, we just met by chance."

"Of course," Nolon agreed, smiling a little. Grissul smiled back but with much less subtlety.

"So I was going to tell you," Grissul began, "that I was out on that field, the one behind the empty buildings at the edge of town where everything just slides down and goes off in all directions. And there's a marsh by there, makes the ground a little, I don't know, stringy or something. No trees, though, only a lot of wild grassy reeds, you know where I mean?"

"I now have a good idea," Nolon replied, a trifle bored or at least pretending to be.

"This was a little before dark that I was there. A little before the stars began to come out. I really wasn't planning to do anything, let me say that. I just walked some ways out onto the field, changed direction a few times, walked a ways more. Then I saw something through a blind of huge stalks, much taller than me, with these great spiky heads on top. And really very stiff, not bending at all, just sort of wobbling in the breeze. They might well have creaked—I don't know—when I pushed my way through to see beyond them. Then I knelt down to get a better look at what was there on the ground. I'm telling you, Mr. Nolon, it was right *in* the ground. It appeared to be a part of it, like—"

"Mr. Grissul, *what* appeared?"

Grissul remembered himself and found a tone of voice not so exhausting of his own strength, nor so wearing on his listener's patience.

"The face," he said, leaning back in his chair. "It was right there, about the size of, I don't know, a window or a picture hanging on the wall, except that it was in the ground and it was a big oval, not rectangular in any way. Just as if someone had partly buried a giant, or better yet, a giant's *mask*. Only the edges of the face seemed not so much buried as, well, woven I guess you would say, right into the ground. The eyes were closed, not *shut* closed—it didn't seem to be dead—but relaxed. The same with the lips, very heavy lips, rubbing up against each other. Even complexion, ashy gray, and soft cheeks. They *looked* soft, I mean, because I didn't actually touch them in any way. I think it was asleep."

Nolon shifted slightly in his chair and looked straight into Grissul's tiny eyes.

"Then come and see for yourself," Grissul insisted. "The moon's bright enough."

"That's not the problem, I'm perfectly willing to go along with you, whatever might be there. But for once I have other plans."

"Oh, other plans," repeated Grissul as if some secret, hidden deep and long, had been revealed. "And what other plans would those be, Mr. Nolon?"

"Plans of relatively long standing and not altered since made, if you can conceive of such a thing these days. Are you listening? Oh, I thought you nodded off. Well, Rignolo—the painter, not the one you might be thinking of—has made a rare move. He's asked me if I would like to have a look around his studio. No one's ever been there that I know of. And no one's actually seen what he paints."

"No one that you know of," added Grissul.

"Of course. Until tonight, that is, a little while from now unless a change of plans is necessary. Otherwise I shall be the first to see what all that talk of his is about. It should really be worth the trouble, and I could invite you to come along."

Grissul's lower lip pushed forward a little. "Thank you, Mr. Nolon," he added, "but that's more in your line. I thought when I told you about my observation this evening—"

"Of course, your observation is very interesting, extraordinary, Mr. Grissul. But I think that that sort of thing can wait, don't you? Besides, I haven't told you anything of Mr. Rignolo's work."

"You can tell me."

"Landscapes, Mr. Grissul. Nothing but landscapes. Exclusively his subject, a point he even brags about."

"That's very interesting, too."

"I thought you would say something like that. I would also think that you might be even more interested if you had ever heard Rignolo discourse on his canvasses. As if he painted them . . . Well, you can see and hear for yourself. What do you say, then? First Rignolo's studio and then straight out to see if we can find that old field again?"

They agreed that these activities, in this sequence, would not be the worst way to fill an evening.

As they got up from the table, Nolon had a last look at the window across the street. The light that once brightened it must have been put out during his conversation with Grissul. So there was no way of knowing whether or not someone was now standing there, perhaps observing them. Buttoning their long overcoats as far as their scarved necks, the two men walked in complete silence across the park where the earth glowed aquamarine below lusterless stars like the dead eyes of countless sculptured faces.

"Don't just walk stepping everywhere," Rignolo told his visitors as they all entered the studio. He was a little out of breath from the climb up the stairs, wheezing his words, quietly muttering to himself, "This place, oh this place." There was hardly a patch of floor that was not in some way cluttered over, so he need not have warned Nolon, or even Grissul. "You see," he said, "how this isn't really a room up here, just a little closet that tried to grow into one, bulging out every which way and making all these niches and alcoves surrounding us, this shapeless gallery of *nooks*.

There's a window around here somewhere, I don't know, under some of these canvasses, I suppose. But those are what you're here for, not to look out some window that who knows where it is. Nothing to see out there, even so."

Rignolo then ushered his visitors through the shrunken maze composed of recesses of one sort or another, indicating to them a canvas here or there. Each was held somehow to a wall or leaning against one, as if with exhaustion. Having brought their attention to this or that picture, he would step a little to the side and allow them to admire his work, standing there like a polite but slightly bored curator of some seldom-visited museum, a pathetic figure attired in loose-fitting clothes of woven . . . dust. His old face was as lifeless as a mask; his skin had the same faded complexion as his clothes, and just as slack, flabby; his lips were the same color as his skin, but more full and taut; his hair shot out in tufts from his head, uncontrolled, weedy; and his eyes showed too much white, having to all appearances rolled up too far toward his forehead, as if they were trying to peek under it. The combination of these facial features gave Rignolo something of the look of an idiot in ecstasy.

While Nolon was gazing at one of old Rignolo's landscapes, Grissul seemed unable to shake off a preoccupation with the artist himself, though he was obviously making the effort. But the more he tried to turn his attention away from Rignolo, the more easily it was drawn back to the flabby skin, the faded complexion, the undisciplined shocks of hair. Finally, Grissul gave a little tug at the sleeve of Nolon's coat and began to whisper something. Nolon looked at Grissul in a way that might have said, "Yes, I know, but have some sense of decorum in any case," then resumed his contemplation of Rignolo's excellent landscapes.

They were all very similar to one another. Given such titles as "Glistening Night," "Marriage of Sky and Shadow," and "The Stars, the Hills," they were not intended to resemble as much as *suggest* the promised scenes. A visual echo of the non-abstract world might strike home on the periphery of one's vision, some effect of color or form, but for the most part they could be described as extremely remote in their perspective on solid reality. Grissul, who was no stranger to the specific locales purportedly depicted in these canvasses, could very well have expressed the objection that these conglomerations of fragmented mass, these whirlpools of distorted light, simply did not achieve their purpose, did not in fact deserve connection with the geographical subjects portrayed therein. Perhaps it was his intuition that just such a protest might be put forth that inspired—in the rapid, frantic voice of a startled sleeper—the following outburst.

"Think anything you like about these scenes, it's all the same to me. Whisper to each other, my hearing is wonderfully bad. Say that my landscapes do not invite one's eyes to pass into them and wander, let alone linger for the briefest moment. Nevertheless, that is exactly their purpose, and as far as I am concerned they are quite adequate to it, meticulously efficient. I have spent extraordinary lengths of . . . time within the borders of each canvas, both as maker and as casual inhabitant, until the borders no longer exist for me and neither does . . . that other thing. Understand that when I say *inhabitant*, I do not in any way mean that I take my clumsy feet tromping up and down staircases of color, or that I stretch out this body of mine on some lofty ledge where I can play the master of all I see. There are no masters of these scenes and no seers, because bodies and their organs cannot function there—no place for them to go, nothing for them to survey with ordinary eyes, no thoughts to think for the mighty brain. And my thoroughfares will not take you from the doorstep of one weariness to the backdoor of another, and they cannot crumble, because they are burdened with nothing to convey—their travelers are already there, continuously arriving at infinite sites of the perpetually astonishing. Yet these cities are also a homeland, and nothing there will ever threaten to become strange in an unpleasant manner. What I mean to say is that to *inhabit* my landscapes one must, in no figurative sense, grow into them. At best they are a paradise for sleepwalkers; but only those sleepwalkers who never rise to their feet, who forget their destination, who even forget they exist at all. On their way to an ultimate darkness beyond dreams, such sleepwalkers may pause to loiter in these lands of mine, which neighbor on nothingness and stand next door to endlessness. So you see, my critics, what we have in these little pictures is a not *quite* utter annihilation, but an incomplete and thoroughly decorative eternity of—"

"All the same," Grissul interjected, "it sounds unpleasant."

"You're interfering," Nolon said under his breath.

"The old bag of wind," Grissul said under his.

"And just where do you see the unpleasantness? Where, show me. Nowhere, in my view. One cannot be unpleasant to one's self, one cannot be strange to oneself. I claim that all will be different when one is joined with the landscape. For the initiated, each of those little swirls is a cove which one may enter into and become; each line—jagged or merely jittery—is a cartographer's shoreline which may be explored at all points at once; each crinkled wad of radiance, a star basking in its own light, and in yours. This, gentlemen, is a case of making the most of one's talent for pro . . . jec . . . tion. There indeed exist *actual* locales on which my pictures are based, I admit that. But these places keep their distance from the spectator: whereas my new landscapes make you feel at home, those old ones put you off, hold you at arm's length. That's the way it is out there—everything looks at you with strange eyes. But you can get around this intolerable situation, jump the fence, so to speak, and trespass into a world where you *belong* for a change. If my landscapes look unfamiliar to you, it is only because everything looks different from the other side. All this will be understood much more clearly when you have seen my masterwork. Step this way, please."

Nolon and Grissul glanced blankly at each other and then followed the artist up to a narrow door. Opening the door with a tiny key, Rignolo ushered his guests inside. It was a tight squeeze through the doorway.

"Now *this* place really is a closet," Grissul whispered to Nolon. "I don't think I can turn around."

"Then we'll just have to walk out of here in reverse, as if there were something wrong with that."

The door slammed closed and a for a moment there was no place on earth darker than that little room.

"Watch the walls," Rignolo called through the door.

"Walls?" someone whispered.

The first images to begin to appear in the darkness were those crinkled wads of radiance Rignolo spoke of, except that these were much larger, more numerous, and after all became more radiant than the others bound within their cramped little canvasses. And these emerged on all sides of the spectator, above and below as well, so that an irresistible conviction was instilled that the tiny, gravelike room had collapsed or expanded into a star-strewn corridor of night, the certainty created that one was suspended in space without practical means of remaining there. And reaching out for the solid walls, crouching on the floor, only brought confusion rather than relief from the sense of impossibility. From faint pinpoints, very precise, the irregular daubs of brightness grew, each taking on any of the infinite shades between silver and bluish-gray, each ragged at its glowing rim. And each grew to a certain size, where it held. Then another kind of growing began: threadlike filaments of light, grayish-green in color, started sprouting in the spaces between and behind those bulbous thistles of brilliance, running everywhere like cracks up and down a wall. And these threadlike, hairlike tendrils eventually spread across the blackness in an erratic fury of propagation, until all was webbed and stringy in the universal landscape. Then the webbing began to fray and grow shaggy, cosmic moss hanging in luminous clumps, beards. But the scene was not muddled, no more so, that is, than the most natural marsh or fen-like field. Finally, enormous stalks shot out of nowhere, quickly criscrossed to form interesting and well-balanced patterns, and suddenly froze. They were greenish-blue and wore burry crowns of a pinkish color, like prickly brains.

The scene, it appeared, was now complete. All the actual effects were displayed before the spectator: *actual* because the one further effect now being produced was most likely an illusion. It seemed to the spectator, or *might* seem, that deep within the shredded tapestry of webs and hairs and stalks, something else had been woven, something buried beneath the marshy morass but slowly rising to the surface.

"Is that a face?" someone said.

"I can begin to see one, too," said another, "but I don't know if I want to see it. I don't think I can feel where I am now. Let's try not to look at those faces."

A series of cries from within the little room got Rignolo to open the door, which sent Nolon and Grissul tumbling backwards into the artist's studio. They lay among the debris of the floor for some time. Rignolo swiftly secured the door, and then stood absolutely still beside it, his upturned eyes taking no interest in his visitors' predicament. As they regained their feet, a few things were settled in low voices.

"Mr. Nolon, I recognized the place that that room is supposed to be."

"I'm sure you did."

"And I'm also sure I know whose face it was that I saw tonight in that field."

"I think we should be going."

"What are you saying?" demanded Rignolo.

Nolon gestured to a large clock high upon the wall and asked if that was the time.

"Always," replied Rignolo, "since I've never yet seen its hands move."

"Well, then, thank you for everything," said Nolon.

"We have to be *leaving*," added Grissul.

"Just one moment," Rignolo shouted as they were making their way out. "I know where you're going now. Someone, I won't say who, told me what you found in that field. I've done it, haven't I? You can tell me all about it. No, it's not necessary. I've put myself into the scene at last. The infinite with a decor, the ultimate flight! Oh, perhaps there's still some work to be done. But I've made a good start, haven't I? I've got my foot in the door, my face looking in the window. Little by little, then . . . forever. True? No, don't say anything. Show me where it is, I need to go there. I have a right to go."

Having no idea what sort of behavior a refusal might inspire in the fantastical Rignolo, not to mention reprisals on the part of his anonymous informant, Nolon and Grissul respected the artist's request.

*

Into a scene which makes no sound, three figures arrive. Their silhouettes move with distinct, cautious steps across a clearing in a field, progressing slowly, almost without noticeable motion. Around them, crisscrossing shafts of tall grasses are entirely motionless, their pointed tips sharply outlined in the moonlight. Above them, the moon is round and bright; but its brightness is a dull sort, like the flat glow of whiteness that appears in the spaces of complex designs embellishing the page of a book. The three figures, one of which is much shorter than the other two, have stopped and are standing completely still before a particularly dense clump of oddly-shaped stalks. Now one of the taller figures has raised his arm and is pointing toward this clump of stalks, while the shorter figure has taken a step in the direction indicated. The two taller figures are standing together as the short one has all but disappeared forwardly into the dark, dense overgrowth. Only a single shoe, its toes angled groundward, and a square patch of trouser leg are visible. Then nothing at all.

The two remaining figures continue to stand in their places, making no gestures, their hands in the pockets of their long overcoats. They are staring into the blackness where the other one has disappeared. Around them, crisscrossing shafts of tall grasses; above them, the moon is round and bright.

Now the two figures have turned themselves away from the place where the other one disappeared. They are each slightly bent over, and for some time their hands are held tightly against the sides of their heads. Then, slowly, almost without noticeable motion, they move out of the scene.

The field is empty once again. And now everything awakes with movement and sound.

After their adventure, Nolon and Grissul returned to the same table under the trees that had been their point of departure earlier that evening. But where they had left a bare tabletop behind them, not considering the candleflame within its unshapely green bubble, there were at the moment two shallow glasses set out, along with a tall, if somewhat thin bottle placed between them.

They methodically looked at the bottle, the glasses, and each other, as if they did not want to rush into anything.

"Is there still, you know, someone in the window across the street?" Grissul asked.

"Do you think I should look?" Nolon asked back.

Grissul stared at the table, allowing moments to accumulate, then said, "I don't care, Mr. Nolon, I have to say that what happened tonight was very unpleasant."

"Something like that would have happened sooner or later," Nolon replied. "He was too much the dreamer, let's be honest. Nothing he said made any sense to speak of, and he was always saying more than he should. Who knows *who* heard what."

"I've never heard screaming like that."

"It's over," Nolon said quietly.

"But what could have happened to him?" asked Grissul, gripping the shallow glass before him, apparently without awareness of the move.

"Only he could know that for certain," answered Nolon, who mirrored Grissul's move, and seemingly with the same absence of conscious intent.

"And why did he scream that way, why did he say it was all a trick, a mockery of his dreams, that 'filthy thing in the earth.' Why did he scream not to be 'buried forever in that strange, horrible mask'?"

"Maybe he became confused," said Nolon. Nervously, he began pouring from the thin bottle into each of their glasses.

"And then he cried out for someone to kill him. But that's not what he wanted at all, just the opposite. He was afraid to you-know-what. So why would he—"

"Do I really have to explain it all, Mr. Grissul?"

"I suppose not," Grissul said very softly, looking ashamed. "He was trying to get away, to get away with something."

"That's right," said Nolon just as softly, then looking around. "Because he wanted to escape from here without having to you-know-what. How would that look?"

"Set an example."

"Exactly. Now let's just take advantage of the situation and drink our drinks before moving on."

"I'm not sure I want to," said Grissul.

"I'm not sure we have any say in the matter," replied Nolon.

"Yes, but—"

"Shhh. Tonight's our night."

Across the street a shadow fidgeted in the frame of a lighted window. An evening breeze moved through the little park, and the green glow of a candleflame flickered upon two silent faces.

CHET WILLIAMSON

. . . To Feel Another's Woe

CHET WILLIAMSON was born in Lancaster, Pennsylvania, and he currently lives in Elizabethtown with his wife Laurie and son Colin. His first short story was published in 1981, since when his fiction has appeared in *The New Yorker*, *Playboy*, *The Magazine of Fantasy and Science Fiction*, *Twilight Zone*, *New Black Mask* and many other magazines and anthologies.

His first novel was *Soulstorm*, published in 1986, which he followed with *Dreamthorp*, *Ash Wednesday* (a Horror Writers of America Bram Stoker Award nominee), *Lowland Rider*, *McKain's Dilemma* and the latest, *Reign*. His novella, "The Confessions of St. James", appeared in *Night Visions 7*.

". . . To Feel Another's Woe" is an unusual twist on the vampire theme that benefits from the author's knowledgeable depiction of the New York theatre scene.

I HAD TO ADMIT SHE LOOKED like a vampire when Kevin described her as such. Her face, at least, with those high model's cheekbones and absolutely huge, wet-looking eyes. The jet of her hair set off her pale skin strikingly, and that skin was perfect, nearly luminous. To the best of my knowledge, however, vampires didn't wear Danskin tops and Annie Hall flop-slacks, nor did they audition for Broadway shows.

There must have been two hundred of us jammed into the less than immaculate halls of the Ansonia Hotel that morning, with photo/résumés clutched in one hand, scripts of *A Streetcar Named Desire* in the other. John Weidner was directing a revival at Circle in the Square, and every New York actor with an Equity card and a halfway intelligible Brooklyn dialect under his collar was there to try out. Stanley Kowalski had already been spoken for by a new Italian-American film star with more *chutzpah* than talent, but the rest of the roles were open. I was hoping for Steve or Mitch, or maybe even a standby, just something to pay the rent.

I found myself in line next to Kevin McQuinn, a gay song-and-dance man I'd done Jones Beach with two years before. A nice guy, not at all flouncy. "Didn't know this was a musical," I smiled at him.

"Sure. You never heard of the Stella aria?" And he sang softly, "I'll never stop saying Steh-el-*la* . . ."

"Seriously. You going dramatic?"

He shrugged. "No choice. Musicals these days are all rock or opera or rock opera. No soft shoes in *Sweeney Todd*."

"*Sweeney Todd* closed ages ago."

"That's 'cause they didn't have no soft shoes."

Then she walked in holding her P/R and script, and sat on the floor with her back to the wall as gracefully as if she owned the place. I was, to Kevin's amusement, instantly smitten.

"Forget it," he said. "She'd eat you alive."

"I wish. Who is she?"

"Name's Sheila Remarque."

"Shitty stage name."

"She was born with it, so she says. Me, I believe her. Nobody'd *pick* that."

"She any good?"

Kevin smiled, a bit less broadly than his usually mobile face allowed. "Let's just say that I've got twenty bucks that says she'll get whatever part she's after."

"Serious?"

"The girl's phenomenal. You catch *Lear* in the park last summer?" I nodded. "She played Goneril."

"Oh *yeah*." I was amazed that I hadn't recalled the name. "She *was* good."

"You said good, I said phenomenal. Along with the critics."

As I thought back, I remembered the performance vividly. Generally Cordelia stole the show from Lear's two nasty daughters, but all eyes had been on Goneril at the matinée I'd seen. It wasn't that the actress had been upstaging, or doing anything to excess. It was simply (or complexly, if you're an actor) that she was so damned *believable*. There'd been no trace of *acting*, no indication shared between actress and audience, as even the finest performers will do, no self-consciousness whatsover, only utterly true emotion. As I remembered, the one word I had associated with it was *awesome*. How stupid, I thought, to have forgotten her name. "What else do you know about her?" I asked Kevin.

"Not much. A mild reputation with the boys. Love'em and leave'em. A Theda Bara vampire type."

"Ever work with her?"

"Three years ago. *Oklahoma* at Allenberry. I did Will Parker, and she was in the chorus. Fair voice, danced a little, but lousy presence. A real poser, you know? I don't know what the hell happened."

I started to ask Kevin if he knew where she studied, when he suddenly tensed. I followed his gaze, and saw a man coming down the hall carrying a dance bag. He was tall and thin, with light-brown hair and a nondescript face. It's hard to describe features on which not the slightest bit of emotion is displayed. Instead of sitting on the floor like the rest of us, he remained standing, a few yards away from Sheila Remarque, whom he looked at steadily, yet apparently without interest. She looked up, saw him, gave a brief smile, and returned to her script.

Kevin leaned closer and whispered. "You want to know about *Ms.* Remarque, *there's* the man you should ask, not me."

"Why? Who is he?" The man hadn't taken his eyes from the girl, but I couldn't tell whether he watched her in lust or anger. At any rate, I admired her self-control. Save for that first glance, she didn't acknowledge him at all.

"Name's Guy Taylor."

"The one who was in *Annie?*"

Kevin nodded. "Three years here. One on the road. Same company I went out with. Used to drink together. He was hilarious, even when he was sober. But put the drinks in him and he'd make Eddie Murphy look like David Merrick. Bars would fall apart laughing."

"He went with this girl?"

"Lived with her for three, maybe four months, just this past year."

"They split up, I take it."

"Mmm-hmm. Don't know much about it, though." He shook his head. "I ran into Guy a week or so ago at the *Circle of Three* auditions. I was really happy to see him, but he acted like he barely knew me. Asked him how his lady was—I'd never met her, but the word had spread—and he told me he was living alone now, so I didn't press it. Asked a couple people and found out she'd walked out on him. Damn near crushed him. He must've had it hard."

"That's love for you."

"Yeah. Ain't I glad I don't mess with women."

Kevin and I started talking about other things then, but I couldn't keep my eyes off Sheila Remarque's haunting face, nor off the vacuous features of Guy Taylor, who watched the girl with the look of a stolid, stupid guard dog. I wondered if he'd bite anybody who dared to talk to her.

At ten o'clock, as scheduled, the line started to move. When I got to the table, the assistant casting director, or whatever flunky was using that name, looked at my P/R and at me, evidently approved of what he saw, and told me to come back at two o'clock for a reading. Kevin, right beside me, received only a shake of the head and a "thank you for coming."

"Dammit," Kevin said as we walked out. "I shouldn't have stood behind you in line, then I wouldn't've looked so un-macho. I mean, didn't they *know* about Tennessee Williams, for crissake?"

When I went back to the Ansonia at two, there were over thirty people already waiting, twice as many men as women. Among the dozen or so femmes was Sheila Remarque, her nose still stuck in her script, oblivious to those around her. Guy Taylor was also there, standing against a wall as before. He had a script open in front of him, and from time to time would look down at it, but most of the time he stared at Sheila Remarque, who, I honestly believe, was totally indifferent to, and perhaps even ignorant of, his perusal.

As I sat watching the two of them, I thought that the girl would make a stunning Blanche, visually at least. She seemed to have that elusive, fragile quality that Vivien Leigh exemplified so well in the film. I'd only seen Jessica Tandy, who'd originated the role, in still photos, but she always seemed too horsey-looking for my tastes. By no stretch of the imagination could Sheila Remarque be called horsey. She was exquisite porcelain, and I guess I must have become transfixed by her for a moment, for the next time I looked away from her toward Guy Taylor, he was staring at me with that same damned expressionless stare. I was irritated by the proprietary emotion I placed on his face, but found it so disquieting that I couldn't glare back. So I looked at my script again.

After a few minutes, a fiftyish man I didn't recognize came out and spoke to us. "Okay, Mr Weidner will eliminate some of you without hearing you read. Those of you who make the final cut, be prepared to do one of two scenes. We'll have the ladies who are reading for Blanche and you men reading for Mitch first. As you were told this morning, ladies, scene ten, guys six. Use your scripts if you want to. Not's okay too. Let's go."

Seven women and fifteen men, me and Guy Taylor among them, followed the man into what used to be a ballroom. At one end of the high-ceilinged room was a series of raised platforms with a few wooden chairs on them. Ten yards back from this makeshift stage were four folding director's chairs. Another five yards in back of these were four rows of ten each of the same rickety wooden chairs there were on the stage. We sat on these while Weidner, the director, watched us file in. "I'm sorry we can't be in the theater," he said, "but the set there now can't be struck for auditions. We'll have to make do here. Let's start with the gentlemen for a change."

He looked at the stage manager, who read from his clipboard, "Adams."

That was me. I stood up, script in hand. Given a choice, I always held book in auditions. It gives you self-confidence, and if you try to go without and go up on the lines, you look like summer stock. Besides, that's why they call them readings.

"Would someone be kind enough to read Blanche in scene six with Mr Adams?" Weidner asked. A few girls were rash enough to raise their hands and volunteer for a scene they hadn't prepared, but Weidner's eyes fell instantly on Sheila Remarque. "Miss Remarque, isn't it?" She nodded. "My congratulations on your Goneril. Would you be kind enough to read six? I promise I won't let it color my impressions of your scene ten."

Bullshit, I thought, but she nodded graciously, and together we ascended the squeaking platform.

Have you ever played a scene opposite an animal or a really cute little kid? If you have, you know how utterly impossible it is to get the audience to pay any attention to you whatsoever. That was exactly how I felt doing a scene with Sheila Remarque. Not that my reading wasn't good, because it was, better by far than I would have done reading with a prompter or an ASM, because she gave me something I could react to. She made Blanche so real that I had to be real too, and I was good.

But not as good as her. No way.

She used no book, had all the moves and lines down pat. But like I said of her Goneril, there was no *indication* of acting at all. She spoke and moved on that cheapjack stage as if she were and had always been Blanche DuBois, formerly of Belle Rêve, presently of Elysian Fields, New Orleans in the year 1947. Weidner didn't interrupt after a few lines, a few pages, the way directors usually do, but let the scene glide on effortlessly to its end, when, still holding my script, I kissed Blanche DuBois on "her forehead and her eyes and finally her lips," and she sobbed out her line, "'Sometimes—there's God—so quickly!'" and it was over and Blanche DuBois vanished, leaving Sheila Remarque and me on that platform with them all looking up at us soundlessly. Weidner's smile was suffused with wonder. But not for me. I'd been good, but she'd been great.

"Thank you, Mr Adams. Thank you very much. Nice reading. We have your résumé, yes. Thank you," and he nodded in a gesture of dismissal that took me off the platform. "Thank you too, Miss Remarque. Well done. While you're already up there, would you care to do scene ten for us?"

She nodded, and I stopped at the exit. Ten was a hell of a scene, the one where Stanley and the drunken Blanche are alone in the flat, and I had to see her do it. I whispered a request to stay to the fiftyish man who'd brought us in, and he nodded an okay, as if speaking would break whatever spell was on the room. I remained there beside him.

"Our Stanley Kowalski was to be here today to read with the Blanches and Stellas, but a TV commitment prevented him," Weidner said somewhat bitchily. "So if one of you gentlemen would be willing to read with Miss Remarque . . ."

There were no idiots among the men. Not one volunteered. "Ah, Mr Taylor," I heard Weidner say. My stomach tightened. I didn't know whether he'd chosen Taylor to read with her out of sheer malevolence, or whether he was ignorant of their relationship, and it was coincidence—merely his spotting Taylor's familiar face. Either way, I thought, the results could be unpleasant. And from the way several of the gypsies' shoulders stiffened, I could tell they were thinking the same thing. "Would you please?"

Taylor got up slowly, and joined the girl on the platform. As far as I could see, there was no irritation in his face, nor was there any sign of dismay in Sheila Remarque's deep, wet eyes. She smiled at him as though he were a stranger, and took a seat facing the "audience."

"Anytime," said Weidner. He sounded anxious. Not impatient, just anxious.

Sheila Remarque became drunk. Just like that, in the space of a heartbeat. Her whole body fell into the posture of a long-developed alcoholism. Her eyes blurred, her mouth opened, a careless slash across the ruin of her face, lined and bagged with booze. She spoke the lines as if no one had ever said them before, so any onlooker would swear that it was Blanche DuBois's liquor-dulled brain that was creating them, and in no way were they merely words that had existed on a printed page for forty years, words filtered through the voice of a performer.

She finished speaking into the unseen mirror, and Guy Taylor walked toward her as Stanley Kowalski. Blanche saw him, spoke to him. But though she spoke to Stanley Kowalski, it was Guy Taylor who answered, only Guy Taylor reading lines, without a trace of emotion. Oh, the *expression* was there, the nuances, the rhythm of the lines and their meaning was clear. But it was like watching La Duse play a scene with an electronic synthesizer. She destroyed him, and I thought back, hoping she hadn't done the same to me.

This time Weidner didn't let the scene play out to the end. I had to give him credit. As awful as Taylor was, *I* couldn't have brought myself to deny the reality of Sheila Remarque's performance by interrupting, but Weidner did, during one of Stanley's longer speeches about his cousin who opened beer bottles with his teeth. "Okay, fine," Weidner called out. "Good enough. Thank you, Mr Taylor. I think that's all we need see of you today." Weidner looked away from him. "Miss Remarque, if you wouldn't mind, I'd like to hear that one more time. Let's see . . . Mr Carver, would you read Stanley, please." Carver, a chorus gypsy who had no business doing heavy work, staggered to the platform, his face pale, but I didn't wait to see if he'd survive. I'd seen enough wings pulled off flies for one day, and was out the door, heading to the elevator even before Taylor had come off the platform.

I had just pushed the button when I saw Taylor, his dance bag over his shoulder, come out of the ballroom. He walked slowly down the hall toward me, and I prayed the car would arrive quickly enough that I wouldn't have to ride with him. But the Ansonia's lifts have seen better days, and by the time I stepped into the car he was a scant ten yards away. I held the door for him. He stepped in, the doors closed, and we were alone.

Taylor looked at me for a moment. "You'll get Mitch," he said flatly.

I shrugged self-consciously and smiled. "There's a lot of people to read."

"But they won't read Mitch with *her*. And your reading *was* good."

I nodded agreement. "She helped."

"May I," he said after a pause, "give you some advice?" I nodded. "If they give you Mitch," he said, "turn them down."

"Why?" I asked, laughing.

"She's sure to be Blanche. Don't you think?"

"So?"

"You heard me read today."

"So?"

"Have you seen me work?"

"I saw you in *Annie*. And in *Bus Stop* at ELT."

"And?"

"You were good. Real good."

"And what about today?"

I looked at the floor.

"Tell me." I looked at him, my lips pinched. "Shitty," he said. "Nothing there, right?"

"Not much," I said.

"She did that. Took it from me." He shook his head. "Stay away from her. She can do it to you too."

The first thing you learn in professional theater is that actors are children. I say that, knowing full well that I'm one myself. Our egos are huge, yet our feelings are as delicate as orchids. In a way, it stems from the fact that in other trades, rejections are impersonal. Writers aren't rejected—it's one particular story or novel that is. For factory workers, or white-collars, it's lack of knowledge or experience that loses jobs. But for an actor, it's the way he looks, the way he talks, the way he moves that make the heads nod yes or no, and that's rejection on the most deeply personal scale, like kids calling each other Nickel-nose or Fatso. And often that childish hurt extends to other relationships as well. Superstitious? Imaginative? Ballplayers have nothing on us. So when Taylor started blaming Sheila Remarque for his thespian rockslide, I knew it was only because he couldn't bear to admit that it was *he* who had let his craft slip away, not the girl who had taken it from him.

The elevator doors opened, and I stepped off. "Wait," he said, coming after me. "You don't believe me."

"Look, man," I said, turning in exasperation, "I don't know what went on between you and her and I don't care, okay? If she messed you over, I'm sorry, but I'm an actor and I need a job and if I get it I'll *take* it!"

His face remained placid. "Let me buy you a drink," he said.

"Oh Jesus . . ."

"You don't have to be afraid. I won't get violent." He forced a smile. "Do you think I've *been* violent? Have I even raised my voice?"

"No."

"Then please. I just want to talk to you."

I had to admit to myself that I *was* curious. Most actors would have shown more fire over things that meant so much to them, but Taylor was strangely zombielike, as if life were just a walk-through. "All right," I said, "all right."

We walked silently down Broadway. By the time we got to Charlie's it was three thirty, a slow time for the bar. I perched on a stool, but Taylor shook his head. "Table," he said, and we took one and ordered. It turned out we were both bourbon drinkers.

"Jesus," he said after a long sip. "It's cold."

It was. Manhattan winters are never balmy, and the winds that belly through the streets cut through anything short of steel.

"All right," I said. "We're here. You're buying me a drink. Now. You have a story for me?"

"I do. And after I tell it you can go out and do what you like."

"I intend to."

"I won't try to stop you," he went on, not hearing me. "I don't think I could even if I wanted to. It's your life, your career."

"Get to the point."

"I met her last summer. June. I know Joe Papp, and he invited me to the party after the Lear opening, so I went. Sheila was there with a guy, and I walked up and introduced myself to them, and told her how much I enjoyed her performance. She thanked me, very gracious, very friendly, and told me she'd seen me several times and liked my work as well. I thought it odd at the time, the way she came on to me. Very strong, with those big, wet, bedroom eyes of hers eating me up. But her date didn't seem to care. He didn't seem to care about much of anything. Just stood there and drank while she talked, then sat down and drank some more. She told me later, when we were together, that he was a poet. Unpublished, of course, she said. She told me that his work wasn't very good technically, but that it was very emotional. "Rich with feeling,", were the words she used.

"I went to see her in Lear again, several times really, and was more impressed with each performance. The poet was waiting for her the second time I went, but the third, she left alone. I finessed her into a drink, we talked, got along beautifully. She told me it was all over between her and the poet, and that night she ended up in my bed. It was good, and she seemed friendly, passionate, yet undemanding. After a few more dates, a few more nights and mornings, I suggested living together, no commitments. She agreed, and the next weekend she moved in with me.

"I want you to understand one thing, though. I never loved her. I never told her I loved her or even suggested it. For me, it was companionship and sex, and that was all. Though she was good to be with, nice to kiss, to hold, to share things with, I never loved her. And I know she never loved me." He signaled the waiter and another drink came. Mine was still half full. "So I'm not a . . . a victim of unrequited love, all right? I just want you to be sure of that." I nodded and he went on.

"It started a few weeks after we were living together. She'd want to play games with me, she said. Theater games. You know, pretend she was doing something or say something to get a certain emotion out of me. Most of the time she didn't let me know right away what she was doing. She'd see if she could get me jealous, or mad, or sullen. Happy too. And then she'd laugh and say she was just kidding, that she'd just wanted to see my reactions. Well, I thought that was bullshit. I put it down as a technique exercise rather than any method crap, and in a way

I could understand it—wanting to be face-to-face with emotions to examine them—but I still thought it was an imposition on me, an invasion of my privacy. She didn't do it often, maybe once or twice a week. I tried it on her occasionally, but she never bit, just looked at me as if I were a kid trying to play a man's game.

"Somewhere along the line it started getting kinky. While we were having sex, she'd call me by another name, or tell me about something sad she'd remembered, anything to get different reactions, different rises out of me. Sometimes . . ." He looked down, drained his drink. "Sometimes I'd . . . come and I'd cry at the same time."

The waiter was nearby, and I signaled for another round. "Why did you stay with her?"

"It wasn't . . . she didn't do this all the time, like I said. And I *liked* her. It got so I didn't even mind it when she'd pull this stuff on me, and she knew it. Once she even got me when I was stoned, and a couple of times after I'd had too much to drink. I didn't care. Until winter came.

"I hadn't been doing much after the summer. A few industrials here in town, some voice-over stuff. Good money, but just straight song and dance, flat narration, and no reviews. So the beginning of December Harv Piersall calls me to try out for *Ahab*. The musical that closed in previews? He wanted me to read for Starbuck, a scene where Starbuck is planning to shoot Ahab to save the Pequod. It was a good scene, a strong scene, and I got up there and I couldn't do a thing with it. Not a goddamned thing. I was utterly flat, just like in my narration and my singing around a Pontiac. But there it hadn't mattered—I hadn't had to put out any emotion—just sell the product, that was all. But *now*, when I had to feel something, had to express something, I couldn't. Harv asked me if anything was wrong, and I babbled some excuse about not feeling well, and when he invited me to come back and read again I did, a day later, and it was the same.

"That weekend I went down to St. Mark's to see Sheila in an OOB production—it was a new translation of *Medea* by some grad student at NYU—and she'd gotten the title role. They'd been rehearsing off and on for a month, no pay to speak of, but she was enthusiastic about it. It was the largest and most important part she'd done. Papp was there that night, someone got Prince to come too. The translation was garbage. No set, tunics for costumes, nothing lighting. But Sheila . . ."

He finished his latest drink, spat the ice back into the glass. "She was . . . superb. Every emotion was real. They should have been. She'd taken them from me.

"Don't look at me like that. I thought what you're thinking too, at first. That I was paranoid, jealous of her talents. But once I started to think things through, I knew it was the only answer.

"She was so loving to me afterward, smiled at me and held my arm and introduced me to her friends, and I felt as dull and lifeless as that poet I'd seen her with. Even then I suspected what she'd done, but I didn't say anything to her about it. That next week when I tried to get in touch with the poet, I found out he'd left the city, gone home to wherever it was he'd come from. I went over to Lincoln Center, to their videotape collection, and watched *King Lear*. I wanted to see if I could find anything that didn't jell, that wasn't quite *right*. Hell, I didn't know what I was looking for, just that I'd know when I saw it."

He shook his head. "It was . . . incredible. On the tape there was no sign of the performance I'd seen her give. Instead I saw a flat, lifeless, amateurish performance, dreadfully bad in contrast to the others. I couldn't believe it, watched it again. The same thing. Then I knew why she never auditioned for commercials, or for film. It didn't . . . *show up* on camera. She could fool people, but not a camera.

"I went back to the apartment then, and told her what I'd found out. It wasn't guessing on my part, not a theory, because I *knew* by then. You see, I *knew*."

Taylor stopped talking and looked down into his empty glass. I thought perhaps I'd made a huge mistake in going to the bar with him, for he was most certainly paranoid, and could conceivably become violent as well, in spite of his assurances to the contrary. "So what . . ." My "so" came out too much like "sho," but I pushed on with my question while he flagged the waiter, who raised an eyebrow, but brought more drinks. "So what did she say? When you told her?"

"She . . . verified it. Told me that I was right. 'In a way,' she said. In a way."

"Well . . ." I shook my head to clear it. ". . . didn't she probably mean that she was just studying you? That's hardly, hardl\[y\] *stealing* your emotions, is it?"

"No. She stole them."

"That's silly. That's still silly. You've still got them."

"No. I wanted . . . when I knew for sure, I wanted to kill her. The way she smiled at me, as though I were powerless to take anything back, as though she had planned it all from the moment we met—that made me want to kill her." He turned his empty eyes on me. "But I didn't. Couldn't. I couldn't get angry enough."

He sighed. "She moved out. That didn't bother me. I was glad. As glad as I could feel after what she'd done. I don't know *how* she did it. I think it was something she learned, or learned she had. I don't know whether I'll ever get them back or not, either. Oh, not from *her*. Never from her. But on my own. Build them up inside me somehow. The emotions. The feelings. Maybe someday."

He reached across the table and touched my hand, his fingers surprisingly warm. "So much I don't know. But one thing I do. She'll do it again, find someone else, *you* if you let her. I saw how you were looking at her today." I pulled my hand away from his, bumping my drink. He grabbed it before it spilled, set it upright. "Don't," he cautioned. "Don't have anything to do with her."

"It's absurd," I said, half stuttering. "Ridiculous. You still . . . show emotions."

"Maybe. Maybe a few. But they're only outward signs. Inside it's hollow." His head went to one side. "You don't believe me."

"N—no . . ." And I didn't, not then.

"You should have known me before."

Suddenly I remembered Kevin at the audition, and his telling me how funny and wild Guy Taylor had gotten on a few drinks. My own churning stomach reminded me of how many we had had sitting here for less than an hour, and my churning mind showed me Sheila Remarque's drunk, drunk, perfectly

drunk Blanche DuBois earlier that afternoon. "You've had
. . ." I babbled, ". . . how many drinks have you had?"

He shrugged.

"But . . . you're not . . . showing any *signs* . . ."

"Yes. That's right," he said in a clear, steady, sober voice.
"That's right."

He crossed his forearms on the table, lowered his head onto
them, and wept. The sobs were loud, prolonged, shaking his
whole body.

He wept.

"There!" I cried, staggering to my feet. "There, see? See?
You're *crying*, you're *crying!* See?"

He raised his head and looked at me, still weeping, still
weeping, with not one tear to be seen.

When the call came offering me Mitch, I took the part. I didn't
even consider turning it down. Sheila Remarque had, as Kevin,
Guy Taylor, and I had anticipated, been cast as Blanche DuBois,
and she smiled warmly at me when I entered the studio for the first
reading, as though she remembered our audition with fondness.
I was pleasant, but somewhat aloof at first, not wanting the others
to see, to suspect what I was going to do.

I thought it might be difficult to get her alone, but it wasn't.
She had already chosen me, I could tell, watching me through
the readings, coming up to me and chatting at the breaks. By
the end of the day she'd learned where I lived, that I was single,
unattached, and straight, and that I'd been bucking for eight years
to get a part this good. She told me that she lived only a block away
from my building (a lie, I later found out), and, after the rehearsal,
suggested we take a cab together and split the expense. I agreed,
and the cab left us out on West 72nd next to the park.

It was dark and cold, and I saw her shiver under her down-filled
jacket. I shivered too, for we were alone at last, somewhat hidden
by the trees, and there were no passersby to be seen, only the taxis
and buses and cars hurtling past.

I turned to her, the smile gone from my face. "I know what
you've done," I said. "I talked to Guy Taylor. He told me all
about it. And warned me."

Her face didn't change. She just hung on to that soft half smile of hers, and watched me with those liquid eyes.

"He said . . . you'd be after me. He told me not to take the part. But I had to. I had to know if it's true, all he said."

Her smile faded, she looked down at the dirty, ice-covered sidewalk, and nodded, creases of sadness at the corners of her eyes. I reached out and did what I had planned, said what I had wanted to say to her ever since leaving Guy Taylor crying without tears at the table in Charlie's.

"Teach me," I said, taking her hand as gently as I knew how. "I'd be no threat to you, no competition for roles. In fact, you may need me, need a man who can equal you on stage. Because there aren't any now. You can take what you want from me as long as you can teach me how to get it back again.

"Please. Teach me."

When she looked up at me, her face was wet with tears. I kissed them away, neither knowing nor caring whose they were.

ROBERT WESTALL

The Last Day of
Miss Dorinda Molyneaux

ROBERT WESTALL is one of the most acclaimed contemporary writers of children's fiction and has twice been awarded the Carnegie Medal for his novels. He was born in Tynemouth, Northumberland, and reveals: "I was blessed with a dead grandfather who glared down on my early years from his photograph on the wall; my mother's greatest desire was that we had known each other . . . One day I found what I thought was a little stone marble in a drawer, and began to play with it. Until my aunt told me it was the gallstone that killed him. With such a start, I suppose I was doomed to write ghost stories . . ."

His idol is M.R. James (". . . for the *economy* of his effects—he can get more horror out of an old blanket than Stephen King can get out of a whole town"), and the following story owes much to that classic writer's mastery of subtle chills.

Westall's books include *Break of Dark*, which is about a haunted bomber over Berlin; *The Haunting of Chas McGill* featuring cats versus an unmentionable horror; *Ghosts and Journeys* boasting a haunted toilet ("when you gotta go, you gotta go"); *Rachel and the Angel* which has a lost angel as dangerous as an atomic missile off course, and *The Call and Other Stories* involving the telephone Samaritans. "I try to get away from haunted mansions when I can," he remarks.

L IFE'S IRONICAL; BUT SOMETIMES nice-ironical. Take the time I was struggling with all my might and main to overtake Clocky Watson in the antique trade. As you know, I failed. What I never noticed, in the middle of my exertions, was that I was becoming a very solid, prosperous citizen in the eyes of my fellow-citizens.

Not, that is, until people began having a quiet word with me, putting in a quiet word for me, ringing me up and conducting rambling, ambiguous, awkward conversations that always ended up with me being invited to join something.

The Freemasons I refused; if I have one belief, it's that I must make my own way by my own bloody efforts, and my sense of humour would never let me appear in a funny little apron. The invitation to be a magistrate I put off for years; in my game the line between crook and Honest John is drawn in some very funny places (as it is in most games, if the truth be known) and I would not play the hypocrite. But I joined Rotary without a qualm, though I never did much apart from eat, drink and gossip. My starring moment always came in their annual sale of second-hand goods in aid of the hospital radio. I think at first they hoped I'd find a long-lost Rembrandt. But in the end they put me in charge of the old lawn-mowers, in the rain outside. (It always seemed to be raining.) And if I got the odd sideboard as a bargain, or a set of good Victorian chairs, I always paid more than the price they'd put on them, in their ignorance. Of course, *they* reckoned they were making my fortune . . .

But the invitation I liked best was to be a school manager at Barton Road Primary. I was still unmarried at thirty-four—though not from lack of wining and dining young women—and having despaired of ever having children, the chance to acquire three hundred at one blow was too great a temptation.

The third meeting I attended was to appoint a new teacher. I found it amusingly boring at first. My fellow-managers were not a brilliant lot, being mainly the weaker hangers-on of the local political parties. Each seemed to have a set question which he asked every candidate in turn, with an air of profound wisdom. We interviewed three worthy female mice, in tweed skirts and jumpers, and the only difference I could make between them was that one was rather tall, one rather fat, and one amazingly minute.

The fourth candidate was Miss Dorinda Molyneaux. That caused a stir, I can tell you. The Molyneaux were a county family, living five miles away at Barlborough Hall. There were five daughters, born one a year over twenty years before, while their mother was getting breeding over with so that she could return with undivided interest to riding horses, all duty done. The girls had a name for being spirited. One had run off to South Africa with a Count Clichy, who had once tried to run our local country club. Another went far left, emigrated to America and got involved in the Berkeley campus troubles. I looked forward with interest to what eccentricity the eldest, Miss Dorinda (or rather, to be correct, Miss Molyneaux), should display.

Miss Molyneaux's eccentricity was doing good; to the children of the underprivileged workers. For I must explain that although Barlborough is a pretty half-timbered little town, it has its black spots, and most of them are centred round Barton Road.

She came in, closed the door behind her decisively, and shook hands firmly with our madam chairman, without giving her the option to shake hands or not. She then shook hands with the rest of us, with that raised eyebrow of privilege that requires introductions. She followed up the introductions with questions as to our occupations and well-being, and her general thoughts on life. She was definitely interviewing us. In all it must have taken up nearly a quarter of an hour. And we had allowed twenty minutes for each candidate.

Then she sat down, crossed her legs, and gave us, with a smile, her undivided attention.

The first thing I noticed was how remarkably fine those legs were . . . Miss Molyneaux was a very fine young woman indeed. Long, glossy hair below her shoulders, expensively cut to look casual. The pearls would be real, and old. A tan not acquired in English weather. A big girl, though not fat, and eyes as bold a blue as those of the first Baron Molyneaux who had crossed with the Conqueror and stolen his bit of England.

They asked her their usual questions. Did she believe in

corporal punishment? She put her head on one side, crinkling up her face in schoolgirl thought.

"I'm not *against* it. Not *really* against it. But I believe in training by kindness. I had a horse once . . ." She kindly explained her theory of animal welfare to Councillor Byerscough, who was not half as senile as he looked, and a near Communist to boot . . . I sat back, waiting for her to lose one vote after another. Pity; she was by far the brightest person we'd seen that afternoon.

But it wasn't as simple as that. I wasn't allowing for the weight of prejudice. There were four left-wingers who wouldn't have voted for her if she'd talked like Ernest Bevin and sung like Caruso. There was the Headmistress, who sat with a look of spreading outrage on her face. But there were also five Tories, shopkeepers mainly, though they called themselves Independents, who were not only almost touching their forelocks to Miss Molyneaux but asking to be remembered kindly to her father. And both sides would have voted to spite the other, if the candidate had been the Queen herself.

And then there was me. I'd sat quiet, as Miss Molyneaux had swept out with a final gracious smile round the table, and hostilities had commenced. I'd sat quiet as old battles were re-fought, and old wounds, like the Dinner Ladies' Christmas Present, re-opened. And in the end, deadlocked, they turned to me.

Which class, I asked gravely, might she be destined for?

"Upper year, bottom stream," said the Headmistress, her eyes going remote and frosty, sensing a traitor in her camp. "Our worst problem—they need an experienced teacher who will keep them in hand—not someone fresh from training college, like . . ." She stopped herself just in time. "I can't upset the whole school system in mid year by moving my staff about."

Why did I vote for Dorinda Molyneaux? To begin with, I fancied her. Then, I had slightly cruel curiosity about what she and 4C would do to each other. But above all, I thought Barton Road needed a good shake-up. I longed to set a cat among the mice . . .

So she got the job, and thanked us graciously. And I earned the Headmistress's undying hatred.

School managers do not have a lot of say in the daily running of the school; but Dorinda's arrival was so spectacular that stories kept reaching me, third-hand.

The class horror (there's one in every class) moved in on her quickly. By the end of the second morning, during an altercation concerning a broken ruler, he called her a silly tart ... Now Dorinda might be opposed to corporal punishment, but the Molyneaux did not get where they are today by not knowing how to cope with English peasants. And the vigour with which "Molly" Molyneaux could hurl a lacrosse ball still lived as a legend in the halls of Roedean.

The class horror, Henry Winterbottom by name, was back-handed across the ear so hard he teetered on his toes five yards before he hit the painting-cupboard, which was rather insecurely fixed to the wall. Then he fell down, and the cupboard fell on top of him. The noise was heard as far off as the caretaker's house.

The Head rushed in and extricated Henry from the wreckage. Miss Molyneaux's teaching career looked doomed to early death. But blows were the coin of affection in the Winterbottom family, the only coin in an emotionally bankrupt household. And besides, the disaster had been so widespread as to bring renown on Henry's head also. Both he and Miss Molyneaux would linger in legend ... So he uttered the gallant words, "I just opened the cupboard door and it fell on me, Miss."

The Head, sensing she was being robbed of her great opportunity, swivelled her eyes around the class, looking for a dissenting verdict. But the class was too firmly under Henry's thumb; and Miss Molyneaux's violence was much too treasured a possession. Not a lip moved. But Henry Winterbottom became from that day on as faithful to Miss Molyneaux as any of her many family dogs.

And that was the way it went. Miss Molyneaux was used to being firm with dogs and horses, and 4C became her foxhounds.

From 4C's point of view, she was the greatest of treasures, a genuine eccentric. Where the earnest little mice would have nagged 4C about bad handwriting, or not handing in their homework in time (death to any child's soul) Miss Molyneaux gave detailed instructions on how to groom a horse, generously brandishing a curry-comb in huge strokes that carved an invisible horse out of the air.

Then there were those thrilling moments of silence, after Henry asked such questions as: "Have you ever drunk champagne, miss?" Which were rewarded not only with the news that Bollinger '48 was the best champagne to buy, but that Miss Molyneaux had actually consumed a whole jeroboam with a feller in a punt on the river at Cambridge, at the incredibly aristocratic hour of four in the morning.

The Head tried a few sneaky tricks. Classes had to be marched in crocodile to the playing-field a mile away for games. It was said that many such journeys had turned the Deputy-Headmaster's hair grey.

But Miss Molyneaux had a good eye and a vigorous disposition. She not only took over the girls' hockey team, but joined in the boys' soccer in her flaring-blue tracksuit, laying out the school captain with a magnificent foul.

Soon, the whole school was eating out of her hand, and to 4C she was a goddess. Several parents complained about requests for ponies at Christmas . . .

It was at about this time that I came back upon the scene. She nailed me at the Autumn Fayre, held in aid of a school minibus.

"Their minds need broadening," she said. "No good teaching history without *showing* them. I hear you know about old things." So I turned up one afternoon with the least breakable items from my shop. And, as we've learnt to say now, she counted them all out and she counted them all back, heavily thumb-printed. And Henry Winterbottom got the silver salt-cellar back out of Jack Hargreaves's trouser-pocket before I'd even missed it. Henry gave Jack a well-aimed kidney-punch by way of retribution, saying, "You can't nick off him—he's miss's *feller*, ain't he?"

Miss, who also overheard this infant dialogue, had the grace to blush, and I suddenly felt I had a chance. "We ought to take them round a stately home," I said, ever the good citizen.

"How nice," she said, with the kind of smile you give the Spanish chargé d'affaires.

"But we'd better spy out the land first," I added. "So you can make up a project. Do you know Tattersham Hall?"

"No, I don't know Tattersham," she said, suddenly sharp. "Who lives there now?" I felt I was moving into a different league.

"A lot of butterflies."

"Oh, that silkworm lot," she said ungraciously. "They bought out Bertie Tattersham after he'd got the DTs, silly old sod."

The Headmistress passed, giving a look that would cheerfully have crucified us both.

"You free Saturday afternoon?" said Dorinda. She was never one to wait to be asked.

I drove up to Barlborough Hall prompt on two. Dorinda was in the formal garden with two rather disreputable Pekinese called Marco and Polo; she was either teaching them to pull up weeds, or instructing the flowers how to grow. Something was certainly getting it in the neck.

Marco peed on my best cavalry-twill slacks, by way of greeting.

"Not used to animals, then?" asked Dorinda brutally. "It's a sign of affection—he's marking you out as his property." Obviously, Polo felt hurt about Marco's pre-emptive strike on my garments; he walked up casually and buried his teeth in the tatty fur round Marco's neck. Together they rolled into some rather depressed laurels, making a sound like feeding-time at the zoo.

"They're *great* friends," said Dorinda.

She looked at my Chrysler station-wagon, parked on the rather thin and rutted gravel. "Is it foreign?"

"It's illegitimate," I said gravely. "Its mother was a Rolls, but they left her out one night and she was raped by a rather common single-decker bus."

"I suppose it will get us there?"

"And your best Sheraton commode, six Chippendale dining-chairs and all your family portraits."

"Oh, yes, you're a dealer, aren't you?"

Not a propitious start, and the trip got steadily worse. We walked into the entrance-hall at Tattersham, which is lined with dead and glorious foreign butterflies in celluloid boxes, which some people will pay up to four hundred pounds for.

"Yu-uk!" said Dorinda; a noise of disgust so explosive it would have made Earl Harold flee the field at Hastings. It turned every head in the room.

"I thought your lot liked dead animals?" I said.

"Only ones we've shot ourselves. Anyway, when . . . if I ever invite you for tea, you won't find a single dead animal at Barlborough. We are not a 'lot'—we're individual people, and I've never met the Duke of Edinburgh, either."

I had hoped it might be romantic in what the Tattersham people call the Jungle: the old palm-house, still full of palms and little tinkling power-driven waterfalls, but now alive with huge tropical butterflies that will actually settle on your hand.

"Bloody hot in here. Worse'n a Turkish bath," said Dorinda. A blue swallowtail from Malaya settled on her shoulder. "Tatty-looking thing," she observed. "Falling to pieces. Should be put out of its misery."

Then she dragged me from room to room, questioning everyone she could lay her hands on about the processes of silk-farming. I left her side for a moment. It was a mistake. I heard her hoot, "You mean they have to *kill* the poor things, to get the silk? Kill them by boiling them alive? Monstrous. Should be abolished. I'd rather wear nylon knickers, now I know."

I got her away from the blushing curator with, as the RAF used to say, maximum boost.

"Not bringing the kids here," she announced, as we tumbled down the front steps. "Nothing but a bloody abattoir. What's that?" She stopped abruptly, so that I banged into her, which was not unpleasant.

"That's Tattersham church."

"But it's three miles from the village."

"But very close to the Hall. The gentry could walk there without even getting wet. The villagers could walk it in an hour—nothing to peasants."

The blue frost of her eyes travelled slowly up and down my face.

"I wasn't aware there was a Peasants' Union, Mr Ashden," she said at last, "and I wasn't aware you'd appointed yourself shop-steward. I suppose your father was a docker or something, and you're not going to allow me to forget it. I suppose you left school at twelve, and worked polishing the gentry's boots for two shillings a week, and a half-day off every fortnight."

"My father," I said, "is a bank manager in Cottesden, and I took a second in History at Durham."

"More the Petty-Bourgeois Union, then?"

"Do you want to see the church?"

It might have been the sudden frost in the May of our relationship, but I shuddered as we approached that church. It wasn't the sort of church I like. It might have been medieval once, but it had been badly got at during the Gothic Revival. The worst thing they'd done was to re-case the outside in some pale, marble-like stone, as smooth and nasty as a marshmallow. The years are not kind to that sort of stone; green algae had gathered in every crevice and ledge, and dribbled its pale-green-ness down the walls. It looked like a hollowed-out tombstone, with windows.

The door was open. In fact, from the rusted lock and the porchful of dead leaves, I guessed nobody ever bothered to close it; the nearest village was three miles away, and there was no fear of vandals. All the notices flapping on the notice-board were yellow and held on with drawing-pins that had deteriorated into blobs of rust. The vicar, the Reverend Ernest Lacey, lived five miles away, at Tettesden; if it was still the same vicar.

We pushed on, through the inner door. Inside, purple and blue windows, in the black darkness. We stood for a moment, unable to see even our feet.

Then the family tombs began to loom towards us out of the darkness. They reared up to left and right, the whole length of the wall, a flowering of white marble pillars and marble faces lying on gilt cushions, trophy of shield and sword and trumpet, and pot-bellied exulting cherub with dust piled in his navel. They crowded inwards across the black-and-white tiled floor, like a crowd at a road accident, bare white marble arms outflung pleadingly in frozen futile gestures; white marble eyes seeing nothing, but seeming to know a great deal. Between them, the space for the living, a few short box-pews, seemed to cower and shrink. Even if that church was packed, the dead would surely outnumber the living.

> IN THE FAMILY VAULT UNDER THE ALTAR
> ARE DEPOSITED THE REMAINS OF
> JOHN ANSTEY ESQUIRE
> SECOND SON OF THE LATE CHRISTOPHER
> ANSTEY ESQUIRE
> AND ONE OF HIS MAJESTY'S COMMISSIONERS
> FOR
> AUDITING PUBLIC ACCOUNTS
> WHO DEPARTED THIS LIFE THE 25TH NOVEMBER
> 1810

So many wanting to be remembered, and so few coming to remember them. It struck me that the ignored dead might get angry, like tigers in a zoo that have been left hungry for too long.

"Oh, that's *beautiful*," breathed Dorinda. She was staring at a grille that bordered the altar; a thing that the blue window behind reduced to a skeleton, but which on closer inspection still disclosed a lick of gilt. I went up and fingered it. Very fine wrought-iron work, of curiously individual design. It closed off a pointed arch, and seemed to my bemused gaze to be almost woven out of odd-shaped distorted crosses, overlapping, and weaving through each other.

"It is by Tijou?" whispered Dorinda, awed for once.

"Too late for Tijou—Tijou's your 1680s—St Paul's. This is more your 1760s. Still, a good piece of blacksmithing."

"Peasant! But the children could make rubbings of the patterns on it—they could copy out the words on the tombs, and draw the cherubs. And Henry would love to draw all those spears and shields."

"And there's a couple of monumental brasses, I'll bet." I pulled back a faded red carpet, unpleasantly damp to my fingers, to reveal a six-foot knight and his lady, engraved flat in brass, inlaid in the black-and-white marble of the floor.

"Oh, this would make a *lovely* project—we could have an exhibition in the school hall. But how can we get them here?"

She turned to me, flushed with enthusiasm, mouth open. I wanted to kiss her, but settled for saying, "Well, the school's getting the minibus soon. Can you drive it?"

"Of course."

"And if I bring my illegitimate Rolls, I can park twelve into that."

"Will it be safe?"

"Never lost a grandfather-clock yet, and they're worth money."

"Oh, let's *do* it, Geoff!"

One part of me was elated; she'd never called me "Geoff" before. But the other half of me, the antique-dealer, was doubtful.

This church felt wrong. I do not say this lightly. Dealers are undertakers of a sort. When a man dies, the undertaker comes for his body, and quite often the dealer comes for the rest. How often I have been left alone to break up the home a man has built up over fifty years, and sell the pieces where I can. As I break up the home, I know the man. I have known a cracked teapot yield enough evidence of adultery to satisfy ten divorce-court judges. I learn that he was mean from his boots; that trapped for ever inside the sepia photographs are seven of his children. From his diary, that he believed in God or the Devil or Carter's Little Liver Pills. I deal in dead men's clocks, pipes, swords and velvet breeches. And passing through my hands, they give off joy and loneliness, fear and optimism. I have known more evil in a set of false teeth than in any so-called haunted house in England.

And this church felt wrong . . . I tried to temporise. "It's . . . not a good example of the style. I have a friend, a vicar, with the most beautiful church. He's studied it for years. He'll explain everything to the kids . . . it's got bells they can ring . . ."

She set her chin stubbornly. "No. *I* found this. If you won't help me, I'll come on my own. Hire a coach . . ."

I disliked the idea of her and the kids being here alone even more. So against my better judgement, I said "OK."

Then she said, suddenly more sensitive than I'd known her, "You don't like the place, do you, Geoff?"

"It feels wrong."

"We're not going to *feel* it; we're going to draw it." And the brave invulnerable smile came back, like a highwayman putting on his mask. I think, in that moment, I fell in love with her.

And knowing that, I still didn't stop the awful thing that happened.

"Cor, sir, there ain't half a niff down there," said Henry Winterbottom, sticking his nose through the gilded grille. "What is it, the bog?"

"Clot," said Jack Hargreaves. "That's the Crip. Dracula's down there." He started chewing avidly at Henry's filthy neck, until Henry gave him a punch that sent him rattling against the ironwork.

"Yer mean . . . bodies?" Henry's eyes glowed with what might have been described as an unearthly light. "Bodies all rotting, with their eyes falling out an' the flesh hanging off their bones, an' *skulls*."

"Can we go down an' get one out of the coffin, sir?" asked Jack Hargreaves.

"No," I said firmly.

"Aw, sir, *please*. We wouldn't do it no harm. We'd put it back, after."

"It's unhygienic, shows no respect for the dead, and besides, the grille's locked," I said.

"Oh, yeah," said Jack Hargreaves, rather professionally. "Reckon you could pick that lock, Winterbottom?"

"Try me."

But I shooed them on and got them distracted in brass-rubbing a knight in armour, to the sound of tearing rubbing-paper, and cries of "Stupid bastard" and "*You* did that."

I prowled on, I couldn't keep still in that place. It wasn't just the cold. I thought I'd come prepared for that, with a quilted anorak and three sweaters. No, I kept having, not delusions, not even fears, but odd little anxieties . . . preoccupations. I had the conviction the walls weren't vertical . . . or was it the floor, that seemed to slope down towards the middle of the nave? Certainly the floor was hollow; no one could walk on it and listen to the echo of his footsteps without realizing that. Then

... the windows didn't seem to be letting in as much light as they should. I kept going outside to check if the sky was getting cloudy, but it was still bright and sunny, thank God, and I went back feeling the better for it.

Then I stared at the cross in a side-chapel. It just looked like two bits of wood nailed together. I mean, it *was* just two bits of wood nailed together; but though I'm not a religious sort, I tend to see any cross as a bit more than two bits of wood nailed together.

And that smell. Or niff, as Henry would have it. It wasn't strong, but it was everywhere; you never got it out of your nostrils. The only thing I can liken it to was when I got in a new lavatory-bowl at the shop; it had to be left for the sealant to dry overnight, so the builder stuffed wet paper down the hole, but the biting black smell of the sewer filled my shop and dreams all night.

For a while, till lunch, the children made things better. There's an atomic bomb of enthusiasm in a lively class of thirty-five let loose from school for the day. I could almost feel their vitality invading every part of the dark affronted silence. But, little by little, the silence absorbed it ... Lunchtime was still happy, with the children asking what the big house was for. But they were curiously reluctant to get back to work afterwards, and then the grumbles started.

"Miss, this Sellotape won't stick!"

"Sir, me pencil's broken again."

Dorinda was a tower, a fury of strength, coursing round the church non-stop. I began to realize just how hard a good primary teacher can work. But the complaints began to overtake even her speed. Soon, in spite of both our efforts, only half the children were working; the rest were standing round in little dispirited groups.

Then there was a god-awful scream from the chancel: one of the younger girls screaming, on and on. Dorinda ran, I ran. The child was standing tearing at her cheeks with her fingers, eyes shut and a noise issuing from her open mouth like a demented steam-whistle.

"It's a spider, miss. Behind that man's head." They pointed to the recumbent effigy of the tenth Lord Tattersham, who had a smirk of dying satisfaction on his face, and who appeared to have been carved from some singularly pale and nasty Cheddar cheese.

"Garn, only a spider . . ." Henry flicked with his hand behind the tenth lord's ear and the spider dropped to the floor. We all gaped; it was impressively huge. Henry raised his hobnailed boot . . .

"No," I said. "It's just an ordinary spider—just got rather old and big—a grandspider, maybe!"

There was a thin and nervous titter; then I picked up the spider and let it run up my anorak. "They're very useful," I said. "If it weren't for them, the flies of the world would poison us all." I carried the spider out, saying encouragingly to him, "Come on, Eustace." It seemed important just then to dispel fear, discourage killing. When I got back, most of them were working, and the cheerful noise was back.

"Thanks," said Dorinda. "You wouldn't make a bad teacher, you know."

"Thanks" I said. "But I *am* a good dealer. Eustace'll fetch a pound for somebody's stuffed spider collection." She looked as if she half believed me, then turned away laughing. That was good, too. Though I thought there was something a little shaky in her laugh.

I went to check my pile of gear by the door. Cameras, gadget-bag. But also my first-aid kit and two big lanterns. I had come prepared for a siege. Two large thermos-flasks of coffee; a box of Mars bars. I hadn't the slightest idea what I was expecting, but nothing good.

A memorial on the wall caught my eye.

TO THE MEMORY OF THOMAS DORE
AN HONOURED AND PAINEFUL
SCHOOLEMASTER
LAY PREACHER AND BENEFACTOR OF THIS
PARISH.
HE PUBLICKLY REBUKED VICE AND
DISCRETELY PRACTISED VIRTUE
AND LEFT HIS INTIRE ESTATE

TO BUY TRACTS FOR THE POOR.
THIS MONUMENT WAS ERECTED BY
PUBLICK SUBSCRIPTION
AMONG HIS GRIEVING FRIENDS AND
PUPILS
MDCCCX
BLESSED ARE THEY THAT REST IN THE
LORD

There was the crash of a drawing-board, the tinkle of paperclips and a wail of "Oh, miss, he's tore it!"

"Thomas Dore, where art thou," I muttered. "We could do with some reinforcements."

But there was no crack of thunder in response, no rending of the tomb, only echoing cries of "Henry's took my rubber, sir."

I did my utmost; I whizzed up and down with my flashgun and camera, taking pictures of everybody working; I gave out coffee, then followed up with a round of Mars bars. But more and more, in my rounds, I came across a scatter of work abandoned. And more and more I found children gathered miserably in the shelter of the porch, on any excuse: a stone in the shoe; the need for a loo; feeling faint, feeling sick. I ferried many across to the loos in the house. Their eyes caught the butterflies in the entrance-hall. The demands to go to the loo reached epidemic proportions as word of the butterflies got back; one would have thought cholera or dysentery was raging.

In the end, I made a bargain with them. If they'd go back and finish their work and clear up nicely, I'd fix a quick trip round the butterflies.

"That's bribery," hissed Dorinda in the live-silkworm room.

"Do you want to put on a good exhibition or not?" I hissed back, reaching forward just in time to stop Henry stuffing three live silkworms into an empty cigarette packet (though all the display-cabinets appeared locked and sealed . . .).

I must admit I was glad to see Tattersham church fading back into the dusk in my rear-view mirror as I herded the minibus towards home like an anxious sheepdog. I was grateful that nothing really bad had happened . . . even though the minibus ahead seemed full of the fluttering shapes of swallowtail butterflies.

They tumbled out of the transport happily enough in the school-yard. In fact, they'd sung the first two lines of old pop-songs over and over, all the way home, a sure sign of well-being.

"Where's he taking you tonight, miss?" inquired Jack Hargreaves, loudly.

"What do you mean?" bridled Dorinda.

"'e's taking you to the flicks, ain't he? Your feller? I mean, 'e's not stingy . . . they've got Elvis on at the Roxy."

"It's a cowboy film, miss—'Love me Tender'."

"Oh, it's lovely, miss—he gets killed in the end," chorused the girls.

"It's dead wet," chorused the boys.

"Let me run you home," I said to her tactfully, as she was about to explode.

When I dropped her, I said, "What about old Elvis, then?"

She invited me to a point-to-point at Meersden on Saturday; and it poured all afternoon. I can't think of a worse punishment than that.

There, the whole thing might have died. But it rained all Sunday as well, and I spent the time in my little darkroom, developing the photographs I'd taken in the church. They'd come out remarkably sharp, for flash, and I blew them up to ten-by-eight, to console her. They'd look quite nice round the classroom walls . . . the one thing I couldn't make out was a face that appeared in one, peering round one of the tombs. It wasn't my face, and it certainly wasn't Dorinda's. Far too ugly. And as it had a bald head, it certainly wasn't one of the children's.

It was well back in the harsh shadows thrown by the flash, watching two of the girls rubbing a brass-lettered tablet set in the floor. The girls were very intent (or pretending to be very intent) on what they were doing, and were obviously quite unaware of being watched. The face didn't look like a real person, somehow; I might have put it down as the face of an effigy from one of the tombs, except that the eyes were dark and alive and watching. It worried at my mind all the time I was printing and developing.

I kept on going across to the print where it was hanging up to dry, and staring at the face; I think I was trying to reason it out of existence, as a trick of the flash on a piece of crumbling stonework. As a projection of my own eye and mind. But it looked . . . it looked, let's face it, hungry and evil. I didn't like the thought that I was making it up out of my own imagination; I've always had a down-to-earth trouble-free imagination.

Anyway, I ran down to the school with the photographs on Wednesday and the kids were pleased to see me, and so was Dorinda—and so, by a miracle, was the Headmistress. The kids had been busy, working from what they'd done in the church, and the lively results hung all over the walls. It appeared that as soon as they'd got back into the classroom, they'd come back to rumbustious life and produced the best stuff ever seen. So good that an inspector had been summoned. I was introduced to him: a pushy young man who went wild over my photographs and said it was seldom that a school manager took such an interest, and who went on about having the whole exhibition laid out in the foyer at County Hall. I wondered whether he was just angling to get a date with Dorinda, but his enthusiasm seemed genuine enough and had sent the Head into seventh heaven.

I pointed out the strange watching head in the photograph. Dorinda insisted it was a trick of the light. But Jack Hargreaves said "Yeah, sir, he was there. An old bloke. He didn't say nothing. Just hung around in the shadders, watching the girls, dirty old sod. I thought 'e was the caretaker."

The Headmistress gave Dorinda a very funny look, and Dorinda went a bit pale. The Inspector changed the subject rather quickly, and went back to his praise of the drawings of cross-eyed cherubs and the very fine picture of a tomb that Henry was busy on. It had a mournful draped lady on top, in the Regency style, and the inscription:

TO THE MEMORY OF MARY CRAIG
A WOMAN OF EXEMPLARY PIETY AND
DISCRETION
WHO WAS CALLED HENCE AT THE EARLY AGE OF

29

YET HAVING IN AN EMINENT DEGREE ATTAINED
THAT

"You'll have to hurry and finish this," said the Inspector.

"Can't sir—this is far as we copied. We had to rush at the end."

"Pity," said the Inspector. "It certainly can't be hung up in County Hall in that unfinished state."

I saw a look pass from Henry to Jack Hargreaves; I thought it was a look of pure disgust. How wrong I was, I was only to discover later.

On Monday morning at the shop, the phone rang, sounding like trouble. It was the Head, and even over the phone I could tell she was tight-lipped and shaking with fury.

"You'd better get down here straight away, Mr Ashden. I knew this church business would lead to nothing but trouble. I feel I must call a meeting of the managers, but I think you are entitled to be consulted first."

I covered the mile to school in record time. The Head was waiting just inside the entrance, and pounced immediately. She *was* tight-lipped and shaking. She led me to the hall where Dorinda's exhibition had been hung before going to County Hall. She gestured a quivering hand at the big central exhibit. It was Henry and Jack Hargreaves's drawing of the Regency tomb; the draped lady on top still looked like a wilting lettuce-leaf, but the inscription had been completed:

TO THE MEMORY OF MARY CRAIG
A WOMAN OF EXEMPLARY PIETY AND
DISCRETION
WHO WAS CALLED HENCE AT THE EARLY AGE OF
29
YET HAVING IN AN EMINENT DEGREE ATTAINED
THAT MATURITY
WHICH CONSISTETH NOT IN LENGTH OF DAYS
DIED MCCLXXX

Unfortunately, other words had been scrawled over this chaste message, huge words in a wild hand. Words like "whore" and "strumpet" and "doxy".

"That," said the Head, "is what comes of ill-advised expeditions." She led me to her office. The Inspector was there, rather white round the gills in the face of such massive female wrath. And Dorinda, who if anything looked rather red in the face, and defiant.

"Have you faced the lads . . . with this?" I asked.

"Certainly not."

"Can I see them?" I asked, as calmly as I could. "I think it might stop us making fools of ourselves."

"What *do* you mean, Mr Ashden?"

"I mean these are not words commonly found in the twentieth-century child's vocabulary."

The Inspector nodded; he was no fool. The Head picked up that nod, and Henry was duly summoned.

"Henry," I said. "Suppose I was to send you out for a strumpet . . . where would you go to get one?"

Henry looked at our assembled faces warily; too old a hand not to smell trouble coming a mile off. But then a look of genuine bafflement came over his face. "Music-shop?" he offered.

"That's a *trumpet*, Henry."

"Cake-shop?" A flicker of a grin crossed his face.

"That's *crumpet*, Henry."

"Dunno, sir." His face was utterly still again.

"So, Henry, what would you call . . . a woman . . . who took money for going with men?"

Henry's face froze in a look of pure horror. Never had such words been uttered in this holy of holies.

"You may answer, Henry" said the Head, without moving her lips at all.

"A . . . tart, miss. On the game. Or a scrubber." The whites were showing all round his eyes.

"So if you didn't know what a strumpet was, Henry, why did you write it on your picture of the tomb?"

"Cos it was on the tomb when Jack an' I got there, Saturday

afternoon, sir. We didn't know whether to copy it or not, but we thought it must be official."

I beat the Inspector to our cars by a full ten yards . . .

"Never in my forty years as a servant of God have I known such a thing," boomed the Reverend Ernest Lacey. "One opens one's church to schools for the benefit of the community as a whole, and *this* happens. Children today . . ."

"Can you suggest," I said, "how children today could possibly have reached up that high? I mean, is there a ladder available that they could have used?"

The young police-sergeant whom Lacey had brought with him nodded thoughtfully.

"There is no ladder," said the Reverend Lacey. "They must have brought one with them."

"On their bicycles?"

"That's an adult's work, sir," said the sergeant. "You can tell by the sweep of their arm, in the lettering." He stood up on a pew, and stretched up. "Big fellow—almost as big as me. That's adults, Reverend."

"Disgusting."

"Henry," I said. "Was that bald man here again, when you came?"

"Yeah," said Henry, very chastened. "He was hanging about, peeping at us. Didn't say nothing. I thought he might stop us, but he didn't say nothing. He's only really interested in girls . . . He was a rum 'un, though." Henry blushed delightfully, and stopped.

"Why, Henry?"

"Can I whisper, sir?" He drew close. "Jack Hargreaves reckoned he were only wearing a shirt . . . a raggy shirt, all dirty. Reckon he was one o'*them*, sir."

"One of what, Henry?" asked the Head in dire tones.

"An escaped lunatic, miss," said Henry, dissimulating. "A nutter."

"Nutter or not," said the sergeant, "if it's adults, it's a crime. Now if you'll pardon me, Reverend, I'll take evidence. Then you can get the place cleaned up." He went to the tomb and

began to scrape some of the black paint of the vile lettering off
with a knife, into a little envelope. I noticed the paint could not
have been dry; it came off the white marble too easily. I saw the
sergeant wrinkle his nose.

We left him and drove back to school, the Head emitting sighs
all the way, like a dragon cooling down after breathing fire; and
Dorinda making subtle little self-righteous noises that seemed to
be demanding an apology from her superior.

My shop-bell rang while I was brewing coffee. It turned
out to be the young uniformed sergeant from the church.
I offered him a cup; he drifted round my shop looking at
things.

"It's all paid for, sergeant," I said, half sharply, half a joke.

"That's all right, sir," he said soothingly. "I'm into old things
a bit myself. That's a nice Viennese regulator . . . the trade price
is twenty pounds, I see."

I raised my eyebrows. "Nineteen to you, sergeant. Or is that
bribing a policeman in the course of his duties?"

Surprisingly, he laughed, and got out a cheque-book. "I'm
afraid I'm not the usual sort of police-sergeant; I've got A-levels.
It worries my superintendent. He doesn't think I'm quite human.
First he sent me off to Bramshill College to get rid of me, and
now he keeps me at headquarters for dealing with the nobs, and
anything funny that crops up, like this church business."

"There have been developments, then?"

"Oh, yes. Of a sort. We know he's got a key to the church."

I gave a grunt of surprise.

"The vicar got a woman in to clean up, then he locked the
church; thought he had the only key. A week later he went to
look round, and the joker had been at it again. And three times
since, in the last fortnight. I've been spending a few sleepless
nights in that vestry . . . but nothing happens while I'm around.
Then the first night I'm not, it happens again."

"I don't envy you," I said. "It's a nasty building. I don't think
I'd spend a night alone there for a superintendent's wages."

"I wasn't alone, sir," he said with a wry grin. "Local bobby
was with me."

"What does he think?"

"Hasn't a clue. He's new—came last year from Stropping. I'm afraid village bobbies aren't what they were. I'd like you to come and see the place again, sir, if you will. I'd like your professional opinion."

"It wasn't those kids, you know."

"I know it's not kids."

As we went, I slipped the pictures I'd taken in church into my pocket. Or rather, one of them.

I looked at the interior of the church aghast. Every tomb seemed to have been vandalized.

WILLIAM TRENTON
VICAR OF THIS PARISH FOR FORTY YEARS
AND AN INDUSTRIOUS HARBINGER OF CHURCH
MUSICK
THE SWEETNESS OF HIS HARMONIES CHARMED
THE EAR
AND THE MILDNESS OF HIS MANNERS THE
HEART
DIED MDCCCV

That one carried, scrawled in furious letters:

THEEFE, EXTORTIONER. GIVE BACK THE TITHES
YOU RUINED JACK BURTON FOR

And, on the tomb of a lady of Invincible Virtue and Great Condescension:

SHE PLAYED THE HARLOT WITH HER OWN SON

I walked from one to the other.

"Nasty," I said. "But not brainless. It's almost as if he knew all about them. A mad local historian?"

"It's funny you should say that. I've checked the church records. There was a farmer called John Wilberforce Burton —died in 1783. Dispossessed of his land—killed himself—not buried in sacred ground. And the lady he made that comment on, she had a son who never married. She outlived him. The comments are all *relevant*. Almost like he'd known them personally."

"Has everyone copped it?"

"He's left the Victorian ones alone . . . and the schoolmaster, Dore."

"Oh, the pillar of virtue, yes. Well, he would, wouldn't he?"

"Funny thing is . . ." the sergeant paused in embarrassment ". . . I had a writing expert in—a graphologist. Superintendent went mad about the expense of getting him over from Muncaster. I got all the kids in that class to scribble stuff down for me. He went over them—that's how I know it wasn't the kids—but he did say one funny thing. Apparently the writing's very old-fashioned. It seems that every century makes it own kind of mark . . ." He ground to a halt.

"You mean, like the young Georgian gents who carved their names so elegantly on the pews at Newhurst during the long sermons . . ." And I ground to a halt too. We looked at each other in the gloom of the nave, then shrugged, as men do, and changed the subject. How different Dorinda's story might have been if we hadn't.

I pulled out my photograph. The one with the bald head, watching the little girls brass-rubbing. I suppose now we'd got on to daft topics, I wasn't afraid to raise the matter.

"What do you make of that, sergeant?"

"Oh, this is the famous photograph? I'd meant to ask you about that. Only I reckoned the lads were making up a tale, to get out of trouble. Rum-looking bloke, if it *is* a bloke . . . hard to tell . . . could be a lump of marble . . . statue's hand or something . . ."

"Let's line it up from where I took it."

We looked. There was nothing on any of the tombs where the "head" appeared in my photograph.

"Could be anything. Maybe one of the kids left a packet of sandwiches on a ledge. It looks crumpled . . . crumpled and yet . . . bloated . . . bit like a turnip lantern. Could even be the head of another kid."

"A *bald* kid?"

"Could be a trick of the flash, making him look bald. If he's real, I wouldn't fancy meeting him up an alley on a dark night."

We both laughed uneasily. Then he said: "D'you mind if I hang on to this? I'll get some copies made. Somebody in the district might recognize him. Somebody who's been to Madame Tussaud's maybe." We laughed uneasily again.

And there we left it.

I must say the official opening of our exhibition at County Hall was quite a do. That was in the days when money was no object; the catering was elegant, and the whisky flowed like water. The exhibition looked great; they'd borrowed my negatives and blown them up to a yard square and very sharp, and the kids looked far keener and more industrious than they really had been. But their work was good, and beautifully mounted; good mounting can make a thing look worth a million dollars.

You must remember that was also in the days before kids were taken out of school a lot; I think the county was trying to encourage project work in the primaries. There were a lot of teachers there that evening, and a lot of inspectors and organizers and advisers, and a lot of councillors who'd mainly come for the whisky (which they drank at incredible speed, never batting an eyelid; they must have had a lot of practice). Form 4C were there as well, brought by the Head from Barlborough on a coach, with four other teachers as reinforcements. The children looked incredibly clean: I didn't recognize them till they spoke.

Dorinda, I remember, came straight from home in her white Mini. She looked so happy and excited. There was such a press of people round her, complimenting her, or just touching their forelocks and asking to be remembered to her father, that I couldn't get near. But I remember to this day how happy she looked . . .

Working round the exhibits, I came face to face with my police sergeant, every inch the gent in natty thornproof; Mike Watkins as I knew him now, from his name on the cheque.

"How's your Vienna regulator doing?"

"Fine. That's about all that is."

"Not caught your mad local historian, then?"

"Nobody recognized the photograph. Though I got some damned funny looks. You know, what strikes me is the way it all started after 4C had been to the church."

"It wasn't them!"

"I know it wasn't. But things started happening immediately after . . . like they'd *disturbed* something. Something pretty nasty. I've got one new piece of evidence."

All the time we'd been moving round the exhibition. Now something old and beautiful and shiny caught my dealer's eye, among all the cross-eyed cherubs and dim brass-rubbings. A padlock, thin and elegant, and polished with Brasso half out of its life.

"Hang on," I said. We went across together. The notice under the padlock, rather wildly written, read:

A MEDIEEVIL LOCK. ON LOAN FROM
TATTERSHAM CHURCH FROM THE CRIP
(DRACULA) DONE UP BY J. HARGREAVES
AND H. WINTERBOTTOM.

The lock was not medieevil, or even medieval. It was elegantly Georgian, with an interlacing pattern of crosses: the lock from the grille of the vault under the altar.

An awful premonition gripped me.

"What's your nasty piece of evidence?" I asked. He shuffled uncomfortably.

"Well, you remember I scraped some of the black paint off that first tomb that was vandalized? I sent it to Forensic, and they couldn't make head nor tail of it, so they sent it on to the Home Office. Lucky I'd scraped off plenty."

"Well?" I asked sharply.

"Well, old Sir Bernard Spilsbury got to the bottom of it. It wasn't paint at all – it's the decomposed remains of tissue. Animal or human, they can't really tell . . . it's so old."

"How old?"

He gulped. "They reckon . . . centuries old . . ."

"Oh, my God, the lock . . . the crypt. Somebody who knew

the owners of the tombs personally . . . It's crazy, sergeant. If we say anything, they'll throw us in the nuthouse."

He became very constabulary, the way even the best ones can. "I have evidence, sir, that party or parties unknown have entered the crypt and violated the cadavers, and are using their remains to write graffiti on the tombs. All of which are crimes."

As from another world, the voice broke in on us: from the cosy world of pretty girls handing round drinks and art-advisers plotting, and councillors knocking back whisky.

"Ladies and Gentlemen, in honour of this unique occasion, the Chairman of the County Council, Councillor Neil Fogarty, will present certificates of merit to each child who took part."

It went quite smoothly until the name "Hargreaves, J." was uttered. No Hargreaves, J., came forward.

"I'm certain he was on the bus," said the Head, tetchily.

"Perhaps he's gone to the . . ."

"Carry on," said the Head.

They carried on, until they came to the name "Winterbottom, H.". He was not only missing also, but a thorough search of the cloakrooms and corridors had revealed no trace of Hargreaves, J., either.

"Where are they?" hissed Dorinda, realistically taking the form-monitor on one side and shaking the life out of her.

Eventually, there were tears. And the appalling admission that the two had slipped away from the bus, having asked to stop for the loo at Tattersham. The whole form had got off; Jack and Henry had deliberately not got back on. Others had answered their names on the roll-call. Jack and Henry had brought sandwiches and torches. They were going to lie in wait in the church for the bald-headed man who wrote the dirty words.

The next second, Dorinda was running for her car; and the sergeant and I were pounding down the corridors of County Hall behind her.

We nearly caught up with her in the car park; she drove off from under our very noses.

"We'll take my car," I shouted. Which we did, and by putting my foot down on the by-pass, I nearly overtook her at Selmerby. But at that point she took to the little winding lanes that she'd known on horseback since a child. And on those bends, the Mini left my shooting-brake standing.

"We've lost her, sir," said Sergeant Watkins. "Drop me at the next phone-box and I'll summon help straight to the church."

But I couldn't bear to stop. One thing kept ringing through my head: Henry Winterbottom saying that whatever the thing was, it didn't bother *boys*. It was the little *girls* it was interested in.

In the end, Sergeant Watkins took the law into his own hands (as he had every right to do), and jumped out as I slowed down at a crossroads. At least he had the courtesy to slam the door, so I didn't even have to stop. But the minutes ticked away; I took a wrong turning and got lost. And still the minutes ticked away.

It was half an hour before I pulled up by Tattersham church. The white Mini was parked by the porch. No light on in the church, or in the big house; but in the moonlight, the church door gaped wide. Henry's skill with a lock had worked again.

I ran through the inner door; into pitch darkness.

"Dorinda?"

There was a kind of mindless animal sob.

"Dorinda, for God's sake!" I shouted.

Then I heard a slithering noise, somewhere among the box-pews; I was just beginning to see the outline of the windows now, but nothing else.

Then Henry's voice came, quavering, "Careful, sir. We're in the corner, here. Watch it, he's prowling round."

"He'd better not prowl round me," I shouted, "or I'll break him in half."

"Watch it, sir. He's all slippery . . . pongy . . . he sort of falls apart when you touch him."

Oh, God, the lights. Where were the lights? I realized I'd never known.

"Where are the lights, Henry?" I was moving towards him, slowly, stealthily. Listening for the slithering that was moving between us.

Dorinda began to sob again, softly, mindlessly.

"The lights don't work, sir," quavered Henry. "They must have cut them off."

My outward-groping hand came into contact with something upright, round and hard. I knew what it was; one of the churchwardens' staves that are set upright at the end of the back pews. I got it loose, and felt for the top; a heavy brass bishop's mitre; it would make a good club. I felt a little better, and moved on. The sound of Dorinda's sobbing, the boys' heavy breathing, came nearer. So did the slithering. And I could smell him now; the smell that had always been in this church, but a thousand times stronger. The smell of death; I had smelt it, plunging into the bowels of a crashed bomber in the War.

I could smell him, I could hear him; but I hit him because I *felt* him: a sudden drop in temperature on the right-hand side of my face as he came at me—as if he drew the warmth out of the surrounding air . . .

I had never struck a blow like it before, and I hope never to strike one like it again. It would have killed a man; but I could never have brought myself to hit a living man that hard. It had all the fear in me, all the rage, all the hate. And I could tell from the feel of it that the churchwarden's staff hit him where his neck joined his shoulders. It felt like hitting a rotten marrow, with bone splintering inside. Cold drops splashed my face. But there was no shudder, no gasp of pain or groan; it was hitting a dead thing, and instinctively I gave up hope.

The next second the staff was snatched from my hands so fiercely that I lost all use of my fingers. And the second after that I was flung against the pews with such force that the seat-back, like a horizontal axe, drove all the air from my lungs, and I thought my back was broken. But I had felt the large hands that flung me; cold as ice, even through my trench-coat. I lay on the floor and listened to the slithering go past me towards the corner where Dorinda was.

I don't know how I got back to my feet, but as I did so, a sound came to me from the sane world outside: the wail of a police-car siren. The windows of the church lit up from without, with the cold blue light of car headlights. And I saw him. Or it.

232

For, sensing the flare of light, it turned, and I saw it across the tops of the box-pews. A bald head, with blank black eyes that shone in the light. A broad chest, with what might have been a growth of black hair. And round the head and shoulders, not a ragged shirt, as Henry had said. But the green rags of a shroud . . .

Now there was a second police-car siren. Old Watkins must have had them homing in by radio from every point of the compass.

For a long moment the creature paused, like a badger brought to bay in its own wood. Then it seemed to sense that there would be no end to the lights and the noise, and the men with whom it had little quarrel. Men who could run it to earth and destroy and demolish and block it off for ever. Though the unreadable expression on the bald face never changed, I knew that it despaired.

The next second it was limping at great speed across the nave, towards the altar. I heard the grille to the vault clang, and it was gone.

Seconds later, a torch-beam cut across the nave from the porch. There was a fumbling, and all the lights went on; Sergeant Watkins must have known where the master-switch was. And then the place was full of flat caps and blue uniforms.

"Where?" asked Mike Watkins. I nodded towards the grille that led to the vault. He walked across, took something from his pocket and clicked it into place on the grille. He gave me a certain look, and I nodded. There are some things that are best not entered in policemen's notebooks, if only for the sake of Chief Constables and the judiciary.

"How did you get the lock?" I asked him.

"I confiscated it as material evidence," he said ruefully. "But it's better back where it is. I don't think we'll have any more bother, do you?"

I shook my head; but I rattled the old Georgian lock gently, just to make sure.

There was a gaggle of blue uniforms in the far corner, but it was parting; someone was being led out.

Dorinda was as white as a sheet, silent, eyes looking nowhere — all the signs of deep shock. But at least she was putting one foot in front of the other.

"I've radioed for an ambulance," said Sergeant Watkins. The boys followed Dorinda out, with that same white, glazed look on their faces. Except Henry, who summoned up enough energy for a ghost of a grin and said, "Cor, sir, you didn't 'arf fetch him one . . ."

I went to hospital with Dorinda in the ambulance; the boys went in the police-car. Halfway there, she opened her eyes and knew me.

"Geoff . . . thanks."

But it wasn't the Dorinda Molyneaux I'd known. The unshakeable confidence had gone; the certainty that there was a practical answer for everything.

"I never realized . . ." She closed her eyes and was silent, then continued: "I thought if you were decent . . . and kept the rules . . . God wouldn't let things like that . . . happen to you."

I didn't ask what had happened to her. I just said, "God lets road accidents happen to decent people every day. Why should that kind of thing be so different?"

"Yes," she said, with the sadness you expect from an old, old woman. "Yes." She reached out and grabbed my hand, and played with the knuckles. "I like you—you're *warm*." She went on holding my hand till we got to the hospital.

Mike Watkins joined me in the waiting-room; with his notebook.

"I suppose you're after the name and address of the accused," I said, with a weak attempt at humour.

"Only for my own interest."

"Must have been old Anstey, the Public Auditor. It was the Anstey vault."

"Well, I'm not going down again to look—not for a superintendent's wages. But I don't reckon it was Anstey. Anstey's memorial was desecrated too. And I've seen a painting of him, in old age—a thin, elegant old gent, with lots of frizzy grey hair."

"What I saw hadn't got grey hair." I shuddered at the memory. "Who d'you reckon it was, then?"

"The only memorial that wasn't desecrated was Thomas Dore's."

"The honoured and paineful schoolmaster and benefactor of this parish . . ."

"Still publickly rebuking vice . . ."

"And discretely practising virtue . . . God, I feel sick. I'd like to blow the place to smithereens and him with it."

"Nasty thing, repressed sex," said Sergeant Watkins. "We were shown a lot of that at Bramshill College. Prefer a pint of beer and a game of darts, meself. Don't fret, Geoff. He won't get loose again. I'll have a word with the vicar. He'll believe us . . . nobody else would."

I took good care of Dorinda after that. Eventually, she got so she could walk into a church again; if I held her hand tight. She did that just before we got married. Which was the last day of Miss Dorinda Molyneaux.

BRIAN LUMLEY

No Sharks in the Med

BRIAN LUMLEY was born on England's North-East coast, and currently lives with his wife, Dorothy, in Devon. As a young man he joined the British army, and in his spare time commenced writing horror stories. His first books were published in the mid-1970s by Arkham House, and after leaving the army ten years ago he took up writing full time.

The author of more than two-dozen books, including *The Burrowers Beneath*, *Khai of Ancient Khem*, the *Dreams* trilogy, *Psychomech*, *Psychosphere*, *Psychamok*, *The House of Doors* and the bestselling five-volume *Necroscope* series, he won the 1989 British Fantasy Award for his short story "Fruiting Bodies".

A regular visitor to the Greek islands, Lumley draws on first-hand experience in the following story to weave a terrifying chiller that just *could* happen.

C USTOMS WAS NON-EXISTENT; people bring duty frees *out* of Greece, not in. As for passport control: a pair of tanned, hairy, bored-looking characters in stained, too-tight uniforms and peaked caps were in charge. One to take your passport, find the page to be franked, scan photograph and bearer both with a blank gaze that took in absolutely nothing unless you happened to be female and stacked (in which case it took in everything and more), then pass the passport on. Geoff Hammond thought: *I wonder if that's why they call them passports?* The second one took the little black book from the first and hammered down on it with his stamp, impressing several pages but no one else, then handed the important document back to its owner—but grudgingly, as if he didn't believe you could be trusted with it.

This second one, the one with the rubber stamp, had a brother. They could be, probably were, twins. Five-eightish, late twenties, lots of shoulders and no hips; raven hair shiny with grease, so tightly curled it looked permed; brown eyes utterly vacant of expression. The only difference was the uniform: the fact that the brother on the home-and-dry side of the barrier didn't have one. Leaning on the barrier, he twirled cheap, yellow-framed, dark-lensed glasses like glinting propellers, observed almost speculatively the incoming holiday makers. He wore shorts, frayed where they hugged his thick thighs, barely long enough to be decent. *Hung like a bull!* Geoff thought. It was almost embarrassing. Dressed for the benefit of the single girls, obviously. He'd be hoping they were taking notes for later. His chances might improve if he were two inches taller and had a face. But he didn't; the face was as vacant as the eyes.

Then Geoff saw what it was that was wrong with those eyes: beyond the barrier, the specimen in the bulging shorts was walleyed. Likewise his twin punching the passports. Their right eyes had white pupils that stared like dead fish. The one in the booth wore lightly-tinted glasses, so that you didn't notice until he looked up and stared directly at you. Which in Geoff's case he hadn't; but he was certainly looking at Gwen. Then he glanced at Geoff, patiently waiting. and said: "Together, you?" His voice was a shade too loud, making it almost an accusation.

Different names on the passports, obviously! But Geoff

wasn't going to stand here and explain how they were just married and Gwen hadn't had time to make the required alterations. That really *would* be embarrassing! In fact (and come to think of it), it might not even be legal. Maybe she should have changed it right away, or got something done with it, anyway, in London. The honeymoon holiday they'd chosen was one of those get-it-while-it's-going deals, a last-minute half-price seat-filler, a gift horse; and they'd been pushed for time. But what the Hell—this was 1987, wasn't it?

"Yes," Geoff finally answered. "Together."

"Ah!" the other nodded, grinned, appraised Gwen again with a raised eye-brow, before stamping her passport and handing it over.

Wall-eyed bastard! Geoff thought.

When they passed through the gate in the barrier, the other wall-eyed bastard had disappeared. . .

Stepping through the automatic glass doors from the shade of the airport building into the sunlight of the coach terminus was like opening the door of a furnace; it was a replay of the moment when the plane's air-conditioned passengers trooped out across the tarmac to board the buses waiting to convey them to passport control. You came out into the sun fairly crisp, but by the time you'd trundled your luggage to the kerbside and lifted it off the trolley your armpits were already sticky. One o'clock, and the temperature must have been hovering around eighty-five for hours. It not only beat down on you but, trapped in the concrete, beat up as well. Hammerblows of heat.

A mini-skirted courier, English as a rose and harassed as Hell—her white blouse soggy while her blue and white hat still sat jaunty on her head—came fluttering, clutching her millboard with its bulldog clip and thin sheaf of notes. "Mr Hammond and Miss—" she glanced at her notes, "—Pinter?"

"Mr and Mrs Hammond," Geoff answered. He lowered his voice and continued confidentially: "We're all proper, legitimate, and true. Only our identities have been altered in order to protect our passports."

"Um?" she said.

Too deep for her, Geoff thought, sighing inwardly.

"Yes," said Gwen, sweetly. "We're the Hammonds."

"Oh!" the girl looked a little confused. "It's just that—"

"I haven't changed my passport yet," said Gwen, smiling.

"Ah!" Understanding finally dawned. The courier smiled nervously at Geoff, turned again to Gwen. "Is it too late for congratulations?"

"Four days," Gwen answered.

"Well, congratulations anyway."

Geoff was eager to be out of the sun. "Which is our coach?" he wanted to know. "Is it—could it possibly be—air-conditioned?" There were several coaches parked in an untidy cluster a little farther up the kerb.

Again the courier's confusion, also something of embarrassment showing in her bright blue eyes. "You're going to—Achladi?"

Geoff sighed again, this time audibly. It was her business to know where they were going. It wasn't a very good start.

"Yes," she cut in quickly, before he or Gwen could comment. "Achladi—but not by coach! You see, your plane was an hour late; the coach for Achladi couldn't be held up for just one couple; but it's OK—you'll have the privacy of your own taxi, and of course Skymed will foot the bill."

She went off to whistle up a taxi and Geoff and Gwen glanced at each other, shrugged, sat down on their cases. But in a moment the courier was back, and behind her a taxi came rolling, nosing into the kerb. Its driver jumped out, whirled about opening doors, the boot, stashing cases while Geoff and Gwen got into the back of the car. Then, throwing his straw hat down beside him as he climbed into the driving seat and slammed his door, the young Greek looked back at his passengers and smiled. A single gold tooth flashed in a bar of white. But the smile was quite dead, like the grin of a shark before he bites, and the voice when it came was phlegmy, like pebbles colliding in mud. "Achladi, yes?"

"Ye—" Geoff began, paused, and finished: "—es! Er, Achladi, right!" Their driver was the wall-eyed passport-stamper's wall-eyed brother.

"I Spiros," he declared, turning the taxi out of the airport. "And you?"

Something warned Geoff against any sort of familiarity with this one. In all this heat, the warning was like a breath of cold air on the back of his neck. "I'm Mr Hammond," he answered, stiffly. "This is my wife." Gwen turned her head a little and frowned at him.

"I'm—" she began.

"My *wife!*" Geoff said again. She looked surprised but kept her peace.

Spiros was watching the road where it narrowed and wound. Already out of the airport, he skirted the island's main town and raced for foothills rising to a spine of half-clad mountains. Achladi was maybe half an hour away, on the other side of the central range. The road soon became a track, a thick layer of dust over pot-holed tarmac and cobbles; in short, a typical Greek road. They slowed down a little through a village where white-walled houses lined the way, with lemon groves set back between and behind the dwellings, and were left with bright flashes of bougainvillea-framed balconies burning like after-images on their retinas. Then Spiros gave it the gun again.

Behind them, all was dust kicked up by the spinning wheels and the suction of the car's passing. Geoff glanced out of the fly-specked rear window. The cloud of brown dust, chasing after them, seemed ominous in the way it obscured the so-recent past. And turning front again, Geoff saw that Spiros kept his strange eye mainly on the road ahead, and the good one on his rearview. But watching what? The dust? No, he was looking at . . .

At Gwen! The interior mirror was angled directly into her cleavage.

They had been married only a very short time. The day when he'd take pride in the jealously of other men—in their coveting his wife—was still years in the future. Even then, look but don't touch would be the order of the day. Right now it was watch where you're looking, and possession was ninety-nine point nine percent of the law. As for the other point one percent: well, there was nothing much you could do about what the lecherous bastards were thinking!

Geoff took Gwen's elbow, pulled her close and whispered: "Have you noticed how tight he takes the bends? He does it so we'll bounce about a bit. He's watching how your tits jiggle!"

She'd been delighting in the scenery, hadn't even noticed Spiros, his eyes or anything. For a beautiful girl of twenty-three, she was remarkably naïve, and it wasn't just an act. It was one of the things Geoff loved best about her. Only eighteen months her senior, Geoff hardly considered himself a man of the world; but he did know a rat when he smelled one. In Spiros's case he could smell several sorts.

"He . . . *what*—?" Gwen said out loud, glancing down at herself. One button too many had come open in her blouse, showing the edges of her cups. Green eyes widening, she looked up and spotted Spiros's rearview. He grinned at her through the mirror and licked his lips, but without deliberation. He was naïve, too, in his way. In his different sort of way.

"Sit over here," said Geoff out loud, as she did up the offending button *and* the one above it. "The view is much better on this side." He half-stood, let her slide along the seat behind him. Both of Spiros's eyes were now back on the road . . .

Ten minutes later they were up into a pass through gorgeous pine-clad slopes so steep they came close to sheer. Here and there scree slides showed through the greenery, or a thrusting outcrop of rock. "Mountains," Spiros grunted, without looking back.

"You have an eye for detail," Geoff answered.

Gwen gave his arm a gentle nip, and he knew she was thinking *sarcasm is the lowest form of wit—and it doesn't become you!* Nor cruelty, apparently. Geoff had meant nothing special by his "eye" remark, but Spiros was sensitive. He groped in the glove compartment for his yellow-rimmed sunshades, put them on. And drove in a stony silence for what looked like being the rest of the journey.

Through the mountains they sped, and the west coast of the island opened up like a gigantic travel brochure. The mountains seemed to go right down to the sea, rocks merging with that incredible, aching blue. And they could see the village down there, Achladi, like something out of a dazzling dream perched on both sides of a spur that gentled into the ocean.

"Beautiful!" Gwen breathed.

"Yes," Spiros nodded. "Beautiful, thee village." Like many Greeks speaking English, his definite articles all sounded like *thee*. "For fish, for thee swims, thee sun—is beautiful."

After that it was all downhill; winding, at times precipitous, but the view was never less than stunning. For Geoff, it brought back memories of Cyprus. Good ones, most of them, but one bad one that always made him catch his breath, clench his fists. The reason he hadn't been too keen on coming back to the Med in the first place. He closed his eyes in an attempt to force the memory out of mind, but that only made it worse, the picture springing up that much clearer.

He was a kid again, just five years old, late in the summer of '67. His father was a Staff-Sergeant Medic, his mother with the QARANCs; both of them were stationed at Dhekelia, a Sovereign Base Area garrison just up the coast from Larnaca where they had a married quarter. They'd met and married in Berlin, spent three years there, then got posted out to Cyprus together. With two years done in Cyprus, Geoff's father had a year to go to complete his twenty-two. After that last year in the sun . . . there was a place waiting for him in the ambulance pool of one of London's big hospitals. Geoff's mother had hoped to get on the nursing staff of the same hospital. But before any of that . . .

Geoff had started school in Dhekelia, but on those rare weekends when both of his parents were free of duty, they'd all go off to the beach together. And that had been his favourite thing in all the world: the beach with its golden sand and crystal-clear, safe, shallow water. But sometimes, seeking privacy, they'd take a picnic basket and drive east along the coast until the road became a track, then find a way down the cliffs and swim from the rocks up around Cape Greco. That's where it had happened.

"Geoff!" Gwen tugged at his arm, breaking the spell. He was grateful to be dragged back to reality. "Were you sleeping?"

"Daydreaming," he answered.

"Me, too!" she said. "I think I must be. I mean, just *look* at it!"

They were winding down a steep ribbon of road cut into the mountain's flank, and Achladi was directly below them. A coach coming up squeezed by, its windows full of brown, browned-off faces. Holidaymakers going off to the airport, going home. Their holidays were over but Geoff's and Gwen's was just beginning, and the village they had come to *was* truly beautiful. Especially beautiful because it was unspoiled. This was only Achladi's second season; before they'd built the airport you could only get here by boat. Very few had bothered.

Geoff's vision of Cyprus and his bad time quickly receded; while he didn't consider himself a romantic like Gwen, still he recognized Achladi's magic. And now he supposed he'd have to admit that they'd made the right choice.

White-walled gardens; red tiles, green-framed windows, some flat roofs and some with a gentle pitch; bougainvillea cascading over white, arched balconies; a tiny white church on the point of the spur where broken rocks finally tumbled into the sea; massive ancient olive trees in walled plots at every street junction, and grapevines on trellises giving a little shade and dappling every garden and patio. That, at a glance, was Achladi. A high sea wall kept the sea at bay, not that it could ever be a real threat, for the entire front of the village fell within the harbour's crab's-claw moles. Steps went down here and there from the sea wall to the rocks; a half-dozen towels were spread wherever there was a flat or gently-inclined surface to take them, and the sea bobbed with a half-dozen heads, snorkels and face-masks. Deep water here, but a quarter-mile to the south, beyond the harbour wall, a shingle beach stretched like the webbing between the toes of some great beast for maybe a hundred yards to where a second claw-like spur came down from the mountains. As for the rest of this western coastline: as far as the eye could see both north and south, it looked like sky, cliff and sea to Geoff. Cape Greco all over again. But before he could go back to that:

"Is Villa Eleni, yes?" Spiros's gurgling voice intruded. "Him have no road. No can drive. I carry thee bags."

The road went right down the ridge of the spur to the little church. Half-way, it was crossed at right-angles by a second motor road which contained and serviced a handful of shops. The rest of the place was made up of streets too narrow or too perpendicular for cars. A few ancient scooters put-putted and puttered about, donkeys clip-clopped here and there, but that was all. Spiros turned his vehicle about at the main junction (the *only* real road junction) and parked in the shade of a giant olive tree. He went to get the luggage. There were two large cases, two small ones. Geoff would have shared the load equally but found himself brushed aside; Spiros took the elephant's share and left him with the small-fry. He wouldn't have minded, but it was obviously the Greek's chance to show off his strength.

Leading the way up a steep cobbled ramp of a street, Spiros's muscular buttocks kept threatening to burst through the thin stuff of his cut-down jeans. And because the holidaymakers followed on a little way behind, Geoff was aware of Gwen's eyes on Spiros's tanned, gleaming thews. There wasn't much of anywhere else to look. "Him Tarzan, you Jane," he commented, but his grin was a shade too dry.

"Who you?" she answered, her nose going up in the air. "Cheetah?"

"*Uph, uph!*" said Geoff.

"Anyway," she relented. "Your bottom's nicer. More compact."

He saved his breath, made no further comment. Even the light cases seemed heavy. If he was Cheetah, that must make Spiros Kong! The Greek glanced back once, grinned in his fashion, and kept going. Breathing heavily, Geoff and Gwen made an effort to catch up, failed miserably. Then, toward the top of the way, Spiros turned right into an arched alcove, climbed three stone steps, put down his cases and paused at a varnished pine door. He pulled on a string to free the latch, shoved the door open and took up his cases again. As the English couple came round the corner he was stepping inside. "Thee Villa Eleni," he said, as they followed him in.

Beyond the door was a high-walled courtyard of black and white pebbles laid out in octopus and dolphin designs. A split-level patio fronted the "villa," a square box of a house whose one redeeming feature had to be a retractable sun-awning shading the windows and most of the patio. It also made an admirable refuge from the dazzling white of everything.

There were whitewashed concrete steps climbing the side of the building to the upper floor, with a landing that opened onto a wooden-railed balcony with its own striped awning. Beach towels and an outsize lady's bathing costume were hanging over the rail, drying, and all the windows were open. Someone was home, maybe. Or maybe sitting in a shady taverna sipping on iced drinks. Downstairs, a key with a label had been left in the keyhole of a louvered, fly-screened door. Geoff read the label, which said simply: "Mr Hammond." The booking had been made in his name.

"This is us," he said to Gwen, turning the key.

They went in, Spiros following with the large cases. Inside, the cool air was a blessing. Now they would like to explore the place on their own, but the Greek was there to do it for them. And he knew his way around. He put the cases down, opened his arms to indicate the central room. "For sit, talk, thee resting." He pointed to a tiled area in one corner, with a refrigerator, sink-unit and two-ring electric cooker. "For thee toast, coffee—thee fish and chips, eh?" He shoved open the door of a tiny room tiled top to bottom, containing a shower, wash-basin and WC. "And this one," he said, without further explanation. Then five strides back across the floor took him to another room, low-ceilinged, pine-beamed, with a Lindean double bed built in under louvered windows. He cocked his head on one side. "And thee bed—just one. . ."

"That's all we'll need," Geoff answered, his annoyance building.

"Yes," Gwen said. "Well, thank you, er, Spiros—you're very kind. And we'll be fine now."

Spiros scratched his chin, went back into the main room and sprawled in an easy chair. "Outside is hot," he said. "Here she is cool—*krio*, you know?"

Geoff went to him. "It's *very* hot," he agreed, "and we're sticky. Now we want to shower, put our things away, look around. Thanks for your help. You can go now."

Spiros stood up and his face went slack, his expression more blank than before. His wall-eye looked strange through its tinted lens. "Go now?" he repeated.

Geoff sighed. "Yes, go!"

The corner of Spiros's mouth twitched, drew back a little to show his gold tooth. "I fetch from airport, carry cases."

"Ah!" said Geoff, getting out his wallet. "What do I owe you?" He'd bought drachmas at the bank in London.

Spiros sniffed, looked scornful, half turned away. "One thousand," he finally answered, bluntly.

"That's about four pounds and fifty pence," Gwen said from the bedroom doorway. "Sounds reasonable."

"Except it was supposed to be on Skymed," Geoff scowled. He paid up anyway and saw Spiros to the door. The Greek departed, sauntered indifferently across the patio to pause in the arched doorway and look back across the courtyard. Gwen had come to stand beside Geoff in the double doorway under the awning.

The Greek looked straight at her and licked his fleshy lips. The vacant grin was back on his face. "I see you," he said, nodding with a sort of slow deliberation.

As he closed the door behind him, Gwen muttered, "Not if I see you first! *Ugh!*"

"I am with you," Geoff agreed. "*Not* my favourite local character!"

"Spiros," she said. "Well, and it suits him to a tee. It's about as close as you can get to spider! And that one *is* about as close as you can get!"

They showered, fell exhausted on the bed—but not so exhausted that they could just lie there without making love.

Later—with suitcases emptied and small valuables stashed out of sight, and spare clothes all hung up or tucked away—dressed in light, loose gear, sandals, sunglasses, it was time to explore the village. "And afterwards," Gwen insisted, "we're swimming!"

She'd packed their towels and swimwear in a plastic beach bag. She loved to swim, and Geoff might have, too, except . . .

But as they left their rooms and stepped out across the patio, the varnished door in the courtyard wall opened to admit their upstairs neighbours, and for the next hour all thoughts of exploration and a dip in the sea were swept aside. The elderly couple who now introduced themselves gushed, there was no other way to describe it. He was George and she was Petula.

"My *dear*," said George, taking Gwen's hand and kissing it, "such a *stunning* young lady, and how sad that I've only two days left in which to enjoy you!" He was maybe sixty-four or five, ex-handsome but sagging a bit now, tall if a little bent, and brown as a native. With a small grey moustache and faded blue eyes, he looked as if he'd—no, in all probability he *had*—piloted Spitfires in World War II! Alas, he wore the most blindingly colourful shorts and shirt that Gwen had ever seen.

Petula was very large, about as tall as George but two of him in girth. She was just as brown, though, (and so presumably didn't mind exposing it all), seemed equally if not more energetic, and was never at a loss for words. They were a strange, paradoxical pair: very upper-crust, but at the same time very much down to earth. If Petula tended to speak with plums in her mouth, certainly they were of a very tangy variety.

"He'll flatter you to death, my dear," she told Gwen, ushering the newcomers up the steps at the side of the house and onto the high balcony. "But you must *never* take your eyes off his hands! Stage magicians have nothing on George. Forty years ago he magicked himself into my bedroom, and he's been there ever since!"

"She seduced me!" said George, bustling indoors.

"I did not!" Petula was petulant. "What? Why he's quite simply a wolf in . . . in a Joseph suit!"

"A Joseph suit?" George repeated her. He came back out onto the balcony with brandy-sours in a frosted jug, a clattering tray of ice-cubes, slices of sugared lemon and an eggcup of salt for the sours. He put the lot down on a plastic table, said: "Ah!—glasses!" and ducked back inside again.

"Yes," his wife called after him, pointing at his Bermudas and Hawaiian shirt. "Your clothes of many colours!"

It was all good fun and Geoff and Gwen enjoyed it. They sat round the table on plastic chairs, and George and Petula entertained them. It made for a very nice welcome to Achladi indeed.

"Of course," said George after a while, when they'd settled down a little, "we first came here eight years ago, when there were no flights, just boats. Now that people are flying in—" he shrugged, "—two more seasons and there'll be belly-dancers and hotdog stands! But for now it's . . . just perfect. Will you look at that view?"

The view from the balcony was very fetching. "From up here we can see the entire village," said Gwen. "You must point out the best shops, the bank or exchange or whatever, all the places we'll need to know about."

George and Petula looked at each other, smiled knowingly.

"Oh?" said Gwen.

Geoff checked their expressions, nodded, made a guess: "There are no places we need to know about."

"Well, three, actually," said Petula. "Four if you count Dimi's—the taverna. Oh, there are other places to eat, but Dimi's is *the* place. Except I feel I've spoilt it for you now. I mean, that really is something you should have discovered for yourself. It's half the fun, finding the best place to eat!"

"What about the other three places we should know about" Gwen inquired. "Will knowing those spoil it for us, too? Knowing them in advance, I mean?"

"Good Lord, no!" George shook his head. "Vital knowledge, young lady!"

"The baker's," said Petula. "For fresh rolls—daily." She pointed it out, blue smoke rising from a cluster of chimneypots. "Also the booze shop, for booze—"

"—Also daily," said George, pointing. "Right there on that corner—where the bottles glint. D'you know, they have an *ancient* Metaxa so cheap you wouldn't—"

"*And*," Petula continued, "the path down to the beach. Which is . . . over there."

"But tell us," said George, changing the subject, "are you married, you two? Or is that too personal?"

"Oh, of *course* they're married!" Petula told him. "But very recently, because they still sit so close together. Touching. You see?"

"Ah!" said George. "Then we shan't have another elopement."

"You know, my dear, you really are an old idiot," said Petula, sighing. "I mean, elopements are for lovers to be together. And these two already *are* together!"

Geoff and Gwen raised their eyebrows. "An elopement?" Gwen said. "Here? When did this happen?"

"Right here, yes," said Petula. "Ten days ago. On our first night we had a young man downstairs, Gordon. On his own. He was supposed to be here with his fiancée but she's jilted him. He went out with us, had a few too many in Dimi's and told us all about it. A Swedish girl—very lovely, blonde creature—was also on her own. She helped steer him back here and, I suppose, tucked him in. She had her own place, mind you, and didn't stay."

"But the next night she did!" George enthused.

"And then they ran off," said Petula, brightly. "Eloped! As simple as that. We saw them once, on the beach, the next morning. Following which—"

"—Gone!" said George.

"Maybe their holidays were over and they just went home," said Gwen, reasonably.

"No," George shook his head. "Gordon had come out on our plane, his holiday was just starting. She'd been here about a week and a half, was due to fly out the day after they made off together."

"They paid for their holidays and then deserted them?" Geoff frowned. "Doesn't make any sense."

"Does anything, when you're in love?" Petula sighed.

"The way I see it," said George, "they fell in love with each other, and with Greece, and went off to explore all the options."

"Love?" Gwen was doubtful. "On the rebound?"

"If she'd been a mousey little thing, I'd quite agree," said Petula. "But no, she really was a beautiful girl."

"And him a nice lad," said George. "A bit sparse but clean, good-looking."

"Indeed, they were much like you two," his wife added. "I mean, not *like* you, but like you."

"Cheers," said Geoff, wryly. "I mean, I know I'm not Mr Universe, but—"

"Tight in the bottom!" said Petula. "That's what the girls like these days. You'll do all right."

"See," said Gwen, nudging him. "Told you so!"

But Geoff was still frowning. "Didn't anyone look for them? What if they'd been involved in an accident or something?"

"No," said Petula. "They were seen boarding a ferry in the main town. Indeed, one of the local taxi drivers took them there. Spiros."

Gwen and Geoff's turn to look at each other. "A strange fish, that one," said Geoff.

George shrugged. "Oh, I don't know. You know him, do you? It's that eye of his which makes him seem a bit sinister. . ."

Maybe he's right, Geoff thought.

Shortly after that, their drinks finished, they went off to start their explorations. . .

The village was a maze of cobbled, white-washed alleys. Even as tiny as it was you could get lost in it, but never for longer than the length of a street. Going downhill, no matter the direction, you'd come to the sea. Uphill you'd come to the main road, or if you didn't, then turn the next corner and *continue* uphill, and then you would. The most well-trodden alley, with the shiniest cobbles, was the one that led to the hard-packed path, which in turn led to the beach. Pass the "booze shop" on the corner twice, and you'd know where it was always. The window was plastered with labels, some familiar and others entirely conjectural; inside, steel shelving went floor to ceiling, stacked with every conceivable brand; even the more exotic and (back home) wildly expensive stuffs were on view, often in ridiculously cheap, three-litre, duty-free bottles with their own chrome taps and display stands.

"Courvoisier!" said Gwen, appreciatively.

"Grand Marnier, surely!" Geoff protested. "What, five pints of Grand Marnier? At that price? Can you believe it? But that's to take home. What about while we're here?"

"Coconut liqueur," she said. "Or better still, mint chocolate — to compliment our midnight coffees."

They found several small tavernas, too, with people seated outdoors at tiny tables under the vines. Chicken portions and slabs of lamb sputtering on spits; small fishes sizzling over charcoal; *moussaka* steaming in long trays . . .

Dimi's was down on the harbour, where a wide, low wall kept you safe from falling in the sea. They had a Greek salad which they divided two ways, tiny cubes of lamb roasted on wooden slivers, a half-bottle of local white wine costing pennies. As they ate and sipped the wine, so they began to relax; the hot sunlight was tempered by an almost imperceptible breeze off the sea.

Geoff said: "Do you really feel energetic? Damned if I do."

She didn't feel full of boundless energy, no, but she wasn't going down without a fight. "If it was up to you," she said, "we'd just sit here and watch the fishing nets dry, right?"

"Nothing wrong with taking it easy," he answered. "We're on holiday, remember?"

"Your idea of taking it easy means being bone idle!" she answered. "*I* say we're going for a dip, then back to the villa for siesta and you know, and—"

"Can we have the you know before the siesta?" He kept a straight face.

"—And then we'll be all settled in, recovered from the journey, ready for tonight. Insatiable!"

"OK," he shrugged. "Anything you say. But we swim from the beach, not from the rocks."

Gwen looked at him suspiciously. "That was almost too easy."

Now he grinned. "It was the thought of, well, you know, that did it," he told her. . .

*

251

Lying on the beach, panting from their exertions in the sea, with the sun lifting the moisture off their still-pale bodies, Gwen said: "I don't understand."

"Hmm?"

"You swim very well. I've always thought so. So what is this fear of the water you complain about?"

"First," Geoff answered, "I don't swim very well. Oh, for a hundred yards I'll swim like a dolphin—any more than that and I do it like a brick! I can't float. If I stop swimming I sink."

"So don't stop."

"When you get tired, you stop."

"What was it that made you frightened of the water?"

He told her:

"I was a kid in Cyprus. A little kid. My father had taught me how to swim. I used to watch him diving off the rocks, oh, maybe twenty or thirty feet high, into the sea. I thought I could do it, too. So one day when my folks weren't watching, I tried. I must have hit my head on something on the way down. Or maybe I simply struck the water all wrong. When they spotted me floating in the sea, I was just about done for. My father dragged me out. He was a medic—the kiss of life and all that. So now I'm not much for swimming, and I'm absolutely *nothing* for diving! I will swim—for a splash, in shallow water, like today—but that's my limit. And I'll only go in from a beach. I can't stand cliffs, height. It's as simple as that. You married a coward. So there."

"No I didn't," she said. "I married someone with a great bottom. Why didn't you tell me all this before?"

"You didn't ask me. I don't like to talk about it because I don't much care to remember it. I was just a kid, and yet I knew I was going to die. And I knew it wouldn't be nice. I still haven't got it out of my system, not completely. And so the less said about it the better."

A beach ball landed close by, bounced, rolled to a standstill against Gwen's thigh. They looked up. A brown, burly figure came striding. They recognized the frayed, bulging shorts. Spiros.

"Hallo," he said, going down into a crouch close by, forearms resting on his knees. "Thee beach. Thee ball. I swim, play. You swim?" (This to Geoff.) "You come swim, throwing thee ball?"

Geoff sat up. There were half-a-dozen other couples on the beach; why couldn't this jerk pick on them? Geoff thought to himself: *I'm about to get sand kicked in my face!* "No," he said out loud, shaking his head. "I don't swim much."

"No swim? You frighting thee big fish? Thee sharks?"

"Sharks?" Now Gwen sat up. From behind their dark lenses she could feel Spiros's eyes crawling over her.

Geoff shook his head. "There are no sharks in the Med," he said.

"Him right" Spiros laughed high-pitched, like a woman, without his customary gurgling. A weird sound. "No sharks. I make thee jokes!" He stopped laughing and looked straight at Gwen. She couldn't decide if he was looking at her face or her breasts. Those damned sunglasses of his! "You come swim, lady, with Spiros? Play in thee water?"

"My . . . *God!*" Gwen sputtered, glowering at him. She pulled her dress on over her still-damp, very skimpy swimming costume, packed her towel away, picked up her sandals. When she was annoyed, she really *was* annoyed.

Geoff stood up as she made off, turned to Spiros. "Now listen—" he began.

"Ah, you go now! Is OK. I see you." He took his ball, raced with it down the beach, hurled it out over the sea. Before it splashed down he was diving, low and flat, striking the water like a knife. Unlike Geoff, he swam very well indeed. . .

When Geoff caught up with his wife she was stiff with anger. Mainly angry with herself. "That was *so* rude of me!" she exploded.

"No it wasn't," he said. "I feel exactly the same about it."

"But he's so damned . . . persistent! I mean, he knows we're together, man and wife . . . 'thee bed—just one.' How *dare* he intrude?"

Geoff tried to make light of it. "You're imagining it," he said.

"And you? Doesn't he get on your nerves?"

"Maybe I'm imagining it too. Look, he's Greek—and not an especially attractive specimen. Look at it from his point of view. All of a sudden there's a gaggle of dolly-birds on the beach, dressed in stuff his sister wouldn't wear for undies! So he tries to get closer—for a better view, as it were—so that he can get a wall-eyeful. He's no different to other blokes. Not quite as smooth, that's all."

"Smooth!" she almost spat the word out. "He's about as smooth as a badger's—"

"—Bottom," said Geoff. "Yes, I know. If I'd known you were such a bum-fancier I mightn't have married you."

And at last she laughed, but shakily.

They stopped at the booze shop and bought brandy and a large bottle of Coca-Cola. And mint chocolate liqueur, of course, for their midnight coffees . . .

That night Gwen put on a blue and white dress, very Greek if cut a little low in the front, and silver sandals. Tucking a handkerchief into the breast pocket of his white jacket, Geoff thought: *she's beautiful!* With her heart-shaped face and the way her hair framed it, cut in a page-boy style that suited its shiny black sheen—and her green, green eyes—he'd always thought she looked French. But tonight she was definitely Greek. And he was so glad that she was English, and his.

Dimi's was doing a roaring trade. George and Petula had a table in the corner, overlooking the sea. They had spread themselves out in order to occupy all four seats, but when Geoff and Gwen appeared they waved, called them over. "We thought you'd drop in," George said, as they sat down. And to Gwen: "You look charming, my dear."

"Now I feel I'm really on my holidays," Gwen smiled.

"Honeymoon, surely," said Petula.

"*Shh!*" Geoff cautioned her. "In England they throw confetti. Over here it's plates!"

"Your secret is safe with us," said George.

"Holiday, honeymoon, whatever," said Gwen. "Compliments from handsome gentlemen; the stars reflected in the sea; a full moon rising and bouzouki music floating in the air. And—"

"—The mouth-watering smells of good Greek grub!" Geoff cut in. "Have you ordered?" He looked at George and Petula.

"A moment ago," Petula told him. "If you go into the kitchen there, Dimi will show you his menu—live, as it were. Tell him you're with us and he'll make an effort to serve us together. Starter, main course, a pudding—the lot."

"Good!" Geoff said, standing up. "I could eat the saddle off a donkey!"

"Eat the whole donkey," George told him. "The one who's going to wake you up with his racket at six-thirty tomorrow morning."

"You don't know Geoff," said Gwen. "He'd sleep through a Rolling Stones concert."

"And *you* don't know Achladi donkeys!" said Petula.

In the kitchen, the huge, bearded proprietor was busy, fussing over his harassed-looking cooks. As Geoff entered he came over. "Good evenings, sir. You are new in Achladi?"

"Just today," Geoff smiled. "We came here for lunch but missed you."

"Ah!" Dimitrios gasped, shrugged apologetically. "I was sleeps! Every day, for two hours, I sleeps. Where you stay, eh?"

"The Villa Eleni."

"Eleni? Is me!" Dimitrios beamed. "*I* am Villa Eleni. I mean, I owns it. Eleni is thee name my wifes."

"It's a beautiful name," said Geoff, beginning to feel trapped in the conversation. "Er, we're with George and Petula."

"You are eating? Good, good. I show you." Geoff was given a guided tour of the ovens and the sweets trolley. He ordered, keeping it light for Gwen.

"And here," said Dimitrios. "For your lady!" He produced a filigreed silver-metal brooch in the shape of a butterfly, with "Dimi's" worked into the metal of the body. Gwen wouldn't like it especially, but politic to accept it. Geoff had noticed several female patrons wearing them, Petula included.

"That's very kind of you," he said.

255

Making his way back to their table, he saw Spiros was there before him.

Now where the Hell had he sprung from? And what the Hell was he playing at?

Spiros wore tight blue jeans, (his image, obviously), and a white T-shirt stained down the front. He was standing over the corner table, one hand on the wall where it overlooked the sea, the other on the table itself. Propped up, still he swayed. He was leaning over Gwen. George and Petula had frozen smiles on their faces, looked frankly astonished. Geoff couldn't quite see all of Gwen, for Spiros's bulk was in the way.

What he could see, of the entire mini-tableau, printed itself on his eyes as he drew closer. Adrenalin surged in him and he began to breathe faster. He barely noticed George standing up and sliding out of view. Then as the bouzouki tape came to an end and the taverna's low babble of sound seemed to grow that much louder, Gwen's outraged voice suddenly rose over everything else:

"Get . . . your . . . filthy . . . paws . . . *off* me!" she cried.

Geoff was there. Petula had drawn as far back as possible; no longer smiling, her hand was at her throat, her eyes staring in disbelief. Spiros's left hand had caught up the V of Gwen's dress. His fingers were inside the dress and his thumb outside. In his right hand he clutched a pin like the one Dimitrios had given to Geoff. He was protesting:

"But I giving it! I putting it on your dress! Is nice, this one. We friends. Why you shout? You no like Spiros?" His throaty, gurgling voice was slurred: waves of ouzo fumes literally wafted off him like the stench of a dead fish. Geoff moved in, knocked Spiros's elbow away where it leaned on the wall. Spiros must release Gwen to maintain his balance. He did so, but still crashed half-over the wall. For a moment Geoff thought he would go completely over, into the sea. But he just lolled there, shaking his head, and finally turned it to look back at Geoff. There was a look on his face which Geoff couldn't quite describe. Drunken stupidity slowly turning to rage, maybe. Then he pushed himself upright, stood swaying against the wall, his fists knotting and the muscles in his arms bunching.

Hit him now, Geoff's inner man told him. *Do it, and he'll go clean over into the sea. It's not high, seven or eight feet, that's all. It'll sober the bastard up, and after that he won't trouble you again.*

But what if he couldn't swim? *You know he swims like a fish—like a bloody shark!*

"You think you better than Spiros, eh?" The Greek wobbled dangerously, steadied up and took a step in Geoff's direction.

"No!" the voice of the bearded Dimitrios was shattering in Geoff's ear. Massive, he stepped between them, grabbed Spiros by the hair, half-dragged, half-pushed him toward the exit. "No, *everybody* thinks he's better!" he cried. "Because everybody *is* better! Out—" he heaved Spiros yelping into the harbour's shadows. "I tell you before, Spiros: drink all the ouzo in Achladi. Is your business. But not let it ruin *my* business. Then comes thee *real* troubles!"

Gwen was naturally upset. It spoiled something of the evening for her. But by the time they had finished eating, things were about back to normal. No one else in the place, other than George and Petula, had seemed especially interested in the incident anyway.

At around eleven, when the taverna had cleared a little, the girl from Skymed came in. She came over.

"Hello, Julie!" said George, finding her a chair. And, flatterer born, he added: "How lovely you're looking tonight—but of course you look lovely all the time."

Petula tut-tutted. "George, if you hadn't met me you'd be a gigolo by now, I'm sure!"

"Mr Hammond," Julie said. "I'm terribly sorry. I should have explained to Spiros that he'd recover the fare for your ride from me. Actually, I believed he understood that but apparently he didn't. I've just seen him in one of the bars and asked him how much I owed him. He was a little upset, wouldn't accept the money, told me I should see you."

"Was he sober yet?" Geoff asked, sourly.

"Er, not very, I'm afraid. Has he been a nuisance?"

Geoff coughed. "Only a *bit* of one."

"It was a thousand drachmas" said Gwen.

The courier looked a little taken aback. "Well it should only have been seven hundred."

"He did carry our bags, though," said Geoff.

"Ah! Maybe that explains it. Anyway, I'm authorized to pay you seven hundred."

"All donations are welcome," Gwen said, opening her purse and accepting the money. "But if I were you in the future I'd use someone else. This Spiros isn't a particularly pleasant fellow."

"Well he does seem to have a problem with the ouzo," Julie answered. "On the other hand—"

"He has *several* problems!" Geoff was sharper than he meant to be. After all, it wasn't her fault.

"—He also has the best beach," Julie finished.

"Beach?" Geoff raised an eyebrow. "He has a beach?"

"Didn't we tell you?" Petula spoke up. "Two or three of the locals have small boats in the harbour. For a few hundred drachmas they'll take you to one of a handful of private beaches along the coast. They're private because no one lives there, and there's no way in except by boat. The boatmen have their favourite places, which they guard jealously and call 'their' beaches, so that the others don't poach on them. They take you in the morning or whenever, collect you in the evening. Absolutely private . . . ideal for picnics . . . romance!" She sighed.

"What a lovely idea," said Gwen. "To have a beach of your own for the day!"

"Well, as far as I'm concerned," Geoff told her, "Spiros can keep his beach."

"Oh-oh!" said George. "Speak of the devil. . ."

Spiros had returned. He averted his face and made straight for the kitchens in the back. He was noticeably steadier on his feet now. Dimitrios came bowling out to meet him and a few low-muttered words passed between them. Their conversation quickly grew more heated, becoming rapid-fire Greek in moments, and Spiros appeared to be pleading his case. Finally Dimitrios shrugged, came lumbering toward the corner table with Spiros in tow.

"Spiros, he sorry," Dimitrios said. "For tonight. Too much ouzo. He just want be friendly."

"Is right," said Spiros, lifting his head. He shrugged helplessly. "Thee ouzo."

Geoff nodded. "OK, forget it," he said, but coldly.

"Is . . . OK?" Spiros lifted his head a little more. He looked at Gwen.

Gwen forced herself to nod. "It's OK."

Now Spiros beamed, or as close as he was likely to get to it. But still Geoff had this feeling that there was something cold and calculating in his manner.

"I make it good!" Spiros declared, nodding. "One day, I take you thee *best* beach! For thee picnic. Very private. Two peoples, no more. I no take thee money, nothing. Is good?"

"Fine," said Geoff. "That'll be fine."

"OK," Spiros smiled his unsmile, nodded, turned away. Going out, he looked back. "I sorry," he said again; and again his shrug. "Thee ouzo . . ."

"Hardly eloquent," said Petula, when he'd disappeared.

"But better than nothing," said George.

"Things are looking up!" Gwen was happier now.

Geoff was still unsure how he felt. He said nothing. . .

"Breakfast is on us," George announced the next morning. He smiled down on Geoff and Gwen where they drank coffee and tested the early morning sunlight at a garden table on the patio. They were still in their dressing-gowns, eyes bleary, hair tousled.

Geoff looked up, squinting his eyes against the hurtful blue of the sky, and said: "I see what you mean about that donkey! What the Hell time is it, anyway?"

"Eight-fifteen," said George. "You're lucky. Normally he's at it, oh, an hour earlier than this!" From somewhere down in the maze of alleys, as if summoned by their conversation, the hideous braying echoed yet again as the village gradually came awake.

Just before nine they set out, George and Petula guiding them to a little place bearing the paint-daubed legend: "Brekfas Bar."

They climbed steps to a pine-railed patio set with pine tables and chairs, under a varnished pine frame supporting a canopy of split bamboo. Service was good; the "English" food hot, tasty, and very cheap; the coffee dreadful!

"*Yechh!*" Gwen commented, understanding now why George and Petula had ordered tea. "Take a note, Mr Hammond," she said. "Tomorrow, no coffee. Just fruit juice."

"We thought maybe it was us being fussy," said Petula. "Else we'd have warned you."

"Anyway," George sighed. "Here's where we have to leave you. For tomorrow we fly—literally. So today we're shopping, picking up our duty-frees, gifts, the postcards we never sent, some Greek cigarettes."

"But we'll see you tonight, if you'd care to?" said Petula.

"Delighted!" Geoff answered. "What, Zorba's Dance, moussaka, and a couple or three of those giant Metaxas that Dimi serves? Who could refuse?"

"Not to mention the company," said Gwen.

"About eight-thirty, then," said Petula. And off they went.

"I shall miss them," said Gwen.

"But it will be nice to be on our own for once," Geoff leaned over to kiss her.

"Hallo!" came a now familiar, gurgling voice from below. Spiros stood in the street beyond the rail, looking up at them, the sun striking sparks from the lenses of his sunglasses. Their faces fell and he couldn't fail to notice it. "Is OK," he quickly held up a hand. "I no stay. I busy. Today I make thee taxi. Later, thee boat."

Gwen gave a little gasp of excitement, clutched Geoff's arm. "The private beach!" she said. "Now that's what I'd call being on our own!" And to Spiros: "If we're ready at one o'clock, will you take us to your beach?"

"Of course!" he answered. "At one o'clock, I near Dimi's. My boat, him called *Spiros* like me. You see him."

Gwen nodded. "We'll see you then."

"Good!" Spiros nodded. He looked up at them a moment longer, and Geoff wished he could fathom where the man's eyes were. Probably up Gwen's dress. But then he turned and went on his way.

"Now we shop!" Gwen said.

They shopped for picnic items. Nothing gigantic, mainly small things. Slices of salami, hard cheese, two fat tomatoes, fresh bread, a bottle of light white wine, some feta, eggs for boiling, and a liter of crystal-clear bottled water. And as an afterthought: half-a-dozen small pats of butter, a small jar of honey, a sharp knife and a packet of doilies. No wicker basket; their little plastic coolbox would have to do. And one of their pieces of shoulder luggage for the blanket, towels, and swim-things. Geoff was no good for details; Gwen's head, to the contrary, was only happy buzzing with them. He let her get on with it, acted as beast of burden. In fact there was no burden to mention. After all, she was shopping for just the two of them, and it was as good a way as any to explore the village stores and see what was on offer. While she examined this and that, Geoff spent the time comparing the prices of various spirits with those already noted in the booze shop. So the morning passed.

At eleven-thirty they went back to the Villa Eleni for you know and a shower, and afterwards Gwen prepared the foodstuffs while Geoff lazed under the awning. No sign of George and Petula; eighty-four degrees of heat as they idled their way down to the harbour; the village had closed itself down through the hottest part of the day, and they saw no one they knew. Spiros's boat lolled like a mirrored blot on the stirless ocean, and Geoff thought: *even the fish will be finding this a bit much!* Also: *I hope there's some shade on this blasted beach!*

Spiros appeared from behind a tangle of nets. He stood up, yawned, adjusted his straw hat like a sunshade on his head. "Thee boat," he said, in his entirely unnecessary fashion, as he helped them climb aboard. *Spiros* "thee boat" was hardly a hundred percent seaworthy, Geoff saw that immediately. In fact, in any other ocean in the world she'd be condemned. But this was the Mediterranean in July.

Barely big enough for three adults, the boat rocked a little as Spiros yanked futilely on the starter. Water seeped through boards, rotten and long since sprung, black with constant damp and badly caulked. Spiros saw Geoff's expression where he sat with his sandals in half an inch of water. He shrugged. "Is nothings," he said.

Finally the engine coughed into life, began to purr, and they were off. Spiros had the tiller; Geoff and Gwen faced him from the prow, which now lifted up a little as they left the harbour and cut straight out to sea. It was then, for the first time, that Geoff noticed Spiros's furtiveness: the way he kept glancing back toward Achladi, as if anxious not to be observed. Unlikely that they would be, for the village seemed fast asleep. Or perhaps he was just checking landmarks, avoiding rocks or reefs or what have you. Geoff looked overboard. The water seemed deep enough to him. Indeed, it seemed much *too* deep! But at least there were no sharks. . .

Well out to sea, Spiros swung the boat south and followed the coastline for maybe two and a half to three miles. The highest of Achladi's houses and apartments had slipped entirely from view by the time he turned in towards land again and sought a bight in the seemingly unbroken march of cliffs. The place was landmarked: a fang of rock had weathered free, shaping a stack that reared up from the water to form a narrow, deep channel between itself and the cliffs proper. In former times a second, greater stack had crashed oceanward and now lay like a reef just under the water across the entire frontage. In effect, this made the place a lagoon: a sandy beach to the rear, safe water, and the reef of shattered, softly matted rocks where the small waves broke.

There was only one way in. Spiros gentled his boat through the deep water between the crooked outcrop and the overhanging cliff. Clear of the channel, he nosed her into the beach and cut the motor; as the keel grated on grit he stepped nimbly between his passengers and jumped ashore, dragging the boat a few inches up onto the sand. Geoff passed him the picnic things, then steadied the boat while Gwen took off her sandals and made to step down where the water met the sand. But Spiros was quick off the mark.

He stepped forward, caught her up, carried her two paces up the beach and set her down. His left arm had been under her thighs, his right under her back, cradling her. But when he set her upon her own feet his right hand had momentarily cupped her breast, which he'd quite deliberately squeezed.

Gwen opened her mouth, stood gasping her outrage, unable to give it words. Geoff had got out of the boat and was picking up their things to bring them higher up the sand. Spiros, slapping him on the back, stepped round him and shoved the boat off, splashed in shallow water a moment before leaping nimbly aboard. Gwen controlled herself, said nothing. She could feel the blood in her cheeks but hoped Geoff wouldn't notice. Not here, miles from anywhere. Not in this lonely place. No, there must be no trouble here.

For suddenly it had dawned on her just how very lonely it was. Beautiful, unspoiled, a lovers' idyll—but oh so very lonely . . .

"You alright, love?" said Geoff, taking her elbow. She was looking at Spiros standing silent in his boat. Their eyes seemed locked, it was as if she didn't see him but the mind behind the sunglasses, behind those disparate, dispassionate eyes. A message had passed between them. Geoff sensed it but couldn't fathom it. He had almost seemed to hear Spiros say "yes," and Gwen answer "no."

"Gwen?" he said again.

"I see you," Spiros called, grinning. It broke the spell. Gwen looked away, and Geoff called out:

"Six-thirty, right?"

Spiros waggled a hand this way and that palm-down, as if undecided. "Six, six-thirty—something," he said, shrugging. He started his motor, waved once, chugged out of the bay between the jutting sentinel rock and the cliffs. As he passed out of sight the boat's engine roared with life, its throaty growl rapidly fading into the distance. . .

Gwen said nothing about the incident; she felt sure that if she did, then Geoff would make something of it. Their entire holiday could so easily be spoiled. It was bad enough that for her the day had already been ruined. So she kept quiet, and perhaps a little too quiet. When Geoff asked her again if anything was wrong she told him she had a headache. Then, feeling a little unclean, she stripped herself quite naked and swam while he explored the beach.

Not that there was a great deal to explore. He walked the damp sand at the water's rim to the southern extreme and came up against the cliffs where they curved out into the sea. They were quite unscalable, towering maybe eighty or ninety feet to their jagged rim. Walking the hundred or so yards back the other way, the thought came to Geoff that if Spiros didn't come back for them—that is, if anything untoward should happen to him—they'd just have to sit it out until they were found. Which, since Spiros was the only one who knew they were here, might well be a long time. Having thought it, Geoff tried to shake the idea off but it wouldn't go away. The place was quite literally a trap. Even a decent swimmer would have to have at least a couple of miles in him before considering swimming out of here.

Once lodged in Geoff's brain, the concept rapidly expanded itself. Before . . . he had looked at the faded-yellow and bone-white facade of the cliffs against the incredible blue of the sky with admiration; the beach had been every man's dream of tranquility, privacy, Eden with its own Eve; the softly lapping ocean had seemed like a warm, soothing bath reaching from horizon to horizon. But now . . . the place was so like Cape Greco. Except at Greco there had always been a way down to the sea—and up from it. . .

The northern end of the beach was much like the southern, the only difference being the great fang of rock protruding from the sea. Geoff stripped, swam out to it, was aware that the water here was a great deal deeper than back along the beach. But the distance was only thirty feet or so, nothing to worry about. And there were hand- and footholds galore around the base of the pillar of upthrusting rock. He hauled himself up onto a tiny ledge, climbed higher (not too high), sat on a projecting fist of rock with his feet dangling and called to Gwen. His voice surprised him, for it seemed strangely small and panting. The cliffs took it up, however, amplified and passed it on. His shout reached Gwen where she splashed; she spotted him, stopped swimming and stood up. She waved, and he marvelled at her body, her tip-tilted breasts displayed where she stood like some lovely Mediterranean nymph, all unashamed. *Venus rising from the waves.* Except that here the waves were little more than ripples.

He glanced down at the water and was at once dizzy: the way it lapped at the rock and flowed so gently in the worn hollows of the stone, all fluid and glinting motion; and Geoff's stomach following the same routine, seeming to slosh loosely inside him. *Damn* this terror of his! What was he but eight, nine feet above the sea? God, he might as well feel sick standing on a thick carpet!

He stood up, shouted, jumped outward, toward Gwen.

Down he plunged into cool, liquid blue, and fought his way to the surface, and swam furiously to the beach. There he lay, half-in, half-out of the water, his heart and lungs hammering, blood coursing through his body. It had been such a little thing—something any ten-year-old child could have done—but to him it had been such an effort. And an achievement!

Elated, he stood up, sprinted down the beach, threw himself into the warm, shallow water just as Gwen was emerging. Carried back by him she laughed, splashed him, finally submitted to his hug. They rolled in twelve inches of water and her legs went round him; and there where the water met the sand they grew gentle, then fierce, and when it was done the sea laved their heat and rocked them gently, slowly dispersing their passion. . .

About four o'clock they ate, but very little. They weren't hungry; the sun was too hot; the silence, at first enchanting, had turned to a droning, sun-scorched monotony that beat on the ears worse than a city's roar. And there was a smell. When the light breeze off the sea swung in a certain direction, it brought something unpleasant with it.

To provide shade, Geoff had rigged up his shirt, slacks, and a large beach towel on a frame of drifted bamboo between the brittle, sandpapered branches of an old tree washed half-way up the sand. There in this tatty, makeshift teepee they'd spread their blanket, retreated from the pounding sun. But as the smell came again Geoff crept out of the cramped shade, stood up and shielded his eyes to look along the wall of the cliffs. "It comes . . . from over there," he said, pointing.

Gwen joined him. "I thought you'd explored?" she said.

"Along the tideline," he answered, nodding slowly. "Not along the base of the cliffs. Actually, they don't look too safe, and they overhang a fair bit in places. But if you'll look where I'm pointing—there, where the cliffs are cut back—is that water glinting?"

"A spring?" she looked at him. "A waterfall?"

"Hardly a waterfall," he said. "More a dribble. But what is it that's dribbling? I mean, springs don't stink, do they?"

Gwen wrinkled her nose. "Sewage, do you think?"

"*Yecchh!*" he said. "But at least it would explain why there's no one else here. I'm going to have a look."

She followed him to the place where the cliffs were notched in a V. Out of the sunlight, they both shivered a little. They'd put on swimwear for simple decency's sake, in case a boat should pass by, but now they hugged themselves as the chill of damp stone drew off their stored heat and brought goose-pimples to flesh which sun and sea had already roughened. And there, beneath the overhanging cliff, they found in the shingle a pool formed of a steady flow from on high. Without a shadow of a doubt, the pool was the source of the carrion stench; but here in the shade its water was dark, muddied, rippled, quite opaque. If there was anything in it, then it couldn't be seen.

As for the waterfall: it forked high up in the cliff, fell in twin streams, one of which was a trickle. Leaning out over the pool at its narrowest, shallowest point, Geoff cupped his hand to catch a few droplets. He held them to his nose, shook his head. "Just water," he said. "It's the pool itself that stinks."

"Or something back there?" Gwen looked beyond the pool, into the darkness of the cave formed of the V and the overhang.

Geoff took up a stone, hurled it into the darkness and silence. Clattering echoes sounded, and a moment later—

Flies! A swarm of them, disturbed where they'd been sitting on cool, damp ledges. They came in a cloud out of the cave, sent Geoff and Gwen yelping, fleeing for the sea. Geoff was stung twice, Gwen escaped injury; the ocean was their refuge, shielding them while the flies dispersed or returned to their vile-smelling breeding ground.

After the murky, poisonous pool the sea felt cool and refreshing. Muttering curses, Geoff stood in the shallows while Gwen squeezed the craters of the stings in his right shoulder and bathed them with salt water. When she was done he said, bitterly: "I've *had* it with this place! The sooner the Greek gets back the better."

His words were like an invocation. Towelling themselves dry, they heard the roar of Spiros's motor, heard it throttle back, and a moment later his boat came nosing in through the gap between the rock and the cliffs. But instead of landing he stood off in the shallow water. "Hallo," he called, in his totally unnecessary fashion.

"You're early," Geoff called back. And under his breath: *Thank God!*

"Early, yes," Spiros answered. "But I have these troubles." He shrugged.

Gwen had pulled her dress on, packed the last of their things away. She walked down to the water's edge with Geoff. "Troubles?" she said, her voice a shade unsteady.

"Thee boat," he said, and pointed into the open, lolling belly of the craft, where they couldn't see. "I hitting thee rock when I leave Achladi. Is OK, but—" And he made his fifty-fifty sign, waggling his hand with the fingers open and the palm down. His face remained impassive, however.

Geoff looked at Gwen, then back to Spiros. "You mean it's unsafe?"

"For three peoples, unsafe—maybe." Again the Greek's shrug. "I thinks, I take thee lady first. Is OK, I come back. Is bad, I find other boat."

"You can't take both of us?" Geoff's face fell.

Spiros shook his head. "Maybe big problems," he said.

Geoff nodded. "OK," he said to Gwen. "Go just as you are. Leave all this stuff here and keep the boat light." And to Spiros: "Can you come in a bit more?"

The Greek made a clicking sound with his tongue, shrugged apologetically. "Thee boat is broked. I not want thee more breakings. You swim?" He looked at Gwen, leaned over the side and held out his hand. Keeping her dress on, she waded into

267

the water, made her way to the side of the boat. The water only came up to her breasts, but it turned her dress to a transparent, clinging film. She grasped the upper strake with one hand and made to drag herself aboard. Spiros, leaning backwards, took her free hand.

Watching, Geoff saw her come half out of the water—then saw her freeze. She gasped loudly and twisted her wet hand in Spiros's grasp, tugged free of his grip, flopped back down into the water. And while the Greek regained his balance, she quickly swam back ashore. Geoff helped her from the sea. "Gwen?" he said.

Spiros worked his starter, got the motor going. He commenced a slow, deliberate circling of the small bay.

"Gwen?" Geoff said again. "What is it? What's wrong?" She was pale, shivering.

"He . . ." she finally started to speak. "He . . . had an erection! Geoff, I could see it bulging in his shorts, throbbing. My God—and I know it was for me! And the boat . . ."

"What about the boat?" Anger was building in Geoff's heart and head, starting to run cold in his blood.

"There was no damage—none that I could see, anyway. He . . . he just wanted to get me into that boat, on my own!"

Spiros could see them talking together. He came angling close in to the beach, called out: "I bring thee better boat. Half an hour. Is safer. I see you." He headed for the channel between the rock and the cliff and in another moment passed from sight. . .

"Geoff, we're in trouble," Gwen said, as soon as Spiros had left. "We're in serious trouble."

"I know it," he said. "I think I've known it ever since we got here. That bloke's as sinister as they come."

"And it's not just his eye, it's his mind," said Gwen. "He's sick." Finally, she told her husband about the incident when Spiros had carried her ashore from the boat.

"So that's what that was all about," he growled. "Well, something has to be done about him. We'll have to report him."

She clutched his arm. "We have to get back to Achladi before we can do that," she said quietly. "Geoff, I don't think he intends to let us get back!"

That thought had been in his mind, too, but he hadn't wanted her to know it. He felt suddenly helpless. The trap seemed sprung and they were in it. But what did Spiros intend, and how could he possibly hope to get away with it—whatever "it" was? Gwen broke into his thoughts:

"No one knows we're here, just Spiros."

"I know," said Geoff. "And what about that couple who . . ." He let it tail off. It had just slipped from his tongue. It was the last thing he'd wanted to say.

"Do you think I haven't thought of that?" Gwen hissed, gripping his arm more tightly yet. "He was the last one to see them—getting on a ferry, he said. But did they?" She stripped off her dress.

"What are you doing?" he asked, breathlessly.

"We came in from the north," she answered, wading out again into the water. "There were no beaches between here and Achladi. What about to the south? There are other beaches than this one, we know that. Maybe there's one just half a mile away. Maybe even less. If I can find one where there's a path up the cliffs. . . ."

"Gwen," he said. "Gwen!" Panic was rising in him to match his impotence, his rage and terror.

She turned and looked at him, looked helpless in her skimpy bikini—and yet determined, too. And to think he'd considered her naïve! Well, maybe she had been. But no more. She managed a small smile, said, "I love you."

"What if you exhaust yourself?" He could think of nothing else to say.

"I'll know when to turn back," she said. Even in the hot sunlight he felt cold, and knew she must, too. He started toward her, but she was already into a controlled crawl, heading south, out across the submerged rocks. He watched her out of sight round the southern extreme of the jutting cliffs, stood knotting and unknotting his fists at the edge of the sea. . .

For long moments Geoff stood there, cold inside and hot out. And at the same time cold all over. Then the sense of time fleeting by overcame him. He ground his teeth, felt his frustration overflow. He wanted to shout but feared Gwen would hear him and turn back. But there must be something he could do. With his bare hands? Like what? A weapon—he needed a weapon.

There was the knife they'd bought just for their picnic. He went to their things and found it. Only a three-inch blade, but sharp! Hand to hand it must give him something of an advantage. But what if Spiros had a bigger knife? He seemed to have a bigger or better everything else.

One of the drifted tree's branches was long, straight, slender. It pointed like a mocking, sandpapered wooden finger at the unscalable cliffs. Geoff applied his weight close to the main branch. As he lifted his feet from the ground the branch broke, sending him to his knees in the sand. Now he needed some binding material. Taking his unfinished spear with him, he ran to the base of the cliffs. Various odds and ends had been driven back there by past storms. Plastic Coke bottles, fragments of driftwood, pieces of cork . . . a nylon fishing net tangled round a broken barrel!

Geoff cut lengths of tough nylon line from the net, bound the knife in position at the end of his spear. Now he felt he had a *real* advantage. He looked around. The sun was sinking leisurely toward the sea, casting his long shadow on the sand. How long since Spiros left? How much time left till he got back? Geoff glanced at the frowning needle of the sentinel rock. A sentinel, yes. A watcher. Or a watchtower!

He put down his spear, ran to the northern point and sprang into the sea. Moments later he was clawing at the rock, dragging himself from the water, climbing. And scarcely a thought of danger, not from the sea or the climb, not from the deep water or the height. At thirty feet the rock narrowed down; he could lean to left or right and scan the sea to the north, in the direction of Achladi. Way out on the blue, sails gleamed white in the brilliant sunlight. On the far horizon, a smudge of smoke. Nothing else.

For a moment—the merest moment—Geoff's old nausea returned. He closed his eyes and flattened himself to the rock, gripped tightly where his fingers were bedded in cracks in the weathered stone. A mass of stone shifted slightly under the pressure of his right hand, almost causing him to lose his balance. He teetered for a second, remembered Gwen . . . the nausea passed, and with it all fear. He stepped a little lower, examined the great slab of rock which his hand had tugged loose. And suddenly an idea burned bright in his brain.

Which was when he heard Gwen's cry, thin as a keening wind, shrilling into his bones from along the beach. He jerked his head round, saw her there in the water inside the reef, wearily striking for the shore. She looked all in. His heart leaped into his mouth, and without pause he launched himself from the rock, striking the water feet first and sinking deep. No fear or effort to it this time; no time for any of that; surfacing, he struck for the shore. Then back along the beach, panting his heart out, flinging himself down in the small waves where she knelt, sobbing, her face covered by her hands.

"Gwen, are you all right? What is it, love? What's happened? I *knew* you'd exhaust yourself!"

She tried to stand up, collapsed into his arms and shivered there; he cradled her where earlier they'd made love. And at last she could tell it.

"I . . . I stayed close to the shore," she gasped, gradually getting her breath. "Or rather, close to the cliffs. I was looking . . . looking for a way up. I'd gone about a third of a mile, I think. Then there was a spot where the water was very deep and the cliffs sheer. Something touched my legs and it was like an electric shock—I mean, it was so unexpected there in that deep water. To feel something slimy touching my legs like that. *Ugh!*" She drew a deep breath.

"I thought: *God, sharks!* But then I remembered: there are no sharks in the Med. Still, I wanted to be sure. So . . . so I turned, made a shallow dive and looked to see what . . . what . . ." She broke down into sobbing again.

Geoff could do nothing but warm her, hug her tighter yet.

"Oh, but there *are* sharks in the Med, Geoff," she finally went on. "One shark, anyway. His name is Spiros! A spider? No, he's a shark! Under the sea there, I saw . . . a girl, naked, tethered to the bottom with a rope round her ankle. And down in the deeps, a stone holding her there."

"My God!" Geoff breathed.

"Her thighs, belly, were covered in those little green swimming crabs. She was all bloated, puffy, floating upright on her own internal gasses. Fish nibbled at her. Her nipples were gone. . ."

"The fish!" Geoff gasped. But Gwen shook her head.

"Not the fish," she rasped. "Her arms and breasts were black with bruises. Her nipples had been bitten through—*right* through! Oh, Geoff, Geoff!" She hugged him harder than ever, shivering hard enough to shake him. "I *know* what happened to her. It was him, Spiros." She paused, tried to control her shivering, which wasn't only the after-effect of the water.

And finally she continued: "After that I had no strength. But somehow I made it back."

"Get dressed," he told her then, his voice colder than she'd ever heard it. "Quickly! No, not your dress—my trousers, shirt. The slacks will be too long for you. Roll up the bottoms. But get dressed, get warm."

She did as he said. The sun, sinking, was still hot. Soon she was warm again, and calmer. Then Geoff gave her the spear he'd made and told her what he was going to do. . .

There were two of them, as like as peas in a pod. Geoff saw them, and the pieces fell into place. Spiros and his brother. The island's codes were tight. These two looked for loose women; loose in their narrow eyes, anyway. And from the passports of the honeymooners it had been plain that they weren't married. Which had made Gwen a whore, in their eyes. Like the Swedish girl, who'd met a man and gone to bed with him. As easy as that. So Spiros had tried it on, the easy way at first. By making it plain that he was on offer. Now that that hadn't worked, now it was time for the hard way.

Geoff saw them coming in the boat and stopped gouging at the rock. His fingernails were cracked and starting to bleed, but the job was as complete as he could wish. He ducked back out of sight, hugged the sentinel rock and thought only of Gwen. He had one chance and mustn't miss it.

He glanced back, over his shoulder. Gwen had heard the boat's engine. She stood half-way between the sea and the waterfall with its foul pool. Her spear was grasped tightly in her hands. *Like a young Amazon*, Geoff thought. But then he heard the boat's motor cut back and concentrated on what he was doing.

The put-put-put of the boat's exhaust came closer. Geoff took a chance, glanced round the rim of the rock. Here they came, gentling into the channel between the rock and the cliffs. Spiros's brother wore slacks; both men were naked from the waist up; Spiros had the tiller. And his brother had a shotgun!

One chance. *Only one chance.*

The boat's nose came inching forward, began to pass directly below. Geoff gave a mad yell, heaved at the loose wedge of rock. For a moment he thought it would stick and put all his weight into it. But then it shifted, toppled.

Below, the two Greeks had looked up, eyes huge in tanned, startled faces. The one with the shotgun was on his feet. He saw the falling rock in the instant before it smashed down on him and drove him through the bottom of the boat. His gun went off, both barrels, and the shimmering air near Geoff's head buzzed like a nest of wasps. Then, while all below was still in a turmoil, he aimed himself at Spiros and jumped.

Thrown about in the stern of his sinking boat, Spiros was making ready to dive overboard when Geoff's feet hit him. he was hurled into the water, Geoff narrowly missing the swamped boat as he, too, crashed down into the sea. And then a mad flurry of water as they both struck out for the shore.

Spiros was there first. Crying out, wild, outraged, frightened, he dragged himself from the sea. He looked round and saw Geoff coming through the water—saw his boat disappear with only ripples to mark its passing, and no sign of his brother—and started at a lop-sided run up the beach. Towards Gwen. Geoff swam for all he was worth, flew from the sea up onto the land.

Gwen was running, heading for the V in the cliff under the waterfall. Spiros was right behind her, arms reaching. Geoff came last, the air rasping in his lungs, Hell's fires blazing in his heart. He'd drawn blood and found it to his liking. But he stumbled, fell, and when he was up again he saw Spiros closing on his quarry. Gwen was backed up against the cliff, her feet in the water at the shallow end of the vile pool. The Greek made a low, apish lunge at her and she struck at him with her spear.

She gashed his face even as he grabbed her. His hand caught in the loose material of Geoff's shirt, tearing it from her so that her breasts lolled free. Then she stabbed at him again, slicing him across the neck. His hands flew to his face and neck; he staggered back from her, tripped, and sat down in chest-deep water; Geoff arrived panting at the pool and Gwen flew into his arms. He took the spear from her, turned it towards Spiros.

But the Greek was finished. He shrieked and splashed in the pool like the madman he was, seemed incapable of getting to his feet. His wounds weren't bad, but the blood was everywhere. That wasn't the worst of it: the thing he'd tripped on had floated to the surface. It was beginning to rot, but it was—or had been—a young man. Rubbery arms and legs tangled with Spiros's limbs; a ghastly, gaping face tossed with his frantic threshing; a great black hole showed where the bloated corpse had taken a shotgun blast to the chest, the shot that had killed him.

For a little while longer Spiros fought to be rid of the thing—screamed aloud as its gaping, accusing mouth screamed horribly, silently at him—then gave up and flopped back half-in, half-out of the water. One of the corpse's arms was draped across his heaving, shuddering chest. He lay there with his hands over his face and cried, and the flies came swarming like a black, hostile cloud from the cave to settle on him.

Geoff held Gwen close, guided her away from the horror down the beach to a sea which was a deeper blue now. "It's OK," he kept saying, as much for himself as for her. "It's OK. They'll come looking for us, sooner or later."

As it happened, it was sooner. . .

D. F. LEWIS

Mort au Monde

DES LEWIS was born in 1948 and is married with two children. In 1968 August Derleth rejected two of his tales for being "pretty much pure grue", since when he has been published widely in the genre in small press publications on both sides of the Atlantic.

His disparate literary influences include H.P. Lovecraft, Lord Dunsany, Robert Aickman and Philip K. Dick, and Lewis' growing reputation in the genre resulted in the award-winning small press magazine *Dagon* publishing a special issue devoted to his fiction last year.

With "Mort au Monde" we hope to introduce his distinctive, disturbing prose to an even wider audience.

I SLEPT HEAVILY . . . too heavily by half. For things had crept on all fours through the open door, which I could have sworn I left shut, squawking heads quietly turning from side to side in search of cast-off human meat to suck upon.

I woke with the dream still going on in a small part of my brain. For I convinced myself that I actually saw a pair of widely set eyes searing the darkness with beams of bloodshot fire.

But it was no doubt daytime in the real world and I suddenly recalled my own name. Muirfield came back first . . . then David . . . and, finally, the place, named St Perrin. With some pain, I rose from the bed and staggered towards the window . . . which I proceeded to unshutter with some amazement at the brightness of the sun already shafting along the tips of the distant hills.

It all fitted somehow. But, for some reason, I could not fathom why my loved one, Marianne, was sleeping in a separate room. I knew that if I walked along the musty corridor from my door numbered 2, I would find a screwed-on plate showing 5. Those who slept between us, those unseen, unnamed chaperones, were only just to be heard stirring in their beds, as I crept past their doors towards number 5. It was dark on the landing, and it was difficult to make out the hazy cross-hatching of the banisters leading down to the lower storeys; I was dizzy for a moment, but gathered myself for meeting my loved one.

Marianne had allowed her hair to fall to her shoulders since I last saw her at dinner the previous evening. The unrevealing mouth . . . the deceptive drapes of the night-dress . . . the hollow in the throat . . . the peeping toes . . . all gave me an impression that she had struggled against the odds not to be taken unawares. What gave the game away were the red eyes.

It was when a deep grunt from further inside her room commanded the shutting of the door, that I decided I ought to return to my own territory, to retrieve different dreams from under the bedclothes, dreams that I could more easily live with.

Hot croissants with coffee are too light for an Englishman. I yearned for toast and marmalade, eggs and bacon, steaming pots of strong tea, honey on the cornflakes, milk by the church, freshly squeezed oranges. Marianne sat opposite, staring into her large bowl of coffee, as if she were trying to read the future. I could have told her that the past is more mysterious—but I didn't.

I don't know if I'd noticed it before, but her eyes were nearly all white, carrying upon their surface small round yolks of darting brown like particles under the microscope. Unlike most people I'd met, I could not read her soul through such deceptive apertures. It was as if I had indeed been defeated by someone who was using *my* eyes to race me to the bottom of my own soul.

"Where shall we go today?" She spoke towards the sounding board of my face. "I think we should take advantage of a sunny day, by going to the coast."

"I don't know. Why don't we stay in these grounds, and read or something?" I never discovered whether these words of mine made any sense, for her next statement did not follow them on. Even in the most crudely formulated conversations, there is at least a thin thread of logic weaving in and out of the various tangents and non-sequiturs. But, evidently, not in a conversation with dear Marianne.

"I expect we wouldn't have come here at all, if it hadn't been for your Mother, David."

I was pleasantly surprised, nevertheless, to hear her use my name when addressing me. This gave me renewed encouragement to respond: "Well, it *was* very kind of her to let us have this place for the summer . . ."

"The nights are so long in this chateau. Sleep is insufficient to cover them."

What the hell was she talking about? My upbringing had taught me that sleep was not a pleasure, merely a necessity . . . "for entropy to be slowed down", as my late grandfather had always said.

Well, we did go to the seaside that day, despite the slanting rainclouds that swept in by lunchtime from across the sea. I had been hoping to see some of those old-fashioned girls sun-bathing; in the event, there was just a mass of twirling umbrellas along the promenade.

Finally, the pair of us resorted to the old part of the town, full of climbing alleys and countless spired churches hogging the skyline. Being abroad had ceased to be a novelty long since, but the foreignness of that place really got under my skin. I felt the whole thing was an episode from an alternate universe, one in which I was the unsung hero and Marianne the singer.

She cut me dead at every turn, just with her eyes. I felt diminished to the quick, for she only had eyes for complete strangers (or, at least, for people who seemed strange to me). Until I realised that they must have slept in the bedrooms between us ... for a fleeting moment, I thought they were distant relations, who had remained incognito, just for the sake of appearances. Like all people not in your immediate vicinity nor party to your conversation, they sounded like Undergrunts, with squeezed-up eyes and thin lips.

I snatched Marianne's hands and, running towards the harbour, we were only just in time to catch the last rollonrolloff for England ... which carved a slow path into the rising moon. As night came upon us again, we were soon to discover that our respective cabins were decks apart.

Too late to realise that it was sailing in the wrong direction, Marianne clasped me tight: even her eyes could not hide her fear. And we kept vigil for what could be an endless night, without even resorting to our cabins, calling each other by our names in case we forgot; careful not to betray any emotions that would give the chaperones a reason to come out of hiding.

THOMAS TESSIER

Blanca

THOMAS TESSIER was born in Connecticut, where he currently lives. Educated at University College, Dublin, he spent several years in London, where he worked as a publisher and was a regular contributor to *Vogue*.

His superior horror novels include *The Fates, Shockwaves, The Nightwalker, Phantom* (nominated for the 1982 World Fantasy Award), *Finishing Touches* and his latest, *Secret Strangers*.

"Blanca" is a eloquent ghost story, told in Tessier's immaculate prose, that has disturbing echoes in today's headlines.

W HEN I TOLD A FEW close friends that I was going to Blanca, their reaction was about what I had expected. "Why?" they asked. "There's nothing to see in Blanca. Nothing to do except disappear." Sly smiles. "Watch out you don't disappear." "Maybe that's why I chose it," I said with a smile of my own. "It might be nice to disappear for a while."

For a travel writer who has been on the job ten years, as I have, it isn't so easy to escape. The good places have been done, the mediocre ones too. You name it and I've probably been there, evaluating the hotels, sampling the cuisine, checking out the facilities and amenities, chatting up the locals. It's a great job, but I was tired of the regular world. What I needed was a therapeutic getaway, to spend a couple of weeks in an obscure backwater doing nothing more than sipping cold beer on a terrace and reading a good book.

I knew people in the business who'd been to Blanca. It's boring, they told me. Miles and miles of rolling plains and rangeland. There's a dead volcano somewhere in Blanca, but it isn't worth climbing. Yes, the towns are neat and the people are pleasant enough. There's never any difficulty getting a clean room and bed for the night. But nothing happens, there's nothing to do. No monuments or ancient ruins. No carnival, no festivals or feasts. The night life is said to be fairly low-key, so if you're looking for that kind of action, which I wasn't, there are much better places to go. Blanca was cattle country, and the only good thing I ever heard about it was that the steaks were excellent.

Blanca is not a nation but a territory, overlapping several borders in that region of the world. The native Indians were crushed nearly two centuries ago. They survive, a sullen minority now thoroughly domesticated by generations of servitude as cheap labor cowhands, meat packers, and household help. The European settlers tried to create Blanca as an independent state, but numerous rebellions failed and it was eventually carved up by its larger neighbors. But Blanca is Blanca, they still say there, regardless of the boundaries that appear on maps.

Because Blanca has comparatively little to offer the visitor, it is not on any of the main routes. I had to catch two flights, the second of which stopped at so many featureless outposts along the way that it seemed like days before I finally reached Oranien. With a population of nearly one hundred thousand it is easily the largest city in Blanca.

I checked into the Hotel des Vacances, which was within walking distance of the central district but just far enough away to escape the noise. My room was large and airy and had a small balcony that overlooked two residential streets and a park. It was comfortable, and not at all like a modern luxury hotel.

I slept for nearly eleven hours that first night, had steak and eggs for brunch, and then took a lazy walk around the center of Oranien. The narrow side streets had a certain pioneer charm—the original hard-clay tiles had never been paved over and remained neatly in place. But the most remarkable feature of the city was its state of cleanliness. I began to look for a piece of litter and couldn't find so much as a discarded cigarette butt. It reminded me of parts of Switzerland, or Singapore.

On the top floor of a department store I caught a view of the southern part of the city, a vast stretch of stockyards, abattoirs, and railroad tracks. All the beef in Blanca passed through Oranien on its way to the outside world. I'd come to a dusty, three-story cowtown, and it was the tidiest, best-scrubbed place I'd ever seen.

But then I'd heard stories about the police in Blanca. They *were* the law, and if you had any sense at all you never challenged them. Littering ranked close to treason by their way of thinking, and while that might seem harsh to some, I had no problem with it. I've seen immaculate places and I've seen squalor; on the whole, I prefer the former. Besides, it had nothing to do with me. I was on vacation, recovering from a personal mess, exorcising old demons (including a wife). The first few days I was in Oranien the only cops I saw were chubby little men in silly uniforms, directing traffic. They looked like extras in some Ruritanian operetta.

"Not them," Basma said quietly. "The ones you must worry about are the ones you can't see. The men in plain clothes. They are everywhere."

"Even here?" I asked, amused but intrigued.

"Yes, surely."

We were in the small but very pleasant beer garden behind the Hotel des Vacances. There were perhaps two dozen other people scattered about the umbrella-topped tables in the late afternoon sun. A few neighborhood regulars, the rest visitors and hotel guests like myself, passing through. Everyone looked happy and relaxed.

My companion was both a foreigner and a local resident. Basma had taken it upon himself to join me at my table the day before, when I had just discovered the beer garden and was settling into *The Thirteenth Simenon Omnibus*. At first I resented the intrusion and tried to ignore the man, but he would not be denied. Finally I gave in and closed my book.

We spent two hours or more drinking and chatting, with Basma carrying most of the load. But he was easy company. A middle-aged Lebanese, he had reluctantly fled Beirut while he still had a cache of foreign currency. The city had become unbearable, impossible, and he believed he was a target of both the Christians ("Because I am a Muslim") and the Shiites ("Because they think all international businessmen are working for the CIA"). Besides, business had pretty much dried up. Basma had been in Oranien for the best part of three years, doing the odd bit of trade and otherwise depleting his capital. He was eager to move on to more fertile ground, but had not yet decided where that might be. By then I was tired and tipsy and went to bed early. But we agreed to meet again the next day and have dinner in town, which is how we came to be discussing the police.

"Who, for instance?" I asked.

"Let's not be looking around and staring," Basma said softly. "But that couple at the table by the wall on your right. I've seen them many times and wondered about them."

A handsome man and a beautiful woman, both in their late twenties. He wore a linen suit, a white shirt, and no tie. He had dark hair and a strong, unmarked face. She was dressed in a smart, obviously foreign outfit—skirt, matching jacket, and a stylish blouse. I imagined her to be the daughter of a local big shot; she had that air of privilege and hauteur. They made me feel old, or perhaps just envious of their youth and good looks.

"I don't care," I said. "I'm just passing through. All I want to do is relax for a couple of weeks."

"Of course." Basma smiled indulgently.

So that night he gave me the grand tour of Oranien, such as it is. After the mandatory steak dinner we strolled through the main shopping arcade, which was full of the latest European fashions and Asian electronic equipment, all carrying steep price tags. We took in a couple of bars, briefly surveyed a dance hall that doubled as an economy-class dating service, and then stopped for a while at a neon-riddled disco called Marlene's, where the crowd was somewhat interesting. There the sons and daughters of local wealth came to dance, flirt, play their social games, and get blitzed. Basma called them second-raters, because the brightest of their generation and class were away in America or England, studying at the best private schools and universities.

By the time we'd squandered some money at a posh gaming club and had a frightening glimpse of a very discreet place where you could do whatever you wanted with girls (or boys) as young as thirteen, I'd seen enough for one night. Oranien's dull and orderly exterior masked the usual wanton tendencies. It didn't bother me, but it didn't interest me.

Back in my room, I poured one last nightcap from my bottle of duty-free bourbon and lit a cigarette. I'd had a lot to drink, but it had been spaced out over many hours, with a meal thrown in somewhere along the line. I wasn't drunk, just tired, reasonably buzzed. I know this for sure, because whenever I have gotten drunk in the past I've never dreamed, or at least I've never remembered it. That night I did have a dream, and it was one I would not forget.

I was sleeping in my bed, there in the Hotel des Vacances. It was the middle of the night. Suddenly I was awakened by a loud clattering noise. I jumped out of bed. I was at the window, looking out on what seemed to be a historical costume pageant. It confused me, and I couldn't move. The street below, brightly lit by a three-quarters moon, was full of soldiers on horseback. They carried torches or waved swords. The horses continued to make a dreadful racket, stamping their hooves on the clay tiles. Every house in sight remained dark, but the soldiers went to several different doors, roused the inhabitants, and seized eight or ten people altogether. They were thrown into horse-drawn carts already crowded with prisoners. The night was full of terrible sounds—soldiers shouting, men arguing or pleading in vain, women and children wailing, a ghastly pandemonium. It seemed they had finished and were about to move on when one of the soldiers, obviously an officer, turned and looked up directly at me. I was standing out on the little balcony, gripping the wrought-iron railing tightly. The officer spoke to one of his comrades, who also looked in my direction. The officer raised his sword, pointing to me. I knew his face—but I had no idea who he was. A group of soldiers, apparently responding to instructions, hurried across the street to the hotel. Still, I couldn't move. A terrible fear came over me as I realized they would take me away with the others. The rest is sensation—the twisting, falling, hideous sweetness we all dream more often than we would like before it actually happens—dying.

I slept late—it was becoming a welcome habit—and woke up feeling remarkably cheerful and energetic. I remembered the dream, I thought about it through my shower, over brunch, and during my walk to the news-stand for the most recent *Herald Tribune*. I sat outdoors at a café, drank two cups of coffee, smoked cigarettes, and read about Darryl Strawberry's 525-foot home run in distant Montreal.

It was great to be alive. Any sense of menace or fear had dissolved out of the dream. It had already become a kind of mental curio that I carried around with me. Maybe I was happy simply because I knew I could never have had that nightmare in New York. What it seemed to say to me in the light of day was: "Now you know you're in Blanca."

"It's local history," Basma agreed when we met in the beer garden later that afternoon and I told him about the dream. "You must have known about it before you came here."

"Sure. Well, vaguely." I lit a cigarette while the waitress delivered our second round of beers. "I've heard the jokes about people being taken away in the dead of night and never seen again."

"Yes, but they are not jokes. What you dreamed is exactly how it used to happen—and by the way, it still does, from time to time."

"Really?"

"Of course."

"Well, that's politics, which never interested me. I'd just as soon get back to dreaming about sex."

"Aha." Basma smiled broadly. "No need just to dream about it, you know."

"It'll do for now."

Basma shrugged sadly. I knew I was doing a bad job of living up to his mental image of American tourists as people hell-bent on having an extravagantly good time. We had a light dinner together and then I disappointed him further by deciding to make an early evening of it. I was still a bit tired from our night out on the town, and I wanted nothing more than to read in bed for a while and then get about twelve hours of sleep. I had it in mind to rent a car the next day and see a bit of the nearby countryside, however flat and dull it might be.

Simenon worked his usual magic. I was soon transported to rainy Paris (even in the sweltering heat of August, Simenon's Paris seems rainy), where Inspector Maigret had another nasty murder to unravel. It was bliss, but unfortunately I drifted off to sleep sooner than I expected. I woke up a little after four in the morning, the paperback in my hand. I dropped the book to the floor and crawled under the covers. But it was no good. Finally I sat up and groaned, realizing that I would not be able to get back to sleep. For a while I simply stayed there, lying still.

I got out of bed when I noticed a strange flickering of light reflected on the half-open window. It came from the street below, a lamp-post or car headlights most likely. But when I stepped onto the balcony and looked down, I was paralyzed by what I saw. They were all there again. The horses, the carts, the soldiers with their swords and torches, the pitiful souls being dragged from their homes, the mothers and wives, the children. It was a repeat performance of the grim nightmare I'd had only twenty-four hours ago, but this time I was wide-awake. I forced myself to be sure: I took note of the cold, harsh wrought iron beneath my bare feet, I sucked in huge breaths of chilly night air, and I looked over my shoulder into the hotel room to reassure myself in some way. But when I turned back to the street below they were still there; the scene continued to play itself out. I was awake, and it was happening.

I realized there were certain differences. Noise—there was none. The horses stamped, the soldiers shouted, the men argued, and their families sobbed, but I heard none of this; I could only see it taking place. Silence ruled the night. And then there was the officer, the one in charge, who had pointed his sword at me in the dream. I spotted him again and he still looked familiar to me, but I didn't know who he was. This time he never once glanced in my direction. He and his troops went about their business as if I didn't exist, though they could hardly fail to notice me standing there on the second-floor balcony, the room lit up behind me. The fact that they didn't may account for the other difference, the lack of fear in me. The scene had a terrible fascination, I was transfixed by it, but at the same time I felt detached from it, uninvolved. I didn't know what to make of it. I felt puzzled rather than threatened.

Finally I did something sensible. I looked up the street, away from the scene, and sure enough, I saw the usual line of parked cars that I knew belonged there. It was a comforting sight. But then, when I turned back, the dream drama was still just visible. The soldiers and the carts had formed a wavy line and were marching away from me toward the main road, a hundred yards or so in the distance. I watched them until they reached the intersection with that broad avenue, at which point my eyes could make out nothing more than the bobbing, meandering flow of torch flames.

It took another few minutes for me to realize that what I was looking at was a stream of headlights. Then I became aware of the sound of that traffic; the silence was broken. The early shift, I told myself. Hundreds of workers on their way to the abattoirs, stockyards, and packing plants on the south side of the city. The news agents, short-order cooks, and bus drivers. All the people who open up the city before dawn every morning. Any city. I stepped back into the room, sat on my bed, and lit a cigarette, wondering how yesterday's nightmare could turn into today's hallucination.

"Do you take drugs?" Basma asked me casually.

We were walking through the park, toward a bar I'd never been to in my life. It was about five that afternoon, and I'd blurted out the story of the hallucination—which was what I still took it to be—as soon as we met for our daily drink and chat.

I laughed. "No, it's been a few years since I did any drugs, and even then it wasn't much."

"You are quite certain that you were fully awake when you saw this—whatever it was?"

"Yes."

"And you were awake *before* you saw it?"

"Definitely. I was lying there, feeling sorry for myself for waking up so early. I saw the orange light flickering on the window—it's a glass door, actually, to the balcony."

"Yes, yes," Basma said impatiently.

"Well, as I told you, I sat up, went to the window, stepped out onto the balcony, and there it was."

"I see."

Basma didn't speak again until we reached the bar, a workers' grogshop that offered only the locally brewed beer, Bolero. Once we got our drinks and I had lit a cigarette, Basma returned to the subject.

"You think it was hallucination."

"Yes, of course," I said. "What else would it be?"

"Ghosts." Basma smiled, but not as if he were joking. "Perhaps you saw some ghosts from history."

"Oh, I doubt that very much."

"Why? It makes perfect sense. What is more, I think you may have been awake the first time you saw them, two nights ago. You only thought it was a dream, you were less certain because it was the first time and you had been drinking more—yes?"

"Yes, I had been drinking more, but I still think that I was dreaming. It ended in a panic and I was lost in sleep in an instant—no sensation of getting back into bed or thinking about it." I stubbed out my cigarette and lit another. I didn't like disappointing Basma again, he seemed as eager as a child to believe in ghosts. "Besides, even if I had been awake, that doesn't mean it was not a hallucination."

"The same hallucination, two nights in a row." Basma gave this some thought. "And you have some medical history of this?"

"No, not at all," I had to admit.

"Then why do you think it should suddenly start happening to you now?"

I shrugged. "The stories I'd heard about Blanca. The emotional distress resulting from the break-up of my marriage. Throw in the mild despair I sometimes feel at the approach of my fortieth birthday." I finished the beer and looked around for a waitress—a mistake in that bar. Then I realized how self-pitying I sounded, and it annoyed me very much. "To tell you the truth, I really have no idea at all why this kind of kind thing should be happening to me."

"Hallucination?" Basma asked again, quietly.

"That makes a lot more sense than an army of ghosts."

"As long as it makes sense to you."

It didn't, in fact, but I was fed up with talking about it, fed up with even thinking about it, so I fetched two more Bolero beers and then changed the subject. I told Basma about my day trip. I'd hired an Opel Rekord that morning and driven past miles and miles of cattle ranches, through small but impeccable villages, in a wide looping route north of Oranien. Altogether, I was out of the city for about five hours, and I'd seen quite enough of the countryside. There was nothing wrong with it—it was agreeably unspoiled rangeland—but it was bland, featureless, utterly lacking in charm or interest. Just as I'd been told.

"Yes." Basma nodded. "I have heard that once you leave the city it's much the same in every direction, for hundreds of miles. Although I've never seen for myself."

"You've never left Oranien, since you got here?"

"Why should I? There's nothing to see." His smile broadened into a grin. "Is there?"

"Well, no."

"Do you still have the car?"

"Yes, until tomorrow noon," I told him. "It's parked back near the hotel."

"Good. If you don't mind driving, I would like to show you something. Not exactly a tourist attraction, but I think you'll find it worthwhile."

He wouldn't tell me where we were going, but there was still plenty of daylight left when we drove away a few minutes later. I followed his directions, and it was soon obvious that we were heading toward the south end of the city.

"The stockyards?" I guessed.

"Ah, you've seen them."

"Only from a distance." I told Basma about the view from the department store.

"Now you will see it all close up."

I was mildly curious. We passed through the commercial district and then a residential area not unlike the one in which I was staying. The houses and apartment buildings became shabbier and more dilapidated the farther we went from the center of the city; the middle class in-town neighborhood gave way to the worker-Indian tenements on the outskirts. I wanted to drive slowly so that I could see as much as possible, and in the fact I had to because there were so many people out on the streets. Kids playing games and ignoring the traffic, grown-ups talking in small groups (men to men, women to women, mostly), and the old folks sitting stoically wherever they could find a quiet spot. Most of the social life, including the cooking and eating of food, seemed to take place outdoors.

Almost before I realized it, we were there. The industry and the workers' lodgings had sprung up together over the years, without benefit of design or long-term planning. There were row houses right up to the open doors of an abattoir, apartment buildings wedged between a canning factory and a processing plant, and a vast maze of corrals holding thousands of cattle bumping against dozens of tiny backyards. After we had cruised around for a while, I began to understand that these people literally lived in their workplaces: you would go home when your shift was finished, but home was hardly any different. The interminable stupid bawling of the cattle, the mingled stench of blood, raw meat, and cowshit, the constant rattling of trains, the drumming vibrations of the factories—everything here, everything you saw or heard or felt or smelled was about decay and death. You could taste it in the air.

We reached the worst of it, a mean stretch where finally the people themselves seemed only marginally alive. They stood or sat about in front of their shacks looking dazed. The streets, no longer paved, became increasingly difficult to navigate. Ditches ran along both sides, and they ran red with blood from the slaughterhouses. In the absence of traffic and other human noises, the shriek of power-saws carving animal flesh was piercingly clear. At every pile of garbage vicious cats and scarred dogs competed with huge brown roaches and gangs of rats for whatever was going. It was getting dark fast.

"I hope you know the way back."

"Yes, of course."

Basma gave me a series of directions, and it wasn't too long before we were on a better road. Neither of us had spoken much in the course of our slumming tour. As soon as I caught a glimpse of the lights in the center of the city my stomach began to relax. I've been to some of the worst refugee camps in the world and never felt so tense. But refugee camps are at least theoretically temporary, and there is always the hope, however slim, of eventual movement. The people I had just seen were never going anywhere.

"I suppose I've had Blanca beef many times, in all my travels," I said, just to say something.

"I'm sure you have," Basma agreed promptly. "They ship it out in every form. Brains, tongue, heart, kidneys, liver, as well as all the usual cuts, prime rib, steaks and so on, all the way down to hot dogs and Vienna sausages. If it isn't tinned or wrapped in plastic, it's frozen."

We began to joke about becoming vegetarians, describing the best salads we could remember having, and we kept at it until we were comfortably settled with drinks in Number One, which was supposedly the better of Oranien's two topless joints. It was expensive but otherwise all right. That kind of bar, where the music was loud and the women occasionally distracting, was just what Basma and I needed, since our excursion into the south end had left us in no mood for serious conversation. We drank until the place closed, by which time we were both unfit to drive, so we left the rental car parked where it was and hired a taxi.

I wasn't surprised when Basma got out of the cab with me at the hotel. I didn't know exactly where he lived but I assumed it was in the neighborhood because we'd met in the beer garden and we always said good night outside the hotel. ·

"Would you like to have a nightcap in my room?" he asked me as the taxi pulled away.

"No, thank you very much. I couldn't take one more drink."

"Are you sure? I have a bottle of Teachers, pretty good stuff, and I live right there, across the street." Basma pointed vaguely to the first or second building on the opposite corner. "Come on, one more."

"No, really, thanks, but I'm going to fall down and pass out, and I'd rather do that in my bed than on your floor."

Basma shrugged. "Okay. See you tomorrow."

"Sure, good night." I turned away, but then stopped and looked back at him. "Hey, you know what? Your building is one of the ones those ghost soldiers raided."

"Don't be telling me such things," he said from the middle of the street. "I don't want to know that."

"Why? It's just ghosts, and history. Right?"

"Never mind that."

Basma wagged a finger at me and kept going. I made it upstairs, locked my door, and even managed to get my clothes off before spinning dizzily into sleep. It was nearly noon when I opened my eyes again. The first thing that came to me was how nice it felt not to have another hallucination, nightmare, or ghostly apparition to brood about. I'd been truly out of it, and I'd slept straight through, unbothered.

On the negative side, however, I felt terrible the moment I stood up. I took a long shower, which made me feel cleaner but did nothing for my head, and I was going to get some food when I remembered the rental car. I didn't want to pay another day's charges but it was already late. When I got to the car I found a parking ticket under the wiper blade. I shoved it in my pocket, wondering if I could safely tear it up or if the vaunted Oranien police would catch up with me before I flew out next week.

The car rental agency wanted me to pay for the second full day, naturally, since I was well over an hour past the deadline when I finally got there. I had no luck arguing until I pulled out my *Vogue* credentials, at which point the manager suddenly became obsequious and sympathetic. No problem: no extra charges.

Then I got some much-needed food into my stomach. I went back to my hotel room, tore up the parking ticket, and fell asleep again on the bed while trying to read the *Herald Tribune*. It was after four when I dragged myself down to the beer garden. I held off on the alcohol, cautiously sipping mineral water while I waited for Basma. An hour later I began to wonder if I was wrong. We *had* agreed to meet in the usual place at the usual time, hadn't we? Maybe he had business to attend to elsewhere and I'd misunderstood him in the boozy fog last night. I wasn't disappointed or annoyed, because I really wanted a break from Basma's company, for one evening anyway. I stayed a little longer, out of courtesy, and then returned to my room. He'd know where to find me if he turned up later. But he didn't, and I had a very welcome early night.

The next day I felt great, and I did what I had really wanted to do all along. I sat in the shade in the beer garden, reading Simenon. I had breakfast there, followed later by more coffee, then lunch, and, in the middle of the afternoon, lemonade and a plate of watermelon chunks. By five o'clock I'd knocked off both Maigret novels in the volume, and I allowed myself a glass of cold Bolero beer. It was a very pale lager, but I was beginning to develop a taste for it.

Where was Basma? I had a sudden guilty flashback to our drunken parting. I'd teased him about the ghost soldiers, as he thought of them, and now it occurred to me that I might have annoyed him. Perhaps that was why he was staying away.

What you do when you're drunk always seems much worse when you reconstruct it later. I was tired of sitting there, but once again I stayed on for another hour or so, until it was obvious that my Lebanese friend was not going to put in an appearance.

I went looking for him a little while later. I started with the corner building diagonally opposite the hotel. Inside the unlocked screen door was a small entry foyer with a tile floor and a rickety wooden table. The inner door was locked, so I rang the bell, and kept ringing it for nearly five minutes before a heavy-set, middle-aged woman answered.

"I'm looking for Mr. Basma," I told her.

"He go."

"When do you expect him back?" She shrugged and shook her head at this. "Well, can I leave a message for him?" I took out a pen and a piece of paper I'd brought for that purpose. But the woman continued to shake her head.

"He go," she repeated emphatically.

"Isn't he coming back?"

"Men come. He go with men."

Simple enough, and the end of the story as far as she was concerned. I wasn't ready to give up, however.

"What about his things?"

"What."

"Things. Clothes, belongings." Most people in Blanca can speak English because the local dialect is one of those clotted, homegrown curiosities of limited use, like Afrikaans. But this creature's English seemed marginal at best. "His possessions, his personal—his *things*, dammit."

"Gone."

"When did he go?"

"Yesterday."

"Can I see his room?"

"Room?"

"Yes. Basma's room. Please."

"Yes, yes. Come."

It took a while to get there, because the woman moved only with difficulty. She showed me into the front room on the first floor. It was a dreary little place with a couch, a couple of chairs, a table, a hideous wardrobe, and a single bed. There was a small bathroom and, behind a plastic curtain, an even smaller galley kitchen. The few items of furniture were old and worn, the walls faded and unadorned, the carpeting thin as paper. I went to the window and looked out at the park and the quiet streets. I looked at the balcony and window of my room in the hotel across the way.

"Nice view," the woman said.

I nodded absently. There was no doubt in my mind that Basma was gone for good. The room had been completely stripped of all personal items. What was there was what you got when you rented a very modest furnished room.

"Three hundred crown," the woman said.

"What?"

"Three hundred crown. One month." She waved her hand in a gesture commending the room to me. "One hundred U.S. dollar."

"No." I hurried away.

That night I slept by the balcony window in my room. I used the big armchair, and stretched my legs out on the coffee table. It was not a comfortable arrangement, but it wasn't unbearable, and I wanted to be there. It seemed important not to miss the apparition, if it should occur again.

I tried to read for a while, but I could no longer keep my mind on the words. Basma wouldn't have left so suddenly without saying good-bye, I told myself. From what the woman had said in her skeletal English, he had been taken—and that surely meant taken against his will. But by whom, and why? It seemed highly unlikely that his Lebanese enemies would come such a distance to exact revenge, and he'd been so insistent in cautioning me about the Blanca police that I couldn't imagine he'd ever set a foot wrong here. Certainly not in the realm of politics. But Basma was an entrepreneur, so it was not impossible that he'd gotten involved in some shady deal that had landed him in trouble with the authorities.

Could I help him in any way? He had been good company, a friend. He hadn't tried to con me. He'd been a useful guide to the city. It seemed wrong just to shrug it off mentally and forget about him. But I couldn't think of anything to do, other than ask the police about him—and I was reluctant to do that.

It was dawn when I awoke to the sound of car doors slamming. The first thing I saw was a silver Mercedes with black-tinted windows, parked at the corner across from my hotel. The car's yellow hazard lights were flashing. Four men wearing sunglasses and linen suits entered Basma's building. While they were inside, a van with the similarly darkened windows pulled up behind the Mercedes and waited. A moment later the four men reappeared, with a fifth man in their custody—he wasn't even handcuffed, but it was obvious he was their prisoner. I stood up, swung the window open, and stepped out onto the balcony.

"Basma."

I had spoken to myself, barely whispering the name in stunned disbelief. But the five of them stopped immediately and looked up at me. Basma looked terrified. I thought I recognized one of the other men. I was so shocked and frightened, however, that I took a step back involuntarily and stumbled. I had to grab the window frame to catch my balance. Then the scene was finished, gone as if it had never happened, and I was looking down at an empty street corner.

I sat on the bed and lit a cigarette. My hands shook, my head clamored. The smoke was like ground glass in my throat, but I sucked it in deeply, as if trying to make a point with my own pain. I'd been so many miles, seen so much of the world, the best and the worst and the endless in between, but now for the first time in my life I felt lost.

Then I became angry with myself. My feelings didn't matter in this situation. Basma was the one in trouble, and I had to try to help, or at least find out what was happening to him. For all I knew, I was the only friend he had in Blanca. I didn't want to—it scared the shit out of me to think about it—but I had to do something. And now I knew where to start.

They came into the beer garden at four o'clock that afternoon, as they had several times during the past week. The woman was beautiful as ever, cool and formidable. The kind of woman you would fear falling in love with, but love to watch. It was her man, however, who fascinated me. The man in the linen suit. Basma had warned me about them. I was pretty sure the man was the officer on horseback I had seen twice. I *knew* he was one of the men I had seen take Basma away.

Dreams, nightmares, hallucinations, ghosts. Take your pick. But maybe the simplest, truest explanation was that I was in the middle of a breakdown, caused by the collapse of my marriage and my abrupt flight to this miserable place. It made sense, and I hesitated, clinging to my own weakness. But I was there, Basma was gone, and that man in the linen suit was very real. I got up at last and approached him.

"Excuse me," I said. "I'm sorry to intrude, but I wonder if I could speak to you for a moment."

"Yes. Please."

He gestured for me to take a seat. They looked as if they had just been waiting for me to come, which made me feel even more uncomfortable.

"I've seen you around here almost every day since I arrived —I'm on vacation—and the thing is, I can't find a friend of mine. He seems to have disappeared. His name is Basma, he's Lebanese, and he was living in the corner building across the street. Do you know him?"

"I don't think so."

"Can you suggest how I might find out about him?"

"Go to the police."

They seemed to regard me with an impossible mixture of curiosity and disinterest. I was getting nowhere.

"He seemed to think you were a policeman."

At last, something. The barest flicker of an eyebrow, then the man smiled, as if at some silly misunderstanding. The woman was keenly attentive now, and it was hard not to return the all-consuming look in her eyes.

"I work in the government," the man said. "I am not a policeman. But you are a visitor here. Let me ask some people I know about your friend for you. Of course, I cannot promise you anything."

"I understand."

"Are you staying here?"

"Yes." I gave him my name and room number and told him I would be staying five more days. "Thank you for your help. I'm sorry to trouble you."

"No trouble."

Later I felt disgusted at how deferential I'd been, all but groveling for a scrap of information. The man knew Basma, knew the whole story far better than I did; he was a primary player. "Thank you for your help." But how else could I have handled it? It would have been crazy to confront the man and accuse him of arresting Basma. It would have been absurd to tell him that history replays itself every morning on that street corner, and that I'd seen what he and his colleagues had done.

So the possibilities for action on my part were extremely limited. I'd done what I could. I began to think that I should let it go, that it was just one more thing in my life to put behind me. Basma was rotting in some filthy jail cell, if he wasn't already a ghost. In any event, nothing I could do would make the least difference. I might try to write about Basma and Blanca, something political with teeth in it—but not here, not until I was safely back in New York. I'd never done anything like that before.

I slept well that night and did very little the next day. I took a couple of short walks, but mostly hung around the hotel reading and relaxing. The government man and his beautiful woman did not put in an appearance. Then I enjoyed another peaceful night, free of dreams and ghosts. It was so pleasant to idle away afternoons in the beer garden, sipping iced tea and nibbling slivers of cold melon. I was glad that the man in the linen suit failed to show up for the second day in a row.

I did think about Basma at odd moments, but in my line of work I meet so many people, all over the world. Already he was slipping away from me. And I had calmed down enough to realize I would never write that article. I wasn't equipped to do that kind of thing properly. Tourism was my beat, not politics or ghosts or disappearances. To hell with Blanca. Maybe it was a surrender of sorts, but by admitting these things to myself I felt

I was on the way to a full mental recovery, and that had been the whole purpose of the trip in the first place.

That evening I intended to find a new restaurant, have anything but steak for dinner, and then scout a few bars. I was in the mood for serious female contact at last. It was a little past seven when I stepped out of the hotel. At that instant the silver Mercedes braked sharply to a halt and the man in the linen suit jumped out. He came right at me. I was determined not to let this nasty little hood intimidate me anymore.

"Do you want to see your friend?"

"Yes. Where is he?"

"I will take you." He gestured toward the open car door. "Please. It is still light."

I was aware that the other people on the street all stood motionless, watching. Calmly, at my own pace, I walked to the car and sat down inside. I was in the backseat, between the man I knew and another fellow, who ignored me warily. I was not surprised to see the beautiful young woman in the front seat, along with the driver. She glanced at me once, then looked away. We raced through the center of the city. We were heading south, I knew that much. I asked a few questions, but the only answers I got were vague and unsatisfactory.

The driver never slowed down. If anything, he pushed the car a little faster when we reached the crowded working-class district. People and animals sometimes had to jump out of the way at the last second to save themselves. I could sense the others in the car trying not to smile. We passed the factories, the slaughterhouses, the tenements, the stockyards, the grim processing, canning, and freezing plants. We ripped through the sprawling shantytown and continued beyond the point where Basma and I had ended our exploration. Finally we were on a dirt road, crossing a vast scrubby wasteland. We had gone a couple of miles when I saw that we were approaching a cluster of vehicles parked with their headlights on, pointing in the same direction.

They walked me to the edge of a long ditch, about eight feet deep. It was dusk, not yet too dark to see, but spotlights had been hooked up to a generator to illuminate the scene.

It was all so bright it hurt my eyes. Perhaps a dozen other men stood about, smoking, talking quietly, taking notes and photographs. When my eyes adjusted, I forced myself to look carefully.

There were a lot of bodies in the ditch, I would say at least twenty. All the same: hands tied behind the back, the back of the head partially blown away, bloating features. I noticed the swarming insects, the ferocious smell. I stood there for a while, staring, but so help me I could not put together a single thought. A couple of men wearing goggles and masks were getting ready to spray the ditch with some chemical.

"Can you identify that person?" the man in the linen suit asked me, pointing to a particular corpse. "There."

"Yes, that's him." In spite of the puffed face, parts of which had already been nibbled at by animals, I had no difficulty picking out my late friend. "That's Basma."

"I am sorry," he said casually. "A terrible way to die."

As if there were any good ones.

"Why did this happen to him?" I asked. "He was a harmless little man, a foreign guest in this country. Why should they"—I almost said "you" but managed to avoid it—"do this to him?"

"Come here, please."

He led me back to the car, where the young woman waited. She looked smart as ever, this time in a tropical pantsuit with a white blouse open three buttons deep. The man nodded to her. She reached into a briefcase I hadn't noticed and handed him something. He held it up for me to see.

"Did you do this?"

I could feel the blood vacating my cheeks, then rushing back as I tried to muster a sense of embarrassed contempt. He had a large rectangle of cardboard, on which were pasted all the torn pieces of my parking ticket.

"Yes, we do that all the time back in New York. I hope it's not a felony here. I'm willing to pay the fine, whatever it is, and I'll pay it now, if you like."

"Did you refuse to pay a late fee to Bolero Rent-a-Car, and did you threaten to write negative comments about that agency in your travel articles?"

I took a deep breath, exhaled slowly. "I was about an hour late, but I explained the situation to them and they seemed to be satisfied. If they're not, then I'd be glad to pay the fee."

"May I have your passport."

I gave it to him. "Why?"

"You can get in the car now. An officer will drive you back to your hotel. Thank you for your help."

"I need my passport," I told him. "I'm flying home in three days. Sunday afternoon."

"I know," he replied. "We will contact you."

I tried to talk to the driver on the journey back into town, but he ignored me. I was furious, but frightened as well. The whole thing was a grotesque charade. They didn't need me to identify Basma, but they made me go through with it, knowing that I wouldn't have the courage to accuse them of his murder. Take a good look in that ditch, they were saying to me, this is the kind of thing we can do. They were toying with me, because it's their nature to toy with people.

What, if anything, could Basma have done to bring about his own destruction at the hands of these people? Had he been involved in some way with a radical faction in Lebanon? Did the authorities here think they were eliminating a Muslim terrorist? Was he a crook or a smuggler, a charming criminal who had escaped from Beirut only to run out of luck in Blanca? To me he seemed a pleasant, fairly idle fellow with an agreeable manner and a taste for godless liquor. But, in fairness, I hardly knew him. We had a few dinners together, a lot of drinks, that's all. It was a brief acquaintance. Our backgrounds and our circumstances were totally different. They couldn't do *that* to me.

Common sense told me I had nothing to fear. The parking ticket and the rental agency were trivial matters that could be settled with a little cash. I was an American, a travel writer for a major international magazine. They might push me around, but they wouldn't hurt me.

All the same, I decided to take certain precautions. The next morning I tried to contact the nearest American consulate, which was some four hundred miles away. At first the operator of the hotel switchboard told me that all long-distance lines out of

Oranien were engaged. After an hour of fruitless attempts she said she had learned that they were "down," and that she had no idea how long it would be before they were working again. So I went to the central post office and tried their telephones, but with the same result.

I tried to rent another car—at a different agency. I'm not sure what I intended to do with it, but I was refused one because I could not produce my passport.

I didn't bother with lunch. I drank a couple of beers and smoked a lot of cigarettes. I wandered around until I found the railroad station. I bought a ticket on the next departing train, although I wasn't even sure where it was going. Then a uniformed policeman confiscated the ticket, smiling.

"We don't want you to disappear on us, sir."

Of course. They got the parking ticket from the wastebasket in my room. They'd talked with the rental agency about me. They'd been watching and following me all the time. It was pointless to wonder why. I went back to the hotel and, as calmly as possible, I wrote a letter to my lawyer in New York, telling him where I was, that I had a problem with the authorities, and that if he hadn't heard from me—my voice on the telephone—by the time he got the letter, he was to do whatever it took to get me out of Blanca—press conferences, congressmen, the State Department, the works. I wrote more or less the same thing to my editor. I used hotel stationery and did not write my name on the envelopes. The hotel was unsafe and so were the streets, but I thought my chances were a little better outdoors. I went for a walk and slipped the letters into the mailbox on the corner as inconspicuously as possible. I crossed into the park and sat on a bench for a while, smoking. Nothing happened. I got back to my room just in time to look out the window and see a silver Mercedes pull away from the mailbox.

This is my last nigh in Blanca. Tomorrow I am supposed to be on the noon flight out of here. I still have that ticket. I do not have my passport. For two days and two nights I have waited. Nothing happens. I am waiting. There's nowhere to go, nothing to do, except smoke and drink and wait.

I think of them all the time, the handsome man in the linen suit and the beautiful young woman. Mostly I think of her, with her blouse open three buttons deep. Her breasts are not large because I saw no cleavage, but I know they are perfect. Her skin finely tanned with the faintest trace of sun-bleached down. I would like to have her, to lick her, but she is impossible to touch. You can only look at a woman like that and wonder what it would be like to fuck death.

Tonight when I ask at the desk for a wake-up call they smile and say yes, of course, and smile some more. No one writes it down. The porter says I don't look well. Would I like dinner in my room? Some company? Clean, he adds encouragingly.

It'll be over long before noon. Around four or five in the morning the silver Mercedes will arrive, the van right behind. The men in the van are there to strip the room of my possessions after I'm gone. Some morning in the future you can look out one of these windows and see how it happened, too late for me—and for you.

I hope I'm not alone, I hope there are others. Many will be arguing, begging, screaming, shitting their pants, but some will walk unaided, with quiet dignity. If I have to, that's what I want to do.

Not that it matters.

I crush out a cigarette. I open another bottle of beer, reach for another cigarette. I don't have to go to the window to see what is happening outside. There is light in the sky.

Look for me.

IAN WATSON

The Eye of the Ayatollah

IAN WATSON was born and raised on Tyneside, and after receiving a first class honours degree in English and a research degree from Oxford, he lectured on literature for several years in Tanzania and Tokyo. He currently lives with his wife and daughter in the small Northamptonshire village of Moreton Pinkney, and is an active member of CND and the Labour Party.

His novel *The Embedding* was nominated for the John W. Campbell Memorial Award in 1974 and won the Prix Apollo in its French translation the following year. Since then he has written many acclaimed book and stories in both the science fiction and horror genres. Recent titles include the novel *The Flies of Memory* and the collection *Stalin's Teardrops*, as well as a gaming novelisation for GW Books, *Inquisitor*. *The Work of Ian Watson: An Annotated Bibliography & Guide* by Douglas A. Mackey appeared earlier this year from Borgo Press.

Interzone had the courage to originally publish the following story, and despite being a work of fiction it touches upon some important recent issues that affect us all.

THREE YEARS EARLIER Ali lost his right eye and part of his face during one of the battles against Iraq. Which battle? Where? He didn't know. His cloaked, hood-clad mother had joyfully seen him off en route to paradise on the back of a fume-coughing truck packed with trainee revolutionary guards, all of about his own age, which was sixteen. Blood from Mother's finger adorned his forehead; she had cut herself deep with a kitchen knife.

What did Mother look like? Almond eyes, broad nose, big creamy cheeks, generous lips. The only time Ali ever saw more of her body was briefly when he was born, an incident which he neither understood at the time nor subsequently remembered. Her blood on his forehead was sacramental.

The truck drove all day and all night through dust— towards, latterly, the dawning thud and *crump* of heavy artillery. The recruits chanted and sang themselves hoarse and prayed for death, the door to paradise.

Arriving at a shattered moonscape masked by smoke, Ali and his companions were issued with hand grenades and sent out across a mine-field in the direction of the thunder. Ahead, a torrent of boulders could have been tumbling from the sky—as though here he stepped close to the very heartbeat of God, the compassionate, the merciful. The land-mine which blew his neighbour apart, arms and legs flying separately in the direction of heaven, tore off the side of Ali's face.

The next few weeks were nebulous for Ali. He himself existed inside a black, mute thunder-cloud occasionally riven by the red lightning of pain. Finally the crowded hospital released him, since he could walk and his mattress was needed; and hidden Mother welcomed half a martyr home. Neighbours admired Ali's scars and the remains of his empty eye socket.

Yet the war ended inconclusively.

Ali often visited the Fountain of Blood downtown to gape at the plumes of red-dyed water spurting as though from severed arteries. Part of a host half a million strong, he screamed for the death of the Satan-author, blasphemous apostate lurking in that Western devil-land.

Yet it wasn't the Satan-author who died; it was the Ayatollah, father of truth, beloved of God, the merciful, the compassionate.

Grief racked Ali, grief wrenched a million hearts, five million. Ali burrowed like a mole through the dense conglomerate of one of the hugest crowds in history, millions of pebbles of flesh cemented by the sand of rageful sorrow—through into the Beshte Zahar Cemetery. No, not so much cemented as surging, *churning* like the ballast and cement and liquid in some giant, horizontal concrete-mixer. Fainting, shrieking, reaching, clawing, crazed with bitter woe: a million locusts, and only one leaf to feed at—the coffin, soon to arrive. He fought his way into the inner square built of freight containers. Thousands of mourners were beating their heads with their fists in unison. Mystics were harvesting bowls of earth from the bottom of the grave, and passing these out—the crowd ate the precious soil.

A helicopter landed. Moments later, a tumult of young men hauled the shrouded body from its coffin. Hands tore the shroud to pieces, each scrap a precious relic. "Ya Ali, Ya Hussein," cried ten thousand voices. The thin white legs of the holy man jutted aloft like bare sticks, as his corpse slumped.

Ali, clawing, was in the forefront but his defective vision foxed him. As he fought his way to the rear through the tide of bodies he puzzled at what his right hand clutched, something resembling a slippery ping-pong ball. Panting, he paused long enough to glance. His palm cupped a glazed, naked eye. With a tail of optic nerve: a kind of plump, ocular tadpole.

Had a miracle happened? Had a piece of the shroud transmuted itself into Ali's own lost eye, now restored to him? Was he not himself named in honour of the martyr Ali, who founded the true school of Islam?

At last his brain caught up with what his fingers and their nails had done: he, Ali the half-faced, had torn out one of the Ayatollah's eyes.

Behind him, shots rang out. The helicopter landed once more . . .

Later, Ali heard how the corpse eventually entered its hole in the ground, to be covered by flagstones heaved hand over hand, and how a dozen of the cargo containers were piled across the grave. No one would or could say what state the body had been in finally.

The eye sat on a shelf by Ali's bed, staring unblinkingly at him. (For, lacking eyelids, how could an eye blink?) Its gaze appeared to track him about the little room, the pupil stretching into a squint to follow him.

Ali prayed. He thought about preservatives. He wondered what best to do. How could he possibly plunge that holy eye into alcohol even of the medicinal variety? So he visited a pharmacy to ask advice about—so he said—pickling a dead frog; he returned with a jar of formalin. Once afloat in that solution of formaldehyde, the eyeball definitely swung from side to side keeping an eye on him.

On him, on mere Ali the half-face? Oh no. Simply alert, awaiting, on the look-out. Ali prayed. Ali dreamed. A vision visited him. The holy man had been a hawk. What was that hawk's eye hunting for? Why, it was surveying all of the Earth, searching for the hiding place of the Satan-author.

Events deployed as the will of God decreed. Truly dreams were troubled in Tehran during those days. Angels guided Ali to the office of Dr Omar Hafiz, doyen of the country's ballistic missile programme, who for his part had dreamt originally—

—of exploding a nuclear weapon on Tel Aviv to free the Palestinians. Those high-explosive birds aimed at Baghdad were a side-show. Alas, lack of a warhead derailed the project. So next, Dr Hafiz dreamed of a reconnaissance satellite to spy on Iraqi army positions; but peace had been declared. Lately Hafiz dreamt of using the prototype rocket to put a communications satellite into orbit to criss-cross the whole face of the Earth: the *Voice of God*, broadcasting the truth . . .

An angel had also visited Dr Hafiz.

"We *can* fly your hawk," he assured Ali. "The cold of space will preserve the eye from corruption. It will look down on Europe, America, Africa. That Satan-author may have hidden anywhere. He may have bought plastic surgery. The eye will find him. With its miraculous perception it will recognize him.

He is what it seeks; for fifty years, if need be."

"And I, the half-face," said Ali, "need to be on hand when our hawk finds its prey, do I not? For the eye was given into my hand, was it not?"

Events unfolded like a fragrant rose from a bud. Surgeons renovated Ali's face, rebuilt his orbital bone, gave him a glass eye. Tutors nurtured his smattering of English and French into something resembling fluency. Commandos offered him the sort of weapons training he'd sorely lacked when he rode to war. His forged passport identified him as a naturalized Australian.

Soon his country launched its first Earth satellite named the *Eye of the Ayatollah*, and announced to the world (as well as to the Satan-author, wherever he was) that the orbiting instrument package did indeed contain exactly that. Benighted infidels outside the harbour of Islam laughed—uneasily. Corrupted souls within the harbour of Islam glanced askance at the night sky.

No one beyond the inner hierarchy knew the whole truth about Ali. Whenever Ali shut his left eye, he looked down through his artificial eye upon the countries of the Earth from space. For his glass eye was more than a bauble. Through it, miraculously, the youth could see whatever the holy man's searching eye could see through the zoom-lenses of the satelite; as had been promised in the vision confided to Dr Hafiz . . .

In the cold void above the topmost air, the *Eye of the Ayatollah* orbited for a year, two years, five years . . . Disguised as a dinkum Aussie immigrant on holiday, Ali wandered the world as frugally as he could, financed by an American Express gold card. Universally acceptable; he still regretted the expedient.

The orbiting eye seemed to twitch as it was passing over Pakistan, and there went Ali; a solar flare must have been responsible. Again, over Nicaragua, it spasmed; thus Ali went to that strife-torn land. Perhaps a cosmic ray had hit the eye.

He found himself in Sweden, in Ireland, in America, England, France. Always keeping watch. From his hiding place the Satan-author published another book, redoubling Ali's fervour.

Seven years passed. The eye watched. Ali watched.

At long last the eye throbbed. It was gazing down upon an island off the south-west coast of Scotland; upon a tiny isle that nestled against a bay of its parent island like a new-born baby whale beside its leviathan of a mother. The eye passed over, but not before imprinting Ali vividly.

He flew to London, collected a gun and grenades from a certain embassy, and caught a train to Glasgow.

He would need to wait there for some weeks till the satellite would be poised to pass over the same part of Scotland again. Buying maps and guides, he soon learned that the name of the mother island was Arran, and of the islet: Holy Island, a title which set his teeth on edge.

As the time approached, Ali took a bus to the coast then a ferry to Arran. Renting a modest car, he reconnoitred this pinnacled island of granite bens and fells, glens of bracken and frisky streams rushing amidst great boulders, mounds of moraine, dark conifers, and wild red deer—suddenly giving way in the south to rolling heathery hills, calm pastures, sandy beaches with a few palm trees.

Ali checked in to a hotel in the small sea-side town of Lamlash opposite Holy Island. He had brought a hammer, and was pretending to be an enthusiastic amateur geologist. Binoculars too; he was an eager bird-watcher.

How that islet dominated the shore. Its two-mile stretch of jagged cliffs and rugged moorland sheltered wild goats, long-legged diminutive Soay sheep, shaggy Highland cattle; and birds, birds. Holy Island was a nature reserve, a field study centre. From its southernmost tip a lighthouse beaconed across the Firth of Clyde.

Unholy island, thought Ali.

Apparently a Christian saint called Molaise lived on the isle in the time of the prophet Mohammed, bless his name. The saint's cell could still be visited; Vikings had defaced it with runic inscriptions. The Satan-author also skulked in a kind of cell. Did he think he could walk free in safety upon those moors amongst the goats? The bars of his cell were the eye-beams of an authentic holy man, whose organ of vision lived on.

But first the instrument package enshrining that organ of vision must re-enter the atmosphere and parachute down to Earth; for such had been Dr Hafiz's design. Thus the hawk would pounce.

Studying his maps, Ali chose a glen leading to a ben. He telephoned a cover number in Australia, to alert Tehran. Next evening, the important part of the *Eye of the Ayatollah* descended and soft-landed in the bonnie upland heather.

The following morning, Ali took the ferry over to Holy Island in company with half a dozen ornithologists. The sea was choppy, the breeze was brisk, so spindrift soon coated the lens-studded box that held the eye, which Ali wore around his neck like some gold-plated camera. Already that camera-that-wasn't had attracted a few curious glances. Was Ali some aviphile oil sheikh travelling incognito who couldn't forsake at least one token of ostentation?

"Ah," he told himself, "I'm but the humblest servant."

Fortunately the crossing did not coincide with a time for prayer; however he found that his vision was fogging. Ducking down out of sight behind some cargo, he opened the golden box and cradled the holy eyeball naked in his palm once more. The soft ball seemed to burn icily as though still frozen. Inspired, the Half-Face popped his glass prosthetic from its rebuilt orbit and replaced it with the Ayatollah's own.

His vision swam. He saw two scenes at once: the hellishly gaunt, approaching cliffs licked by sea-spume, and what he could only interpret as a glimpse of paradise, the slope of a verdant valley where fountains of milk gushed, spilling down in streams, where all manner of jewels glittered—a landscape girt with a dance of scintillating pastel auroras like diaphanous rose-and-pink veils of maidens, though minus the maidens. Ahead was a curiously imprecise promise of ecstasies without substance, as if he was seeing this terrain in some warmer Eden of the past, courtesy of an angel.

Some such subconscious, submerged vista must always have lurked in his inner gaze, as a cynosure, a focus. In this mystical moment he appeared to remember the lost object of all his buried desires. The whole island swelled with the light of joyful creation, the conjuring of mischievous beauty. Honey flowed like lava from one hilltop.

He shut the eye that was his own; and through that other, holy eye he saw only the sternness of cliffs again, their stark authenticity. Gulls screamed battle-cries. The sun was an ulcer of yellow pus, its after-image a ball of blood. The impact of waves faintly echoed that torrent of boulders he had heard on a previous occasion at the battlefront.

"Why, Satan-author," Ali said to himself in surprise, "you are in hell already."

When he closed his holy right eye to regard the scenery with his left eye, heavenly auras sparkled again, interference patterns between two modes of vision, awakening deeply hidden memories of a time when he had perceived the world freshly with wonder, long ago; of a time when he had been born and had to create a universe around himself.

"In hell indeed," he added, "unless your eyes see otherwise."

After he left the ferry to mount the island, he hiked with either his right eye open or his left, the holy eye mapping out barren geometries of rock and sky and grass, the other eye teasing the tastebuds of his soul with that shimmer of scanty pastel veils behind which raw beauty beckoned.

He stepped out, he halted, he stepped out. The holy eye led him along a stony track towards what had once been a crofter's cottage and was now a sprawling homestead with mirror-glass windows surrounded by a high wire fence, supposedly to deter goats. The only guards these days were gulls.

The Satan-author sat at a desk. Haggard, yes. A nervous twitch in one eye; almost totally bald. Yet as he looked at this intruder who pointed a pistol as though out of habit, the author smiled.

"So it has come at last."

That damnable smile, of sanity still sustained!

Ali shut his holy eye. Seen through his left eye, a nimbus surrounded the author's head. Ali reverted to his right eye, tightening his grip on the gun as he scanned the despicable face. A moment later he looked with his left eye too, and his vision swam again dizzyingly, so he closed the left eye.

"You look like a human traffic light," remarked the author as though choosing wry last words for posterity, fit for some future dictionary of quotations.

Ali's holy attention was caught by a paper-knife used to open the author's voluminous, redirected correspondence, all his envelopes full of cheques paying him lavishly for his blasphemy in the currencies of Satan: dollars, pounds, francs, marks.

Now Ali's left eye also noted the knife with the sharp point. A roseate halo stained the blade with diluted blood. The handle was iridescent mother-of-pearl. Ali remembered the battle against Iraq and suddenly felt cheated. Strange desire surged within him.

"Which," he asked, as if this was a riddle, "which is my real eye? My true eye?"

Perhaps amazed at the idiosyncrasy of human nature, the author stared at this man who opened one eye then the other turn by turn, squinting at him. Was he really being offered a choice as though in a fairy tale? A choice between life and death—or only a choice between types of death?

He hesitated, then spoke at random. "The left eye."

"An angel guides your words." Ali snatched up the knife, opened both eyes at once, and pointed the steel tip at the holy one.

The author tensed, imagining that he had chosen wrongly —perhaps could never have chosen correctly!—but Ali skewered the eye of the Ayatollah, drew it forth dripping humours, and stabbed the knife and its jelly burden down upon the desk.

"This," said Ali, "is the eye that sees hell."

A weight of years-long possession drained away from Ali's heart; and for the first time since he could recall, his own left eye leaked tears.

KARL EDWARD WAGNER

At First Just Ghostly

KARL EDWARD WAGNER was born in Knoxville, Tennessee, and trained as a psychiatrist before becoming a British and World Fantasy Award-winning writer and editor. His first novel, *Darkness Weaves With Many Shades*, introduced Kane in the first of an unusually intelligent and brutal heroic fantasy series that continued with *Death Angel's Shadow*, *Bloodstone*, *Dark Crusade* and the collections *Night Winds* and *The Book of Kane*.

He expanded the exploits of two of Robert E. Howard's characters, Conan and Bran Mak Morn respectively, in the novels *The Road of Kings* and *Legion from the Shadows*, while his superior horror stories have been collected in *In A Lonely Place*, *Why Not You and I?* and *Unthreatened by the Morning Light*. He has edited eleven volumes of *The Year's Best Horror Stories* (currently being hardcovered as *Horrorstory*), three *Echoes of Valor* anthologies and the recent *Intensive Scare*.

Wagner is a regular visitor to London, and "At First But Ghostly" reflects his enthusiasm for that ancient city, its arcane mysteries, and the popular '60s television series *The Avengers*. It is also part of a novel he has been working on for the past few years.

I. Beginning Our Descent

H IS NAME WAS Cody Lennox, and he was coming back to England to die, or maybe just to forget, and after all it's about the same in the long run.

He had been dozing for the last hour or so, when the British Airways stewardess politely offered him an immigration card to be filled in. He placed it upon the tray table beside the unfinished game of solitaire and the finished glass of Scotch, which he must now remember to call whisky when asking at the bar, and this was one of the few things he was unlikely to forget.

Lennox tapped his glass. "Time for another?"

"Certainly, sir." The stewardess was blonde and compactly pretty and carefully spoke BBC English with only a trace of a Lancashire accent. Her training had also taught her not to look askance at first class passengers who declined breakfast in favor of another large whisky.

Lennox's fellow passenger in the aisle seat favored him with a bifocaled frown and returned to his book of crossword puzzles. Lennox had fantasied him to be an accountant for some particularly corrupt television evangelist, doubtlessly on an urgent mission to Switzerland. They had not spoken since the first hour of the flight, when after pre-flight champagne and three subsequent large whiskies Lennox had admitted to being a writer.

Fellow passenger (scathingly): "Oh, well then—name something you've written."

Lennox (in apparent good humor): "You go first. Name something you've read."

In the ensuing frostiness Lennox played countless hands of solitaire with the deck the stewardess had provided and downed almost as many large whiskies, which she also dutifully provided. He considered a visit to the overhead lounge, but a trip to the lavatory convinced him that his legs weren't to be trusted on the stairs. So he played solitaire, patiently, undeterred by total lack of success, losing despite the nagging temptation to cheat. Lennox had once been told by a friend in a moment of drunken insight that a Total Loser was someone who cheated

313

at solitaire and still lost, and Lennox didn't care to take that chance.

Eventually he fell asleep.

Cody Lennox liked to fly first class. He stood a rangy six-foot-four, and while he still combed his hair to look like James Dean, his joints were the other side of forty and rebelled at being folded into a 747's tourist-class orange crates. He was wont to say that the edible food and free booze were more than worth the additional expense on a seven-hour flight, and his preventive remedy for tedium and for jet-lag was to drink himself into a blissful stupor and sleep throughout the flight. Once he and Cathy had flown over on the Concorde, and for that cherished memory he would never do so again.

He still hadn't got used to traveling alone, and he supposed he never would.

He looked through the window and into darkness fading to grey. As they chased the dawn, clouds began to appear and break apart; below them monotonous expanses of grey sea gave way to glimpses of distant green land. Coming in over Ireland, he supposed, and finished his drink.

He felt steadier now, and he filled out the immigration card, wincing, as he knew he would, over the inquiry as to marital status, etc. He placed the card inside his passport, avoiding looking at his photograph there. There was time for another hand, so he collected and reshuffled his cards.

"We are beginning our descent into London Heathrow," someone was announcing. Lennox had nodded off. "Please make certain your seatbelts are fastened, your seat backs are in the upright position, your tray tables are . . ."

"The passengers will please refrain," prompted Lennox, scooping up the cards and locking back his tray. "Batten the hatches, you swabs. Prepare to abandon ship."

"Do you want to know why you never won?"

"Eh?" said Lennox, startled by his seatmate's first attempt at conversation since the Jersey shore.

The mysterious accountant pointed an incisive finger toward the cabin floor. "You haven't been playing with a full deck."

The Queen of Spades peeked out from beneath the accountant's tight black shoes.

"The opportunity to deliver a line such as that comes only once in a life-time," Lennox said with admiration. He reached down to recover the truant card, but the impact of landing skidded it away.

Probably the really and truly best thing about flying first class across the Atlantic was that you were first off the plane and first to get through immigration and customs. Lennox had a morbid dread of being engulfed by gabbling hordes of blue-haired widows from New Jersey or milling throngs of students hunchbacked by garish knapsacks and sleeping bags. "Americans never queue up," he once observed to an icily patient gentleman, similarly overrun while waiting for a teller at a London bank. "They just mill about and make confused sounds."

"The purpose of your stay here, sir?" asked the immigrations officer, flipping through Lennox's passport.

"Primarily I'm on holiday," said Lennox. "Although for tax purposes I'll be mixing in a little business, as I'm also here to attend the World Science Fiction Convention in Brighton some days from now."

The officer was automatically stamping his passport. "So then, you're a writer, are you, sir?" His eyes abruptly focused through the boredom of routine, and he flipped back to the passport photo.

"Cody Lennox!" He compared photo and face in disbelief. "Lord, and I've just finished reading *They Do Not Die!*"

"Small world," said Cody imaginatively. "Will you still let me in?"

"First celebrity I've had here." The immigrations officer returned his passport. "Your books have given me and the wife some fair shivers. Working on a new one, are you?"

"Might write one while I'm here."

"I'll want to read it, then."

Lennox passed through to baggage claim and found his two scruffy suitcases. They were half-empty, as he preferred to buy whatever he needed when he needed it, and he hated to pack.

He also hated carry-on luggage, people who carried on carry-on luggage, and cameras of all sorts. Such eccentricities frequently excited some speculation as to his nationality.

Cody Lennox was, however, American: born in Los Angeles of a Scandinavian bit-player and a father who worked in pictures before skipping to Mexico; educated across the States with two never-to-be-completed doctorates scattered along the way, and now living in New York City. He had had eight best-selling horror novels over the last five years, in addition to some other books that had paid the bills early on. His novels weren't all that long on the best-seller lists, but they were there, nonetheless, and film rights and script work all added up to an enviable bundle. He had been on *Johnny Carson* twice, but he had never hosted *Saturday Night Live*. His books could be found at supermarket check-out counters between the tabloids and the *TV Guides*, but only for a month or so. It was a living. Once he had been happy with his life.

Cody Lennox hauled his pair of cases through the green lane at Heathrow customs. He had made this trip a dozen times or more, and he had never been stopped. Sometimes he considered becoming a smuggler. Probably he looked too non-innocent for the customs officers to bother examining his luggage.

He looked a little like an on-the-skids rock star with his designer jeans and t-shirt and wrinkled linen jacket. He still had the face of a young James Dean, but his ash-blond hair was so pale as to seem dead-white. His left ear was pierced, but he seldom bothered to wear anything there, and his week-old smear of a beard was fashionable but too light to be noticed. He wore blue-lensed glasses over his pale blue eyes, but this was more of necessity than style: Lennox was virtually blinded by bright sunlight.

Lennox adjusted his scarred watch to London time while he waited to cash a traveler's check at the bank outside the customs exit. He saw no sign of his seatmate, and for this he was grateful. Bastard might have told him about the missing card.

The Piccadilly Line ran from Heathrow to where Lennox meant to go, but he was in no mood for the early morning crush on the tube. Still feeling the buzz of a long flight and too

316

many drinks, he joined the queue for a taxi—nudging his cases along with his foot, as he endured confused American tourists and aggressive Germans who simply shoved to the front of it all.

Lennox was very tired and somewhere on the verge of a hangover, when the next black Austin stopped for him. He tossed his cases into the missing left-side front seat and pulled himself into the back. After the 747 the back seat was spacious, and he stretched out his long legs.

He said: "The Bloomsbury Park Hotel. Small place on Southampton Row. Just off Russell Square."

"I know it, guv," said the driver. "Changed the name again, have they?"

"Right. Used to be the Grand. God only knows what it was before that."

II. Lost Without a Crowd

IT WAS NOT much after nine when the cab made a neat U-turn across Southampton Row and landed Lennox and his cases at the door of his hotel. In addition to changing its name, the Bloomsbury Park Hotel had changed management half a dozen times in the dozen or so years that Lennox had been stopping there, but the head porter had been there probably since before the Blitz, and he greeted Lennox with a warm smile.

"Good to see you again, sir."

"Good to be back, Mr. Edwards."

It had been about a year since his last stay here, and Edwards remembered not to inquire about his wife.

The newest management had redone the foyer again; this time in trendy Art Deco, which fitted as well with the original Art Nouveau décor as did the kilt on the golden-ager tourist who was complaining his way across the lobby in tow of his wife.

Jack Martin was at the reception desk, scribbling away at a piece of hotel stationery.

"Hello, Jack."

"Cody! I don't believe it! I was just writing you a note telling you where I was staying."

"Synchronicity, good buddy. When'd you get here?"

"Flew in Sunday from L.A. Still coping with jet-lag, but I walked over here to see whether you'd checked in yet. Had breakfast? Guess they fed you on the flight. How was it?"

"OK. Anything you can walk away from is OK. Here, better let me register."

Lennox filled in forms while Martin worked on a cigarette. No, his room wasn't ready yet, but Lennox had expected that, and the porters would see to his cases in the meantime.

The girl at the desk was auburnhaired, Irish, and half Lennox's age, and he wondered if she'd been here last time. Probably so, or else she was instinctively cheeky.

"You're very popular, sir. Two calls for you already."

"More likely ten, judging by my usual luck with hotel switchboards." Lennox studied the messages. "Mike Carson says to give him a ring and I owe him a pint. And the other one—from a Mr. Kane?"

"He said he'd be getting in touch."

"Never heard of him. Social secretary from Buckingham Palace, isn't he? Come on, Jack. Let's go get something to drink."

"Pubs won't open until eleven," Martin pointed out.

"Let me show you my private club."

There was a minimart just down Southampton Row from the hotel, and Lennox bought Martin a carton of orange juice and two cans of lager for himself. Cosmo Place was the alleyway that connected onto Queen Square, where there were vacant benches beneath the trees. Lennox was just able to keep his hands from shaking as he popped his first lager.

Martin was trying to solve the juice carton. "So, Cody. How are things going?"

It was more than a casual question and Lennox hated the glance of watchful concern that accompanied it, but he had grown accustomed to it all and it no longer hurt so bitterly.

"Can't complain, Jack. *They Do Not Die!* is still hanging high on the lists, and Mack says the sharks are in a feeding frenzy to bid on my next one."

"How's that been coming along?"

Lennox killed his lager, stretched out with a sigh, and thoughtfully opened the second can. He said: "Cathy and I used to come here and sit. Place close by on Theobald's Road sells some of the best fish and chips I've ever had. Used to carry them back, sit and eat here, and then we'd walk back to The Sun and wash it all down with pints of gut-wrenching ales."

He closed his eyes and took a long pull of lager, remembering. When he opened his eyes he saw the worn benches stained with pigeon droppings, the dustbins overstuffed with cider bottles, the litter of empty beercans and crisps packets. The square smelled of urine and unwashed bodies; the derelicts slept all about here at night.

"Let it go, Cody."

"Can't. Nothing left to hang onto but memories."

"But you're just killing yourself."

"I'm already dead."

The church steeple tolled ten. Lennox had always suspected that its bells were an array of old iron pots. A deaf gnome banged on them with a soup ladle. The steeple was a ponderous embarrassment that clashed with what remained of the simple Queen Anne architecture.

"The Church of St. George the Martyr," Lennox said. "Loads of history here. See that steeple? Hawksmoor had a hand in it."

"Who's Hawksmoor?"

"The hero of a famous fairyland fantasy trilogy. Did you know, for example, that the church crypts here are connected by a tunnel beneath Cosmo Place to the cellars of that pub on the corner—The Queen's Larder?"

"Didn't know you read guidebooks."

"Don't. Old pensioner Cathy and I used to drink with there told us. Name was Dennis, and he always drank purple velvets—that's stout mixed with port. Haven't seen him since then."

"With that to drink, I'm not surprised." Martin tossed his juice carton into a bin. "So why St. George the Martyr? I always thought old George slew that dragon. Must have been another George somewhere."

"Or another dragon," said Lennox. "Let's just see if my room is ready by now."

His room was ready. Lennox poured himself a glass of Scotch from the coals-to-Newcastle bottle in his suitcase, then phoned Mike Carson. Carson said he'd meet them at The Swan soon after eleven, and he did.

Lennox was at the bar buying the first round. The day was turning warm and bright after last night's rain, and they had seats at an outside table on Cosmo Place.

"You ever notice," observed Carson, "how Cody always seems to bring good weather when he's over?"

"No, I hadn't," said Martin. "Just must be luck."

Carson offered a cigarette, and they both lit up. "Cody once said to me," he said, inhaling, "that the English carry umbrellas because they expect it to rain. Cody says he never does, because he expects the day to be clear."

"First optimistic thing I've ever heard about that Cody said."

"It's not optimism," Carson explained. "It's bloody arrogance."

Martin turned to peer into the pub. Lennox was still waiting to be served. Martin said: "God knows it can't be good luck. Not with Cody."

"So, then. How is he?"

"God knows. Not taking it well. I'm worried."

Jack Martin was short for his generation, neatly groomed with a frost of grey starting in his carefully trimmed beard, and there was a hint of middle-age spread beneath his raw silk sports jacket. He had known Lennox from when they were both determined young writers in Los Angeles, before Lennox had connected and split for New York; and while his own several books in no way competed with Lennox's sales figures, he had scripted at least three successful horror films (one from an early Lennox novel), and he had a devoted following among discriminating readers of the genre. Martin's ambition was to become an emerging mainstream writer. He had known Lennox as a friend since high school days.

Mike Carson was taller than Martin, shorter than Lennox, and spare of frame, with short black hair and a brooding face. He wore a long overcoat, loose shirt and baggy trousers, and stopped just short of punk. He looked like an unbalanced and consumptive artist who was slowly starving in a garret; in fact he was Irish and scraping out a fair living between moderately frequent assignments and his wife's steady job. Carson had done the British paperback covers for the last five of Lennox's novels, and, although Lennox had never said so, Carson knew that Lennox had insisted that his choice of artist be included in his contracts. Carson had known Lennox since the first time Cody and Cathy had visited London—when West End pints cost 30p, and Carson had made the mistake of trying to drink him under the table.

"Two bitters, and here's your lager, Jack," said Lennox, sloshing their pints on the pebble-grained aluminum table. "Christ, I hate these straight-sided glasses. They look like oversized Coca-Cola glasses."

"Cheers."

"Oh, thanks, Cody."

They drank.

"Well," said Lennox, halfway through his bitter at a gulp. "So who else is over here?"

"Haven't seen very many stray American writers," Martin told him. "Still a bit early, I guess. Geoffrey Marsh is here—staying over at the Wansbeck. Saw Sanford Vade coming out of an off-license with two jail-baits and a bottle of Beam's Choice. Oh, and I did run into Kent Allard in the lobby this morning. He asked if you were coming over."

"He would." Lennox finished his pint. "You said you were staying at the Russell?"

"That's right."

"I'll get these." Carson downed his pint.

"I'm still OK." Martin sipped at his lager.

Lennox belched. "Crazy town where you have to do your

drinking between eleven and three—and then try to find a loo. At least this time next year they'll have twelve-hour opening."

"Why don't you come down to Mexico with me sometime?" Martin suggested. "We could stay a week for what a day here costs. I know some great places."

"My destiny lies here."

"Bullshit. You can get just as drunk in Mexico for a lot less money."

"Money means nothing to me."

"Bullshit."

"Besides, in Mexico I might run into my father."

Carson crashed down three pints. Martin had started to raise a hand in protest. The aluminum table tipped. Martin's fresh pint of lager rocked and tilted. Lennox reached across his own pint glass to catch Martin's. His heavy wristwatch band shattered the top off of the straight-sided glass. Lennox caught Martin's pint and set it safely upright.

"Reflexes," said Lennox proudly.

"You're bleeding," said Martin.

"No, I'm not."

Carson pointed. "Then where's all this blood coming from?"

Lennox examined his wrist, then pulled out the splinter of glass. "Shit. I've ruined my pint."

It was a minor cut, but it bled stubbornly. Martin gave him a crumpled tissue to use until Carson returned with several paper serviettes and another pint of bitter.

"Don't drink the other," Carson advised. "It's all full of glass and blood."

"I'll hide the evidence," said Lennox, dabbing at his cut wrist. He carried his broken glass to the sewer grating between The Swan and The Queen's Larder. As he bent to pour out the blood-tinged mess, he noticed a playing card balanced against the grating. It was the Queen of Spades.

Lennox reached down for it clumsily, but a splash of his blood was faster and struck the edge of the card, flipping it into the darkness below.

III. Wicked Malt

"I UNDERSTAND YOU just slashed your wrist."

"Hello, Kent," said Lennox without enthusiasm. "Nice to see you again. Been over here long?"

Kent Allard had joined their table while Lennox was disposing of his shattered glass. Kent looked like any well-to-do Hollywood hustler—permanently tanned and forever 35. He wrote about writers, made books about books, and had ghosted half the celebrity kiss-and-tell autobiographies of the past decade. Lennox had heard that Allard was somehow related to one of the Great Departed. Martin liked Allard and called him a demonic genius in wolf's clothing; Lennox saw in Allard most of the reasons why he had fled from Los Angeles.

"What a coincidence," said Lennox, reaching for his fresh pint.

"Slashing your wrist?"

"No. Running into you here."

"It's all because of the Harmonic Convergence," said Allard. "Synchronicity is in the air. Besides, I'm staying down the block at the Russell, and Jack said you might be meeting here for lunch. So, how are things going for you, Cody?"

"Keeping busy. What's the Harmonic Convergence?"

"You mean you missed it? August 16–17? Scant hours ago."

"I was in transit. Just got in scant hours ago."

"Didn't really miss anything. Now, what about lunch?"

"I'm on jet-lag," Lennox begged off. "Think I'll just mellow out with a few more of these and hit the sack."

"I ate just before coming over," Carson lied.

"You and me then, Jack," said Allard. "I'm in a mood for Italian. Anyone know a good place?"

Martin pointed. "One right here's a good one."

They left, and Lennox said to Carson: "Let's get out of here."

Lennox kept dabbing at his wrist, but it had long since quit bleeding. He and Carson ended up at the Nellie Dean in Soho, for no particular reason. Inside it was crowded, loud, smoky and hot, so they leaned against the wall outside and drained many pints. Lennox had twice already bashed his head on the rafters going downstairs to the gents'.

"English pubs have a distinct aura," said Lennox.

"What's that?"

"A smell of strong tobacco, spilled bitter, stale clothing, sweat and breath."

"That's aroma you meant."

"Very possibly." Lennox glanced at his watch, saw no blood, decided they had less than half an hour to drink. "Have you noticed that all the women are dressed in black?"

"It's the fashion," Carson explained.

"Black everything. Neck to their shoes. Everything very tight. And those wide belts to cinch their waistline. Do you know what it all signifies?"

"My round," said Carson.

"It's the return of *fin de siècle* decadence. This is 1987, the dawn of a new *fin de siècle*. A new age of decadence. All of it kicked off by the Harmonic Emergence."

Carson remembered that Martin had asked him to look after Lennox. He bought another round.

"Some wicked malt," Carson nodded.

She was dressed in a black leather mini and might have been 17. They solemnly watched her parade by on her stiletto heels.

"Christ, I'm horny." Lennox downed his pint. "And I need to piss. And I need some sleep."

"It's your round," prompted Carson.

And soon it was three o'clock closing time.

The walk back to the hotel was a staggering muddle of crowded side-walks and near-misses when crossing streets. Carson served as a guide of sorts.

"Here, have you seen these?"

They were leaning against a telephone kiosk, catching their breath and getting their bearings.

"Seen what?"

"These here."

The inside of the booth was papered with a dozen handprinted stickers, all offering sexual services and a phone number to call:

... PUNISHMENT FOR WENDY—NAUGHTY SCHOOL-GIRL & UNIFORMS ... LET'S GET ON YOUR KNEES, BOY ... TIE & TEASE TV RUBBER ... WANT SAFE SEX? GET BREAST RELIEF ... PUNK BOYS AGAINST THE WALL ... NAUGHTY BOYS GET BOTTOM MARKS ...

"Here." Carson abruptly began peeling off stickers, handing them to Lennox. "In case you get lonely."

Lennox dutifully stuck the torn patches into his notebook. "I don't think I'm really into caning punk boys until they cry and all that. I'm just horny. Do any of them say anything about just that? I mean, just screwing?"

"You said you were decadent."

"Well, not that way. What happens when you call one of these numbers? Do the cops come around?"

"Don't know. Never tried. But I know this geezer who did. Woman comes up to his hotel room, and there's a big bloke lurking back down the corridor to make sure there's no trouble for her."

"What happened?"

"She let the ponce in, he bashed the geezer, and they took his wallet and watch."

"Did he have to pay extra for all that?"

It was about four by the time they managed to get back to his hotel. Lennox was feeling the double effects of jet-lag and too much booze on an empty stomach. Carson dutifully saw him to his room, had a glass of whisky with him, then left Lennox with the advice that he have a lie-down. Lennox did.

He slept soundly, which was rare for him these days, and it was past ten when he awoke. Lennox sensed the familiar throb of an incipient hangover, so he washed his face, changed shirt and jacket, and headed for the residents' bar.

He was briefly confused, as the new management had moved the residents' bar into the former restaurant on the ground floor. In the course of remodeling the foyer, they had evidently inserted some striking stained-glass panels beside the steps leading to the downstairs bar. Some sort of heraldic designs, Lennox noted in passing, one of them a little garish.

Lennox decided on a large whisky, then chased it with three aspirin and a pint of lager. The lager settled in nicely, and he had another—drinking it slowly as his hangover receded. He began to feel almost alive once again, and with his third pint he was chatting up the willowy blonde barmaid. She was patient, if not receptive. The bar was nearly empty, and Lennox might have pressed onward, were it not for the table of blue-haired widows who were discussing the quaintness of the British in voices that probably carried all the way back to New Jersey.

Lennox finished his fourth pint and gave up. He stopped by the front desk on the way to his room. There were two messages: one from his British agent and one from a Mr. Kane. Both said they would ring back.

Lennox was just able to manage the plastic card that unlocked his door. Supposedly this improvement over the old metal keys made his room secure from hotel thieves. Lennox wished said thieves the possession of his dirty socks.

He poured himself a generous shot of Scotch and slumped into a chair. The nightcap had no apparent effect, so he tried another. The long nap had left him restless, and it was still early bedtime in New York. Digging out his pocket notebook, Lennox decided to tally the day's expenses. Must keep the IRS happy.

And there he found the peeled-off stickers from the phone booths. Lennox had almost forgotten the incident, and he chuckled as he re-read them:

"MISS NIPPLES"

"SLAP HAPPY BITCH"

"FUN AND GAMES"

It might be fun to phone one of them, just to hear what they'd say.

Lennox studied his collection. Most of the stickers had torn when Carson pulled them off, and Lennox had stuck them all in a jumble onto the pages. No, he didn't want to talk to the enema specialist. Lennox closed his eyes, stabbed a finger onto the notebook. There was a phone number under his finger, but nothing more; the sticker had torn in half in coming away, and all Lennox had left was a badly smudged phone number.

Better that way. Strictly random. Besides, he had no intention of telling Ms. Switch or whoever where he was staying. Was that a 2 or a 7?

Lennox had a third drink and just was able to sort out the buttons on the phone. He was still chuckling while it rang.

Three rings, and someone picked up the receiver.

"Howdy there!" Lennox answered the silence. "My name's Bubba Joe McBob, and I'm here from Texas, and I sure could use a little action. What you all got for me, honey?"

"Do you wish me to come to you?" The voice was coldly formal, but at least it was a woman's voice.

"You bet I do, sugar britches."

"As you wish, Cody Lennox."

Lennox stared stupidly at the phone. There was only an empty buzzing from the receiver. He started to dial again, then began to laugh.

"That barmaid," he chuckled, hanging up. "She's watching switchboard, now that the bar's closed down. Cut into my call."

He struggled out of his shoes and considered trying another call. Was that barmaid going to come up to his room after work? She just might. She'd taken the trouble to remember his name. Why miss a chance to sleep with a famous author?

That last drink had made him sleepy. Lennox turned off most of the lights and stretched out on his bed to await the hot-to-trot blonde barmaid. Almost immediately he began to snore.

Lennox was certain he was awake when his door opened and the woman entered his room.

Passkey, he thought, raising himself on his elbows.

It wasn't the barmaid.

"Well, hello now," he said, thinking, *so much for plastic keys and burglar-proof locks*.

She stared at him as if he were part of the furnishings—her eyes slowly taking stock of the room. She was dressed entirely in black, and he could barely see her pale face beneath her low cap. If her eyes hadn't so dominated, he might have seen her face.

Lennox cleared his throat, wondering how to handle the situation. Was she just a hotel thief, or did these call services have some sort of high-tech tracing device? The hotel management wouldn't be amused if he phoned down for them to evict the call girl he'd summoned. Besides . . .

"Cody Lennox?" she asked, and it was the voice on the phone.

"At your service," said Lennox. "Or vice versa, I suppose."

She pulled off her cap, and her hair was straight and short and black. Its blackness accentuated the paleness of her face—devoid of any color other than the black-red bruise of her lips. Lennox thought her eyes must be black as well.

She had many rings on her fingers and her nails were varnished black. She unclasped the wide cinch at her waist, and when she tugged off the black turtle-neck, her breasts were small and her erect nipples were as pale as the rest of her body. She kicked off her black stiletto pumps, then wriggled free of black tube-skirt and tights with a sinuous motion that reminded Lennox of how a snake would shed its skin. Her hips were small and well-rounded, and her pubic hair was a narrow black vee against her white skin.

Lennox remembered to close his jaw.

She sprang onto the bed—cat-like, thought Lennox—and all of this was moving much too fast. Her black-nailed fingers clawed at his belt and zipper, and his jeans were jerked down and away from his growing erection.

"Whoa!" Lennox protested, trying to unbutton his shirt. "Hey, let me just . . ."

And the door must have opened, because there was another man suddenly in the room.

The woman froze.

"Hey," said Lennox. "You're shit out of luck. I put everything in the hotel's safe deposit."

His voice trailed off. He sensed tension, far too much tension, and he knew this was not just a hotel burglary, and he desperately hoped it was only a dream.

The man was not as tall as Lennox, but he was built like an all-pro NFL lineman. He was wearing kicker boots, punker black leathers, and a lot of chains and badges and things.

His combed-back red hair and short beard were like rust surrounding a brutal face, and his eyes were cold blue and malevolent. Lennox quickly looked away. It was time to try pinching himself. He tried. It hurt.

"Stay out of this, Kane!" said the woman, backing away like a cat before a pit bull.

"It's you who should go," said Kane, "while you still can."

"We grow stronger."

"But not strong enough. I was in time."

"Hey," said Lennox. "Are you two sure you're in the right room? Or, just tell me if I've made a . . ."

She made a gesture. A globe of blue fire darted from her fingers toward Kane. It faded before it reached him.

"Pathetic," said Kane. "Now, get out."

She made a virginal dash for her clothes, clasping their bundle before her, and Lennox almost failed to notice that her feet were changing into cloven hooves. Then she was gone. Like that.

"I'll let myself out," said Kane.

"This is the weirdest dream yet," Lennox congratulated him. "If I can remember this when I wake up, you guys are going into my next book. You got an agent?"

"Remember this, Cody," said Kane. "Just because you're paranoid, it doesn't mean someone isn't really shooting at you."

And Lennox must then have drifted back into dreamless sleep, because he didn't remember when Kane left, and he didn't remember how the pair of black stiletto pumps came to be at the foot of his bed.

IV. Blue Pumps

LENNOX AWOKE at around noon with the grandfather of all hangovers and the maid clattering at his door. He managed to get into his clothes, looked at his face in the mirror and swore never to drink again. As he headed for the bar, he told the maid: "Previous guest left her shoes under the bed. You take them. Not my size."

Two pints of lager put him right, and Lennox remembered that he was supposed to meet Jack Martin for lunch. A third pint, and he was able to paw through his notebook for the time and place. He gazed curiously at the clusters of stickers from the telephone kiosks in Soho. No sign of the number he had dreamt that he called last night.

"We thought you was dead," said Mike Carson, sitting down beside him. "Sorry I'm late, but the bus was held up in traffic. How's the wrist?"

"What?" Lennox was surprised to note a small scab and swelling next to his watchband.

"Don't you remember? You karate-chopped your pint yesterday. Is it lager you're drinking?"

Carson carried over a round just as Jack Martin hustled down the steps into the downstairs bar. "I'm sorry I'm late," he said, "but it's not my fault."

"Is it lager you're having?" asked Carson.

Lennox finally found an indecipherable scrawl that seemed to indicate he was to meet Martin and Carson here at Peter's Bar at noon. He felt a little smug as he closed his notebook.

"So," said Martin, cautiously. "Are you rested up?"

"Slept like the dead," said Lennox. "A lustful lady in black visited my dreams."

"Whoa!"

"She was chased away by Hulk Hogan before I starched the sheets." Lennox was feeling much better. "What do you say we drink up and wander over to The Friend at Hand? They do a super pub lunch there."

Lennox was able to cope with a ploughman's lunch with Stilton, and he only hit his head once on the eccentric copper lanterns that hung from the fake wooden beams. The food steadied him, and after three pints of bitter he felt up to laying waste to London.

Martin dropped all of his change into a fruit machine, despite his avowed prowess with the Vegas slots, and when he asked for just one more 10p, instead Lennox stuffed the coin into the machine himself and collected five pounds.

"Synchronicity," explained Lennox, who had pushed buttons purely at random. Beginner's luck, he decided privately, and converted his winnings into pints.

It was close and crowded inside, so they found a table outside next to the door. They watched the crowds hurry by along Herbrand Street behind the Hotel Russell; it was a shortcut from the Russell Square tube station to Southampton Row and on toward the British Museum. Tourists wandered in confusion, consulting guidebooks. Office workers strode purposefully by.

"Blue pumps," said Lennox.

"Eh?" Carson was headed inside for his round.

"My next book," Lennox confided. "You got your camera, Jack?"

"Sure. Why?" Martin was carefully picking out the bits of kidney from his steak-and-kidney pie.

"In this Our Harmonic August of Our Lord, 1987," said Lennox, "London women are all wearing pumps."

"Training shoes?" Carson glanced at Martin's Reeboks. "I think you mean stilettos." He continued inside.

"Sorry, I do not speaka your language so good. No, look. The tourists are all wearing tennis shoes or something ugly and comfortable. London women all wear stiletto pumps. And they have that quick, purposeful stride, and they never look about; they know where they're going even if they don't want to go there."

"Didn't know you had a foot fetish," Martin said.

"A lovely turn of the ankle," Lennox went on. "Pure *fin de siècle*."

"Skirts are a bit shorter though."

"We'll get a cab," said Lennox. "Drive all around London. You take pictures of their pumps. I'll write the commentary. *Blue Pumps*. Retitle it *Blue Stilettos* for the UK edition. Coffee table book. Pop art. Sell millions of copies. You got enough film?"

"I've got to piss," decided Martin. "You going to be all right here?"

"Steam into this," invited Carson, bringing fresh pints. "You feeling any better?"

"Never better." Lennox was staring back into the pub. "See her?"

"Where?"

"Girl in black."

"Which one?"

"Back by the corner—next to the cigarette machine. Near the Gents'. Jack just walked past her."

"I can't see who you're talking about."

"She's the Lady in Black from my dream."

"Here, sink your pint, Cody. It'll steady you a bit."

"No, wait." Lennox made it to his feet. "I'm going to check this out. Ready for a slash anyway."

Lennox passed Martin as he entered the pub, and Martin gave his back a worried look.

She was standing alone by the bar, her back was to him, and she was dressed all in black. Beside her, talking to one another, stood a group of workmen wearing white boiler suits, somewhat smudged with soot and grime. The side door, which opened onto a sort of tiny alleyway named Colonnade, let circulate a welcome breeze to part the dense tobacco smoke.

She was pretty from the back, and her tight black skirt set off her figure. Lennox figured to walk past her, buy a pack of cigarettes from the machine, then turn to glance at her face. Next he'd casually move beside her at the bar, order a large Glenfiddich (very impressive), open his cigarettes, politely offer her one, and conversation would follow. He was aware that Carson and Martin were observing his progress from beyond the other doorway.

Lennox had almost reached her, but one of the workmen— a rather large bloke—turned away from the chattering group and leaned a thick arm across the bar to block his way. Lennox started to say something.

"Don't," said Kane, turning to face him. "It's another bad move."

Lennox had only a vague memory of his face, but his eyes were not to be forgotten, and the man in the white boiler suit was the man from his dream.

Lennox found drunken *sang-froid*. "Have we met?"

Kane ignored him, not removing his arm from the bar. He said to the Lady in Black: "Turn around, Bright Eyes."

She slowly turned her head toward Lennox. Beneath the black cap, her face was a leathery mask of tattered flesh clinging to a blackened skull.

Lennox felt his beer coming back up.

"Leave us," Kane told her. "Lunchbreak is over."

Lennox closed his eyes tightly, battling to hold his stomach under control. She—whatever he had seen—wasn't there when he opened his eyes again.

Kane was. "That's twice now," he said. "You and I need to talk, Cody. How about over dinner? I'll have my girl get in touch."

Lennox pressed his hand to his mouth and surged toward the Gents'. Kane let him pass.

"Catch you later," Kane called after him.

Kane was gone when Lennox stumbled out of the Gents'. When he had toweled himself clean, his face in the mirror was ghostly pale. He stopped at the bar and quickly downed a large whisky. He was shaking badly, but the second whisky settled him down.

Carson and Martin were studiously trying not to watch him too closely as he stumbled onto his seat.

"You OK, Cody?" asked Martin.

Lennox wanted to say: "I'm all right, Jack." Instead he said: "I'm not sure."

"Ought to go easy," Carson suggested. "Jet-lag."

Lennox swallowed his pint. "Look, did you see her?"

"See who?" Martin exchanged glances with Carson.

"Look. What did I just do?"

"What? Just now?"

"When I got up from this table a minute ago."

Martin put down his cigarette. "Well, Cody, I wasn't really paying much attention. You told Mike you thought you'd recognized some girl at the bar and that you needed to take a leak. Then you groped your way past one of those workmen and vanished into the loo. Mike was about to look in on you when you staggered out, tossed back two shots, and found your way back here. I really think you ought to get a nap."

"The girl! The girl in black at the bar. Where did she go?"

"There was never a girl at the bar," said Carson. "Not that we could see."

"My round, I think." Lennox gathered up their glasses and lurched for the bar.

"Don't let him drink too much," Martin cautioned Carson.

"He's really not taking it well," said Carson, "about Cathy."

Martin shook out another cigarette. "What could you expect? I just hope one good drunken binge of a vacation over here will be the catharsis he needs. Otherwise . . ."

Lennox slammed down the pints, spilling relatively little. He was really feeling lots better. Hair of the dog was a sure cure for DT's. "So, Jack. You got your camera?"

"For *Blue Pumps*?"

"That, too. But mainly so that next time you can take a picture of me with my girl friend."

"Are you Cody Lennox?"

Cody saw her dark blue pumps and followed the nicely filled dark blue hose up to the short denim skirt and jacket. Her breasts were small and firm, and he supposed he could see the rest of them if he unbuttoned her badge-covered jacket. She had that peculiarly perfect British complexion, with a fashion model's features and short red hair in a sort of spiked crewcut. Behind her mirror shades her eyes would have to be blue, and she was almost as tall as Lennox. She was holding out a copy of *They Do Not Die!*

"I apologize for being so forward," she said. "But I'm a fan of yours, and I'd heard you were coming over for the big convention in Brighton. Well, I'd just purchased your latest book at Dillon's, and then I saw you seated here and looked closely at the photograph on the dust jacket. It's a match. Please, do you mind?"

Lennox did not mind. He dug out his pen. "Would you like this inscribed to . . .?"

"Klesst. K-l-e-double-s- and one t."

He was trying to place her accent. Not quite BBC English.

Hint of Irish? "Last name and phone number?"

"Just 'Klesst,' please."

Lennox wrote:

> *All My Best to Klesst.*
> *Signed at Her Request.*
> *Love from London—*
> *Cody Lennox*
> *8/19/87 1:18 PM*

He closed the book and set it down on the table. "Here you go. Care to join me and these other debauched celebrities for a drink?"

"Thanks ever so much, but I've got to run." Klesst scooped up her book. "But I'm sure I'll be seeing you again soon." And she hurried away toward the Russell Square tube station.

"Blue pumps, but too long a stride," observed Lennox. "Can't be a native Londoner."

"Christ, but is she 21?" Martin craned his neck to watch her vanish around the corner.

Carson pointed. "She left you a note, Cody. See if it's her address."

There was an envelope lying where the book had been. Lennox turned it over and read *Cody Lennox*, penned in a large masculine hand across the front. He opened the envelope. There was a short note in the same hand and written upon his hotel's stationery:

> *8/19/87 1:20 PM*
> *Cody—*
> *Let's do dinner.*
> *Meet you in the lobby of the Bloomsbury Park Hotel at 6:30 this evening.*
> *My treat.*
>
> *—Kane*

"Shit," said Lennox.

Martin reached out. "Let me read it."

Martin read it. He handed the note to Carson. "You know what I think?"

"What do you think?"

"Kent Allard. It's just exactly his sort of twisted humor. Got some pretty fan to pass this to you instead of just phoning you at your hotel. Bet he's watching us from his hotel across the street there, laughing his head off."

"Seems more like M. R. James's 'Passing the Runes'," said Carson, returning the note to Lennox.

Lennox wadded note and envelope and stuffed them into the ash tray. "Anyway, I know where I *won't* be at 6:30 this evening. Jack, it's your round."

V. As I Wander Through My Playing Cards

LENNOX MADE it back to his hotel, creatively opened his door, and found his bed. There he remained until 5:30, at which point his headache awakened him. He washed down six aspirin with swigs of Scotch, then decided to kill the rest of the bottle. He sat on the edge of his bed, looking at his hands, thinking about Cathy.

At 6:00 he washed his face, combed his hair, brushed his teeth, and went out in search of adventure. After having parked his lunch in the Gents' at The Friend at Hand, his stomach was raw and uncertain about the whisky. He supposed he really should eat something, so he steamed into a pub by the British Museum and had three pints of lager.

Much improved, Lennox strolled through Soho and into the theatre district. *Follies* was playing at the Shaftesbury Theatre, but he'd already been told that tickets were impossible. He stood outside, wishing he might press his nose against the glass, and a scalper exchanged a stalls ticket for only thirty quid. Lennox was delighted, and he managed to stay awake throughout the performance, despite an overpowering headache and sense of lethargy. He enjoyed himself, and it was quite a disappointment when he had to go back alone to his hotel instead of having a late dinner with Diana Rigg.

Instead, Lennox stopped in at the first pub he passed. By closing time he had drunk six large whiskies and had won twenty quid from the fruit machines on an investment of 50p. He was getting looks from the barmen as he left. Lennox had played the machines out of boredom, never really understanding what the buttons were supposed to do. Jack Martin, eat your heart out. Lennox decided he'd present Jack with a handful of tokens when they met for lunch tomorrow.

Lennox was in good voice by now. He considered that a walk back through Soho to his hotel would count as an evening constitutional, all the better because the narrow side streets provided superb echo for his medley of Bon Jovi hits. Lennox had screamed out all that he could remember of "You Give Love a Bad Name," when he found the Queen of Diamonds.

She was lying in the gutter, somewhat soiled: a lost playing card with a buxom and nude lady, very much early 1960s *Playboy* centerfold, and quite demure by Times Square standards. He pocketed this.

Another chorus, a sudden turning, and he found the Queen of Clubs. She had been trod upon, but was in fair repair: a lovely black girl with dusky skin and a fetching smile. Lennox added her to his jacket pocket and proceeded along the turning.

He was quite lost by now, but completely confident, when he found the Queen of Hearts. She was propped against a lamp post, and she was a tall redhead who reminded him of Klesst, whose name had stayed in his memory. Lennox carefully included her with the others and stumbled into another darkened side street, certain he would find the Queen of Spades.

His voice was growing hoarse, and he reckoned he could use another drink, and he realized that he was seriously lost, and then he noticed that five people were closing around him from out of the darkness.

One was the Queen of Spades, dressed all in black, her face a pale shape in the darkness. The others were four ragged, shuffling winos—blowlamps, was that the expression in cockney rhyming slang for tramps? Whatever. More to the point, they had very long knives.

Of additional interest, as they closed in, Lennox saw that their clothes weren't actually ragged, but rather they were rotted, as were their faces.

"Take him now," said the Lady in Black.

Lennox started to run.

Kane stepped out of a black passage-way as Lennox flung past. He was wearing a three-piece pin-striped business suit that was obviously the best of Bond Street, and he had a distinctly professional appearance with his neat beard, bowler, and umbrella.

Kane petulantly threw the closest attacker against the wall. As the wall was on the opposite side of the street, the man hung there for a moment, before sliding down like a filthy and shattered doll. By then Kane had pulled the head off the next assailant and tossed that bit somewhere in the direction of the Lady in Black. The third dead thing lunged for Kane with his knife, but Kane disarmed him, throwing arm and knife into the darkness, and then deftly ripped out his heart.

Hanging back, the last assailant threw his knife at Kane, and, while Kane was catching the blade, rolled behind a large dustbin and pulled an Uzi from beneath his raincoat.

Kane shoved Lennox onto the pavement, as a burst of 9 mm slugs ripped over them. Twisting away, Kane tugged some sort of pistol from his shoulder holster and pointed it at the dustbin. Dustbin, gunman, a parked car, and most of the wall opposite blew apart into glowing cinders.

The Queen of Spades had disappeared.

Tires howled, and a black Jaguar convertible took the turning on two wheels.

"Pitch him in!" Klesst shouted. She was wearing a black leather jumpsuit, and she was already reversing as Kane tossed in his bowler, umbrella, and Lennox, then tumbled in after—all but crushing the lot.

Perhaps thirty seconds had elapsed from Kane's first appearance. Lennox was in a state of shell shock.

Kane propped up Lennox against the back seat, as Klesst turned Soho streets into Le Mans.

"Well then, Cody," Kane shouted. "I really don't think you

should have broken our dinner engagement."

VI. This Ain't the Summer of Love

"YOU'VE GOT dead bits all over your suit," Klesst scolded.

Kane muttered and dropped Lennox onto a leather sofa; he had been carrying him pendulant from his jacket collar, and Lennox collapsed like a stringless puppet.

Lennox said: "I need a drink."

"Single-malted. No ice." Kane nodded to Klesst. "Rather a large one, I think. Same for me."

"You just blew up half of Soho," Lennox remembered.

Kane was shrugging out of his suit jacket, eyeing his carrion-smeared hands in distaste. "Threw in a mundane this time. Wonder whether for you or for me? Play hostess, Klesst. I need a quick wash-up."

Lennox noticed the weapon in Kane's left-hand draw shoulder holster. It seemed to be made of almost translucent black plastic, and it reminded Lennox of the Whitney Lightning .22 automatic he had lusted over in the outdoors magazine ads of his youth.

"He just blew up half of London," said Lennox, accepting the glass from Klesst. "Is that really a raygun?"

"Cosmic ray laser, as close as you'd understand."

Lennox watched Klesst over his glass as he drank. "Oh, sure. I've read too much science fiction for that. Which hand holds the fusion reactor or something?"

"That's just a selective transmitter. Broadcast power on tight-contain. Trans time-time. Two black holes locked in an anti-matter matrix. Dad worked on it for a long real-time."

"Am I supposed to believe any of that?"

"No, Cody. It's really just magic."

"Carried off by Emperor Ming and his charming daughter. This is where writers get their ideas, you know." And for a while he sipped his drink and waited to wake up.

"May I have another?" Lennox handed her his empty glass. She was very longlegged and very lovely in tight black leather.

He decided that DT's were nothing to be afraid of, after all.

"You know, my friends did warn me it would come down to this in the end," he told Klesst.

"Still think you're hallucinating, Cody?" Kane had scrubbed his large hands and switched into formal evening attire. They seemed to be in a spacious sort of oak-paneled study. Lennox looked about for the butler and a stuffed moose's head.

"I'm not prepared to argue with a hallucination."

"You might, if I began to pull off your fingers, one at a time," suggested Kane.

Lennox turned to Klesst. "You're not really related to this ogre? You don't look a bit like Myrna Loy."

Kane nodded to Klesst, and she left the room.

"Have we been properly introduced?" Lennox gulped his imaginary drink. Excellent dream whisky.

"Only if you bother to count the three times I've recently pulled your ass out of the fire. I'm Kane."

"Charles Foster Kane?"

"Just Kane."

"So, Kane," said Lennox, sitting up. "How you been? I heard your old folks got evicted. You and your brother still not getting along?"

"Chance?" wondered Klesst, returning with an agate box.

"Not likely. He has the power, but not the control. That's why they want him. And why they can still get to him."

Kane opened the box. It was filled with a white powder. "Care to partake of a few numbers, Cody? Time you were getting back to some semblance of lucidity."

"You Brits manage some awesome coke," Lennox approved. "Let's toot up and party till dawn. You're a great host, Kane, you know, and I'm sorry I called you on ogre. I'm really going to miss you when I wake up. By the way, how old's your daughter?"

"Old enough to break your back," Klesst assured him.

"Kinky." Lennox dipped a golden coke spoon into the white powder, snorted, and refilled for his other nostril. "Smooth." He quickly repeated the process and handed box and spoon to Kane.

"My special blend," said Kane. "Took some work to get right. First one's free."

"Shit," said Lennox. He was experiencing a rush like nothing he'd ever felt before. A moment ago he had been close to dropping off into an alcoholic stupor—assuming he hadn't already passed out somewhere. The drug—clearly not cocaine—cut through the alcohol-soaked blur of his consciousness as shockingly as splinters of ice thrust into his brain. Lennox felt suddenly sober, suddenly aware that he was seated in an opulent study with a leather-clad young lady and a very large and very intimidating man in black tie, and suddenly he began to suspect that this might not be a dream.

"So glad that you could finally join us, Cody," said Kane. "If you care to stay alive very much longer, there are a few things you really need to know about yourself and about those others who already know all about you."

Lennox looked at his hands. They should have been trembling, but they weren't. So, this still had to be a dream.

"Do you understand the popular expression 'synchronicity' as used in the sense of 'coincidence'?"

"Easy one, mine host. Random events or experiences that appear to align in non-random patterns. You start to call your great-aunt Biddie to whom you haven't spoken in years, and as you reach for the phone, it rings, and it's your great-aunt Biddie. Some call it ESP. Paranoids see patterns in it all."

"And you know about the Harmonic Convergence?"

"Some sort of alignment of the planets. Supposed to unleash all sorts of astrological forces, mumbo-jumbo, etc., etc., etc., and change the world forever. What's your sign, by the way?"

"Not on your zodiac. Give him another hit, Klesst."

Lennox helped himself to a couple more generous snorts. "It's some kind of speed, right? Maybe crystal meth mixed with coke?"

"Old world secret," said Kane. "I'll send some home with you, perhaps."

He settled into a leather chair and sipped his drink, watching Lennox. "Suppose a person had the power to control random events?"

"He'd be a very wealthy gambler."

"Won much on the fruit machines, Cody?"

"Now, whoa!"

"Suppose the conscious wish to talk to great-aunt Biddie were powerful enough to cause her to phone up in response to the wish?"

"Suppose great-aunt Biddie's wish to talk to me was the cause of my suddenly thinking of her? *Touché*, I think."

"Rather, that's the whole point, Cody. Cause or effect? Because if synchronicity is not a random phenomenon, then who controls it? Who is the master?"

"Klesst, sweetheart—go fetch your father his nightly Thorazine, while we discuss the one about the chicken and the egg. By the way, where did you buy that outfit?"

"Kensington Market. I have a stall there. Come visit. We also do tattoos and piercing."

Lennox was starting to fade, despite the drug. "Already had my ear pierced."

"That's just a start."

"What a coincidence," said Kane. "Klesst, why not give Cody a sample of your jewelry stock—something to remember us by?"

Lennox was helping himself to the whisky. "I really should be waking up—I mean, getting back. This really has been real, gang. I just hope I can remember it all tomorrow long enough to write it down."

"You will," Kane told him. "I've seen to that."

Lennox tossed back straight whisky, then poured another. It was his dream, so he could do as he pleased. "So what about the Moronic Confluence?"

"The Harmonic Convergence was a cosmic expression of synchronicity. It unleashed certain forces, certain latent powers. Your powers, for instance."

"So now the world will become a better place for all?"

"Afraid not, Cody. It only unleashed forces which you would consider forces of evil."

"Bummer!"

"Try this." Klesst handed Lennox a silver pendant affixed to a French hook. It was a sunburst, about the size of a one-pound coin. A circle of somewhat serpentine sunrays framed a sun whose face was that of a snarling demon.

Lennox gazed at the amulet uncertainly.

"Allow me," said Kane. Very quickly he inserted the silver hook through Lennox's left earlobe. Lennox winced, touched his hand to his ear, saw blood on his finger. It had been some time since he had had his ear pierced, and the opening must have begun to close.

"Looks good," approved Klesst.

Lennox remembered that you weren't supposed to feel pain in a dream, but then he also felt like he was about to pass out, and that wasn't right for a dream either.

"Where's that coke?"

"Don't want to overdo it first time, do we, Cody?" said Kane. "I think you've had enough to handle tonight. But not to worry: I'll be in touch tomorrow. Too late for a taxi, I'm afraid, but we'll see you safely to your hotel."

"Keys," said Klesst, and caught them as Kane tossed.

"I was really very sober there for a minute or two," Lennox explained, bouncing against Kane's huge shoulder.

"Short-term effect," said Kane. "Just be glad of that."

"How come only evil forces were released?"

"Because there are no good forces."

"So, then. You don't believe that there is a God."

"There was a god."

"Well, then. Where is he now?"

"I killed him," said Kane.

VII. Strange Days Have Found Us

LENNOX AWOKE when his bedside phone began ringing at noon. He was in his hotel room, but he hadn't the slightest as to how he had arrived there. He had some confused memories of the night before . . . But first, the phone.

It was Carson. "Wake up, you lazy sod. We're all waiting on you."

"Where?"

"In the downstairs bar. Me and Jack, Geoffrey Marsh and Kent Allard. Come on, you're missing your breakfast."

"Be right down."

Lennox automatically went through the motions of dressing. The morning after a blackout was nothing new for him. He wished he had time to shower, but settled for splashing cold water over his face and shoulders, toweling vigorously. The towel caught on something on his left ear, tugged painfully. Lennox wiped cold water from his eyes and saw the sunburst amulet dangling from his left ear.

"Get serious," he told his reflection. Must have bought it off a stall during one of his blackouts. But it was all coming back. Vivid memories of Kane and zombie assassins. No way. Another all-too-real nightmare. Maybe he really should cut down on the booze.

Lennox fingered the silver amulet, but the French hook seemed to be fixed within his earlobe, and it hurt to try to draw it free. No time to fool with it now. Lennox splashed a little whisky onto his ear to guard against infection, finished dressing, and took the stairway to the downstairs bar. Art Nouveau stained-glass windows, brightened by the midday sun, made each landing a sort of kaleidoscope, and Lennox was winded and dizzy by the time he reached Peter's Bar.

"Steam into this," Carson said. "Reckoned you'd fancy a lager."

Lennox wedged into the table and drained half the pint in a long swallow. "God, that feels good!" He was surprised to notice that his hands were steady. Must have made it an earlier evening than he'd thought. Good job, that. He was aware that they were all trying not to watch him.

"So, where do you guys want to go for lunch?" Jack Martin asked. "Is there someplace near here where we could, like, get a real pizza?"

"Pizza Express in Soho has American-style pizza," offered Geoffrey Marsh. "How've you been, Cody? Enjoying your trip?"

"So far, so good." Cody shook hands across the table. "Good to see you, Geoffrey. Jack said you were over."

Marsh was an athletically fit man whose hair was starting to thin and whose brown beard was showing grey. As he was the same age as Lennox and Martin, the two consoled one another that workouts and tennis evidently could not slow the aging process, and that therefore there was no point in their mending their ways. Marsh wrote what he liked to call "quiet horror" under various pseudonyms, several of which sold very well indeed. He, Martin, and Lennox had been friends and colleagues long enough to become regarded as "the Old Guard" of the horror genre.

"Nice earring, Cody," said Kent Allard. "Are you turning cyberpunk on us?"

"More likely cyberdrunk," Lennox said, finishing his pint. "I caught *Follies* last night, then crawled back here somehow. Look at all the loot I won on the way."

As he poured forth a handful of fruit machine tokens, Lennox asked casually: "Hear about anything going down in Soho last night? Could have sworn I heard some sort of gunfire or something."

"Probably just yobbos," suggested Carson.

"Check the papers, maybe," said Marsh.

"I never read beyond page three," Allard said.

Martin was looking hungrily at the fistful of tokens. "Let's try the machine here. Will it take these same tokens?"

"Just watch me," Lennox said. "I'm on a streak. Has to do with the Harmonic Convergence."

As he and Martin made for a fruit machine, Marsh watched them with concern. He asked Carson: "How's Cody doing? Really."

Carson was acutely aware of Allard's attention, and Allard was a notorious gossip. "He's doing OK," he lied. "Good as any man might after his wife and her lover are found dead in bed in some posh hotel room. He'll get through it."

"I wonder," said Allard.

"Just watch him, Mike," worried Marsh. "I don't think he's in control just now."

"Was he ever?" Carson wondered.

It took Martin most of ten minutes to lose all of Lennox's tokens in the fruit machine, plus the five quid Lennox won for him by suggesting when to hold. Martin then said: "I'm ready to . . ."

Lennox was already starting for the door, but he stopped short. Martin's voice had halted, as had the plume of his cigarette smoke. Lennox turned about. No one was moving in the pub. Nothing was moving in the pub. Totally freeze-frame. Awesome.

"Same again, mate?" asked Kane, filling a pint mug from behind the bar. "Lager, isn't it?" He was dressed as a hotel barman.

"What have you done?" Lennox took the pint.

"Time-time," said Kane, helping himself to a pint of Royal Oak. There were bits floating in it. Kane waited for them to settle.

"It isn't three yet," Lennox protested. The pub and all within were entirely motionless.

"I really like your sense of humor. Actually, I meant I'm holding time-time at stop just a bit. Did you know, Cody, that the energy currently being expended could create two moderately large star systems?"

"All right, I'm impressed," admitted Lennox. "Are you real, or am I really over the edge?"

"Right on both counts, Cody." Kane lifted his mug. "Cheers."

Lennox knocked back his pint, set it down on the bar. Nothing moved, save he and Kane.

"Same again?" Kane asked.

"Might as well. Can anyone else see you?"

"Confusing me with Harvey?" Kane refilled their pints. "And after I've just saved your ass yet again."

"How's that?" Lennox drank, because there was little else he could do about matters.

"A horrid and malevolent tentacled thing was lurking about. Here. Just now. Looking for you, I think."

"Didn't notice one. Where? In the Gents'?"

"No. Behind the fireplace over there. Take a closer look at its tiles, by the way."

"I've seen them. It's St. George slaying the dragon."

"I said, a closer look. Take it from an experienced dragon fighter: George isn't doing all that well. Could have been you just now."

"I need to sit down."

"I'll join you later."

"I'm going back to my room."

"In that case, that's four pounds eighty, please."

Lennox passed Kane a five pound note, and suddenly everything was moving again.

". . . go get something to eat," said Martin, banging on the fruit machine.

"I need out of here!" Lennox was headed for the stair.

But Kane was already seated at their table. He was wearing stone-washed jeans, a Grateful Dead t-shirt, and mirror shades. Lennox was grateful for that last.

"Hello, Cody," said Kane. "Been so looking forward to meeting you at last."

"This is Mr. Kane, said Allard, breaking off their earnest conversation. "He's brought us all invitations . . ."

"I'm out of here."

". . . to the publishers' party tonight . . ."

"Please do sit down, Cody," Kane invited.

The tugging pain from his ear pendant abruptly dragged Lennox back onto his vacated seat.

"That's better," said Kane. "I've always wanted the two of us to have a chat."

". . . for all of his authors," Allard concluded.

"And you must be Jack Martin." Kane stood up to shake hands. "I've read all your books. I like the one about Damon."

"Are you a writer?" asked Martin, wincing. "Or what?"

"He's a what," said Lennox, gulping Marsh's lager.

"Mr. Kane here—or is that your first name?"

"It's just Kane. Like Sting or Cher or Donovan."

"Kane here," Allard continued smoothly, "recently acquired Midland Books. He's now our major British publisher. I guess you guys hadn't heard the news."

"Just cut the deal. I know it will prove to be a good investment. But, hey, we're all of us in this outlaw profession together." Kane raised his mug. "Death to publishers."

"And Midland Books is having a party for its authors tonight," Allard informed them, thinking good job he'd phoned his agent this morning for the insider information.

"So, do you write yourself?" Martin persisted.

"Barbarian fantasy," said Kane. "Under a pseudonym. Some time back. I'm sure you've never read any of it."

"Can the rest of you guys see him, too?" wondered Lennox.

"Invitations, Kent, as promised," said Kane, distributing engraved cards. "Relatively small gathering of some of my authors and staff. Please do feel free to bring along friends. It's just over at the Hotel Russell, so I know you can find your way."

"You're not British, are you," said Lennox.

"A citizen of the world," Kane explained helpfully. "And by the way, I believe I owe you 20p change." He handed Lennox a coin.

"A pre-convention bash, is it?" asked Marsh.

"Naturally we'll discuss business matters amidst the champagne. Must do it up proper for taxes, after all. And I'm particularly interested in talking over your current projects, Cody."

"I'm writing a novel about demonic trilobites who gobble people's brains. It's called *The Biting*."

"Much to be explored there. Is the small community in New England or California?"

"How'd you know to find us here?"

"Synchronicity."

"Mike, let's go get something to eat." Lennox stood up.

"Actually, Kent phoned the office to say you were meeting here for lunch."

"Kane is taking us all to lunch," Allard said smugly. "I love this man."

"I got a previous engagement. No time. Come on, Mike."

"Tell Klesst I'll be counting on her as hostess again tonight," Kane called after them.

"You've got to sort of make allowances for Cody," Marsh told Kane. "Sure, he's drinking too much. But he's really been through Hell lately."

"And he's likely to remain there," said Kane, "without a little help from his friends. And I already count him as my friend. My round, I think."

VIII. A Big Chrome Baby and a Black Leather Doll

CARSON WAS examining the engraved invitation. "Do you think I might bring along some prints to show tonight?"

Lennox was searching for a cab. "Kane's no publisher."

"We can take the tube. It's just over there."

"Horrid and malevolent tentacled things lurk beneath underground platforms."

"So, where are we really going?"

"Kensington Market. I need an obscene tattoo and some gross t-shirts."

Lennox secured a cab, and they piled in. "Ken High Street. Anywhere near Holland Road."

"You're missing lunch, and your publisher's paying. What do you think about the prints?"

"Do you know anything about Kane? Anything at all?"

"Never heard of him before today. Kent said Kane's bought Midland, and Kent would know. You know how it is with publishers today—new owners taking over one after another and then selling to the next one. Doesn't do you good to walk out on your publisher. He was going to buy us lunch. Maybe just a few prints, what do you think? He'll have seen some of the covers I've done for Midland."

"The pubs are still open, and it's my round. What was your impression of Kane?"

"Intense. Mega. Crucial. Must work out twice a day." Carson then turned serious. "Buys our lunch, but I wouldn't want to have him come round to the flat after closing. He looks as though he might break you in half if he wanted."

"I never saw Kane before just now. At least, I don't think I *really* did." Lennox found some cigarettes, poked one toward Carson. He'd almost quit. "But I've dreamed about Kane. I've seen Kane before, and I've talked with Kane before, and it all seemed totally real. In my dreams. In my nightmares."

Carson lit their cigarettes. He said, cautiously: "Sometimes, when you've been drinking bad . . ."

"I only hope that it is just the booze. I can sober up tomorrow or next week. Then, what if Kane's still here?"

"What's your worry? It's just that he's your new publisher. You must have read about him in the papers, seen pictures of him somewhere. Let's just go have a pint, Cody. It'll steady you some."

"We're here," announced Lennox, rapping on the Austin's glass partition. "Just let us out anywhere."

"What's here?" asked Carson.

"Kensington Market. Klesst said she has a stall here."

"The wicked malt whose book you signed yesterday? The original lady in blue pumps?"

"She says she's Kane's daughter."

"And when did she tell you all this?"

"She said she has a stall here. She said that in one of my dreams. What if my dreams are true?"

"Then we'll find her, and then we'll all steam into the closest pub."

"That would mean that it wasn't a dream. That it was all true."

"What's true, then?"

"Kane. And all the madness he's told me."

"You've just met him. All of us just did. He's only your publisher."

"I used to do a whole lot of acid back in my Haight-Ashbury days," Lennox confided.

Carson was getting major worried. "Let's just have a look through, and then we'll find a pub. Maybe an off-license, and we can sit on the benches out behind the church across the way."

Kensington Market enclosed three or so floors crammed with many tiny shops, catering primarily to the latest punk styles. Latex and leather fashions, all glistening black and tailored like a second skin, crowded the aisles—reminding Lennox of the fetish boutiques in L.A. and New York. He guessed that PVC probably meant vinyl or something, and while it was all very shiny and kinky, it looked very hot to wear, and it was sweltering in here. The place smelled like a tire graveyard on a hot day, and was about as organized. It was all a bit too trendy, more sideshow than sordid. Punkers were everywhere, and Lennox suddenly became aware that, for once, his was maybe the straightest appearance on the scene. He felt more secure when he noticed that some eyes were glancing toward the omnipresent photographs of James Dean, then turning back to study his face.

Carson was thoughtfully looking at Dead Kennedys records.

The sunburst pendant in his ear seemed to turn Lennox's head and his attention away from the record stall. It was very, very hot. And claustrophobic. Images came to mind of Doré illustrations for Dante's *Inferno*. He moved aimlessly along the crowded aisles. He wished he had a drink.

"Hello, Cody. So good of you to drop by."

Klesst had a stall just down from Xotique. She was wearing a black leather bra, a very brief black leather miniskirt, an exposed suspender belt holding up black stockings, and black stiletto boots. This much Lennox took in at first glance. At second glance he saw that she wore an ear pendant similar to his own, but it was her face on the sunburst.

"Klesst?" Lennox's voice was uncertain. This was probably just another hallucination. Got to keep thinking of them as dreams. Nothing more.

"So, Cody. You recovered from last night. Dad was off looking for you earlier. You see him?"

Lennox faltered, then gave it up. "He caught up with me at the hotel bar. Gave me an invitation. To a party. To-night. Said to remind you that you're to be hostess."

"Boring."

"What are you?" Lennox's voice held panic.

"Good question. What are we all? Why are we here? Do you know Jean-Paul Sartre?"

"Not socially. He doesn't hang out much these days."

"Next question."

"What's happening to me?"

"I thought Kane started to explain that to you last night."

"Sometimes I can't tell my dreams from reality."

"Sometimes there is no distinction."

"I think I'm starting to lose it."

"Are you going to stand here paralyzed in some existential dilemma, or are you going to buy something?"

Lennox stared without focus at her clutter of punk jewelry and studded leather accessories. Extreme. From the corner of his eye, he could see Carson still flipping through the record display. He supposed he ought to re-enter the real world if he could find it, or at least go through the motions. Did he really need a spiked collar?

"Perhaps an earring."

"Then I'll just pierce your other ear. No charge."

"No problem. I'll just take this one out."

"Can't be done."

"Say, what?"

"Do you remember last night?"

"I got very drunk as is my custom. I had some crazy dreams. You were in them. And Kane. That's all. What would you know about my dreams?"

"That was near-time, but real enough. Kane put his mark upon you. Now you bear the mark of Kane. There's no removing it. Ever."

"Tell that to Vincent van Gogh."

"Never fancied pictures of flowers. You're signed and sealed."

"Come again?"

"And be glad for it. They'll try to kill you, now that they can't possess you. What actually do you think happened to you last night?"

"I got very drunk and walked back to my hotel."

"Kane thinks they were trying for him as much as for you. They never else would have called in a mundane. The Harmonic Convergence has increased their powers, but they still have no control of time-time."

"Look. I read *The Sun* today, page three and all of it. Nothing about Soho being devastated or stray bits of zombies found strewn all about."

"I told you: that took place in near-time. Very dangerous. Kane has much less power there, and that's why they lured you there. But now that you're aligned with Kane, they'll come looking for you in real-time as well."

"Are you from around here?"

"Not hardly."

"And is Kane really your father?"

"Obviously."

"He doesn't look old enough."

"You'd be surprised."

"And your mother?"

"Kane killed her."

"And how did you feel about that?"

"She meant to sacrifice me to a well-known demon. She'd made a pact at my birth."

Lennox wondered if he were the only sane person here. And how sane was that?

"Klesst, you're a really beautiful person. May I even say, you're devilishly intriguing. And if I were twenty years younger I'd deck myself out in some of these outrageous costumes they sell here, and I'd carry you off to some dingy basement club where people dance till dawn by bashing their heads together, and afterward I'd tell Kane we were running off to live together in my gentrified loft in New York's SoHo, and if he objected I'd just have to punch him out. However, I'm not twenty years younger, and Kane is bigger than me, so instead I'd like to fix you up with a really good psychiatrist."

"I'm lots older than you think."

"Delighted to hear you say that. I wasn't sure about British laws on the matter."

"So, are you going to buy anything?"

"I haven't really looked about. Maybe a nice leather bra for my closet."

"Have you had your nipples pierced? I can do it here, and I have some lovely golden rings."

"Not today."

"But I'd like that." Klesst moved toward him suddenly, and Lennox as suddenly was afraid.

"Christ, you really did find your lady here." Carson wandered into the stall, holding a Nico album in a plastic bag. He was looking at his watch, calculating how many pints might be sunk before closing.

"She wants to pierce my nipples," complained Lennox.

"Why not just get a tattoo?" Carson compromised. He rolled up his left sleeve. Lennox saw a devil's head above the numbers 666. "Can't remember where I had it done. I'd been pissed for weeks before I noticed it."

"I did it," said Klesst. "Looks great."

"This is Kane's daughter," said Lennox. "I've mostly seen her in my dreams, but I think she's real enough."

"You might find out how real tonight."

"See there, Carson. They throw themselves at me. Klesst, why did you say that I was aligned with Kane?"

"Ought to be more careful about what you sign your name to, Cody. Yesterday. The book."

"I like the British," said Lennox. "You just have to get used to their odd sense of humor."

"I'm not British," said Klesst. "And you still haven't bought anything. Let you have that spiked collar for a fiver."

"Are the pubs still open?" Lennox asked Carson.

"Try it on."

"We'd best be going," said Carson.

Klesst moved very quickly, and it was over before Lennox could think to struggle.

"Radical," she said. "That's a fiver."

"Klesst, you're beautiful, but you're a true space cadet. Close up, and I'll buy you lunch. You're really from California, aren't you? That can be cured."

"So can reality, Cody. See you tonight."

Lennox fingered his studded leather collar. It chafed his neck, but he paid her anyway. He was aware that he was in serious danger of becoming sober, and he intended to remedy that without further delay.

"I think I'm on to something here," he told Carson. "She was coming on strong to me. Real strong."

Carson looked back. "She's not there now."

Lennox turned around. The labyrinthine aisles of stalls seemed to be shimmering in the stagnant air. He couldn't pick out Klesst's stall. He couldn't see Klesst.

"Whoa! Wait a minute here." He started to go back.

Carson took his arm. "Let's just go have a pint."

Lennox fumbled with his collar. "I think this is locked."

"Get the key after the pubs close."

IX. Say a Prayer in the Darkness for the Magic to Come

LENNOX NEARLY slept past the party, but his hangover and the pain from his earlobe woke him up around seven. He found a half-bottle of Scotch and medicated himself. In the mirror his earlobe did not appear to be inflamed, and it no longer hurt. He tugged at the ear pendant, but it didn't want to come loose. Probably encrusted. Lennox dabbed more whisky onto his earlobe as a safeguard.

He wondered what he was doing wearing a spiked collar, then remembered that Klesst had locked it there and kept the key. He fumbled with its lock, wishing it would open, and the catch snapped. Must be a trick to it, he thought, dropping the collar onto his table.

Just time for a quick shower. The cold water helped to wake him up. He had some vague memories of sitting on a bench behind some church in Kensington and drinking several cans of strong lager, while he explained to Carson all about synchronicity. Carson had managed to get him into a cab and back to his hotel.

Lennox felt much better after he finished with the shower, and he took time to trim his near-beard. He put on a baggy cotton designer shirt and matching trousers, a narrow necktie loosely knotted, and his favorite linen jacket. Got to look the part for your publisher, and besides there was Klesst.

Kane had reserved a large suite of rooms at the Hotel Russell, so it was just a short walk along Southampton Row. Lennox found his somewhat crumpled invitation, rechecked his image in the mirror, and sailed off in high spirits.

The party had already started, and a hulking biker in a dinner jacket met him at the door and wanted to see his invitation.

"Let him in, Blacklight," Klesst called out. "He's one of us."

Klesst gave him her hand. "Champagne?"

"For sure."

She was wearing some sort of gleaming black sheath dress that laced openly across her breasts and back. The latex dress and stockings clung tightly to her very lovely body, and Lennox decided that these kinky London fashions weren't all that bad, and that having an affair with his publisher's spaced-out daughter was worth checking out.

"Here we are." Klesst lifted two glasses from a passing tray and handed one to Lennox.

"Cheers," he said, touching their glasses.

"Ah! There you are, Cody. So glad you could make it. I see Klesst is taking care of you."

Kane shook his hand. He was casually dressed, as were most of those in the room, and he was playing the perfect host.

"Lots to munch on over there. I imagine you already know most of the people here. Mingle and enjoy. We'll talk later on."

Lennox downed his champagne and reached for another glass. He did know most of the thirty or so people here. It really was just another publisher's party. Jack Martin had seen Lennox and was working his way over to him.

"Well, Klesst," Lennox said. "That's a very lovely dress you almost have on. Are you the Queen of Spades?"

"Wrong card. Have another drink, Cody."

"You're right. She's not a redhead. But you're both in my dreams." Cody grabbed another glass. "And you're much cuter."

"How's it going, Cody?" Martin had just been talking with Mike Carson about the afternoon's adventures. He was close to panic and wondering about commitment laws in England.

"Ms. Klesst Kane, meet famous writer, Jack Martin."

"I already know her," said Martin. "Blue pumps. We all met yesterday at The Friend At Hand. Nobody told us you were the publisher's daughter."

"My secret identity," said Klesst, and then she smiled and left them to greet the always fashionably late Kent Allard.

"Everything OK?" asked Martin.

"No. I don't think so." Lennox emptied his glass.

"You missed a really great lunch. You really ought to eat something. Just look at all this food here!"

"Had a late lunch with Carson. Wonder if Klesst might like a late dinner?"

"Cody!" Kane's massive arm gripped his shoulders. "Grab a glass of champagne, and let's sit down for a minute in the other room. I want to talk about your next book. Jack, please excuse us for a minute. Business."

"Business," echoed Lennox, reaching for another glass as he followed Kane.

Kane closed the door behind them. "So, how's your day been?"

Lennox sipped his champagne. Kane was pulling a fresh bottle from the ice. "Very pleasant. I dropped by Klesst's shop. Nice place for your daughter to work."

"Kids these days." Kane popped the cork. "Heard you bought some neckwear from her. Not wearing it tonight."

"Took it off. Didn't go with my tie. Had trouble with the catch, though."

"Good job, Cody. There was no key to that lock." Kane refilled their glasses. "I'm impressed."

Cody stood up and bunched his fists. "No way do I believe any of this. I'm blitzed out of my skull just now, and I know I need to cut down on my drinking. Let's do lunch tomorrow, if you really exist, and then we can talk about the next novel. I'm sorry if I'm perhaps not making a lot of sense just now, but life's been a bitch."

"Do a couple hits of this, and then you'll be sober enough." Kane tossed him a phial of white powder. "I need you tonight."

Lennox delved into the phial with the attached spoon. "Kane, you are very weird."

"Take a couple hits. Nice big ones."

Lennox blinked and looked about him. He was sitting in a hotel room across from a huge individual who at best just might be mad. And Lennox suddenly felt sober for the first time in months. Then last night . . .

"Much better," said Kane, retrieving the phial. "Just take a moment to get used to it all."

"You're not a publisher."

"For the moment I am. Needed a realtime framework. Bought Midland Books and kept the staff. Nice cover, and I may even turn a profit. Want to talk about the advance for your next book?"

"Those other times when I saw you. All of that really did happen?"

"Trust me, Cody. It really happened."

"So, I'm not losing my mind."

"Afraid not, Cody."

"So, then." Lennox rubbed his forehead and wondered whether he was over the edge beyond return. "If I'm not crazy, and you're for real, then who are you?"

"A friend, Cody. Haven't I saved your life?"

"That was real?"

"All of it. And anyway, you already knew that beneath the alcoholic fog you've been hiding in. Head in the sand, Cody. Doesn't work. *They* can still see you."

"No, *this* is reality: I'm sitting in a hotel room in London talking with my publisher and there's a party going on. One or both of us is quite mad. I think I'll mingle."

"It takes a bit of getting used to," said Kane, escorting him back to the others. "That's why I'm trying to bring you along slowly." He squeezed Lennox's shoulder in a comradely way, and Lennox sensed that beneath the friendly grip there was latent strength that might crush him in an instant. "Now go enjoy yourself. Busy night ahead."

Carson greeted him with a glass of champagne. "So then, did you make a deal?"

"I'm afraid I may have." Lennox tossed back the champagne. "Mike, I'm beginning to think that all of this is really happening to me."

"Best get some food inside you," Carson said, looking about for Martin for help. Martin was chatting up Klesst.

"What I need is some air. I'll just have a stroll around Russell Square. Back in a flash."

"I'll come with you."

"No. I just want to be alone for a minute. Stay here and talk to Kane. See what you make of him."

Allard had cornered Kane, and Lennox waved as he made for the door. "Just getting some air."

"Catch you later, Cody," Kane shouted back, and Blacklight let Lennox out the door.

Feeling somewhat conspiratorial, Lennox did not cross into Russell Square, but instead walked along Southampton Row and turned down Cosmo Place into Queen Square. With a shudder he made to ignore the human wreckage hunched over their bottles and their benches about the cobbled pavement, and he passed through an iron gate onto the green. It smelled less of urine and unwashed bodies here, if he kept away from the shrubbery which sheltered the enclosing iron fence. The trees deadened the noise of London at night, and the grass felt cool beneath feet bruised by endless pavement.

Lennox walked slowly toward the end of Queen Square, toward the woman's statue there, formerly thought to be a statue of Queen Anne but now believed to be that of Queen Charlotte, Consort of King George III. He paused there, his thoughts aimless—vaguely wondering, as he had so often done before, as to what Queen Charlotte's downward stretched right hand might be pointing.

It was there and then that Lennox found the Queen of Spades.

She was dressed all in black, and at first he just saw her face, ghostly in the darkness. Lennox stared, and the rest of her emerged from the night.

He said: "Hello, Cathy."

"Hello, Cody."

"You're dead, Cathy."

"You should know, Cody."

"So this is it, then. It's not just the booze and all that. I really am completely mad."

"You must have been to cast your lot with Kane."

She moved toward him, swaying bewitchingly as she balanced forward to keep her stiletto heels from digging into the sod. She had on glossy black stockings and a black ciré sheath minidress that would have clung to her waist even without the wide leather cinch. Her dress was strapless and exposed a swath of pale skin from above her breasts to her bare shoulders, where the tops of her long black evening gloves reached the neckline.

Her black hair was gathered in a high chignon, so that her pale face and shoulders seemed to be an alabaster bust floating out of the darkness. Perhaps a plaster deathmask. Lennox recognized the familiar sensuous mouth and finely boned features, and he knew the shade of green of her eyes even before she gazed into his own.

Lennox grasped her bare shoulders. Her flesh was cool but certainly solid beneath his touch.

"Are you really Cathy?"

"If that's what you want."

"Cathy is dead. There was a funeral, and I stood there. It's been more than a year."

"There's nothing permanent about death, Cody. Not when you have power."

"This is another of Kane's tricks."

"I'm not one of Kane's minions. You are. I'm trying to help you break away from Kane."

"All right, that does it. I've been called a lot of things, but never a minion. No more of Kane's white powder, because God knows what's in it, and it's too much for my mirror. I'm going back to my hotel room, where I will curl up with a bottle of Scotch and find oblivion. If I'm still like this tomorrow, I'm really and truly this time for sure going to seek professional help."

Cathy seized his arm and firmly halted his departure. "I can take you to someone who can help you."

As Lennox spun about, the sunburst pendant on his left ear faced her. She instantly released him and stepped back.

"Please," she said. "Please come with me, Cody. Anyway, what have you got to lose?"

"Plainly, not my wits. My sanity is history. I'm standing in a London park talking with my dead wife. You can not be Cathy."

"I can be anyone you want me to be."

"Really? Did you leave your shoes in my room the other night? And did you develop severe acne in the pub the next day? And do you loiter about non-existent streets in Soho in the company of rotting zombies? Because if you answer yes to any or all of the above, then you are not Cathy. Cathy had her secret life, but nothing this extreme."

"I think you need a drink, Cody. Let's go to my place. There we can talk." Cathy took his right arm.

"You know," Lennox told her. "I think I'm handling all of this very well. It's that mega coke that Kane gave me, isn't it? I learned back when I used to do lots of acid that if the trip starts to get too weird, it's best not to fight it and just go with the flow. So, take me to your leader."

Cathy held fast to his right arm and steered Lennox in the direction of the Russell Square tube station. "You really haven't a clue, do you?"

"I am totally clueless."

There were still meth-men and blow-lamps sprawled in the bushes and folded onto benches.

"Promise no more zombies."

"You're marked by Kane."

There were tired tourists and late revelers hurrying along the streets toward the underground for the last trains. Cabs busily scooted past, braking as they dared a zebra crossing, and all of this was very reassuring to a man out on a stroll with his deceased wife.

"Can you see her, too?" Lennox asked a cluster of blue-haired ladies who were puzzling over their maps outside the tube station. He received bifocaled glares and a muttered "Disgusting!" as Cathy dragged him through.

"Let's get a cab," he protested.

"I'm just down the way."

"We'll need tickets."

Lennox stumbled and touched one of the automatic ticket machines. The machine spat out two tickets, and Cathy captured them before he could react.

"I hate these lifts," she said. "Let's take the stairs."

The Russell Square station had a pair of wooden-slat lifts that probably dated back to its Victorian construction. Their open cages crawled down a sooty shaft of geological strata to the depths of London, and often they stuck there when overloaded with too much compressed humanity. Present construction to replace the aged lifts with new shiny steel boxes only added to the congestion.

"These steps go down a hundred miles," Lennox argued, pointing to a sign which advised caution to all those rash enough to attempt the descent. "It's like climbing to the top of the Empire State Building."

"But this is all downhill, Cody. Stop whining and come along."

The stairway bored into the depths in a tight spiral. Cathy's heels made a rhythmic echo, and Lennox began to feel dizzy. Not many people took these stairs, and just now they met no one at all.

"Cathy," said Lennox, pausing for breath. "If it's really you, I just want to say how glad I am to see you again."

The stairwell was hot and claustrophobic, and Lennox felt certain they should have reached the platform by now.

"Cathy, do you remember when we saw that film, *Deathline*? Parts of it were shot down here."

"Come on, Cody."

"I think the print we saw was retitled *Raw Meat*."

"Right. That was some birthday treat, Cody."

"We had fun afterward."

"Right. You pulled one of my stockings over your head and chased me around the apartment, waving a rubber chicken and yelling: 'Mind the doors!'"

"Was that before you began seeing Aaron?"

"Just keep walking, Cody. We're nearly there."

"I can't hear the trains."

"So, what made you throw in with Kane?"

Lennox grasped at the railing. The brass was warm and seemed to be filmed over with slime. He stumbled and leaned hard against Cathy.

"He bought out my British publisher, acquired all my contracts. Hey, I just met the guy. He has some awesome coke and a lovely daughter. Inasmuch as you're dead, you'll forgive my lust, won't you?"

There seemed to be steam filling the spiral stairway. Droplets of something fell onto his face, and Lennox wiped them away curiously. The brass railing began to look more like an uncoiled intestine. He hoped he wouldn't throw up on the steps.

"I think we've been walking too far." The steps were so slimy as to feel gelatinous beneath his feet. Lennox clung to Cathy.

"You're more likely to recognize his name when it's spelled C a i n," she said.

"As in the fratricidal horticulturist? Surely, he's dead by now."

"Immortal," said Cathy. "Unless you can help us stop him. That's why he's bonded you."

The stairway ended, and they walked onto an underground platform of sorts. The overhead tunnel was oozing tendrils of gluey foulness through misshapen tiles, the rails seemed to be writhing like salted worms, the platform and all were clogged by enveloping steamy mist.

For as far as Lennox could see into the mist, hundreds of would-be passengers aimlessly shuffled against one another, rotting in their tatters of medieval clothing.

"Sorry about the mess," said a figure standing on the platform. "Been holding this lot here for quite some years. Really in remarkably good state of preservation though, all things considered—don't you think?

"Cody Lennox?" The man stepped closer. "Please allow me to introduce myself. My name is Satan."

"I think this has gone far enough," Lennox decided. "And anyway, I'm an atheist."

"No problem," said Satan, but he did not offer his hand. He was a tall, dark man with a widow's peak and neatly trimmed black beard, dressed rather theatrically in cape and medieval costume.

"There are no horns and tail," said Satan. "Or would you feel better if there were?"

"You're a theatrical overstatement."

"First impressions," said Satan. His image blurred, and he was much the same but attired in formal dinner dress, fashionable about 1900. Cathy was suddenly wearing a black evening gown from the same period.

"Go away!" begged Lennox, anxiously hoping to awaken.

"Doesn't really matter, does it?" said Satan. "Appearances are deceiving. Like yours. We need to talk."

"That's what Kane told me."

"Cody, I can see that you're confused. Who wouldn't be? So you cut your first deal with Kane. We can renegotiate. What do you want? I've already brought Cathy back. No obligation."

"That's not Cathy," Lennox insisted.

"She could be Cathy. Or whoever you want. Look about you, Cody. Anything you want. Name it. It's yours."

"This is not a mountain top. This is a very horrible subway tunnel, and I don't see anything here that I like. Get thee behind me."

"Good job, Cody," said Kane. He was carrying two glasses of champagne, and he handed one to Lennox. "We missed you at the party, so I came to look."

"Clever move, Kane," Satan said. "So, he led you here."

"Sorry. I should have brought another glass. Satan, is it? Is that what you're going by now? Don't mind if I slip and call you Sathonys out of old acquaintance?"

"Kane, you shouldn't have meddled into this."

"Nice place," approved Kane. "I like the décor. Giger out of Bosch. It's the catacombs beneath Coram's Fields Playground, isn't it? Connects through beneath Queen Square. Very convenient. And I see you've been recruiting from the plague pits."

Lennox made his voice calm. "Kane, are we in Hell or something?"

"What we're in is deep shit," Klesst answered him. "Dad, we're going to run out of champagne."

"The delectable Klesst!" said Satan. "My, how you've grown up!"

"Blacklight can ring room service," Kane told her.

"Klesst," Lennox asked, "is this the well-known . . ."

"We've all been around for a long, long time, Cody."

"Best be getting back to the party," Kane decided. "Can't trust Blacklight to cope on his own."

"A truce," Satan offered. "We've fought on the same side often enough before."

"But this is my turf now," Kane warned him. "And I don't like your plans for renovation."

"You can't stop this."

"Lighten up, Sathonys. You're like a brother to me."

"Oh, shit!" said Klesst.

Kane's left hand moved, and there was a gun in it, and Kane fired the gun.

Satan had instantly vanished, but the point where he had stood coalesced into a seething mass of flaming destruction.

"Cody, get your ass behind me!"

Dead creatures began tumbling from the walls, crawling over the slime-covered paving. Kane fired another annihilating burst. Part of one wall melted into glowing rubble.

Klesst tugged what might have been a derringer from beneath her skirt. She aimed it at the line of rails just as their tentacled lengths were reaching outward. Most of the platform and rails vanished in a consuming flash that hurtled the three of them backward over the slime and toward where the staircase no longer was.

The ceiling began to crumble. Kane fired pointblank into a collapsing tier of ravenous dead creatures. Stones were falling heavily from above. In seconds nauseous smoke clogged the warren of tunnels. Continuous bursts from Kane's and Klesst's weapons provided a strobelight vision of disintegrating masonry and mindlessly advancing dead. Beyond that spasmodic glow of destruction, ill-defined shapes hunched toward them.

"What do you say, Cody?" Kane shouted. "Want to go back to the party?"

Something long dead reached out of the buckling catacomb walls and clawed at Lennox's throat. The sunburst pendant at Lennox's ear blazed with instant power, and the desiccated arm vanished into ash.

"I want out of here!" Lennox screamed.

It was instantly quiet. It was very dark. Dank walls still compressed them.

"Just up these stairs, I think," said Kane, holding his gun at alert. Cover our back, Klesst. Move along, Cody."

"Where are we?" Lennox cursed as he stumbled and bashed his knee against the unseen steps. Klesst powerfully grasped his arm and kept him from falling into uncertain darkness.

"Not on the Russell Square station staircase, as I'd hoped," Kane answered. "That's where we began to follow you. At a guess, we're coming up from beneath Queen Square."

Lennox stumbled again, but Klesst held him upright.

"Can you both see in the dark?" Lennox asked her.

"Yes." Klesst squeezed his arm comfortingly.

"I want out of here."

"Good one, Cody!" Kane congratulated him. "Here's a door that should open onto the cellars beneath the Queen's Larder. We're going to make an awesome team."

Kane snapped the bolt and pushed open the trap door.

"Or, maybe not," said Kane.

Kane shoved away the debris, and they emerged.

The Queen's Larder was a blackened ruin, as were all of the buildings in sight, save for the Church of St. George the Martyr across the way. The sky was a sodium-flame yellow and outlined an endless horizon of blackened heaps of fused stone and glass. There was no clear evidence of sun or moon through the glowing haze. Occasional and distant shapes seemed to sail on black wings across the dead skies; otherwise there was no sign of life. No sign of any sort of life whatsover.

"Shit," said Kane.

"You sure threw one hell of a party," Lennox managed. He sat down on a seared heap of wall. "Look, my sanity reserve has been running on empty for too long. Where does one get a drink here?"

"You bastard!" Klesst yelled at him. "You brought us through the wrong way!"

"Whoa! I was only following your dad. You're the ones who can see in the dark—remember?"

"This is worse than it looks," Kane told them.

"Well, it looks really bad, Kane," Lennox agreed. "Whatever happened to time-time, and where's the party?"

Kane suddenly turned the full power of his eyes upon Lennox, and for the first time Lennox was irrevocably convinced that all of this was really happening to him. And then Cody Lennox knew real fear.

"I've tried to bring you along by stages," Kane said. "The

problem is that I need you, and I need you now. What you're looking at right now is a near-time reality—for your entire world."

"Global nuclear holocaust?"

"Worse than that, Cody. It's more like Armageddon or the Day of Judgement. The Harmonic Convergence gave them the power. They'll open the Gates of Hell and raise the dead. Only no one's flying up to Heaven. It won't be a pretty sight. Look about you."

"Straight answers this time, Kane. Was that really Satan?"

"To the best that your theology can comprehend: yes. Disregarding Judeo-Christian myth, that was the Demonlord. What you saw was a physical embodiment of a hostile and predatory force alien to this world."

"And are you also a Judeo-Christian myth?"

"Very possibly. But don't believe everything you read. There are at least two sides to every story."

"And are you human?"

"Yes, and no."

"I was just wondering," said Lennox. "Except for all the muscles, I'm having a very difficult time telling you and Satan apart."

"I am a physical entity," Kane promised him. "Just as is Klesst. Just as are you. Satan, as you saw him, is a physical embodiment of a trans-dimensional force."

"And Cathy?"

"What you saw was a succubus. Another demon, as your theology interprets such matters. Don't blame yourself for summoning her. You've been set up all along."

"Why?"

"Because you can control synchronicity, Cody. It was a latent power, unconsciously used. The Harmonic Convergence has intensified your powers. You haven't attained real control yet, but I can teach you."

"Why should I trust you?"

Kane waved his arms. "Just look at what will happen. At what *has* happened. This is reality, Cody."

"I thought you could control time, Kane."

"Time-time, Cody. And real-time within limits. We followed you into near-time to find their center of power. They shunted us future-forward on the way back to real-time. I have only physical power here. I need you, Cody, to get back, to keep all this from happening."

"Do it, Cody," Klesst encouraged him. "This place is really boring."

"So. What do I do? I forgot my ruby slippers."

"If you break open the way," Kane said, "I can draw through the power. Think of it this way: you unlock the door, and I come through with the shotgun."

"Kane, I think we'd best just call a tow-truck."

"I really do admire a sense of humor in a man who's facing an unpleasant end." Kane stepped closer, and Lennox was suddenly uncertain as to where the immediate danger might lie.

"It's all random patterns, Cody. It's like a gigantic interlocking puzzle with infinite and equal solutions. When the pieces come together and form a final pattern, it's real-time. Near-time is still in flux. Synchronicity can determine the way the patterns come together. You can control synchronicity. Do it, and get it right this time."

"Do what? Is this where I make an expressionless face and unfocus my eyes?"

"The monster's from the id, Cody. All you have to do is to want something to happen. I'll see that it does."

"I don't begin to understand any of this."

"You don't have to." Klesst put her arm around him. "Hey, don't you wish we were all back at the party and having a good time? Like, here's the three of us together in the bedroom, talking away. Then Dad leaves you and me alone, while he goes to check on the champagne. Our eyes meet, and then our lips crush together."

"Let's party!" Cody shouted.

This time there were no blasts of weaponsfire to mask the shock of ripping apart the space-time pattern . . .

"Sorry, but there's always business," Kane apologized to his guests. "Blacklight, how are we doing on the champagne?"

"Cool," said Blacklight. "Ordered up two more cases. Had some gate-crashers. Bad-looking dude in a tux and a comely Gibson girl in a black formal. Said they were old friends of yours, so I let them in. Don't see them now. Anyway, they said they'd be back."

"I'm sure they will. Carry on."

"Hey, Kane!" Kent Allard lurched toward him. "Did you find Cody?"

"We did."

"We were worried about him. You know . . ."

"Cody is fine."

Lennox and Klesst chose this moment to emerge from the bedroom. They were arm in arm and talking together furiously.

"Well, well," observed Allard. "Fast mover, our Cody."

"Champagne, Cody?" Kane invited.

"Maybe just one," Lennox said. "Please excuse us for a moment, Kent."

"Of course. Go for it, guy."

Lennox snagged a tray of champagne as he guided Klesst into a corner beside Kane. Each took a glass.

He said: "Kane, I'm not sure I really believe any of this, but I'm throwing in on your side."

"Good decision, Cody."

"Only one thing still bothers me, Kane. Granted, I've met the forces of Evil . . ."

"Only *inimical* forces, Cody. It's all so relative."

"We'll argue this later. So, when do I meet the forces of Good?"

"Already told you, Cody. There are none. I'm the only hope this world has."

Kane and Klesst touched glasses with Lennox.

"To us," said Kane.

RICHARD LAYMON

Bad News

RICHARD LAYMON is the author of fifteen horror novels, including *The Cellar, Resurrection Dreams, Funland, The Stake* and *Alarms*. Born in Chicago, Illinois, he currently lives in Los Angeles with his wife Ann and daughter Kelly.

His novel *Flesh* was named the best horror novel of 1989 by *Science Fiction Chronicle* and nominated for a Horror Writers of America Bram Stoker Award.

Laymon's short stories have appeared in such magazines and anthologies as *Ellery Queen, Mike Shayne, Cavalier, Gallery, The Year's Best Horror Stories, Book of the Dead, Stalkers, Night Visions 7, Slashers* and *Hot Blood*, to name only a few.

"Bad News" is a powerful example of his mastery of unrelenting horror.

T HE MORNING WAS SUNNY and quiet. Leaving the door ajar, Paul crossed the flagstones to his driveway. He sidestepped alongside his Granada, being careful neither to tread on the dewy grass nor to let his robe rub against the grimy side of the car.

As he cleared the rear bumper, he spotted the *Messenger*.

Good. Nobody had beaten him to it.

Every so often, especially on weekends, somebody swiped the thing. Not this morning, though. Getting up early had paid off. The newspaper, rolled into a thick bundle and bound by a rubber band, lay on the grass just beyond the edge of Paul's driveway.

On Joe Applegate's lawn.

Crouching to pick it up, Paul glanced at his neighbor's driveway and yard and front stoop.

There was no sign of Applegate's paper.

Probably already took it inside, Paul thought. Unless somebody snatched it.

Hope the damn redneck doesn't think *this* is his.

Paul straightened up, tucked the paper under one arm, and made his way up the narrow strip of pavement between his car and the grass.

Inside the house, he locked the front door. He tossed the newspaper onto the coffee table, started away, and thought he saw the paper wobble.

He looked down at it.

The *Messenger* lay motionless on the glass top of the coffee table.

It was rolled into the shape of a rather thick, lopsided tube. The wobble he'd noticed out of the corner of his eye must've been the paper settling from the toss he'd given it.

It shimmied.

Paul flinched.

A rat-like, snouted face poked out of the middle of the folds. Furless, with white skin that looked oily. It gazed up at him with pink eyes. It bared its teeth.

"Jesus!" Paul gasped as the thing scurried out, rocking the paper, and rushed straight toward him claws clicking on the table top, teeth snapping at the air.

Paul staggered backward.

What the fuck is it!

The creature left a slime trail on the glass. It didn't stop at the edge of the table. It tumbled off, hit the carpeted floor with a soft thump, and sped toward Paul's feet.

He leaped out of its path. The thing abruptly changed course and kept coming.

Paul hurled himself sideways, lurched a few steps to his easy chair and jumped up onto the seat. His feet sank into the springy cushion. He teetered up there, prancing for balance as he turned around, then dropped a knee onto the chair's padded arm.

He watched the thing rush toward him.

Not a rat, at all. It had a rodent-like head, all right, but beyond its thin neck was a body shaped like a bullet: a fleshy, glistening white cylinder about five inches long, rounded at the shoulders, ending just beyond its hind legs without tapering at all as if its rear was a flat disk. It had no tail.

At the foot of the chair, it dug its claws into the fabric and started to climb.

Paul tore a moccasin off his foot. A flimsy weapon, but better than nothing. He swept it down at the beast. The limp leather sole slapped against the thing's flank, but didn't dislodge it. It kept coming up the front of the chair, eyes on Paul, its small teeth clicking.

He stuffed his hand into the moccasin and shoved at the thing. Its snout burst through the bottom, a patch of leather gripped in its teeth. He jerked his hand free, losing the moccasin, and sprang from the chair. Glancing back as he rushed away, he saw the creature and moccasin drop to the floor.

At the fireplace, he grabbed a pointed, wrought-iron poker. He whirled to face the beast. It worked the rest of its body through the hole in the slipper and charged him. He raised the poker.

Something brushed against Paul's ankle. A furry blur shot by. Jack the cat.

Jack slept in Timmy's room, curled on its special rug beside the boy's bed. The commotion out here must've caught its attention.

"Don't!" Paul blurted.

The tabby leaped like a miniature lion and pounced on the creature.

Stupid cat! It's not a mouse!

Paul's view was blocked by Jack. He bent sideways, trying for a better angle, and saw the blunt rear and tiny legs of the thing hanging out the side of Jack's mouth.

"Nail the bastard!" he gasped.

Jack worked his jaw, biting down. His tail switched.

"Paul? What's going on out there?" Joan's groggy, distant voice.

Before he could answer, the cat squawled and leaped straight up, back hunching.

"PAUL!" Now alarmed.

Jack went silent. All four paws hit the floor at once. The cat stood motionless for a moment, then keeled over onto its side. Its anus bulged. The bloody head of the beast squeezed out.

Paul stared, numb with shock, as the thing slid free of Jack's body. It came at him, a tube of red-brown mush flowing out its stubby rear.

"Christ!" he gasped, stumbling backward. "Joan! Don't come in here! Get Timmy! Get the hell out of the house!"

"What's going . . .?" The next word died in Joan's throat as she stepped past the dining room table. She saw Paul in his robe dropping to a crouch and whacking the floor with the fireplace poker. The hooked end of the rod nearly hit a yucky thing that she thought for a moment was a rat. It scooted out of the way.

It wasn't like any rat that Joan had ever seen.

She saw the cat, the carpet dark with gore near its rump.

"Oh dear God," she murmured.

Paul gasped and leaped aside as the creature darted toward his foot. It chased him across the carpet.

Joan took a step forward, wanting to rush in and help him. But she stopped abruptly. She had no weapon. She was barefoot, wearing only her nightgown.

"Shit!" Paul jumped onto the sofa, twisted around and back-stepped, the poker raised overhead. The thing scurried up the upholstery. "Do like I said! Get Timmy out of here. Get help, for Godsake! Call the cops!"

The little beast suddenly halted.

It looked back at Joan.

Ice flowed up her back.

She whirled around and ran. Straight to Timmy's room. The boy woke up as she scooped him out of bed. "Mommy?" He sounded frightened.

"It's okay," she said, rushing out of the room with Timmy clutched to her chest. Hanging onto him with one arm, she snatched her purse off the dining room table. She raced into the kitchen, put him down while she opened the back door, then hoisted him again and ran outside.

"What's wrong, Mommy?" he asked. "Where's Daddy?"

"Everything's fine," she said, easing him down beside the Granada. "A little problem in the house. Daddy's taking care of it." She fumbled inside her purse, found the car keys, unlocked the driver's door and opened it. "You just wait here," she said, lifting Timmy onto the seat. "Don't come out. I'll be back pretty soon." She slammed the door.

And stood there at the edge of the driveway.

What'll I do?

Go back inside and help him?

He's got the poker. What am I gonna do, go after the thing with a carving knife?

She cut off its tail with a carving knife.

That was no damn mouse.

He said to call the cops. Oh, right. Tell them a *thing* is chasing my husband around the house. And then when they get here in ten or fifteen minutes . . .

Joan snapped her head toward Applegate's house.

Applegate, the red-neck gun nut.

She crouched and looked through the car window at Timmy. The boy wasn't stupid. He knew that, somewhere in the house, shit was hitting the fan in a big way. His eyes looked huge and scared and lonely. Joan felt her throat go tight.

At least you're safe, honey, she thought.

She managed a smile for him, then whirled around and rammed herself into the thick hedge beside the driveway. Applegate's bushes raked her skin, snagged her nightgown. But she plunged straight through and dashed across his yard.

She leaped onto his front stoop.

The plastic sign on Applegate's door read: THIS HOUSE INSURED BY SMITH & WESSON.

What an asshole, she thought.

Hoping he was home, she thumbed the doorbell button.

From inside came the faint sound of ringing chimes.

Joan looked down at herself and shook her head. The nightie had been a Valentine's Day present from Paul. There wasn't much of it, and you could see through what there was.

Applegate's gonna love this, she thought. Shit!

Where *is* he?

"Come on, come on," she muttered. She jabbed the doorbell a few more times, then pounded the door with her fist. "Joe!" she yelled.

No answer came. She heard no footsteps from inside the house.

"Damn it all," she muttered. Being careful not to slip again, she hurried to the edge of the concrete slab. She stepped down, took a few strides across the dewy grass, then made her way into the flower bed at the front of Applegate's house. He must be home and up, she thought; his curtains are open. He always kept them shut at night and whenever he was away.

Joan pushed between a couple of camelias, leaned close to his picture window and cupped her hands around her eyes.

She peered into the sunlit living room.

Applegate was home, all right. But not up. He lay sprawled on the floor in his robe and a swamp of blood.

Paul leaped off the end of the couch. He landed beside the front door.

Get the hell out! he thought.

Sure. And leave the thing in here? You come back and can't even find it.

I've gotta kill the bastard.

He lurched sideways as the creature sprang off the arm of the couch. He was almost fast enough. But he felt a sudden small tug on his robe, and yelped. The thing was hanging by its claws near the bottom of the robe, starting to climb. Paul threw open his cloth belt. He twirled to swing the beast away from his body, and jerked the robe off his shoulders. It dropped down his arms.

He let go of the poker so his sleeve wouldn't hang up on it. The poker thumped against the carpet. With one hand, he gave the robe a small fling. It fell to a heap, covering the beast.

He snatched up the poker. For just an instant, he considered beating the robe with the iron bar. But the rod was so thin, he'd be lucky to hit the beast.

Squealing "SHIT!" he sprang onto the cloth bundle with both feet. He jumped up and down on it. Shivers scurried up his legs. He felt as if cold fingers were tickling his scrotum. The skin on his back prickled. He thought he could feel the hair rising on the nape of his neck. But he stayed on the robe, dancing on it, driving his heels at the floor.

Until his right heel struck a bulge.

He screeched, "Yaaaah!" and leaped off.

He whirled around, poker high, and bent down ready to strike.

The robe was too thick, too rumbled, for Paul to locate the lump he'd just stomped.

Gotta be dead, he thought. I *smashed it. Smashed it good.*

Then he realized he hadn't actually felt it squish.

He whacked the robe with his poker. Stared at it. The rod had left a long, straight dent across the heap. Nothing moved. He struck again. The second blow puffed up the old dent and pounded a new one close to where it'd been. He struck a few more times, but never felt the rod hit anything except the robe and the floor.

Paul stepped a little farther away, then leaned forward and stretched out his arm. He slipped the tip of the poker under a lapel, jostled it until a heavy flap of the rob was hooked, then slowly lifted.

The blanketed area of carpet shrank as he raised the robe higher.

No creature.

Then the end of the robe was swaying above the carpet, covering nothing at all.

Still no creature.

It came scurrying down the slim rod of the poker toward his hand.

Paul screamed.

He hurled the weapon and ran.

Racing up the Applegate's driveway toward the rear of his house, Joan wondered if she should try next door. An older couple lived there. She didn't actually know them. Besides, they might be dead, same as Applegate.

And what if they didn't have a gun?

Applegate had plenty. That, she knew. She and Paul had been in his house just once—enough to find out that he was not their kind of person. A Republican, for godsake! A beer-swilling reactionary with the mean, narrow mind of his ilk. Anti-abortion, anti-women's rights, big on capital punishment and the nuclear deterrent. Everything that she and Paul despised.

But he did have guns. His home was an arsenal.

Dashing around the corner of his house, Joan spotted a rake on the back lawn. It had been left carelessly on the grass, tines upward. She ran into the yard and grabbed it up, then swung around and rushed across the concrete patio.

She skidded to a halt at the sliding glass door. With the handle of the rake, she punched through the glass. Shards burst inward, fell and clinked to the floor, leaving a sharp-edged hole the size of a fist. Reaching through the hole, she unlatched the door. When she pulled her hand out, a fang of glass ripped the back of it.

She muttered, "Fuck."

Not much more than a scratch, really. But blood started welling out.

I'm ruining myself, she thought. But then she remembered how Applegate had looked, remembered Paul scampering over the couch with that little monster on his heels.

He could end up like Joe if I don't hurry, she told herself.

Why doesn't *he* get the fuck out of the house?

Deciding to ignore her bleeding hand, Joan wrenched open the door. It rumbled on its runners. She swept it wide, and entered Applegate's den to the left of the broken glass.

There was the gun rack on the other side of the room. She

hurried toward it, holding the rake ready and watching the floor.

What if Applegate hadn't been killed by one of those horrible *things*? Just because we've got one . . . Maybe he was murdered and the killer's still . . .

One of those horrible *things* scurried out from under a chair and darted straight for Joan's feet.

She whipped the rake down.

Got it!

The tines didn't pierce its slimy flesh, but the monster seemed to be trapped between two of the iron teeth.

Joan dropped the rake.

She rushed to the gun rack. A ghastly thing with the weapons resting on what appeared to be the hooves of deer or stags. Wrinkling her nose, she grabbed the bottom weapon. A double-barreled shot-gun?

She whirled around with it just as the monster slithered free of the rake tines.

Clamping the stock against her side, she swung the muzzle toward the thing, thumbed back one of the hammers, and pulled the front trigger.

The blast crashed in her ears.

The shotgun lurched as if it wanted to rip her hands off.

The middle of the rake handle exploded.

So did the monster. It blew apart in a gust of red and splashed across the hardwood floor.

"Jesus H. Christ," Joan muttered.

Then, she smiled.

Paul slammed the bathroom door. He thumbed in the lock button.

An instant later, he flinched as the thing struck the other side of the door.

Just let it try and get me now, he thought.

Then came quiet, crunching sounds. Splintering sounds.

"Bastard!" he yelled, and kicked the bottom of the door.

He pictured the beast on the other side, its tiny teeth ripping out slivers of wood.

If only he hadn't lost the poker, he could crush its head when it came through.

Rushing to the cabinet, he searched for a weapon. His Schick took injector blades. They'd be no use at all. He grabbed a pair of toenail scissors. Better than nothing. But he knew he couldn't bring himself to kneel down and ambush the thing. Not with scissors four inches long.

If only he had a gun.

If only the cops would show up.

He wondered whether Joan had managed to call them yet. She'd had plenty of time to reach a neighbor's phone. Applegate himself might come charging over with one of his guns, if she went to his place.

The door rattled quietly in its frame as the creature continued to burrow through.

There must be something useful in here!

The waste basket! Trap the thing under it!

Paul crouched for the waste basket. Wicker. Shit! They'd had a heavy plastic one until a couple of weeks ago when Joan saw this at Pier One. The bastard would chomp its way out in about a second.

He looked at the bottom of the door, and two tiny splits appeared. A bit of wood the width of a Popsicle stick bulged, cracked at the top, and started to rise.

He heard a faint boom like a car backfiring in the distance.

The flap of wood broke and fell off. The snout of the beast poked out.

Paul whirled. He rushed to the bathtub and climbed over the ledge. The bathmat draped the side of the tub. He flipped it to the floor.

The shower curtain was bunched at the far end, hanging inside.

With no rug or shower curtain to climb, the thing couldn't get at him.

He hoped.

I don't care how good it is, he thought, it can't climb the outside of the tub.

"Just try," he muttered as the thing scurried across the tile floor. It stopped on the bathmat and looked up at him. It seemed

379

to grin. It sprang and Paul yelped. But the leap was short. The beast thumped against the side inches from the top. Its forelegs raced, claws clittering against the enamel for a moment. Then it dropped. Its rump thumped the mat. As it keeled backward, it flipped over and landed on its feet.

Paul bit down on the scissors. He crouched. With both hands, he twisted the faucets. Water gushed from the spout. As it splashed around his feet, he stoppered the drain. He took the scissors from his mouth, stood up straight and looked at the floor beside the tub.

The beast was gone.

Where . . .?

The waste basket tipped over, spilling out wads of pink tissue. It began rolling toward the tub.

"Think you're smart, huh?" Paul said. He let out a laugh. He pumped his legs, splashing water up around his shins and calves. "BUT CAN YOU SWIM? HUH? HOW'S YOUR BACKSTROKE, YOU LITTLE SHIT?"

The waste basket was a foot from the tub when the beast darted up from the far side. It landed atop the rolling wicker. Paul threw the scissors at it. They missed. The creature leaped.

He staggered backward as it flew at the tub. It landed on the ledge, slid across on its belly, and flopped into the water. It splashed. Then it sank.

"GOTCHA!" Paul yelled.

He jumped out of the tub. Bending over, he gazed at the beast. It was still on the bottom, walking along slowly under a few inches of water.

He jerked the shower curtain over the ledge so it hung outside.

The beast came to the surface, glanced this way and that, then spotted Paul and started swimming toward him.

"Come on and drown," he muttered.

It reached the wall of the tub. Its forepaws scampered against the enamel. Though it couldn't climb the smooth wall, it didn't seem ready to drown, either.

Paul backed away from the tub.

On the counter beside the sink was Timmy's Smurf toothbrush standing upright in its plastic holder. He rushed over to it and snatched it from the Smurf's hand.

He knelt beside the tub.

The beast was still trying to climb up.

Paul poked at it. The end of the toothbrush jabbed the top of its head and submerged it. But the thing squirmed free. It started to come up. Before its snout could break the surface, Paul prodded it down again.

"How long can you hold your breath, asshole?"

It started to rise. He poked it down again and laughed.

"Gotcha now."

Again, the beast escaped from under the toothbrush and headed for the surface.

Paul jabbed down at it. His fist struck the water, throwing a splash into his face. As he blinked his eyes clear, something stung his knuckles.

He jerked his hand up.

He brought the creature with it.

Screaming, he lurched away from the tub and shook his arm as the thing scampered over his wrist. It held fast, claws digging in.

He swiped at it with his other hand. It came loose, ripping flesh from his forearm, and raced up *that* hand.

Raced up his left arm, leaving a trail of pinpoint tracks.

Swinging around, he bashed his arm against a wall. But the beast merely scampered to it underside. Upside-down, it scooted toward his armpit.

"PAUL!"

Joan twisted the knob. The bathroom door was locked. From beyond it came a horrible scream.

She aimed at the knob and pulled the trigger.

As the explosion roared in her ears and the shotgun jumped, a hole the size of a fist appeared beside the knob. The door flew open.

Paul, in his underpants, stood beside the bathtub shrieking. His left arm was sheathed with blood. In what remained of his right hand, he held the monster.

He saw her. A wild look came to his eyes.

"Shoot it!" he yelled, and thrust his fist toward the ceiling. Blood streamed down his arm.

"Your hand!"

"I don't care!"

She thumbed back one of the twin hammers, took a bead on her husband's upraised bleeding hand, and pulled a trigger. The hammer clanked.

"My God! Shoot it!"

She cocked the other hammer, aimed, jerked the other trigger. The hammer snapped down. The shotgun didn't fire.

"RELOAD. FOR GODSAKE RELOAD!"

"With *what*?" she shrieked back at him.

"IDIOT!" He jammed the monster into his mouth, chomped down on it, yanked, then threw the decapitated body at her. It left a streamer of blood in the air. It slapped against Joan's shoulder and bounced off, leaving a red smear on her skin.

Paul spat out the thing's head. Then he dropped to his knees and buried it in vomit.

In the living room, he put on his robe. They hurried outside together.

Timmy was still in the car, his face pressed to the passenger window, staring at the woman in curlers and a pink nightgown who was sprawled on the sidewalk, writhing and screaming.

From all around the neighborhood came the muffled sounds of shouts, shrieks and gunshots. Paul heard sirens. A great many sirens. They all seemed far away.

"My God," he muttered.

He scanned the ground while Joan opened the car door and lifted Timmy out. She kneed the door shut. She carried the boy around the rear of the car.

"Where're you going?" Paul asked.

"Applegate's. Come on. We'll be safer there."

"Yeah," he said. "Maybe." And he followed her toward the home of their neighbor.

STEPHEN JONES & KIM NEWMAN

Necrology: 1989

IN 1989, DEATH TOOK no holiday. We said goodbye to many writers, artists, performers and film-makers, yet they left their work behind to remind us of the important contributions they made to the horror, fantasy, and science fiction genres throughout their lifetimes.

AUTHORS/ARTISTS

Aeron Clement, author of the surprise UK bestseller *The Cold Moons*, died in early January after heart bypass surgery. He was 52.

French writer **Pierre Boileau** died January 16th, aged 87. Half of the Boileau-Narcejac team that wrote the novels filmed as *Les Diaboliques* and *Vertigo*, he also co-scripted *Les Yeaux Sans Visage* (1959).

Author and film historian **Leslie Halliwell** died January 21st from abdominal cancer. He was 59. Compiler of the annual

Filmgoer's Companion and *Film Guides*, his other books included *The Dead That Walk* (film criticism), *The Ghost of Sherlock Holmes* (short stories) and *Return to Shangri-La* (novel).

Major surrealist artist **Salvador Dali** died January 23rd from heart failure brought on by pneumonia. He was 84, and designed sequences for such movies as *L'Age d'Or*, *Un Chien Andalou* and Hitchcock's *Spellbound*.

Screenwriter **T.E.B. Clarke** died February 11th, aged 81. His numerous credits for Ealing Studios include *The Halfway House* and the classic *Dead of Night* (1945).

John W. Hall, a British diplomat who wrote fantasies as "Sarban", died April 11th. He was 78. The name Sarban comes from the Arabic word for travelling storyteller, and his most famous work is the alternative-world novel *The Sound of His Horn* (1952).

Dame **Daphne Du Maurier** died April 19th, aged 81. Films based on her novels and stories include *Rebecca*, *The Birds* and *Don't Look Now*.

Calvin Thomas Beck, the editor/publisher of the 1960s SF/fantasy film magazine *Castle of Frankenstein*, died on May 14th after a long illness. He was 56.

Cartoonist **Dik Browne** died on June 4th from cancer, aged 71. He created the strip *Hägar the Horrible*, which is currently published in more than 1,800 newspapers in 58 countries.

Author, old-time SF fan, and founder member of the British Interplanetary Society, **William F. Temple** died on July 15th, aged 75. First published in the horror anthology *Thrills* in 1935, he went on to write approximately 100 short stories and nine novels, including *The Four-Sided Triangle*, which was filmed by Hammer in 1953.

Cartoon creator **Jay Ward** died of cancer on October 12th, aged 69. With the late Bill Scott he created the characters Rocky and Bullwinkle, along with villains Boris and Natasha. His other cartoon series include *Fractured Fairy Tales* and *Dudley-Do-Right*.

Author and songwriter **Barry Sadler** died on November 5th from wounds received while training Contra rebels in

Guatamala. He was 49. Best known for his song, "Ballad of the Green Berets" (1966), he also wrote twenty volumes in the "Casca" series of military fantasies, beginning in 1979 with *Casca: The Eternal Mercenary*.

Author Jean Paiva died of lung cancer on November 13th. She was 45. Her first novel, *The Lilith Factor*, was published in 1989, while a second, *The Fortean Gamble*, was completed shortly before her death.

Comic strip artist C.C. Beck died on November 22nd after a long illness. He was 79. Beck created *Captain Marvel*, which ran from 1940 until 1953, when National Periodical Publications claimed that it was copied from *Superman* and successfully sued. *The Adventures of Captain Marvel* was made into a serial in 1941.

Major fantasist and pioneer of the "theatre of the absurd", Samuel Beckett died in Paris on December 22nd, aged 83. His plays include *Waiting for Godot*, *Endgame*, *Krapp's Last Tape*, *Not I*, *Footfalls*, and *Catastrophe*. In 1969, he was awarded the Nobel Prize for literature.

ACTORS/ACTRESSES

Kenneth McMillan died January 8th from liver disease. His best-known genre role was as the evil Baron Vladmir Harkonnen in *Dune*, and his other credits include *The Stepford Wives*, *Salem's Lot*, *Heartbeeps* and *Cat's Eye*.

Sleazy character actor Joe Spinell died on January 13th of a heart attack, having been despondent following the death of his mother. He was 51 and appeared in *Maniac*, *The Last Horror Film*, *Starcrash Forbidden Zone* and *Vampire* (TV).

Actor/director John Cassavetes died from cirrhosis of the liver on February 3rd, aged 59. His numerous credits include *Rosemary's Baby*, *The Fury*, *Incubus*, and on TV, *Alfred Hitchcock Presents* and *Voyage to the Bottom of the Sea*.

Actor Joe Silver died on February 27th from cancer. He was 66, and appeared in *Rhinoceros*, *Death Trap*, and two early David Cronenberg movies, *Rabid* and *Shivers* (aka *They Came from*

Within). He was also the voice of The Creep in *Creepshow 2*.

British character actor **Harry Andrews** died on March 6th from viral infection-asthma, aged 77. His numerous film credits include *Moby Dick* scripted by Ray Bradbury, *Burke and Hare*, *Night Hair Child*, *Theatre of Blood*, *The Final Programme*, *The Medusa Touch*, *Superman* and *Hawk the Slayer*.

Maurice Evans died March 12th, aged 87. He appeared in *Scrooge* (1935), *Rosemary's Baby*, *Planet of the Apes* and *Beneath the Planet of the Apes* and *Terror in the Wax Museum*, while his many TV appearances included *The Man from UNCLE*, *Batman* (as The Puzzler), *Tarzan*, *Search*, *The Six Million Dollar Man*, *Fantasy Island* and as a series regular on *Bewitched*.

29-year-old actor **Merritt Butrick**, who played Captain Kirk's son in *Star Trek II* and *III*, died from AIDS on March 17th. He also appeared in *Fright Night Part II* and *From the Dead of Night*.

Matt Willis, who portrayed Bela Lugosi's werewolf assistant in *Return of the Vampire*, died March 30th, aged 75. His other credits include *Invisible Agent* and *A Guy Named Joe*.

Veteran character actor **George Coulouris** died on April 25th from a heart attack. He was 85. During his sixty-year career he appeared in *Citizen Kane*, *The Man Without a Body*, *The Woman Eater*, *The Skull*, *Blood from the Mummy's Tomb*, *Tower of Evil*, and *Antichristo*, as well as episodes of TV's *Dr. Who* and *The Prisoner*.

Lucille Ball died from cardiac arrest on April 26th, aged 77. Besides her long-running TV series, she appeared in the movies *The Magic Carpet*, *Roman Scandals* and *Lured* (with Karloff and Zucco).

Guy Williams (born Armand Catalano), who played the title role in *Zorro* and the father of the castaway Robinsons in *Lost in Space* on TV, was found dead on May 6th at his home in Buenos Aires, Argentina. He was 65, and also starred in the 1963 movie *Captain Sinbad*.

Robert Webber died on May 17th from Lou Gehrig's disease. He was 64. The urbane film and TV actor's credits include Hammer's *Hysteria*, *The Silencers*, *Don't Go to Sleep*, *Starflight One* and *Hauser's Memory*.

Saturday Night Live comedienne **Gilda Radner** died from cancer on May 20th, aged 42. She starred in *Haunted Honeymoon* (with husband Gene Wilder) and *It Came from Hollywood*.

The same day saw the death of **Anton Diffring**, who was 70. His many genre movies included Hammer's *The Man Who Could Cheat Death*, *Circus of Horrors*, *Fahrenheit 451*, *Mark of the Devil Part II*, *The Beast Must Die*, *The Masks of Death* and *Faceless*, while on TV he appeared in *Dr. Who*, *The Invisible Man*, *One Step Beyond* and the 1958 pilot for *Tales of Frankenstein*.

Highway to Heaven regular **Victor French** died June 15th from lung cancer, aged 54. His other credits include the movies *The Other* and *The House on Skull Mountain*, and he played Agent 44 on TV's *Get Smart*.

Ray McAnally died on June 15th, aged 63. He appeared in *High Spirits*, *Jack the Ripper* (TV) and starred in the acclaimed near future TV film *A Very British Coup*.

Actor **John Westbrook**, who played Death in Roger Corman's *Masque of the Red Death*, died on June 16th, aged 66. His other credits include *The Tomb of Ligeia*, *Lord of the Rings* and TV's *Blake's Seven*.

The voice of Bugs Bunny, **Mel Blanc**, died of heart disease and emphysema on July 10th, aged 81. He created the voices for thousands of cartoon characters, including Porky Pig, Tweety Pie, Daffy Duck, the Road Runner, Wile E. Coyote and Yosemite Sam, as well as the robot Twiki in TV's *Buck Rogers in the 25th Century*.

Pro-ball player/actor **John Matuszak**, who acted in *Caveman*, *The Ice Pirates* and *The Goonies*, died on June 17th from massive heart failure. He was 38.

The voice of Mr. Magoo, actor **Jim Backus**, died on July 3rd from pneumonia, aged 76. His many movie credits include *Macabre*, *Man of a Thousand Faces*, *The Wonderful World of the Brothers Grimm*, *Zotz!* and *Miracle on 34th Street* (TV).

Lord **Laurence Olivier** died on July 11th, aged 82. Despite a distinguished stage career he also appeared in such films as *Wuthering Heights*, *Rebecca*, *Hamlet*, *Bunny Lake is Missing*, *The Boys from Brazil*, *Clash of the Titans* and *Dracula* (1979).

Sunshine Sammy Morrison, star of the original Our Gang

comedies during the silent era and later one of the East Side Kids, died on July 24th. He was 76. During the 1940s he appeared in *Spooks Run Wild* and *Ghosts on the Loose*, both with Bela Lugosi.

Richard Alexander, who portrayed Prince Barin in both *Flash Gordon* and *Flash Gordon's Trip to Mars*, died on August 9th from pulmonary edema. He was 86. His other credits include *The Leopard Lady*, *SOS Coast Guard* (with Lugosi), *The Ghost of Frankenstein*, *The House of Fear* and *Spook Busters*.

Write/actor **Graham Chapman** died on October 4th from spinal cancer, aged 48. A founding member of the Monty Python's Flying Circus comedy team for more than twenty years, his film credits include *The Life of Brian*, *Monty Python and the Holy Grail*, *The Meaning of Life* and *The Magic Christian*.

Veteran Hollywood actress **Bette Davis** died on October 6th from cancer. She was 81. Late into her career she made a number of genre movies, including *What Ever Happened to Baby Jane?*, *Hush . . . Hush, Sweet Charlotte*, *The Anniversary*, *The Nanny*, *Madame Sin*, *Scream Pretty Peggy*, *Return to Witch Mountain* (with Christopher Lee), *Burnt Offerings*, *The Dark Secret of Harvest Home*, *The Watcher in the Woods* and *Wicked Stepmother* (which she left during production).

Actor **Paul Shenar**, who portrayed Orson Welles in the TV movie *The Night That Panicked America*, died of AIDS on October 11th. He was 53. He also appeared in the pilot for TV's *Gemini Man* and was the voice of Jenner in *The Secret of NIMH*.

Cornel Wilde died from leukaemia on October 15th, aged 74. He starred in *A Thousand and One Nights*, *No Blade of Grass* (also directed) and *Gargoyles*, as well as episodes of *Night Gallery* and *Fantasy Island*.

Distinguished British actor **Anthony Quayle** died in October, aged 76. He film credits include *Hamlet*, *A Study in Terror*, *Murder By Decree*, and *Holocaust 2000* (aka *The Chosen*).

Roland Winters, who portrayed oriental sleuth Charlie Chan in six films, died on October 22nd from a stroke. He was 84. His other movies included *Abbott and Costello Meet the Killer* (with Karloff), and *Miracle on 34th Street* (1973).

John Payne, who starred in the original *Miracle on 34th Street* (1947), died on December 6th from congestive heart failure. He was 77. He was also published in *Weird Tales* under a pseudonym.

Lindsay Crosby, who appeared in *Bigfoot* and *The Glory Stompers*, shot himself in the head on December 11th when his mother's trust fund ran out. He was 51, and according to Bing's will, none of his sons could inherit any of his money until they were 65.

Former Tarzan, **Jock Mahoney** died on December 14th from a stroke. He was 70, and played the Jungle King in three movies: *Tarzan the Magnificent, Tarzan Goes to India* and *Tarzan's Three Challenges*. He also appeared in *Tarzan's Deadly Silence* and *The Land Unknown*.

Tough-guy actor **Lee Van Cleef** died on December 14th from a heart attack, aged 64. Besides being the star of numerous spaghetti westerns, he appeared in *The Beast from 20,000 Fathoms, It Conquered the World, Eascape from New York* and *Speed Zone*.

Italian actress **Silvana Magnano** died from a heart attack on December 16th. She was 59. Her film credits include the 1955 *Ulysses, La Dolce Vita, Black Magic, The Witches, Dune* and *Slugs*.

FILM/TV TECHNICIANS:

Composer **Lionel Newman** died on February 3rd from cardiac arrest, aged 73. He scored such films as *Heaven Can Wait* (1943), *Man in the Attic, The Rocket Man, Gorilla at Large*, and *Doctor Dolittle*.

Director **Reginald LeBorg** died from a heart attack on March 25th, aged 86. He began his career as a contract director for Universal with such programmers as *Calling Dr. Death, The Mummy's Ghost, Dead Man's Eyes, Jungle Woman* and *Weird Woman*, and went on to helm *The Black Sleep, Voodoo Island, Diary of a Madman, House of the Black Death* (2nd unit) and *So Evil, My Sister* (aka *Psycho Sisters*).

Director/actor **Jack Starrett** died on March 27th from kidney failure. He was 52. As an actor he appeared in *Angels on Wheels* and *Angels from Hell*, and he directed *The Strange Vengeance of Rosalie*, *Race with the Devil* and *Kiss My Grits*, amongst others.

Marc Daniels died April 24th from congestive heart failure, aged 77. He directed the first 38 episodes of *I Love Lucy* and his numerous TV credits include *Man from Atlantis*, *Mission: Impossible*, and fourteen episodes of the original *Star Trek*, including "The Menagerie", "The Man Trap", "The Naked Time", "I, Mudd" and "Spock's Brain".

German-American film and TV director **Gerd Oswald** died on May 22nd. He was 72. He directed the movies *Screaming Mimi*, *Brainwashed* and *Agent for H.A.R.M.*, as well as episodes of *Star Trek*, *Voyage to the Bottom of the Sea*, *Twilight Zone* and *The Outer Limits*.

Director/actor **Richard Quine** shot himself to death on June 10th, aged 68. He helmed *Bell, Book and Candle*, *W*, *Oh Dad Poor Dad Mama's Hung You in the Closet and I'm Feeling So Sad*, and was fired from *The Fiendish Plot of Fu Manchu*.

Director **Franklin J. Schaffner** died of cancer on July 2nd. He was 69, and his films include *The War Lord*, *Planet of the Apes*, *The Boys from Brazil*, *Sphinx* and *Lionheart*.

"King of the Serials" **Nat Levine** died on August 6th from myocardial infarction, aged 90. He produced *King of the Congo* (featuring Karloff), *The Phantom Empire*, *The Galloping Ghost* and *The Lost Jungle*.

Producer **Michael Klinger** died on September 15th from a heart attack, aged 68. His credits include *Repulsion*, *Cul-De-Sac* and *A Study in Terror*.

Italian film director **Brunello Rondi** died of a heart attack on November 7th, aged 64. He scripted Federico Fellini's *8 ½*, *Juliet of the Spirits* and *Satyricon*, and directed the 1963 movie *The Demon*.

Harvey Hart died from a heart attack on November 21st, aged 61. He directed *The Pyx* and such TV movies as *Dark Intruder* (released in US cinemas), *Can Ellen Be Saved?*, *The Aliens Are Coming* and *Massarati and the Brain* (with Cristopher Lee), as well as episodes of *Wild, Wild West*, *Star Trek* ("Mudd's Women"), *The Starlost* and *Alfred Hitchcock Hour*.